MITHRA

MITHRA

Sahana L.

PARTRIDGE
A Penguin Random House Company

To order additional copies of this book, contact
Partridge India
000 800 10062 62
orders.india@partridgepublishing.com

www.partridgepublishing.com/india

CONTENTS

For best friends forever and beyond…

Acknowledgements

Writing is a journey in solitude. Nevertheless I have come across a lot of people who have been instrumental in assisting me to reach my destination.

Prabha and Lokesh: My wonderful parents who have always encouraged and supported me in all my endeavours. I love you both!

Irene Raj, Anupama Dhansoia and Saraswathi Subramanian: My loving and expert English teachers at Poorna Prajna Education Center. Had you not identified my talent and nourished it, I would not have come this far.

Bhasker: My Kannada lecturer at Christ Junior College who inspired me to keep the writer in me alive. Thank you for your constant motivation.

CMR Institute of Technology: My alma mater and the venue where I first began writing this novel. I am sorry if you all thought that I wrote notes in the class!

Kalpana, Jeffina, Nandini and Babitha: My fabulous four friends! You have been the biggest source of support and encouragement all through this journey. You know I love you.

Akshith: He is my really good friend since school. Thank you so much for your cooperation and for always believing in my talents.

Vinoj: My best friend for over two decades! You have been the constant source of support, encouragement and criticism through all these years. Thank you so much for putting up with my unending questions and for always being there in my journey.

I thank the entire team of Partridge publishing for guiding me through this entire process in getting my book published. You have been a pleasure to work with.

Saving the best for the last, I would like to express my heartfelt gratitude to my precious readers.

Thank you!

Dear reader, thank you so much for picking up 'Mithra'. With love, step into my world...

PREFACE

Life of a warrior is always filled with challenges. We never fear death. So here I am looking my opponent in the eye, ready for the duel. Either one of us will die. Death does not dither me. Shaurya is standing with his sword glistening in the sun. I know he is baying for blood! I have to win this for Dhruva. This will not be our last day together!

I take a deep breath and hold my sword up, ready to go for the kill. Shaurya is gazing at me with his smouldering light brown eyes...

Chapter 1

A beautiful morning it was, with the golden rays of the sun streaming in through the window. Agneyastra sat there on the wooden chair looking lovingly at Mandhatri who was sound asleep. Her face had an innocent glow and he simply couldn't take his eyes off her. He remembered the day they had married, with a smile on his face. That day he didn't even have an inkling that this woman would become his life one day. Agneyastra's wedding had taken place with the King's blessing and his parents had chosen his bride. Mandhathri was a dusky beauty with dove eyes. Her beauty was understated and her smile was charming. It was that very smile which had drawn him to her. He could never pinpoint the day or instant when he actually fell in love with her. Love happened gradually and it was a silent realisation between the two. But even after years of marriage they didn't have children. Mandhathri worried about it every single day. But Agneyastra loved her immensely and he was contented with his life. It's just that their family was incomplete.

Mandhatri slowly stirred and opened her eyes. A smile appeared on her face when she saw him watching her.

'Good morning Manni!' said he happily.

'Hey, for how long have you been awake?' asked Mandhatri getting up to sit on the bed leaning against the pillow.

'Long enough to watch my sleeping beauty.'

'You are insane!' she said nodding her head in disapproval. Though she disapproved it, she actually loved it when he would sit watching her sleep.

'I know. How are you feeling?' he asked eagerly. Mandhatri gestured him to come and sit beside her. He went on the bed and sat next to her holding her hand. She rested her head on his chest.

'I am fine and so is our child.' He smiled and kissed her forehead.

'Sankhaji said you could deliver within this week. These many years I have lived without an opportunity to realise this dream. As the day is nearing, I am feeling very nervous and excited,' said Agneyastra. She smiled at his impatience.

'Oh my God! I never thought Chief Agneyastra could ever be so nervous. I too can't wait to see the joy on your face when you hold our son.'

He looked at her raising an eyebrow in surprise.

'How are you so sure that it will be a son?'

'I am not sure but I have a feeling that it is going to be a son. Maybe because I know what a son means to you,' she said looking at him.

'I don't have a choice Manni,' said Agneyastra wryly. She knew it was not easy for him to say those words.

'You will be an excellent father Agneya,' she said softly. She lifted her head and kissed him lightly.

'Do you really think so?' he asked a little unsure.

'I know so,' said Mandhatri confidently. She then hugged him pressing her head to his chest. He wrapped his arms around his small blissful world.

***

King Devarata was seated with Prime Minister Purumithra in his royal chamber.

'How is the prince's education at the gurukul going on?' asked the king.

'Prince Vijayendra is being trained in all the skills your Highness. Though he is still a boy, he is learning it very fast. He will make you proud My Lord,' said Purumithra flattering the king. He was well aware that the prince was just an average student.

'I am always proud of my son,' beamed the king. Just then a royal guard stepped in and bowed.

'Your Highness, Chief Agneyastra seeks your audience.'

'Let him in.'

Agneyastra walked in and saluted the king.

'What is the matter Agneyastra?'

'I have made all the arrangements for your Highness to visit the army camp tomorrow.'

'That is good. Let us leave early tomorrow morning,' said the king. But Purumithra was not happy with it.

'Chief Agneyastra, isn't your wife due to deliver anytime now?'

'Yes Sir,' said he with pride infused in his tone.

'Then you must be with her. You are being bestowed with this joy after many years. I relieve you of your duty Agneya. Just bring us the happy news about the birth of your son!' said the king smiling.

Before Agneyastra could reply a guard rushed in. All of them were surprised at his urgency.

'What is it?' asked the king sternly.

'Pardon my impudence your Highness. Royal doctor Sankhaji has sent word for the Chief. Lady Mandhathri is in a critical condition,' he said hurriedly. The king looked startled at Agneyastra's ashen face. Purumithra squeezed his shoulder and said, 'Chief Agneya you have to go.'

'Royal doctor Sankha is very skilled and he will do his best. May God help you,' said the king. Agneyastra quickly bowed to the king and hurried out. Immense fear gripped at his heart. He madly rode on his horse to reach home as quickly as he could. The fear was suffocating him. All he could focus on was to reach Mandhatri. He reached home as the sun set into the horizon.

***

Agneyastra was standing at the window staring into the blue sky. Wrapped in a clean cotton cloth, his lovely daughter was sleeping in his arms.

You will be an excellent father Agneya.

Mandhathri's words echoed in his ears. He closed his eyes and a tear escaped his eye. That evening, a week ago, his world had come crashing down. When he had entered the house, Sankhaji handed him a baby wrapped delicately. It was a girl. Though he was a little disappointed, the sight of holding his child in his arms gave him ethereal happiness. She had her mother's black eyes. But his happiness didn't last long. Mandhathri had breathed her last giving birth to the girl. When Agneyastra heard that, he was so astonished that his hands gave way and he would have dropped the baby, had it not been for Sankha who held her immediately. Copious tears were flowing from Agneya's eyes.

Sankha placed a hand on his shoulder and said, 'We tried our best but she lost lot of blood. Her last words were that you should always love and protect your daughter.'

'Manni has given me no choice, my daughter is all that I have now. She is the one I will love and live for.'

But for Agneyastra life was miserable without Mandhathri. Though his sister and the attendant nursed the baby, Agneyastra simply couldn't bear the void created by her death. He missed her every day, every moment. His daughter was both pain and pleasure to him. For she was not just his hope for the future but also a reminder of the past which he had loved and lost. He named his daughter Mithraveera.

***

'Do you think he will agree?' asked a concerned Devarata. He had been crowned as the king of Virpur after his father had died in a battle. The king was in the royal gardens with Purumithra. He had already sent word for Agneyastra to meet him there.

'Chief Agneyastra has refused to marry again. Nobody could convince him. He dotes on his daughter. That girl has indeed shattered our hopes your Highness.'

'You are right. Agneyastra's family has been protecting the royal family for generations. Their loyalty and dedication is unquestionable. It's really unfortunate that Chief Agneya will be the last from his family to serve us. I just hope that our decision of finding an alternative serves us right,' he said letting out a sigh. He sat down on the intricately designed chair placed under a canopy. Purumithra sat down on a chair placed one step below the king.

Agneyastra was in the artillery inspecting the weapons when he received the king's message. Though it was really unusual to receive a message with such short notice, he quickly mounted his horse and rode towards the palace. When he reached there, the king gestured him to sit on a chair opposite Purumithra.

'How is your daughter Agneya?' asked the king.

'Mithra is fine my lord. Yashomati, my sister is taking care of her. It is unfortunate that I can't keep my girl with me. Though I visit her, it is impossible to spend more time with her as work is my priority,' said Agneya masking his pain with a rigid face.

'Well, you have been called today to make a very important decision. I want to tell you something which is crucial for our kingdom,' said the king and slightly nodded his head at Purumithra. Agneyastra was listening attentively.

'What is it your Highness?' asked Agneyastra.

'Have you given a thought about marrying again? Don't you think you need a companion and your daughter needs a mother?' asked Purumithra though he was already aware of the answer. Agneyastra let out a long drawn breath and looked away so as to hide the pain in his eyes.

'I am sorry my lord. I cannot marry again. Manni was the one who made me live than just survive. She still lives in my heart. It is impossible for me to marry another woman because I can never love her. For when Manni left me, she took away everything with her leaving me a daughter. Now I live for my daughter, she is all I have', said Agneyastra closing his eyes to stop the tears welling up in his eyes. Purumithra gave a meaningful look at the king.

'We are sorry for your pain Agneya. Since this is your decision, we also have been forced to make a decision. Your family has served the royals for generations. Your valour, courage and loyalty is famed across Virpur. But your daughter disappointed us. Now that you refuse to marry again we have lost all hope of expecting your heir to be your successor. We expected a tiger cub but we were handed a helpless puppy...' said Purumithra hinting at Agneyastra's child.

'How dare you!' roared Agneyastra standing up. Pure rage was burning in his eyes. The father couldn't tolerate his child being insulted. He clenched his fists trying to control his anger. He calmed down only because he was standing before the king.

'Chief Agneyastra calm down. The truth may sound cruel but we have to accept it. Of what use is a daughter to you? She cannot succeed you', said the king. Agneyastra composed himself just to be able to talk but his fists were still clenched.

'What is your decision, your Highness?'

'Purumithra tell him.'

'His Highness wants you to choose an eligible and brave boy from the gurukul. You should train him to succeed you like he were your own son,' said Purumithra.

'What do you have to say Agneya?' asked the king formally.

'I have to agree your Highness. Do I even have a choice?' he asked coldly.

'We gave you a choice, but you chose this. You have to live with the choices you make,' said Devarata evenly.

'I don't regret my decision.' Agneyastra had already made a decision of which only he was aware.

***

'I will train you personally. You are no longer just any other boy in gurukul. You are my student', said Agneyastra holding the boy by his shoulder. He was Dhruva. A slender boy aged about 13 years. Agneyastra saw him when the boy was practising archery. He admired the boy's focus and concentration. It was just not that which actually made him choose this boy. There was something more.

That day the skills of adult men who were on the verge of passing out from the gurukul and young adolescents were being put to test. Examinations based on their skills and age were being conducted at the gurukul. At the adolescents archery examination Agneyastra first saw Dhruva. He was a slender boy with fair complexion. There was nothing different in his appearance compared to other boys. But it was his eyes which made all the difference. Agneyastra took note of him when he aced the archery examination. Later in the day when Agneyastra was casually walking in the gurukul, he saw the same boy talking to the man who had aced the adult's archery examination.

'Brother if you don't mind, can I compete with you?' asked the little boy. The man was clearly surprised by the request. He placed his hand on the boy's shoulder.

'You are too young for that.'

'I know. But I really want to compete,' said Dhruva earnestly.

'Well, then let's do it. I don't want to disappoint you. I will stand at the standard distance prescribed for adults. You stand at the distance meant for juniors', said the man picking up his bow and arrow. The boy didn't move. He looked straight at the man.

'No. I will stand right next to you!'

The man's brow knitted into a frown.

'But then you will not hit the target. What is the point of competing when you know you can't win?'

'I want to test my skill with your standards. Competition is not just about winning, it's about playing fair. If I have to compete with you then it is only fair that I rise up to your standards.'

The man smiled at the boy. He nodded in agreement. Both of them took their position with their bow and arrow.

'Shoot!' bellowed the man. The arrows were released simultaneously. The man's arrow hit the target board right at the centre perfectly. Dhruva's arrow did not hit the target circle but it did pierce the board at a corner. Dhruva was disappointed with his performance. But the man was dumbstruck.

'Excellent! Your arrow did hit the board. I never expected it. You are exceptionally skilled for your age. It is an honour to compete with you brother', said the man patting the boy's back in appreciation.

'Thank you brother', said Dhruva smiling. Agneyastra walked up to the boy after the man left. He had clearly found his search.

'Excellent my boy,' said Agneyastra. Dhruva bowed to the Chief.

'What is your name?'

'My name is Dhruva my Lord'.

'Dhruva, this name will be remembered for generations to come. Who are your parents?'

'My father was a soldier in the army. He died fighting in a battle. My mother didn't live long after losing him. Now I am an orphan', said he looking down, his eyes filled with grief.

'You are no longer an orphan. From now on you belong to me', said Agneyastra holding him by his shoulder. He looked up at the Chief perplexed.

'I can't understand your words my Lord'.

'Call me Guruji. I will train you personally. You are no longer just any other boy in gurukul. You are my student.'

The boy's eyes glittered with hope and respect. Agneyastra embraced Dhruva who hugged him back. That was the start of the relationship of a teacher and a student for Agneyastra. But for Dhruva, it was the relationship of a father and a son. He began training Dhruva in every skill he knew. With passing days Dhruva was clearly transforming into Agneyastra's reflection.

***

The rain was stretching its arms all around the place. Agneyastra saw his daughter playing merrily in the rain. He had brought her to a hill top. Though he always forbade her from drenching in the rain, today he didn't stop her. Rather he stood soaking in the rain. Mithraveera was an eight year old girl now. She was happy with her life. Though her aunt Yashomati did take care of her, Mithra could never see her as her mother. She loved her father and enjoyed every moment with him during his weekly visits. She loved the rain and had developed a relationship with it. She relished this opportunity of getting wet in the rain. Yes, she loved the rain until that day...

'Mithra come here.'

The rain was still pouring without any signs of weakening. She squinted her eyes to look at her father and ran to him.

'What is it father?'

'Today I want you to make a promise to me. Will you?' asked Agneyastra looking at her intently despite the rain.

'Of course I will', said the innocent girl. She was unaware that this promise would change her life forever.

'I am going to train you in sword fighting and archery. I will train you in all warfare skills. Will you obey me?'

Mithra was shocked. Only boys went to war!

'But why father?' she asked curiously. Agneyastra held her shoulders tightly.

'Do you love me?'

'Yes father.'

'Then you will do as I say. You will never question me the reason for it. Promise me that you will become a warrior', said Agneyastra outstretching his right palm. Mithra was ready to do anything for him. Without second thoughts she placed her right hand in his.

'I will do as you say father. I will become a warrior.'

He knew she would never disobey him. He believed in her.

'You will be the first woman warrior in the kingdom. I am proud of you my child. From now on you will be called Veera.'

He embraced Mithra for one last time. After this she ceased to be Mithra anymore, for Agneyastra acknowledged her only as Veera. At that time she never realised the pain of losing Mithra to Veera. For the world Mithraveera no longer existed. There was only Veera!

***

CHAPTER 2

After ten years.......

Chief Agneyastra was standing with his arms crossed across his chest. The years that had passed could only make some of his hair grey but the strength in his arms was still the same. He was overseeing the training of the soldiers at the camp. The threat of an impending war was looming large. Then his eyes fell on his boy, now a man. He was tall with a wheatish complexion. His bare chest was clearly exhibiting his well-toned upper torso. He wore a blue cotton dhoti and his sword was in the scabbard tied to his hip. His hair was short unlike other men, for he was never like them. His eyes still had the same focus and concentration but were sharper now. Agneya's boy was now a fully grown up man. Dhruva, the warrior who would succeed Agneyastra or that is what everyone believed unless fate willed it otherwise.

Chief Agneyastra trained Dhruva in all the skills he knew. Dhruva was a quick learner and Agneyastra was proud that very soon his student would outdo him. He had every quality in him to be his successor. But there was one thing the teacher was worried about. Unlike him who was unequivocally loyal to the royals, Dhruva was loyal only to the truth. He would do something only if he regarded it to be right and not just because the king ordered. It was this devil-may-care attitude of Dhruva which concerned the Chief. Agneyastra knew very well that the royals would not tolerate any kind of impudence or disobedience. But he also knew Dhruva could not be changed. Moreover he admired that quality in him. For men admired those qualities in other men when they didn't possess them. Agneyastra never disobeyed the king, he always believed that the king's order must be followed without questioning. But for Dhruva the king was just any other man. This complicated things for both.

One day when king Devarata and prince Vijayendra had come to the army camp, Agneyastra and Dhruva had joined them in the evening for a meeting. After the meeting Vijayendra ordered, 'Dhruva get me a drink!'

It was something that any soldier there would have gladly done to be in the favour of the prince. But Dhruva looked straight at him.

'I am your bodyguard, your Highness and not your servant. That order should be given to the person meant for it and not me,' he said evenly. Everyone were spellbound at his audacity. Agneyastra recovered quickly and glared at Dhruva. He knew Dhruva had to be sent from there.

'Dhruva go and get prepared for the duel at the sword fighting arena. You will be fighting the duel with one of the best swordsman in the army. Leave now!' commanded the Chief. Dhruva executed a royal salute and left. The king looked furiously at Agneyastra.

'Is this how you train him? To disobey the prince himself?' thundered Devarata.

'How dare he speaks to me that way?' growled prince Vijayendra clenching his fist. Agneyastra met their eyes evenly.

'I have trained him to be the best warrior your Highness. I am sure his achievements will outdo mine. Nobody can protect this army and the royal family better than him.'

'But that does not imply that we should put up with his impudence,' said the king.

'It might be impudence for you, but that is his self-respect. He is the best and your Highness should treat him that way. He will secure the royal family but not serve you. I have given you a warrior, if you are looking for a servant then I am sorry, you have the wrong person.'

Agneyastra's words clearly put an end to the conversation. A slight smile appeared on his face as he remembered that incident. Dhruva walked up to him and saluted.

'How is it going?'

'The training is going on fiercely Guruji. Everyone is kicked about the battle', said an enthusiastic Dhruva. It was going to be his first battle. A real test for his skills.

'Even I was excited like you for my first battle. My first challenge! But now a battle is dreary to me. Those men, their blood, the death, the sorrow, the pain – there is nothing romantic about it. Remember son, battles are woes that don't deserve revelry.'

But Dhruva smiled at those words.

'I may think like you after wielding my sword in as many battles as you have Guruji. But now I am just too excited about my first battle.'

Agneyastra nodded his head and smiled wryly. He placed his hand on Dhruva's shoulder.

'Dhruva, you know I have a daughter right?'

'Yes Guruji. Her name is Mithraveera. That is all I know about her,' said Dhruva plainly. Agneyastra looked into his eyes intensely.

'You will take care of her, until your last breath after me.'

Dhruva was aghast to hear those words. But he didn't question him for he knew that his teacher would always have a strong reason behind his deeds. Moreover Dhruva couldn't refuse Agneyastra, his teacher and a father he didn't have.

'I will,' said Dhruva, those two words, a promise of a lifetime.

'She is my life Dhruva and I trust you. Don't let me down,' he said his voice thick with emotion.

Without second thoughts Dhruva pulled out his knife from the scabbard which was partly hidden and secured at his waist. He made a small cut in his right palm which was bleeding now. He placed his bloodied red palm on Agneyastra's right palm and held it tight.

'I will not let go of Mithraveera ever. I promise!'

Dhruva's eyes glowed with intensity and Agneyastra was astonished. He had not expected it from him. He knew what that promise meant. Dhruva had sworn on his life to protect Veera until his last breath. Agneyastra had always seen him as his student. He trained him in every skill he knew. As a teacher he had succeeded. But today he knew it was not his student but his son who had made that promise. Agneyastra embraced Dhruva with earnest love of a father. Dhruva was overwhelmed. For him, Agneyastra was always his father and today he had sealed that relationship with blood.

***

Agneyastra was walking on a small trail in the forest. The path was not very distinct and dense foliage bordered it on both sides. Then suddenly an arrow landed on the path just one foot way from him. He was surprised. He looked around curiously but could not see anyone. He bent down and pulled out the arrow. It was familiar to him. He walked further on the trail and reached a clearing in the forest. Veera was standing there holding the bow in her left hand. She smiled lightly at her father.

Veera was now a warrior. She had dove eyes like her mother and a dusky complexion. She was tall and curvaceous at the right places. Though she was an eighteen year old lady, she didn't behave like one. She didn't possess any of those coquettish traits of a woman. She was always forced to think and act like a man, a warrior. But Veera never complained about it. Moreover she even dressed like a man in dhoti and waist length kurta. Though she had long hair till her waist, she always plaited it and tied it up.

Agneyastra walked up to his daughter still surprised.

'You shot this arrow. But you couldn't have seen me from here. How did you do it?'

'I heard your footsteps,' said Veera calmly.

'What!? You shot this arrow hearing my footsteps! But that's possible only if ...'

'I learnt the art of Shabdavedi,' she said looking straight at him. Agneyastra couldn't believe her words. It took him a moment to recover from the shock.

'But Veera, I didn't teach you that.'

'I have been practising it on my own from the day you told me about it,' she interrupted.

'Excellent Veera! This Shabdavedi skill will surely come handy in critical situations,' said he proud of his student. Veera was satisfied to see that pride in her father's eyes. She would do anything for it. She kept pushing boundaries to prove herself. It was not an easy ordeal.

Agneyastra then went and sat on a small boulder in the clearing. Veera went and sat on the grass in front of him crossing her legs. She kept the bow next to her.

'We have to talk,' said he in the tone of a Chief and not a father. She knew that he had something really important to discuss when he used that tone with her. She looked intently at him.

'I may not be visiting you for the next few months. An inevitable war will be fought in the coming weeks. This time it is not going to be an easy victory for us,' said Agneyastra intensely.

'I will go to war with you father,' said Veera immediately.

He was not surprised at her words. Rather he had expected it from her. But he nodded his head in disapproval.

'No Veera. You are not required to fight in this war. It is going to be difficult to win but not impossible. I will take you with me when the time is right.'

She was disappointed. He touched her shoulder affectionately.

'You are not yet ready for war. A battlefield is completely different from this training arena. There is no doubt that you are well trained but your skills have not been tested in a real war. You have still not faced a single real adversary yet. Trust me there will always be battles to fight in this world.'

Veera understood and Agneyastra smiled at her.

'As you say,' said she with a slight smile.

'I have one more thing to tell you……,' he said thoughtfully.

'I have told you about Dhruva. He is my student whom I have trained to succeed me. I trust him Veera. If ever you have to live without me, Dhruva is the one you will go to.

After me, it is he you will trust,' said her father. Veera looked at him critically.

'Why are you telling this to me now?'

'I should have told this to you long ago. I want you to know that you will not be alone when I am not with you. Dhruva will always be there for you Veera.'

'You are worried about this war father. I can sense that it is not going to be easy. Nevertheless of what you say, nobody can ever replace you,' she said in a soft tone.

'Veera, we can never predict our fate in war. This time I can't go into war without knowing that you will not be alone if I don't come back. Telling you about Dhruva will give me peace of mind,' said Agneyastra looking affectionately at his daughter.

'Okay father. I will go to Dhruva if you leave me. You just finish your battle and come back to me. I will be waiting. I love you and I always will until my last breath. Nothing can change that,' said Veera, her eyes moist.

'I know and I love you too my child,' said he and kissed her forehead. An unknown consternation suddenly began to weigh heavy on her heart. That day she didn't want to let go of her father but just hold onto him forever. As a daughter she could have done it, but for warrior Veera it was unthinkable. Agneyastra preferred she be a warrior than a daughter.

***

CHAPTER 3

Veera rode on her horse with terrifying speed. Two soldiers were riding their horses flanking her on either side. Copious tears were streaming down her face. She was racing against time to reach her father.

That was a beautiful day. Veera was sitting on the boulder in the clearing. She had just finished her early morning martial arts training. The sun was overhead. Two soldiers rode up to the clearing. Veera was astonished to see them. Their armour indicated that they had come straight from the battlefield. Veera's heart began drumming.

'What happened?' she asked nervously.

'Chief Agneyastra sent us. You have to come to the battlefield right away,' said the soldier.

'Is father alright?'

The two soldiers stayed quiet and glanced at each other.

'For God's sake, tell me what happened?' shrieked Veera impatiently.

'Chief has been injured in the war. He wants to see you immediately,' said the soldier lowering his eyes. Breath was knocked out of Veera. But she immediately recovered and tied the scabbard to her hip. She slung the quiver of arrows across her back. One of the soldier picked up her bow. All the three immediately mounted their horses and rode away.

'Hold on father. I am coming,' said Veera to herself. Tears were already streaming down her cheeks.

***

A medical camp had been set up to tend to the injured soldiers at a little distance from the battlefield. In one of the tents Agneyastra was being treated. Sankha was doing his best to stop the blood loss. But he knew all his efforts would be futile, for Agneyastra had a deep cut in his abdomen and an arrow had pierced his chest. He would have died on the battlefield but his soldier managed to bring him to safety. He wanted to save the Chief. Also Agneyastra had an unfinished task to be completed. He immediately sent for Veera. He implored Sankha to keep him alive until he saw her. Sankha knew the Chief could not be saved but he was doing everything he could to fulfil his request.

Veera barged into the tent as soon as she dismounted from the horse. She caught her breath when she saw her father lying there with blood soaking his torso. She went and took his head and rested it on her lap.

'Father, look at me. Please talk to me. You will be fine. Everything will be alright. Talk to me,' she said hurriedly. Agneyastra opened his eyes slowly.

'Veera... I know I won't survive. The prince is fighting in the war. Dhruva is combating to stop the enemies from destroying our army. You will go to protect the prince........' said he stressing on his last word. Sankha pressed the cloth at his abdomen to control the blood loss. But every time Agneyastra spoke he was bleeding more.

'Just hold on father. You will be fine,' said Veera amidst tears.

'My sword...,' whispered Agneyastra. The soldier picked up the Chief's bloodied sword. Agneyastra gestured Veera to take the sword. Veera took it in her hand. The sword was heavy.

'Take it Veera. From now on that sword is yours. The legacy of our family was written with this sword. This sword has been bloodied in numerous battles and killed many men. So long as you hold it, our family's name will live. The valour of our ancestors was written with this sword. Guard it...,' said he. More blood oozed through the bandage.

'I will, father,' said Veera in a muffled voice.

'I am proud of you Veera. I have not been a good father to you.....'

He was losing his consciousness.

'I love you father. Please don't leave me. Stay with me.....' implored a sobbing Veera.

'I am sorry Mithra......' said Agneyastra and closed his eyes. Veera's world came crashing down. There was silence in the tent. Veera placed his head on the bed. She bent and kissed his forehead. She closed her eyes for a moment and let the last tears slide down her face. Then she stood up. Veera wiped her tears and picked up her father's sword, which was now, hers.

***

It was a quiet evening. The cool breeze swept a few strands of Veera's hair onto her face. She was sitting on the floor leaning against the wall. Veera had come to her father's home after performing his last rites. Until then it was considered as a duty of a son. But Veera broke the rules. Nobody opposed because Dhruva shielded her. He stood by her and nobody dared to question him. Together they performed Agneyastra's last rites. Veera had not cried even for a moment after she picked up the sword. She fought valiantly and protected the prince. They won the battle because Dhruva salvaged most of the army on his side. He took a gamble by not going to protect the prince and it had paid off. Dhruva believed that Chief Agneyastra would guard the prince. He was unaware of the Chief being grievously injured. Dhruva didn't take long to recognise Veera when she joined him at the battlefield. Veera wielded that very sword which he had worshipped for years. His grief was unimaginable when he saw Agneyastra's dead body. Though he didn't cry out loud, tears streamed down his face continuously. Tears were the ultimate sign of breakdown for a warrior. That day Dhruva had lost his teacher and most of all, a father.

Dhruva, with bloodshot eyes walked into Agneyastra's home. The servants and the guards were performing their duties with a heavy heart. Except the guards, he dismissed others from work for the day. He looked around and the silence in the house was unbearable. Everything around wore a deserted look. It was already dark in the house but not a single lamp had been lit up. Dhruva lit a lamp and took a glass of milk. He walked to Veera's room.

Veera had not moved an inch, since the morning, from her place. Her eyes were lifeless and blank. She simply stared at the blank wall before her. Dhruva slowly entered and saw her there. She was dressed in cotton dhoti and kurta like a man. Her hair was untied and still a little damp. She had a dusky complexion. But it was her eyes which caught his attention. Those serene eyes had volumes hidden in them. Veera didn't notice Dhruva, rather she seemed oblivious to her surroundings. He was clueless about how he would console her for he had not overcome his loss yet. He placed the glass of milk near her and sat down next to her without facing her. He swallowed hard and let out a long drawn breath to overcome the emotions saturating his heart.

'Veera…' he called slowly. No response.

'Veera I know how hard it must be for you to lose father. But you…..' stopped Dhruva unable to complete. He didn't know what to tell her. But Veera was motionless.

'Don't be so still Veera. I can see your loss and pain. Just cry your heart out. It's not going to help to burden yourself with pain. Seeing you lifeless is killing me!' said Dhruva looking at the wall.

He could no longer tolerate her silence.

'Please Mithra…..,' said Dhruva looking at her. Suddenly Veera turned at him and her eyes bore a tortured look. Tears streamed down her cheeks.

'What did you call me?' asked Veera in a shaky voice.

'Mithra what happened?' he asked troubled.

'Father had stopped calling me Mithra long ago when he decided to make me a warrior. But, Mithra was the last word he uttered…'

She broke down. She began crying uncontrollably. Her grief was unlocked by that one word. Tears soaked her face. Dhruva didn't console her, but he wanted her to cry so that she could unburden herself. Her tears brought fresh tears in his already exhausted eyes. Dhruva didn't speak anymore. He just placed his arm around her shoulder. Veera was trembling with sorrow. She rested her head on his shoulder and her tears were crushing his heart with pain. With unspoken words, those tears were the only consolation they could give each other. Sometimes the best way to overcome grief is to participate in it together so that you know there is one more person going through the same pain. They were not just taking but also giving strength to each other. That day was the beginning of an unbreakable bond between the two.

***

Veera was awakened by the sound of hooves. The guards had come to relieve the others from their night duty of guarding the house. She slowly opened her eyes. Her head was feeling heavy from the previous day's crying. She rubbed her eyes and looked around. For a moment, she couldn't recognise the place. Then she saw that her head was rested on Dhruva's lap. She woke up immediately. Veera couldn't remember when she had fallen asleep resting her head on his shoulder. But he had slept in the same sitting posture the whole night. He had not moved, lest he should disturb her. Veera's head was hurting and she sat there holding her forehead. She looked at Dhruva. His face looked exhausted and his head was rested against the wall. She knew nothing about him except that her father had told her to go to Dhruva if ever she had to live without him. Yesterday when she was numb with grief, he had made her feel with just one word. For Veera, Dhruva no longer was a stranger though she knew nothing about him.

Dhruva's head moved slightly and his eyes flew open. His eyes had an untold fear and his forehead was sweating.

'What happened?' asked a startled Veera. Dhruva tried to control his erratic breathing and calmed down. He looked at her.

'Nothing. Just a nightmare. When did you wake up?'

'A few moments ago. I am sorry....... Yesterday you had to stay here in discomfort for me. I should have controlled my emotions,' she said slowly.

'Don't apologise for sharing your grief with me. I lived through yesterday only because of you. I don't know what would have become of me after losing...' he couldn't finish his sentence.

'Thank you Dhruva.'

'Anything for you Mithra. I will leave now. The servants will arrive soon and you can ask them anything you want. The guards will be here throughout the day. If there is anything you need, send word for me and I will come here as soon as I can.'

'I will. Take care,' said Veera.

'You too,' said Dhruva and left the place. Veera stood there looking outside the window. When Agneyastra died yesterday, she felt lost and all alone in this world. But today she was not alone. There was hope. There was Dhruva for her.

***

CHAPTER 4

After a few days…

Veera was sitting on a stone bench in the garden outside her home. She was holding the papyrus scroll containing the king's summons for her. She was told to come to the royal court that morning. Veera was confused about whether she should go to the royal court. But she was certain that she couldn't ignore the summons. Then she heard approaching footsteps and looked up. Now she knew she would make her decision soon, for it was Dhruva coming to her.

Dhruva had reported to work the very next day after the Chief's demise. Now it was his responsibility to supervise the army. Everyone firmly believed that Dhruva would succeed Agneyastra. So it was appropriate that he mask his sorrow and take up responsibility. But he spent all his time after work with Veera. She had become a recluse after her father's death but with Dhruva she was slowly returning to normalcy. He made sure not to leave her alone for long. Both of them ate their dinner together and if time permitted they also ate their breakfast together. Today was one such day and he had come early in the morning. But he was surprised to see her sitting in the garden.

'Good morning Veera,' said Dhruva smiling.

'Good morning Dhruva,' said Veera with a slight smile. He noticed the papyrus scroll in her hand.

'What is written?' he asked frowning at it. He could recognise that it was from the palace. Veera handed it over to him. Dhruva read through it.

'What to do now?' asked a worried Veera. Dhruva sat down next to her and handed the scroll back to her.

'It's a summons from the king. You decide what to do with it,' he said shrugging his shoulders. Veera nodded her head in disappointment.

'I thought you would help me decide. Well, I think I can't ignore it. There is no harm in going to the royal court I suppose.'

'See! You have already made your decision to go. So there is nothing I have to say. All I can say is best of luck! By the way you should leave early,' he said as a matter of fact.

'I am not going alone. You are coming with me.' She looked straight at him.

'What?! But why? I am sorry Mithra. I can't go with you,' he said immediately.

'Why can't you? Are you afraid?' she asked sarcastically. Dhruva smiled and nodded his head.

'Let's just say that I don't share a good rapport with them. Moreover the summons is only for you. It doesn't include me,' snapped Dhruva.

'If I have to go, then you also go with me Dhruva,' she said firmly. He could no longer refuse her.

'As you wish,' he said at last giving in to her decision. Though he had refused her initially he knew he could not send her alone to the royal court. It just didn't feel right to him.

***

'Veera saved the battle for us. She fought valiantly to guard the prince,' said Prime Minister Purumithra.

'She was exceptional, father. I had never believed until then that a woman could wield a sword,' said an impressed Prince Vijayendra.

'Veera has undoubtedly inherited Agneyastra's valour and courage. She is a reflection of her father.'

King Devarata nodded his head in agreement.

'I agree with you Purumithra. But this is a big decision to make. Is it feasible to hand over the responsibility of the royal family and our army to her?' asked a concerned king.

'Veera is Agneyastra's daughter my lord.'

'That is exactly my primary concern. She is his "daughter" and not his son. Moreover the Chief had trained Dhruva to succeed him and everyone know this. Isn't it foolishness to handover everything to a girl? What will people say? Other kings will laugh at me!' said he clenching his fist.

'My lord, we all know about Dhruva's attitude. If he is made the Chief, we can have no control over him. It will be disastrous if the Chief cannot be controlled by the king. The men respect Dhruva for his capability and they will certainly oppose anyone we choose to replace him. But that won't happen if we choose Veera. It will be the ultimate tribute to Agneyastra's dedication. Nobody will oppose and we can also reign in Dhruva. In any case it is an advantage,' said Purumithra.

'Puruji is right father. Veera will unquestioningly be loyal to us. Moreover she is inexperienced and we can easily impose our decisions on her. She will not override our decisions,' reasoned Vijayendra.

'If she turns out to be as you say, then we will have no problem. Let us hope we are doing the right thing,' said King Devarata. A royal guard walked in and bowed to him.

'Your Highness, Mithraveera and Dhruva want to meet you.'

The king was surprised to hear that even Dhruva had come.

'Send them in,' he ordered.

Veera and Dhruva walked in. Dhruva executed a royal salute and she bowed to them.

'How are you Veera?' asked the king.

'I am fine, your Highness,' replied Veera politely.

'I wish to convey my condolences for Agneyastra's death. On behalf of the royal court. We are sorry for your loss. Your father was great man.'

'Thank you your Highness. He was honoured to serve you,' said Veera.

'We also want to appreciate the courage you displayed in crisis. Though none of us were aware of your training, we were not very surprised by your skills. For you have proved that you are Agneyastra's heir in every way.'

'I am humbled by your words, your Highness.'

'Today I have called you here to make an important decision Veera,' said King Devarata.

Veera and Dhruva were listening intently.

'But we want to talk to you in private. Therefore we summoned only you. Commander Dhruva may leave,' said Purumithra. Dhruva gave him a sharp look. He didn't want to stand there anymore. He immediately turned to leave. But Veera impulsively held his hand. Dhruva looked at her and she gestured him to stay. He let out a long drawn breath. This was going to be difficult for him.

'Kindly pardon me your Highness. But Dhruva stays with me,' she said firmly.

'But Veera…,' interjected Vijayendra.

'I am sorry my lord. There is nothing to be kept secretive from Dhruva. As long as I am involved, he will be present with me,' said Veera stubbornly. Purumithra glanced at the king.

'Okay Veera. Let Dhruva stay. Both of you sit down,' said Purumithra.

'Veera your father was irreplaceable. We can never fill the void he has left in our hearts and the army. Now we have been forced to choose his successor which is inevitable,' said the king. Veera looked at Dhruva sitting next to her on the wooden chair. His face was blank.

'And we have decided after much thought that Veera, you will be the new Chief for the army of Virpur. You will succeed your father,' said Devarata.

There was complete silence in the royal court. Veera was dumbstruck. This news came out of the blue for her. She turned to look at Dhruva. He had a calm and expressionless face. Veera wanted him to say something but she knew that he was not going to say anything.

'Your Highness, my father trained Dhruva to succeed him. I am inexperienced for this role,' protested Veera. Her voice was shaky and nervous.

'Commander Dhruva was indeed trained by Agneyastra. But no decision was made about him succeeding the Chief. We wanted a member of your family to be the Chief and we were disappointed when you were born. You have now proved us wrong Veera. The right way to honour your father's valour would be to make you his successor,' said King Devarata.

'We also have a few conditions Veera, for this is the first time ever we have selected a woman to be the Chief. To do justice to that position, you will always dress like a man. The next condition is very important. You will never marry or have any relationship with a man so as to bear his child,' said Prime Minister Purumithra firmly. Dhruva could no longer control his temper. His eyes were spewing fire.

'This is atrocious!' roared Dhruva standing up.

'Commander Dhruva, hold your tongue. You will not speak until you are asked to,' ordered Vijayendra. Dhruva clenched his fists at his words but didn't speak back. Veera was astonished to hear Purumithra's conditions. She was spellbound and didn't know what to do. There was silence.

'Veera we understand that you are surprised by our decision. But we are forced to do it. I hope you will understand. Well, think about this and tell us your decision tomorrow. You both may leave now,' said the king. Both of them quietly bowed and left. Veera's mind was blank but Dhruva's mind was crowded with emotions.

***

Veera took two glasses of lemonade with mint and went to the garden. Dhruva was seated on the wooden swing looking at the plants but she knew his mind was thinking about today's conversation in the royal court. She walked up to him and gave him one glass. She sat next to him on the swing. Dhruva quietly sipped his lemonade. Veera was looking at the flowers and avoided eye contact with him.

'What do you think I should do?' asked Veera. Dhruva frowned at her in confusion.

'What is there to think about it? You are going to say no to them tomorrow,' he said casually.

'Should I?' asked Veera softly.

'Their conditions are outrageous Mithra. I am not going to let you choose that life.'

'But don't you think it is a once in lifetime opportunity?'

Dhruva looked at her exasperated.

'Mithra, they have made this decision only to keep me away from becoming the Chief. They hate me for adhering only to the truth. They cannot bend me according to their whims and fancies. Many times they tried convincing Guruji to change his mind. But he didn't budge. Now they think that if you are made the Chief their purpose will be achieved and nobody will oppose it,' reasoned Dhruva. Veera took a few minutes to process the information. She finished her drink and so did he. The attendant came and collected their empty glasses. Dhruva stood up to leave.

'Don't think too much about it Mithra. We will go to the royal court tomorrow and tell our decision. I don't care as to who they appoint as the new Chief. It makes no difference to me. I knew they would come up with some ridiculous suggestion like this,' he said and turned to leave.

'What if I agree to it?' said Veera impulsively. Dhruva turned looking at her disbelievingly.

'What did you just say?'

'You heard me. Are you doubting my capability to be the Chief?' she asked looking straight at him. Dhruva let out a sigh and walked back to her. He took her face in his hands and looked into her eyes.

'If I doubt your capability I would be doubting myself. We both were trained by Guruji. You have proven that you are a great warrior in the war Mithra. I know you will make an excellent Chief of the army. But that is not the issue. Their conditions will take away the very essence of your life...' said Dhruva intensely.

'I lost it long ago Dhruva. There is nothing left to lose now.....,' said Veera slowly. He withdrew his hands and turned away from her. He knew he couldn't let her make that decision, he had to stop her. Veera stood up and went to face him.

'Don't jump to conclusions when you are angry. You have to first think with a clear head. You have to analyse the every possible consequence of our decision Dhruva. Now let us just say that I refuse their proposal. Then what? Certainly they will not make you the Chief. They will find some other excuse and appoint another less capable man. We both know that it is not the right thing to do. It will affect our army and kingdom. Do you want that to happen?' she questioned him. Dhruva glared at her.

'I don't give a damn about them! It is you that I am bothered about. I won't let them rob you of your life!' growled Dhruva. Veera had to quickly think of something that would convince him to agree.

'A ship is always safe in the harbour but that is not what ships are meant for. We are warriors and we shouldn't back out from challenges.'

'I am not saying that we should be cowards Mithra. Being brave is different from being foolish. I promised Guruji that I would take care of you. Let me keep up my promise,' said Dhruva with a tortured look.

'What would have father said? He would certainly have agreed to this, wouldn't he? I think you know the answer better than me,' said Veera looking straight into his eyes. Dhruva was stumped. He knew very well that her father would surely have been proud to see his daughter succeed him.

'Mithra…....' said Dhruva in an imploring tone. He knew he had lost this argument.

'Please Dhruva, at least for father's sake agree to it.'

He closed his eyes in pain.

'As you wish Mithra. I stand by your decision,' said Dhruva opening his eyes.

'Thank you,' she said smiling lightly.

'I will always be your accomplice in every decision you make, no matter what. Don't make me regret this decision more than I already do,' said Dhruva holding her by her shoulder. Veera knew that he was hurting but she had no choice.

'As long as you are with me, even if the whole world turns into ash, I lose nothing,' she said looking into his eyes. The two friends stood there ready to take on the world. So long as they stay together, they win. It was just a matter of time, for in this world forever does not exist.

***

CHAPTER 5

'Do you think she can do this?' asked Vidyut looking at the soldiers assembled before them. Dhruva and Vidyut were standing on the raised platform in the battlefield. Soldiers from all the wings of their army were summoned early in the morning. Veera had to address them today. Major Vidyut was overseeing the arrangements along with Dhruva. The royal court had already made the announcement about the appointment of the Chief. Though Veera succeeding her father was justified, a woman becoming the Chief was unheard of and not easily acceptable. This meant the men had to bow to a woman. Veera had agreed to all the conditions but in return she laid down one condition of her own. She said that Dhruva would be her personal bodyguard and second in command after her. This implied that he would be a part of every decision and discussion. Though the members of the royal court were not happy with her condition, they had to agree as Veera gave them no choice. Today is the first time she would be interacting with the soldiers. Veera was nervous and apprehensive about it.

'Mithra will be fine. She can do it,' said Dhruva in reply. Vidyut smiled at his confidence in her. Dhruva and Vidyut were friends from childhood. They were close to each other from the days they had spent together in Gurukul. Vidyut had met Veera and seen her combat in the war. He was appreciative of her skills but still not convinced that she could shoulder this responsibility. It was surprising for him to see that unfathomable confidence and admiration in

Dhruva's eyes for Veera. Equally confusing to him was the bond they both shared. Vidyut felt that they both connected with each other at a deeper level. Though Vidyut knew Dhruva for a long time, he couldn't understand Dhruva as much as Veera could.

'Keep an eye on the crowd. I will be back,' said Dhruva and hurried towards the tent set up near the raised platform.

Veera was sitting stiff on a chair. Her heart was drumming and she had intertwined her fingers out of nervousness. She didn't notice Dhruva enter the tent.

'Mithra…'

'I am scared,' blurted out Veera on hearing his voice.

He pulled a chair and sat in front of her. He freed her hands and took her hand in his hands. He held her hand securely and looked into her eyes.

'I know you are scared. Who told you that fear is a crime? Do you think I am not scared? Fear haunts everyone, Mithra. But what you should always remember is, courage is not the absence of fear but the defeat of fear. The path to courage is always through the dark tunnels of fear and you have to walk through them. Of course you have an advantage…' said Dhruva and a slow smile entered his face. Veera looked at him quizzically.

'You are not alone. I walk with you.'

Veera smiled at him. Fear was defeated.

'Let's go,' she said confidently.

***

'Comrades!' bellowed Veera from the raised platform. Dhruva was standing with her on her right. She looked at the soldiers, commanders and majors assembled before her.

'I am not here as your Chief today. I am here to be a part of this magnificent army. Chief Agneyastra was a man synonymous with valour and courage. Today I am stepping into his place. Under his leadership this army was undefeated. I know every one of us here doubt my ability in leading all of you. The truth is I don't want to be your leader. I don't want you to be mere followers. I want you to lead this army. Comrades, today let us all pledge that each one of us will lead our army to victory,' shouted Veera.

Everyone was listening to her in rapt attention. Dhruva looked at her with a sense of pride. He knew the men were being influenced by her words. Veera was bringing a new sense of belonging among them.

'My father believed in this army. I believe in each one of you. I am not just one among you but I am you. Let us show the world that Virpur cannot be defeated. Long live Virpur!' bellowed Veera.

'Long live Virpur!'

'Long live Virpur!'

'Long live Virpur!' shouted the men. The whole army looked up to the woman who would lead them from that day onwards.

***

'I am honoured to be under your command, Chief,' said Vidyut after saluting Veera.

'You can call me Veera,' she said smiling.

'You are the Commander-in-Chief of the army. I shouldn't address you by your name. I am sorry but you will have to get used to being addressed as Chief.'

'You are right Vidyut. Do I even have a choice?' said Veera shrugging. Dhruva looked at her meaningfully.

'Now both of you come on, let's go have dinner. I am starving,' said Dhruva rubbing his hand over his stomach. Veera had arranged for dinner at her home for the three of them. The attendant Nila laid out small tables on which the plantain leaf was placed. Then she served them dinner of rice and curry along with some boiled spinach.

'What do you think about my speech today?' asked Veera looking apprehensively at Vidyut.

'You were no doubt excellent!' exclaimed Dhruva enthusiastically. Veera gave him an exasperated look and shook her head.

'I asked him and I expect an answer from him, not you. I know you are biased,' she said sharply.

'Dhruva actually spoke the truth. You are very impressive Chief. To be honest, I too had my doubts about your capability. But I was wrong. I know you will make an exceptional Chief.'

Veera smiled slightly but her eyes were expressionless.

'You were not wrong in doubting my capability Vidyut. Until I prove myself capable I want you to keep those apprehensions alive. Sometimes doubting a person is the first step towards discovering his actual worth.'

'Don't be hard on yourself Mithra. You don't have to prove anything to anyone, because there will always be people to find faults. To how many of them will you keep proving yourself?' asked Dhruva with anger in his tone.

'Until my last breath I will have to keep proving myself Dhruva, for that is the reason I am a warrior today.'

'For me you will always be the best and nothing can change that between us,' said Dhruva looking straight into her eyes. Veera knew that he meant every word that he had just said. She knew her comrade better than anyone.

'You will always be the same for me. I know nothing will change between us for that is the only luxury life has given me, Dhruva,' said Veera.

Vidyut quietly ate his food being a silent spectator to their unfathomable bond.

***

'You don't have to worry uncle, I will take care of Sinhika,' said Veera assuring her father. Sinhika smiled at her. Very soon after Veera had become the Chief she obtained permission from the King to induct women in the army. Though he refused initially, she was very persistent and stubborn. The royal court had to give in to her obstinacy. The women were allowed to serve in the army only until they remained spinsters. Once they marry, they will have to leave the army. The citizens of the kingdom were apprehensive to send their daughters to war. But a few brave parents sent their daughters to be trained by Veera. Sinhika was one such lady. After her father left, she went and joined the other woman who were being trained first in martial arts.

Then Veera looked around scanning each and every practice arenas. She could spot Vidyut near the sword fighting arena. He was preoccupied with demonstrating to soldier about the body posture to be maintained during a combat. Commander Brihateja was overseeing the horse riders. He looked at Veera and smiled. But she couldn't spot Dhruva anywhere. Suspecting that he must have left the camp, she cast a look at the stables. But his horse was still tethered there.

Where did he disappear?

Searching him, she went to the private tent set up in the camp for resting. But Veera found that Dhruva was not there either. As she was about to walk out from there, she saw through the window, two men standing under a tree at a distance. Veera immediately walked out and found that Dhruva was talking to a man whose face was covered with a cloth with only his eyes visible. Within a few moments, the masked man mounted his horse and rode away. Dhruva walked back to the tent and was surprised to see Veera standing there. But he showed no surprise on his face. He remained calm and composed as he walked to her. As he neared her he gave a slight smile.

'It is a very hot day, isn't it?' he said casually.

'Yes it is,' she said evenly.

'I am hungry, let's go and eat.'

He walked past Veera towards the tent. But she called out to him. Dhruva stopped on his way and turned around to look at her.

'Who was it?'

'Who?' asked Dhruva immediately. Veera let out a sigh and narrowed her eyes.

'You know who I am talking about,' she said gesturing towards the tree where he was talking with a masked man just a few moments ago.

'Oh! You mean the man I was talking to? He is just a stranger. He had lost his way. I was giving him directions to get back to the city,' said Dhruva shrugging his shoulders.

For anyone else his words would have been believable but not for Veera.

'Mithra, let's go,' said Dhruva running his hand through his hair. Veera nodded her head and followed him into the tent.

***

Chapter 6

'My lady, shall I serve you dinner?' asked Nila looking at Veera. Veera was reading through the scriptures given to her by Prime Minister Purumithra. The scriptures were about the history and battles fought by Virpur. She looked up at Nila and smiled.

'Has Dhruva arrived?'

Usually Veera dined with him and then he would retire to his home to rest.

'No my Lady. Commander Dhruva has still not come home. But he sent you a message through his guard. He said that he would not be joining you for dinner today. He will meet you tomorrow morning,' said Nila.

Veera frowned at her answer. This was very unusual because even if Dhruva didn't come for dinner in the past, he had always kept Veera informed personally. But today when they parted from the camp, he had not told her anything about it.

'Did the guard tell anything about where Dhruva has gone?'

'No, my lady. It is time for your dinner. Shall I serve?'

Veera let out a sigh and nodded her head in assent. She sat on the carpet laid on the floor. A small table was placed in front of her and a plantain leaf on it. Nila served her roti, curry, rice and a cup of boiled vegetables. She ate her food without paying attention to its taste.

Later Veera retired to her private chamber and lied down on her bed. She closed her eyes but sleep was far from entering her eyes. As much as she tried hard, she couldn't sleep. Suddenly a thought struck her and she woke up. Veera wrapped an angavastram around her and walked out into the garden. She called out a guard. He bowed to her.

'What can I do for you my lady?' asked the guard politely.

'You will go straight to Major Vidyut's house and see if he is at home. In case he is not there, go around the kingdom and see where Commander Dhruva and Major Vidyut are. Remember one very important thing, you will carry out my orders surreptitiously. Keep an eye on their whereabouts and report to me in the morning,' said Veera in a low voice. She kept looking around to be cautious that no one else heard her words. The guard nodded his head absorbing the gravity of her order.

'I will do as you say Chief.' He saluted her and went out immediately. Veera closed her eyes and let out a long drawn breath. That masked man kept occupying her mind and she felt uneasy about him.

***

Veera was sitting on the steps leading to the portico of her home. She was drinking milk boiled with a little jaggry. Just then the guard came riding on his horse. Veera immediately stood up impatient to hear the news he had brought her. The guard bowed to her.

'What happened? Did you find them?'

'Yes my Lady.' Veera felt relief and anxiety at the same time.

'Where did they go last night?' she quickly asked him. The guard lowered his head in embarrassment. He didn't want to answer that question.

'Answer me!' ordered Veera.

'My lady, Commander Dhruva and Major Vidyut were… Last night they were at Rati's mansion,' he said at last.

'What!? You mean that prostitute's mansion?' asked Veera disbelievingly. The guard didn't lift his head up unable to meet her eyes.

'I hope you have evidence to prove this information. You better not lie about it,' she threatened him. He looked at her startled.

'No Chief. Every word I told you is true. I saw them last night at Rati's mansion. They left the place in the wee hours of the morning. Both of them went straight to Commander Dhruva's home.'

Veera took a moment to get a hold on the facts which threw her mind off balance.

'Okay. You may go now. But remember that you will not reveal a single word about this to anyone,' warned Veera. The guard then bowed to her and walked away. Veera quickly tied up her hair and mounted her horse. She gestured her guards not to follow her. She rode as fast as she could towards Dhruva's home.

***

Vani bowed to Veera as she entered the house.

'Where is your master?' she asked, her face hot and flushed due to the horse ride.

'Commander Dhruva is still asleep my Lady.'

'Is Vidyut here?'

'Yes my Lady. He is sleeping in the other room,' said Vani.

Veera made no further queries and walked straight to Dhruva's room. She knocked thrice on the door but there was no response. Since the door was unlatched she pushed it open. Dhruva was sprawling on his bed, bare-chested and in deep sleep with his mouth slightly open. He looked so vulnerable to her. Though she was angry with him until the last minute, now she mellowed down. She went near him and called out his name. But he was so deep in sleep that he hardly stirred. At last she gave up and shook him slightly by his shoulder. After four attempts, he opened his eyes.

'Mithra... what are you doing here?' he asked groggily still half-asleep.

'I have to talk to you. Wake up Dhruva.'

'Later Mithra.... Please let me sleep now,' he mumbled closing his eyes again.

'Wake up Dhruva! This is important,' said Veera jerking his shoulder. He slowly got up and sat resting his back to the pillow against the wall. He rubbed his eyes and looked at her with a childish face.

'What is it Mithra?'

'Where were you last night?' she asked him straightaway. He averted her eyes.

'Answer my question,' she demanded.

'At Rati's mansion,' he answered after a moment's pause. There was silence in the room. Veera sat on the bed in front of him.

'I can't still believe that you did this. I never expected you to demean yourself like this,' she said shaking her head.

'What did I do wrong? Many men in our kingdom go there. How does I going there become a crime? You are just overreacting!' snapped Dhruva.

'Overreacting? Is it really you speaking like this? I can't believe my ears. You were not the one to practice such vices. Yet today you are justifying drinking and visiting a prostitute?' squealed Veera.

'Stop it Mithra! As a Chief you can only interfere with the affairs concerned to my work. You cannot trespass into my personal space. I don't like anyone advising me,' he said irritated.

'I have not come here to talk to you as a Chief. Dhruva, I am worried about you. Why don't you understand that you have a reputation to maintain?' asked a concerned Veera.

'Damn my reputation!' sneered Dhruva. Veera stood up and glared at him.

'Fine! Do as you wish. I am not going to ask you anything more,' she said and stormed out of his room. Dhruva banged his clenched fist to the wall.

'Damn it!' he cursed under his breath. He certainly didn't want her to get involved in this.

***

That whole day Veera avoided meeting Dhruva. They didn't meet up for lunch. In the evening also she went home from the palace without seeing him. That evening once again Dhruva and Vidyut went to Rati's mansion. They were received by an eager Rati. They were seated comfortably in the huge hall where a courtesan was dancing to entertain the assembled guests. Dhruva keenly looked around. He could recognise many men and some he couldn't. He cast a sidelong glance at Vidyut. He gestured at the soldier who was seated in the corner of the hall. The soldier touched his hip and signalled to Vidyut that everything was ready. Just then an attendant walked in with a tray full of liquor glasses. She went about serving every man there. They both picked one glass each from the tray. The attendant's head was covered with a pink veil. Only the lower part of her face could be seen. Her lips appeared to curve into a smile as she served Dhruva. But he tried not to get distracted from the task at hand, though there was something familiar about those lips. He watched the men as they began drinking. Both Dhruva and Vidyut left their glasses untouched.

A man who was seated on the other side of the hall, stood up and walked up to Rati. Dhruva keenly watched him as he spoke to a seductive Rati. After a few moments, she started leading the man towards one of the rooms. Dhruva looked at the soldier seated in the corner. He immediately loaded an arrow to his bow and took a shot at the man. Unfortunately the man suddenly tried to whisper something into Rati's ear and moved closer to her. The arrow missed its target and hit a flower vase placed near the wall. In the next moment there was utter chaos in the mansion. Dhruva and Vidyut pulled out their swords and stood up to take positions. The soldiers who had accompanied them also pulled out their swords and took positions. But to their astonishment, as soon as the flower vase was hit, the man whistled loudly. Immediately his men in and around the mansion trooped into the hall with swords and daggers. This was totally unexpected. Dhruva and his men were clearly outnumbered. Yet he would have readily fought with them but that man pulled Rati closer to him and placed a knife at her throat.

'Don't move from your place or else she will die!' he threatened.

It was a stalemate. Dhruva was thinking hard to find just one loophole through which he could bring down his opponents. Just then he could sense a slight movement on his right in another corner of the hall. The attendant who had served them was standing behind the curtain. In a split second, she pulled out a dagger from the folds of her veils and flung it at the man. It was a neat throw. The dagger lodged itself in his arm making him drop his knife. He shrieked in pain.

'Run Rati!' screamed the attendant. This was the opening Dhruva was waiting for.

He used this moment of distraction and charged towards his opponents. Those men were indeed not easy to defeat. But the soldiers were far more trained and skilled than them. They began inflicting grievous injuries on those men. To everyone's surprise that attendant quickly brought out a bow and quiver of arrows which she had hidden behind the curtain. She began shooting arrows at those men. Her aim was accurate though her face was still partially covered with the veil. For Dhruva, it was not hard to guess who she was. He knew that only one person could be so adept in archery.

Dhruva defeated and injured many of his opponents. But the leader of those men still lay on the ground with his arm injured by Veera's dagger. Dhruva made a mistake of assuming that his blood loss had made the man weak. But he viciously picked up the dagger and threw it aiming at Veera. Dhruva who was now nearing her ran up to her and the dagger pierced through his right shoulder.

'MITHRA!' shrieked Dhruva. Vidyut heard his cry and shot an arrow at the man which pierced straight through his neck. He fell dead on the ground.

'DHRUVA!' cried Veera dropping her bow. She held him tightly. His shoulder was bleeding profusely.

'Dhruva, hold tight! Nothing will happen to you. Look at me! Look at me,' she cried holding his head.

Vidyut and the soldiers captured the remaining men. He ordered the soldiers to imprison them. He rushed to Dhruva. Veera slowly removed the dagger. Dhruva screamed in pain and he was still conscious. She quickly tied her veil around his chest in order to control the loss of blood.

'Let's take him out of here. I have sent word for Sankhaji,' said Vidyut hurriedly. He and two more soldiers lifted Dhruva and took him to the carriage. Tears were streaming down Veera's face but she was not sobbing. More than her pain, her mind was focused only on keeping him out of danger. Rati came to her.

'I am sorry about what happened to Commander Dhruva. Thank you for saving my life.'

'It's my duty. Rati thank you for helping us nab those terrorists. We will always be grateful for your help.'

Rati bowed to her.

'It is an honour to be of any help to you Chief.'

Veera nodded at her.

'Don't worry my Lady. He will be fine,' assured Rati squeezing Veera's hand. Veera then quickly took leave and went to the carriage. Vidyut mounted his horse and all other soldiers also followed suit. The carriage with Veera and Dhruva headed straight to his home. The Chief Doctor Sankha and his assistants were present there to treat him.

***

CHAPTER 7

Veera was sitting on a wooden stool. She leaned back on the wall and rested her head. She looked calm. But in her heart she was fervently telling herself that Dhruva will be fine. Her clothes were smeared with his blood. Sankha and his team were treating Dhruva in his room. The door was closed and she was waiting with bated breath to know how he was feeling. Vidyut was impatiently walking to and fro near the room. Even the pretence of being calm was impossible for him. He stopped and looked at her. He really couldn't understand how she appeared to be so tranquil.

'Thank you for coming there Chief. I was dumbstruck when I saw you throw that dagger. If it were not for you, things could have got worse,' he said intensely.

'It's already more than worse. What made you both hide this issue of terrorists from me?' asked Veera glaring at him. He didn't give an answer.

'Why didn't he tell me?' she asked in a voice saturated with pain. Vidyut let out a long drawn breath and sat down in front of her.

'Veera, how could he tell you when he knew that you wouldn't let him go there without you? This was not a battlefield. These terrorists are men with no rules unlike men in war. You have never faced them until now. Certainly the danger was very high. Dhruva never fears for his life. He will take any risk to perform his duty. But he can never risk your life. He cannot even think of putting you in danger. He is very protective about you,' said he looking into her eyes. A tear slid down Veera's cheek.

'This is so unfair. He can't do this to me. He can't…' she said closing her eyes. Just then the door opened and Sankha walked out. They both immediately stood up.

'How is he now?' she asked quickly.

'You did a good thing by tying a cloth around his wound. Fortunately the blood loss was less. We have cleaned his wound and applied medicine. I have bandaged his wound. But he is still unconscious.'

'He will be fine, right?' asked Veera hurriedly. Her heart was drumming with anxiety. Sankha placed a hand on her shoulder.

'Calm down my child. Dhruva is out of danger. He is exhausted and unconscious due to the medicines and blood loss. It will take a few days for the wound to heal.'

'Thank you so much Sankhaji. What about his medicines?'

'My student will be here until Dhruva gets well. He will change his bandage at the right intervals. Also he will administer him the medicines. Do follow the instructions regarding his food strictly,' said Sankha pointing at his student Ilvala.

'I will do as you say Sankhaji. I just want him to get well soon.'

'Don't worry he will be fine. I will come and visit him again tomorrow. Now I will take leave Veera,' said Sankha. She nodded her head and bowed to him.

'Vidyut I think even you should go and rest. I will meet you tomorrow,' said Veera.

'Alright Chief. But please do send word for me in case you need anything. I will come early tomorrow morning,' he said. Sankha, his team and Vidyut left Dhruva's home. As soon as they left, she slowly entered Dhruva's room so as not to make any noise. Veera asked the two attendants to leave the room. She said she would take care of him for the night.

Veera went and sat on the chair near his bed. Dhruva was unconscious. His right shoulder was bandaged. She touched his forehead and caressed it. She took his hand between her palms and held it tight. She sat there looking at his tired face.

'Why didn't you tell me Dhruva? Why didn't you? I would never have let you go without me. This will never happen again. Come what may, now on, life or death we stay together. I promise,' said Veera kissing his hand. She sat there looking at him, his hand secure in hers.

***

'Mithra, please ask her to take it back. I don't want it,' said Dhruva pouting his lips. Veera nodded her head, smiling at him.

'Vani give it to me,' said Veera and took the bowl from her.

'You may go now. I will take care.' Vani bowed to her and walked out of the room.

'Come on Dhruva, stop making faces and eat this,' she said placing the bowl on the table next his bed. Veera was sitting on the chair near his cot. He was sitting on his bed leaning his back against a cushion. He still couldn't lift his right hand. It was dinner time and Sankha had instructed that he should be given a semi-liquid vegetable broth. Sankha had strictly prohibited spices from being added to the broth except a little salt.

'Ew! How can I eat this? It tastes so bland. I don't want it,' said Dhruva again.

'Sankhaji has told you to follow strict diet for a speedy recovery. You will have to eat this broth for three days only. Please don't refuse,' said Veera trying to convince him.

'It's easier said than done,' he said dejected. Veera went and sat before him on the bed. She picked up the bowl and took a spoonful of the broth to his mouth.

'Now just open your mouth,' insisted Veera. Dhruva glared at her but he had no choice. He opened his mouth and she fed him. She smiled and so did he. She continued feeding him the broth. After sometime Veera looked at him seriously and asked, 'Why didn't you tell me about the terrorists?'

Dhruva was taken aback at her question. After a moment of silence, he spoke.

'That day, the man you saw me speaking to in the camp was not some stranger. He is the head of the secret spy network which I have formed for the security of our kingdom. He gave me the information, about these terrorists planning to attack the royal family and loot the palace. Though the information was credible, it was not an easy task to capture them. But we also got a vital information that the man who led this group had a weakness for women. So we guessed that he might visit Rati. My men kept a close watch on her mansion. The first day we got a clue that they were there, Vidyut and I went there. I sought Rati's help to nab them. We didn't want just that one man but everyone in that group. So we planned on a surprise attack the next day,' said Dhruva.

'Well, that's not what I asked you. Why didn't you tell me?' persisted Veera looking straight into his eyes.

'I didn't want you in danger Mithra. It's one thing to fight in a war and another to deal with terrorists. They are far more dangerous. Moreover I was not very sure about the level of difficulty and risks involved in this. So I wanted to keep you out of it.'

'The biggest danger is when we both are not together. We are supposed to be comrades, Dhruva. We should have been guarding each other's backs,' said Veera strongly. Dhruva smiled at her.

'Nevertheless, you did just that. How did you even get there?' asked Dhruva curiously.

'I had my suspicion that you were lying to me about that man being a stranger. The next day your response about Rati confirmed my suspicions that you were hiding something from me. I am not a fool to believe that you would cultivate such practices. I know you better that that. Then I met Rati in disguise and forced her to tell the truth. That evening I slipped into the mansion in the disguise of an attendant. Luckily none of you recognised me. And then you know the rest…' said Veera smugly.

'I knew there was something familiar about that attendant's smile that day. It was just that I didn't give it much thought. You were exceptional that day. Mithra if it were not for you we might have had severe casualties,' said Dhruva.

'Had it not been for you, I might not have survived that dagger Dhruva,' she said her eyes slightly moist.

'Nothing can harm you as long as I am alive,' said Dhruva intensely. She nodded her head in assent and resumed feeding him. Dhruva's eyes welled up.

'What happened? Are you in pain?' asked a startled Veera.

'I lost my parents at a very young age. I don't remember anyone feeding me Mithra. But I grew up so as to not miss them. Today I realise what it feels like to miss my mother,' said Dhruva his voice thick with emotion.

'I lost my mother the very day I was born. My father was not near to nurture me. I too grew up with no one to feed me. I still don't know what it feels like to have a mother,' she said slowly. There was silence between them. Dhruva took the brass spoon from her in his hand. He took a spoonful of the broth and fed it to Veera. A tear escaped her eye. Nothing had ever tasted so good for them. That night what they fed each other was not just food. It was something more than that. It was a promise of unconventional and unconditional love.

***

Princess Madhumathi was standing on the balcony of her private quarters. Cool breeze was blowing over her face. She had retired to her private chamber in the evening. In the morning she had accompanied Queen Lakshmipriya to the royal temple. Then she was shown around the royal palace. As per the ritual she had cooked a sweet dish in the evening. It was a porridge made of rice, milk, jaggry and cardamom. Though there were cooks in her palace, she had learnt cooking. She was indeed a good cook. The Queen was extremely delighted with her daughter-in-law. King

Devarata was also equally satisfied with the alliance he had found for his son. But life wasn't all that rosy for the two people who actually came together in this alliance – prince Vijayendra and princess Madhumathi.

Princess Madhumathi was a talented lady. Though she was born in a royal family, she was very humble. She had learnt to write, read and was also skilled in painting. In her kingdom of Meru, she lived a happy life. Her brother Aniruddha was crowned the Prince by the king Sanjaya. Meru was a small kingdom compared to Virpur. Due to the small size of its army it was constantly under threat. King Sanjaya wanted to strengthen his kingdom and the only way was to form alliances with his neighbouring kingdoms. With this intention he had a meeting with King Devarata in a neutral place. But King Devarata had already made a strategic move in his mind. He kept before King Sanjaya the marriage proposal of Prince Vijayendra and Princess Madhumathi as a condition for the alliance. Though King Sanjaya was at first taken aback, he agreed as it would certainly be advantageous for his kingdom. Thus the marriage was culminated between two people who actually didn't have a say in it.

Even after the wedding, Madhumathi couldn't put her heart and soul into the relationship. She felt that her marriage was simply a compromise. She felt used, for nobody asked her what she wanted. Her father only ordered her into the marriage and never even tried to know if she was ready for it. Madhumathi also didn't oppose because she always wished the welfare of her people. Nevertheless, that reason couldn't justify the marriage for her. She felt like an object being handed from one person to another. Nobody ever thought, that she too has a heart...

The very next day after the wedding Madhumathi stepped into the royal palace of Virpur as Prince Vijayendra's wife and daughter-in-law of Virpur. Princess Madhumathi closed her eyes in pain as she remembered that night...

Princess Madhumathi went into the private chambers of the Prince in the evening. It was large with beautiful carvings adorning the roof. The room was decorated with various artefacts. In celebration of the wedding the private chambers was specially decorated with aromatic flowers. But none of these could calm the princess. Her heart was drumming dramatically with each passing moment. Now, being left alone for the first time after marriage, was the time when the actual feeling of being married began to sink in. She was overcome with pain and her eyes welled up. She closed her eyes and wiped the tears, lest someone should see them. She stood near the window clasping her hands tightly. Madhumathi was literally unprepared for this confrontation. Just then she caught her breath, she heard the door being opened.

Vijayendra stepped into his private chambers and closed the door. He was dressed in a cotton dhoti. He walked in and looked around. He was also nervous about meeting Madhumathi. Though he was not against the proposal of the wedding, still he couldn't get involved in it wholeheartedly. It all just happened too fast! Today was the first time he would be with her in solitude. His mind was full of questions and his heart was excited with curiosity. He slowly walked towards Madhumathi who was standing near the window.

She was dressed in a beautiful red silk sari. Her breathing was heavy as she heard his footsteps nearing her.

'Madhumathi...' called out Vijayendra standing behind her. But she stood rooted to the place, without moving. A moment passed in silence. Vijayendra steeped closer and placed his hand on her shoulder. Madhumathi's heart skipped a beat at his touch! He turned her around to face her. The prince was awestruck for a moment. Madhumathi looked stunning. She was beautiful and he had never been so close to such a beautiful lady. He had a maddening urge to kiss her lovely red lips. Vijayendra literally lost sense of his surroundings. He held her face in his hands and lifted her face up. In one strike all his emotions were wiped out. Madhumathi's eyes said it all...

Vijayendra withdrew his hands at once. There was no love or even the slightest feeling of submission in her eyes. Those eyes were filled with hatred and pain.

'What happened?' asked Vijayendra placing a hand on her shoulder. But Madhumathi flinched. He immediately stepped back from her. He looked straight at her fiercely.

'Are you unhappy with this marriage?'

'How does it even matter now? Nobody cares about what I think,' she said evenly.

'If you didn't want this wedding, you could have refused,' said the prince impatiently.

'Do you really think I could have done that? You know better about how the royals behave. Neither was I asked nor given a choice. My opinion changes nothing,' said the princess, her voice thick with emotion.

'Of course you feelings matter to me. We made a promise to live together till the end. We cannot keep up that promise if you don't accept this relationship,' said Vijayendra intensely. Madhumathi let out a long drawn breath.

'I will sincerely perform the duties as a wife, daughter-in-law and princess. That is all I can give to this relationship...'

Vijayendra closed his eyes in exasperation. He then opened his eyes and looked at her. His heart was burning to have her in his arms.

'Madhu, I really didn't expect this marriage to cause so much pain to you. I am sorry for everything you had to go through. I don't want to dominate you as a husband. I can as well consummate our marriage right now. I know that you won't refuse but I also know that you can never put your heart into it. I don't want that. I like you Madhumathi and I know very soon, I will fall in love with you. One day I will be ready to give my body, heart and soul to you. I will be waiting for the day when you will accept me wholeheartedly. Until then, this wall of distance will always be there between us,' he said looking straight into her eyes. Madhumathi was dumbstruck. She really didn't expect this reply from him. Vijayendra picked up a blanket from his bed and went to sleep on a small cot placed in his private chambers. Before lying down he turned to look at her.

'Madhu you are very beautiful,' said Vijayendra with a slight smile and lied down on the cot. Madhumathi stood there looking at him. He was not a prince that night. Vijayendra was just a man with a heart for Madhumathi.

Madhumathi was lost in her thoughts of her first evening in the palace when she was brought back to the present by the sound of someone approaching. She turned around. Vijayendra walked onto the balcony dressed in a cream coloured silk dhoti and blue silk kurta.

'It's a beautiful evening,' he said looking at Madhumathi who was dressed in a yellow sari. She nodded her head in agreement. Just then the attendant walked onto the balcony with a silver bowl and a plate. She placed them on the table. Madhumathi gestured her to leave.

'Please sit down,' said Madhumathi politely. Vijayendra looked at her quizzically, but went and sat on the chair placed near the table. She served him the sweet dish that she had prepared. Vijayendra enthusiastically scooped a spoonful of it and put it into his mouth.

'Hmmm…' said he as he relished eating it. He always had a soft corner for sweets. Madhumathi was satisfied that he liked it.

'This is so delicious! I will have to personally reward the cook who made this,' said Vijayendra finishing the sweet dish. Madhumathi looked at him sheepishly.

'Actually… I made it,' said Madhumathi. He was surprised. He leaned forward closer to her and looked into her eyes.

'Thank you. I love it, not only the sweet but also the cook,' he said in a husky voice. Madhumathi could feel his breath on her face. Her heart skipped a beat. Vijayendra was clearly winning her heart. She averted his eyes and stood up. He held her hand.

'Keep denying as much as you want to yourself. But I can see it all in your eyes…'

Madhumathi quickly pulled her hand and went away from him, blushing. Vijayendra knew that she was no longer indifferent to his presence. Now all that he had to do was wait until she admitted her feelings for him. But he had to use every ounce of his self-control when she was near him to stop himself from breaking the wall between them. It sure was not easy...

***

CHAPTER 8

'Why don't you believe me when I say that I am fine?' asked an exasperated Dhruva. But Veera didn't budge. She looked at him evenly. At last Dhruva removed his kurta and let her examine his shoulder. Veera took a closer look at his wound. It was almost healed and forming a scar. She lightly pressed around the wound. At one point he winced a little.

'Does it still hurt?' asked a concerned Veera. Dhruva smiled at her.

'Mithra, it does hurt a little but Sankhaji said it will heal completely in another two days.'

'Why don't you rest for some more time?'

Dhruva nodded his head in refusal and wore his kurta again.

'I will become sicker if I stay at home for even one more day.'

'You are so adamant!' complained Veera.

'I know,' he said shrugging his shoulders.

'I will let you come with me on only one condition Dhruva. You will not do anything which will strain your shoulder,' said Veera firmly. He just nodded his head in agreement.

Both of them entered the army camp. Vidyut walked up to them smiling warmly.

'How are you feeling Dhruva? I thought you would be in bed for some more time,' he said mocking Dhruva.

'Oh shut up, Vidyu! I will no longer stay at home doing nothing. So how is everything going on?' he inquired.

'Well, the men are polishing their skills. The women are yet to master the tactics of warfare. But I am sure they will learn very soon. One thing to be concerned is that they are untested and inexperienced. We will not know their performance until they fight in the battlefield. So it is too early to decide if they are a liability or an asset,' said Vidyut frankly.

'I am sure they won't let me down,' replied Veera proudly. Dhruva smiled at her.

'I also hope for the same, Chief,' replied Vidyut.

'You both go for the supervision of the archery arena. I will go to inspect the sword-fighting warriors,' said Veera getting down to work.

'Archery?! But I usually go to the sword-fighting arena!' protested Dhruva. She narrowed her eyes at him.

'I know. Yet today you will do nothing with the sword. You will never be able to stop yourself from wielding a sword if you go there. And that will strain your shoulder,' she reasoned.

'Mithra, you are —' started Dhruva. But Veera raised her hand to cut him short.

'I am the Chief. You will do as I say!' she said sternly.

'Okay Chief. I will do as you say!' said Dhruva glaring at her.

'Vidyut, you will make sure he doesn't do anything against my words.'

'Absolutely Chief,' said Vidyut smiling. He gave Dhruva a sidelong glance mocking him. Dhruva narrowed his eyes. Veera then went towards the sword-fighting arena.

'Oh my God! I can see Commander Dhruva coming here,' said a surprised Achuta. Today the women archers were being trained in the shooting arena.

'Yes and that's surprising because usually it's Chief Veera who trains us. I heard that he was severely injured during the combat with the terrorists. He put himself in the way of an arrow approaching the Chief,' said Sinhika, admiration in her voice. Achuta kept looking at Dhruva. She had a huge crush on Dhruva. Most of the women in the army admired his valour. But he was always indifferent to them. One by one the archers were asked to shoot at the given target. After a few of them took their shots, Dhruva intervened to stop.

'Soldiers, one common mistake that all of you make is having a wrong posture. While holding your bow. If your posture is not right then your aim will not be accurate. Watch me,' said Dhruva taking a bow from the archer near him. He took an arrow from him. Dhruva stood farther than the line drawn for the trainee archers. He stood with his back ramrod straight and fixed the arrow to the bow. His left hand firmly held the bow and his right hand pulled hard at the arrow. The tension in the bow string was maximum. Dhruva's eyes were focused and glowing with concentration. In one swift motion the arrow hit the target bang in the centre. The soldiers present there applauded. Dhruva smiled lightly.

'Now as you all have seen, the moment you get your posture right, you will certainly not miss the target,' he said firmly. Then again the archers resumed their practice. Dhruva and Vidyut along with other commanders began discussing about various measures to be taken to strengthen the army. Achuta was waiting for her turn to shoot at the target. But all her attention was focused on Dhruva. She was petrified when she heard that he had been shot. Then later she got the news about his recovery. Dhruva had not come to the camp for many weeks. Achuta was very impatient to see him. But she could not openly express her desire as it was uncommon for a woman to express her feelings to the man she loved. Every day she kept hoping against hope to see him. But she was always disappointed until she saw him today. Achuta wanted to immediately walk up to him and inquire about his wellbeing yet she stopped herself. She knew she couldn't do it.

Dhruva was talking to his group enthusiastically as he had to catch up with the events that had occurred during his absence. Then suddenly he began coughing. Vidyut patted on his back lightly but his cough didn't seem to stop. Just then a lady gave him a glass of water. Dhruva drank the water and after a few moments he stopped coughing. He looked up and saw a lady archer standing before him.

'Thank you soldier,' he said with a warm smile. Achuta's heart was drumming with happiness when he smiled at her. Those were the first words he had ever spoken to her. She stood there revelling in his proximity.

'Anything else soldier?' asked Dhruva surprised at her still standing there. But she didn't respond. Achuta was simply mesmerised by his presence. Dhruva frowned and snapped his fingers in front of her eyes. She was startled and she lowered her eyes in embarrassment.

'What is your name?' he asked authoritatively.

'Ach…Achuta,' she said at last finding her voice.

'How can you be so distracted being a soldier? Is this the discipline that you have been trained with?' asked Dhruva sternly. She was very nervous.

'There is no room for distractions in a battlefield. Even one moment of recklessness can cost lives. Be alert Achuta. You may go now.'

Achuta quietly bowed to him and left. Vidyut looked at him in disapproval.

'You are being so rude to her Dhruva. That girl actually cares for you. I think she is interested in you...'

'Shut up Vidyu!' said Dhruva glaring at him.

'What? I mean there is nothing wrong in that. If you like her, then there is no harm in reciprocating,' reasoned Vidyut.

'I am never going to do that...'

Vidyut knew there was something deep hidden in his words. He looked at the men around them.

'Gentlemen kindly excuse us,' said Vidyut politely and took Dhruva away from them. When he made sure nobody could hear them he spoke to him.

'What do you mean Dhruva?' he asked seriously.

'I mean, I don't want to harbour any such feelings for a woman.'

'Don't tell me that you will remain a bachelor forever!' asked Vidyut incredulously.

'You are absolutely right.'

'This is ludicrous! Why are you doing this?'

'If Mithra can do it, then why can't I?'

'Chief Veera is compelled to do it. She is different.'

'I see no difference between the two of us. I have promised to walk with her in whichever path she chooses to go. If she remains unmarried then so do I,' said Dhruva firmly.

'But Dhruva'

He raised his hand to stop Vidyut.

'I have already made my decision Vidyu. There is nothing left to argue about it,' he said and walked away. Vidyut let out a sigh. He was well acquainted with Dhruva's obstinacy. It was not easy making him change his decision. Vidyut knew that now only one person could make him have second thought.

***

It was a starry night. The moon was half less than a full moon. Still it was beautiful to look at. Dhruva was sitting on the swing in the garden after finishing dinner with Veera. She brought two glasses of milk with a pinch of turmeric. She gave one glass to him and sat on the swing next to him.

'Had it not been for you, I would certainly not drink milk with turmeric!' rued Dhruva.

'I know! But this is really good for health and helps to keep the body free from diseases. Sankhaji told me.'

Dhruva nodded his head and gulped down the whole glass of milk at one go. Veera laughed at the expression on his face.

'Happy now?' he asked raising his eyebrows.

'Of course! I am happy beyond limits,' she teased him. Then Veera finished drinking her glass of milk.

'Mithra I think there is going to be a war against Suryapatna in the near future.'

Veera looked at him surprised.

'How are you being so certain about it? Any evidence?'

'Yes. Gudcha said that his spy reported about it. They are accumulating huge resources of arms and ammunition. Their forces are being mobilised,' said Dhruva looking at her.

'Well, we had expected an attack long ago. The kingdom of Suryapatna has been eyeing our kingdom from a long time. We will have to speak about this in the royal court tomorrow. We shouldn't delay any further.'

'Yes, you are right. Then let's go to the royal court tomorrow,' said Dhruva and stood up to leave. Veera caught his wrist and gestured him to sit down. Dhruva frowned at her in surprise.

'What is it Mithra?'

'Sit down. I want to talk to you,' said Veera and he obliged. Veera turned away from him and was looking at the plants in front of her.

'What is the matter Mithra that it can't wait till morning?'

'Vidyut spoke to me today...' she said still not looking at him. Dhruva rolled his eyes. He knew what exactly Vidyut would have told her.

'I will not spare him tomorrow! Vidyu will simply not shut his big mouth,' he said angrily. Veera glared at him.

'Why are you angry with him? At least he told me now. Till when would you have hid this truth from me?' asked Veera looking straight at him.

'As long as I could,' he said evenly.

'Your decision is wrong Dhruva...'

'No, Mithra. I have done the right thing. I have taken this step wholeheartedly.'

'There is no need for you to do this. Give me one good reason for your foolishness,' challenged Veera.

'You are the reason. So long as you remain a spinster, I will remain a bachelor...'

Veera closed her eyes letting out a long drawn breath.

'For me it's a compulsion Dhruva. I cannot go against it. But there is no such thing binding you.'

'You are right Mithra. I have no compulsion and I don't need one! I have a heart to listen to and a conscience to answer to. I made a promise to walk with you in your journey. If life can be unfair to you, how can I let it be fair to me?' he asked looking into her eyes. Veera stood up unable to bear his words, she had to convince him to change his mind.

'You need a life partner Dhruva. You need a family to support you. You need an heir to succeed you. You need a woman to complete you,' said a desperate Veera. Dhruva stood up and came near her. He held her shoulders and looked deep into her eyes.

'Mithra you are my family. You are my companion and you complete me. I cannot think of a better life than the one we are leading now,' said Dhruva intensely. A tear slid down Veera's cheek.

'I am never going to forgive myself for this…' said Veera slowly. Dhruva wiped her tear.

'Mithra, I am happy the way we are. Please don't ruin it.'

Veera leaned her head on his shoulder. Dhruva's arms encircled her securely. Tears did not stop streaming down her face. Though it seemed like a life worth living, they were never destined for it…

***

CHAPTER 9

The very next day, Veera and Dhruva went to the royal court. The impending war with Suryapatna was inevitable. King Devarata ordered the army to start preparing for the war. Virpur was going to fight its first war under Veera. This war was indeed a test for her leadership and she was up for the challenge. The army was divided into three sections. Prince Vijayendra, Chief Veera and Commander Dhruva would lead each one of those sections. This was also the first time Prince Vijayendra was going to lead one section of the army. Within a few days the King of Suryapatna openly challenged Virpur to war. The place and date for the war was fixed. Though both the armies were almost equal in their strengths, Virpur still had an upper hand. They now, had the added troupes from Meru and also Veera's strategic planning. The days for the war were numbered.

The war had created a storm in Madhumathi's heart. She stood near the window looking out at the crescent moon. The cold winter breeze made her shiver. She wrapped her arms around her chest to keep herself warm. It was a quiet night. It was already late into the night but Prince Vijayendra had still not returned to his private chambers. Madhumathi closed her eyes as the thoughts about the war were making her uneasy. She was not new to war. She had seen her father and brother fight battles. Actually she should have been proud that her husband was going to lead a section of the army in the war. But the thought of Vijayendra going to war was squeezing her heart with pain. This was different, and Madhumathi was confused. There were just three more days left for the war to commence. As a dutiful wife and brave princess she had to support and motivate the prince to fight in the war. Nevertheless that was not what she wanted.

Prince Vijayendra entered the private chambers exhausted after a long tiring day. Madhumathi looked up at him. He was amused to see her still awake.

'Madhu, why haven't you slept yet?'

'I couldn't sleep. So I just sat here...' she said hesitantly. Vijayendra knew that there was indeed something bothering her.

'I am exhausted. I will first bathe. The practice in the artillery was hectic.'

Vijayendra went to bathe. Madhumathi let out a sigh and again resumed staring at the moon. Her heart was burdened and there was no way she could bear it any longer. After sometime Vijayendra came back. He had bathed and changed into a light yellow cotton dhoti. Though he badly wanted to go to bed to rest, he went straight to Madhumathi and sat opposite to her near the window.

'What is bothering you so much Madhu?'

She didn't answer him and continued looking at the moon. A few moments of silence passed between them. Madhumathi really didn't know what to tell him.

'Madhu, I can't bear your silence. Say something. What are you upset about?' he asked placing his hand on hers. She stiffened at his touch but didn't look at him. She stood up and walked away from him. Her heart was beating frantically. But Vijayendra lost his temper. He had already exhausted every ounce of his patience for the day. He immediately stood up.

'Fine. You don't have to tell me anything. Who am I to you? Why should I even think so much about a woman who is least bothered about me? I don't know what is in your mind Madhu. But I love you! I fell in love with you the day I first saw you here. I want you to be my companion every single moment in my life. That every moment you stand away from me, I want to just take you in my arms and tell how much I love you. Every time you walk away, it just kills me...' said Vijayendra his voice thick with emotion. Madhumathi could no longer restrain herself. She was indeed in love with him but just didn't realise the depth of her passion until then. Vijayendra's words unlocked all her feelings for him. She turned around and ran up to him wrapping her hands around his neck. Vijayendra was astonished. He stood still for a moment.

'I love you too,' she said in a muffled voice. Happiness swept over the prince. He hugged her back in a tight embrace. It was a moment of sheer joy for both of them. After a few moments Vijayendra released her from his embrace. They looked into each other's eyes lovingly.

'I was scared that I may not get a chance to say this to you before you go to war. I love you so much,' said Madhumathi. Vijayendra smiled at her fondly.

'I know. But your little stubborn heart took so long to admit it. Don't worry about me going to war. I will come back to you. It's a promise,' he said intently. Then he held her face tenderly and bent down to kiss his wife. The cold winter breeze enveloped them. But their fire of passion burnt all night sealing their relationship forever...

***

It was a beautiful evening before the war. The next morning the army had to assemble and march to the battlefield. Veera was sitting in her garden feeding the pigeons. She loved to spend time in her garden surrounded by pigeons and rabbits. It refreshed her mind and she would feel stress-free there. Usually nobody disturbed her at that time, but that evening she heard a commotion near the entrance. Veera called out to her attendant Nila.

'What is all that noise about?' asked Veera frowning.

'Please forgive me, my lady. A boy has come to see you. Though we refused permission he is adamant about meeting you. He is standing at the door,' said Nila concerned about disturbing Veera. After thinking for a moment, she told her to let him in. She was curious to see the boy. After a few moments a boy aged around ten years of age walked up to her. He was slender and of average height. He looked quite confident without even a hint of hesitation in his walk. He bowed to her and she smiled at him politely.

'Do I know you, young man?'

'No. But I know you Chief. My name is Bahu, son of soldier Bhibhatsu. My father is a foot soldier in the army,' said Bahu proudly.

'Well, how can I help you?' she asked him curiously.

'Tomorrow my father will go to war with you Chief. He has fought battles before courageously. Even in this war I know he will fight bravely. One day I want to be a warrior like him and I want him to see me wield a sword. So...' he said hesitantly unable to finish his sentence.

'What do you want me to do, my boy?' asked Veera caringly.

'Chief, I heard my mother say that you are really kind-hearted and you protect our army. I want you to just make sure that my father comes back home after this war,' said the boy sincerely. Veera was stunned into silence. She didn't know how to respond. How could she honour the boy's request? Bahu looked at her with a childlike devotion. He sincerely believed that Veera could bring his father back home alive. She didn't know how to tell him that there were more than ten thousand warriors under her command and she really could not guarantee as to how many would come back home. That man was only a foot soldier and in a battle they were the first line of expendables. The chances of a foot soldier staying alive were not great. But for Bahu, that ordinary foot soldier was his father, his hero. Veera very well knew what his father meant to him. The memories of her father flashed before her and she was overcome with emotions but she composed herself quickly. She asked him to sit next to her. Veera placed her hand around his shoulder assuring.

'You are a brave boy Bahu. Your father must really be proud of you. I never make false promises. A war is a place where life is uncertain. When I can't assure my own safety, how can I assure that your father will be safe?' said Veera softly. The boy's face fell in disappointment. She squeezed his shoulder lightly.

'But remember one thing, you will never be alone. Whatever maybe the consequence of this war you will fulfil your dream of becoming a warrior. Bahu should never give up. This sister's best wishes and your father's blessing will always be with you,' she said affectionately. Bahu looked up at her and smiled. He stood up to leave. He bowed to Veera.

'I may not have got what I wanted but I am certainly not going empty-handed,' said Bahu. Veera stood up clearly impressed but his maturity.

'Send you father to war with your love for him. Hope that his bravery will bring him back home. I will be looking forward to the day when you will join the army. May God bless you brother.'

Veera kissed his forehead.

'I promise I won't let you down Chief,' said Bahu confidently and walked out of the garden. Veera stood there seeing him walk away with his head held high. She looked up at the sky making a silent prayer that all her soldiers make it back home. Though she knew it was impossible, there was no harm in hoping for it. Hope was that which gave strength to families to send their loved ones into the battlefield. The hope that one day they will come back home.

***

Veera threw a small pebble into the flowing river. She was sitting on a boulder on the bank of the river. Her legs were dipped into the cool water. The moon and the stars softly lit up the place. She tried to clear her mind filled with thoughts about the war. Veera continued throwing pebbles into the river. She was unarmed except for the dagger which she had kept surreptitiously in her dhoti tied at her waist. Veera didn't ride to the river on her horse, she preferred to go there by walk. Suddenly she stopped her hand mid-air from throwing the pebble. She quickly looked around and strained her ears to hear more clearly. Veera could hear the sound of hooves. She alertly looked in the direction of the sound. For a moment she considered about flinging her dagger in that direction, but she knew it was foolishness, for the chances of an attacker there was very bleak. After sometime she could vaguely see the outline of the rider and his horse. Veera's lips slowly curved into a smile.

I should have known that he would come.

Dhruva tethered his horse to a tree at a distance and started walking towards her.

'Don't you have a home? Since when did you start spending your nights on a riverbank?' joked Dhruva.

'Why won't you just leave me alone? How did you even find out that I am here?' she asked with mock anger.

'Even if you go to the other end of the world, I will find you. There is no way you can get rid of me Mithra'

Dhruva removed his footwear and sat next to her dipping his legs into the water.

'Since when have you been sitting here? I had to search everywhere to find you,' he complained. Veera let out a sigh.

'I just wanted to stay away from all that madness of a war for some time. So I came here. By the way, why did you come searching for me? Shouldn't you be resting so that you will be able to focus on the big task tomorrow?' she asked looking at him.

'You came here to have some peace of mind. I came searching you for the same reason. I could not think of a better way to calm my mind,' said Dhruva softly. Veera smiled at him lightly.

'Even after trying so much I have not been able to put out the negative thoughts...'

'You will never succeed in it if you keep trying to stop those thoughts. The more you try to escape from them, they will keep resurfacing.'

'Then what should I do?'

'Just let those thoughts flow, don't try to stop them. After sometime you will see that there will be no more thoughts left to haunt you,' said Dhruva shrugging his shoulders. Veera nodded her head in amazement.

'You seem to have an answer to all my questions. Actually today a boy named Bahu visited me at home.'

'Bahu? Who is that?' asked a curious Dhruva. Veera narrated that incident that took place in the evening.

'A very impressive boy indeed!' he said raising his eyebrows in appreciation.

'I could not give him anything Dhruva. He made a simple request and I sent him back without making any promise. I felt so incapable to help that boy...' said Veera softly. He nodded his head in disapproval.

'Don't go there, Mithra. This war is just one of the many that you are going to face. You can't afford to be vulnerable. Tomorrow you are going to lead an army into the battlefield,' said Dhruva on a serious note. Vera let out a long drawn breath.

'I am not sure if I can live up to father's achievements.'

'You shouldn't compare yourself with Guruji. You have already been achieving the unthinkable every single day. You are exceptional and I want you to take my word on this without even an iota of doubt,' he said intently. Veera looked straight into his eyes.

'I am scared...'

Dhruva placed his arm around her shoulder.

'There is nothing to fear Mithra. I know you can do this. I will always be with you. We will come back victorious. Trust me,' he said stressing on his last words. Veera smiled lightly and rested her head on his shoulder. She could feel her mind sailing towards peace. Though Dhruva was also uncertain about tomorrow, he was sure about one thing, that he would always protect her. For Veera, she had never felt more secure then she was right at that moment.

***

CHAPTER 10

The war went on for five days. Both the armies fought fiercely. Actually the king of Suryapatna had made a mistake by underestimating the army of Virpur which was led by a woman – Veera. Initially they mocked her. But on the very first day Veera stumped her opponents with her shrewd planning. Her strategies were unconventional and her army backed her well in executing her plans. Veera, Dhruva and Prince Vijayendra lead their sections of army efficiently. At last Virpur emerged victorious and conquered Suryapatna. Since the king of Suryapatna surrendered, he was designated as the care-taker of Suryapatna and king Devarata was announced as the king of Suryapatna. King Devarata was very happy about the consequence of the war and he was very proud of his son who had led a section of the army in the war. Though Veera's army did lose warriors in the war, it didn't stop them from winning. It is a pity that though soldiers fight the war, it is only the King's name that will be remembered...

'Aah! Slowly Dhruva! Your hands are so hard,' said Veera frowning. Dhruva looked at her apologetically. She had sustained an injury on her right hand during the war. Sankha had instructed her to change the bandage after two days. Dhruva was now wrapping the new cotton cloth bandage over her wound but his hard hands hurt her.

'I am sorry Mithra. I will be more careful now,' he said holding her hand tenderly.

'Have you made all the arrangements?'

'The message has been sent to all the concerned families. They will be assembled at the camp after four days,' he said still concentrating on her bandage. Veera let out a long drawn breath.

'The compensation we give them will certainly not bring back their loved ones. But this is the least we can do for them...' said Veera slowly. Dhruva had finished tying her bandage and he looked at her.

'Mithra, war is all about death and loss. There is nothing glorious about it. Yet we are always hungry for war. People will never even know the name of even a single man who sacrificed his life. History will only speak about the kings and their conquests. Yet it is baffling as to why men are always eager to fight when they gain nothing from it,' he said intently. Veera gave him a wry smile.

'First time I am seeing a man who detests war.'

'I really detest war. But I do admit that I revel in warfare. It's the drawbacks of the war that I detest. I didn't choose to become a warrior. Life chose me and I am doing justice for that choice...'

She nodded her head in agreement because she also was of the same opinion.

'Destiny chose us Dhruva. There is no escape from it. Soldiers are made so that they can protect people. That is their priority even if it means risking their own life. But more than the soldiers who go to war, it's their near and dear ones who are the brave lot. It's not easy to see your loved ones walk into danger. You need exceptional courage to endure that pain...'

'What do they get in return? They go through all this for nothing,' said Dhruva agitatedly.

'They sacrifice for the good of the kingdom. They fight for victory,' reasoned Veera.

'Oh really?! That victory always takes the name of the king who in reality has done nothing in the war. Why don't kings fight their wars?' sneered Dhruva. Veera was not surprised by his words. Somewhere deep down she too agreed with him.

'A king is born with privileges, Dhruva. It is the rule of the land. Nothing will ever change that. Sometimes it is better to just accept the truth rather than question it,' said Veera looking straight into his eyes.

'I wish I could,' said Dhruva evenly. He was not ready to agree with her when he knew he was right. Veera knew him too well to assume that he was convinced. She just hoped that this attitude of his does not put him in any danger.

***

It was early in the morning. Veera walked along the bank of the river. Her mind was still disturbed from the war and she thought the nature would calm her mind. She stood there watching the beautiful pinkish orange colour of the sky. The cold breeze made her shiver slightly. But she liked the chill weather. Casually she looked around and saw two men and a woman seated on the bank of the river. One of the men was a priest. The other man had tonsured his head and the woman seated behind him was weeping in silence. Veera understood that they were performing the last rites of a loved one. She felt their grief tug at her heart. Unable to see it any longer she turned to gaze at the rising sun. After some time the priest left and they stood up to leave. The man saw Veera standing at a distance and recognised her instantly. He walked up to her. Hearing his footsteps she turned. Veera was surprised by his approach. She looked at him questioningly. It was disturbing to look into his eyes. His eyes were hard and cold.

'She was due to be married in a fortnight. She was very adamant about fighting in the war. Now I lost my daughter Anjlika, an archer in your army...' said the man in a voice devoid of any emotion. Veera was dumbstruck.

'I am extremely sorry for your loss sir,' she said softly.

'She considered you as her inspiration. I loved her a lot as she was my only daughter. My son is also a warrior in the army. He has been injured during the battle. After a few days, once his wounds are healed, he will get back into the army. But I have lost my precious little girl forever. I should never have let her convince me into letting her join the army. Had I got her married back then, she would now have been raising her own family...' he said with his eyes moist. Veera understood his regret.

'Sir, you were also a warrior, weren't you?' questioned Veera.

'Yes I was.' He answered with pride colouring his tone.

'Anjlika was your daughter. Your blood of valour coursed through her veins. It is quite natural that she too would like to be a warrior like her father and brother. You should be proud of her.'

'Damn the pride! Sons are born to go into a battlefield. But daughters? No! Her life could have been different. She could still have been living happily for many more years. I would never have had to see her body bloodied with arrows pierced!' roared the man with rage.

'She would have been living but not happy. Anjlika would have spent her entire life with the regret of an unfulfilled dream. But now as long as she lived and died as a warrior, she was surely happy and satisfied with her life. People rarely get a chance to live the life they want. Your daughter was fortunate to live her dream and that was possible only because of a loving father like you. Please don't disgrace her death,' said Veera looking into his eyes.

'Nevertheless of what you say, you will never understand a father's pain,' said the man, his voice thick with emotion.

'I cannot bring back your daughter sir. I would be fortunate if you consider me as your daughter,' she said softly. That man was dumbfounded by her words. After a few moments he looked straight at her.

'I cannot accept you as my daughter because I don't have the strength to bear the loss of another one. As a daughter, with death shadowing you always, all you can give a father is only pain. Had your father been alive, you would have known this,' he said evenly. Veera's heart squeezed with grief and her eyes welled up.

'I am sorry for everything,' she said and touched his feet. After a few seconds the man placed his hand on her head.

'May you live long.'

Veera stood up and tears streamed down her face.

'Hard as you may try, you will never find peace. Warriors will always have blood on their hands. You have to live with that.'

He left the place with the weeping woman without looking back at Veera. Then Veera looked down at her hands and clenched her fists closing her eyes. She stood there letting the tears flow down her cheeks.

***

'Dhruva stay calm. You are not going to lose your temper at any cost once we are inside,' said Veera seriously as they climbed the stairs of the royal palace. Dhruva rolled his eyes at her.

'Do you have to say this every time we go to the royal court? I have no interest in losing my temper with them. It's just that sometimes I can't tolerate their stupid talks.'

'Why do I always make the mistake of thinking that you will pay heed to my warning?' she said nodding her head.

'Relax Mithra! I will behave as you say,' he said smiling. Veera smiled back at him punching his arm lightly.

All the members of the royal court, King Devarata and Prince Vijayendra were seated in their respective seats. Veera and Dhruva bowed to them and executed a royal salute. Vidyut was already present there. He looked at them and smiled.

'Chief Veera, the whole of Virpur is proud of you. You have successfully led our army to victory and we appreciate your valour. You have indeed proved to be worthy successor of your father,' praised King Devarata.

'I am humbled, your Highness. I am grateful to your generous words,' said Veera bowing to him.

'But today you weren't summoned just to be praised Chief Veera. We want you to win a challenge,' said Prince Vijayendra. Veera looked at him intrigued. Then she glanced at Dhruva who looked at her assuring. He was alertly waiting for Vijayendra to tell further.

'In Charanvasi, there is an archery competition being held after three fortnights. The best archers from the neighbouring kingdoms and also farther kingdoms will take part in this competition. We have decided that you will represent Virpur and win that challenge.'

'I am really grateful for this opportunity your Highness. I will do my best,' said Veera. She looked Dhruva who was smiling at her.

'Does anyone have any objections to this decision?' asked Prime Minister Purumithra to the royal court. Just then a Minister in the royal court stood up. Shatayu bowed to the king.

'Kindly pardon my intrusion your Highness. But I think we do have better archers in our kingdom. This decision to choose Veera seems to have been made in haste,' he said glancing towards her.

'But Minister Shatayu, I think Veera is better skilled in archery than any other person in the kingdom,' emphasized the king.

'Well, your Highness I think we should first test her skill before making the decision.'

'Very well then. I can prove right away that Mithra is the best. Your Highness kindly give her a bow and arrow,' said Dhruva strongly.

'Commander Dhruva, how can you prove it here?' asked Prince Vijayendra acidly.

'I will your Highness, kindly give a bow and arrow,' persisted Dhruva. Veera was baffled. The king ordered the guard to give Veera a bow and arrow. Veera was clueless on how she could prove her skill in that royal court. Dhruva promptly took his angavastram and blindfolded her. Though Veera was perplexed she didn't question him. She trusted him at any given instant.

'Shoot the arrow to the point where you hear the noise next,' said Dhruva loudly so that everyone could hear his words. Veera nodded her head. There was pin drop silence in the royal court. All eyes were pinned on Veera. She strung the arrow to the bow. Dhruva removed his amulet and threw it at a pillar at the farther end of the court. It hit the pillar with a clanking sound and fell to the ground. Immediately Veera released the arrow and it hit exactly the spot on the pillar where his amulet had made a small dent. The whole royal court was dumbstruck.

'Now show me an archer who can match this,' said Dhruva proudly pointing at her arrow. The king applauded and the entire royal court gave a huge round of applause. Dhruva untied the angavastram from Veera's eyes. They both looked at each other and grinned.

'Excellent Veera! You have indeed shown that I have made the right choice. You will represent Virpur in that competition,' said a happy Devarata.

'It is an honour your Highness,' said Veera and bowed to him.

'Where is Charanvasi?' asked Veera. Dhruva, Veera and Vidyut were walking to the stables to take their horses.

'It is a place beyond the forest bordering Virpur. It is a three days journey from here,' answered Vidyut.

'I have been there before. It is a barren land, mostly used for small battles and competitions,' said Dhruva.

'I will have to start intense practice from tomorrow. I have to live up to the king's expectations,' said Veera on a serious note.

'After seeing you shoot that arrow today, I am certain you will win that competition. I have never seen anyone shoot like that before,' said an impressed Vidyut.

'Mithra is the best,' said a smiling Dhruva. Vidyut looked at him and smiled in agreement.

'Chief Veera can I ask you something?' he asked hesitantly. Veera stopped in her way and looked at him surprised.

'Sure Vidyut, please go ahead.'

'Dhruva blindfolded you without a word. Then he told you to shoot an arrow. You did as he told without questioning. What if you had hurt someone?'

'I wouldn't have done it had it not been for Dhruva who told me to do it. I trust him,' said Veera looking at Dhruva.

'And I believe in her ability. I know she won't miss her target,' said Dhruva confidently. Vidyut smiled at them and the three resumed walking. There was just one question on his mind.

To what extent can two people trust each other?

The answer to his question was right in front of him.

***

CHAPTER 11

Tethering his horse to the tree Dhruva looked around as usual. The guards were in their positions. They saw him and saluted. He acknowledged them and went into the house. He glanced around but didn't find Veera who usually greeted him at the door. The house was quiet and no attendants were present.

'Mithra…' he called out.

'In here Dhruva,' replied Veera. He went in the direction of her voice and found her in the kitchen. The fire had been lit up in the stove made of mud support for the vessel. Water was boiling in the vessel. Veer put some soaked rice into it. Dhruva smiled at her.

'What are you up to? Are you making some new concoction with which we can easily kill our enemies?' laughed Dhruva. She rolled her eyes at him.

'Shut up Dhruva! I am cooking dinner for us!'

'Oh my God! Had I known, I would never have stepped inside,' he teased.

'I know. That's why I didn't tell!' said Veera and she stuck out her tongue at him. He laughed uninhibitedly crinkling his eyes.

'By the way where are all your attendants?'

'I told them to go home. Today I want to cook for you on my own,' she said stirring the rice. Then she took some vegetables to chop. Dhruva went and sat beside her.

'Well then, let me help you. Give it to me,' he said taking the knife from her hand.

'Dhruva how can I let you do all this? I will do it,' she protested.

'Mithra if you can cook and also wield a sword then why can't I do this?' he said evenly. She smiled in defeat unable to argue.

'Fine, go ahead. But chop the vegetables like I have done. Don't chop them too small or too big,' she said sternly. He rolled his eyes at her. After some time the dinner was ready. They both carried the vessels of food out into the garden. On a stone bench Veera lighted a lamp and served rotis and curry onto their plates.

'I love to have dinner in moonlight. Thank you so much,' said an excited Dhruva.

'My pleasure,' said Veera winking at him. Veera took a piece of roti, dipped it in the curry and fed him. Then she sat looking at him expectantly.

'How does it taste?' she asked eagerly. He smiled chewing his food.

'It's delicious!'

She quickly took a bite of the roti with the curry. She glared at him.

'It doesn't taste good. The curry is so bland. Liar!' she complained.

'Mithra, it's okay. This is the first time you have cooked an entire meal. Next time you can improve,' he said calmly. Dhruva took a piece of roti and fed her.

'I have a better idea. You marry a woman who cooks delicious food. Then we both won't have to suffer like this,' she said. Though Veera said it lightly, deep down in her heart she wished he would take her suggestion and Dhruva didn't miss the edge in her words.

'I have an even better idea. I will learn to cook. Then I won't have to search for another woman,' snapped Dhruva eating his food. Veera let out a defeated sigh.

'You will never listen to me, will you?'

'Of course I won't! Now let me eat my dinner peacefully!'

'You eating this by itself is a huge favour. You don't have to pretend like it's the best dinner you have ever had,' she said like a stubborn child. He smiled at her indulgently.

'This is indeed the best food I have ever had. All I can taste is your love and affection for me. Every moment you spent in preparing this food is what makes it so delicious. As long as we share, any simple meal is a sumptuous feast to me…' said Dhruva looking into her eyes. Veera nodded her head in agreement. Her eyes said it all.

After dinner Dhruva sat on the swing in the garden. Veera walked up to him and handed a glass of milk boiled with cinnamon. He took the glass and she sat next to him sipping the milk from her glass. After a while Dhruva looked at her, she was staring up at the moon.

'What are you thinking?'

'What if I don't win this competition?' she asked softly still looking up at the sky. Dhruva didn't reply. He calmly emptied his glass of milk. A few moments later Veera looked at him irritated.

'What?'

'When I say something you are supposed to respond and not get preoccupied with your drink!'

Dhruva simply shrugged his shoulders. Veera stood up to go. He quickly held her hand and pulled her to sit down. He put his arm around her shoulder.

'Mithra it's not wrong to think about failure. But you shouldn't fear failure. This competition is just a test of your skill in archery and you are an excellent archer.'

She looked at him worried.

'I will be the only woman there amidst so many experienced men.'

'You fought amidst so many men in the battle. You didn't just fight but also led an army to victory!' he emphasized.

'A battlefield was totally different Dhruva. I was not alone there. But in this competition I will be up against so many archers and this is my first time,' she said letting out a sigh.

'There is always a first for everything. Don't underestimate your skills. You have every chance of winning in this competition. Trust me...' he said earnestly. Veera knew that Dhruva was indeed saying it from the bottom of his heart.

'Remember one thing Mithra, you should always first think that you will win. Failure is just another chance to prove that you can do better. This competition is not the end of the world. You win or lose, I will always be with you.'

Dhruva looked into her eyes and she rested her head on his shoulder.

'I know. It is your support that pushes me to achieve. No matter what tomorrow brings with it, nothing ever changes between us,' said Veera slowly. Dhruva smiled in quiet satisfaction. He began staring at the stars. The cool breeze felt good.

Sometime later Dhruva looked down and saw that Veera had fallen asleep. He slowly got up, her head still resting on his arm. Then he lifted her and took her inside. He laid her on her bed. Veera twitched in her sleep. Dhruva slowly patted her head until she again slipped into deep sleep. He put the blanket over her. Veera had a childlike innocence on her face. She looked vulnerable and he felt all the more protective about her. When he was at the door he turned back and looked at her once. She was in deep sleep. Dhruva smiled lightly and closed the door noiselessly. The guards saluted him as he went to his horse.

'Be alert. Keep a close watch on the surrounding,' said Dhruva to one of the guards.

'We will my Lord,' said the guard bowing to him. Dhruva leaped onto his horse and sped away.

***

'His Highness has still not woken up...' said Trivika sheepishly.

'Really? But yesterday —' stopped Ashwasena as realisation dawned on him.

'Okay you may go. I will wake his Highness up,' he said suppressing a smile. Trivika, the royal attendant bowed to him and left. He walked into the private chambers. The silk curtains were still closed and it was dark inside. He went straight to the windows and drew the curtains apart.

'Who the hell is it?' growled Shaurya. The sunlight was piercing his eyes.

'Unfortunately it's me.'

'Ashwa... why do you do this to me?' he said groggily. He sat up on his bed rubbing his eyes.

Shaurya, was the crown prince of Indragiri. A tall and handsome man, well-toned physique, sun-tanned skin.

His jet black wavy hair was dishevelled. His hair was short unlike other men.

'So, who was it?' asked Ashwasena with a mischievous grin. Shaurya stood up and stretched his arms languorously. He gave a lopsided smile.

'I wasn't interested in her name. All I know is that she made my night. The rest is immaterial,' said Shaurya winking at him. Then he went and stood near the window looking out.

'Have you ever thought about any of those women who have shared your bed? I agree you are a prince but that doesn't mean you can recklessly go about bedding woman!' said Ashwasensa intensely. Shaurya gave him a sharp look.

'You sound like I am a bloody womaniser! I don't go in search of them. Women want me and all I do is play to their desires. Ashwa you are in love with one woman but so many women love me. It's not my fault!' he said shrugging his shoulders.

'I really hope you find your love one day...'

'Until now I haven't met a single woman who made me think beyond her beauty. It's not easy to find love Ashwa...' said Shaurya with a distant look. There was an unfathomable expression on his face.

'Now what made you disturb my sleep?'

'How foolish of me to think that you would remember! We have to be present in the royal court today,' said Ashwasena hurriedly.

'Shoot! I had completely forgotten!' he said running his hand through his tousled hair.

'Fine. Let me bathe and dress up. Then we can go together.'

'No way Shaurya! I cannot be late. Even if you don't go, nobody is going to complain. But I could be put in the dungeons my Lord!' he said dramatically bowing to the prince. Shaurya rolled his eyes at him.

'Okay then get out of here. I will see you in the royal court.'

'Come soon,' said Ashwasena and walked out of the private chambers. Shaurya stood staring at the sky. The morning breeze blew over his bare upper torso. His thoughts trailed back to the previous night.

She was beautiful. Nothing more. Just beautiful.

Shaurya smiled wryly. You cannot find love, you just have to feel it…

***

'Don't you think we should go looking for her?' asked Vidyut dismounting from his horse.

'Nah! She will find us without trouble,' said Dhruva winking at him.

'Are you sure you don't want to do this?' asked Dhruva mischievously.

'I have to get back to work later, unlike you!'

Dhruva just shook his head at him. He hurled his angavastram to the ground and removed his cream coloured kurta. He threw it on his angavastram and dived into the river. Vidyut stretched himself out on the riverbank watching him swim. Veera had come to the clearing near the riverbank to practise archery. Both Vidyut and Dhruva had come to accompany her home. But seeing the clear water of the river, Dhruva couldn't resist the temptation to swim. He loved swimming and never let go of the opportunity ever.

Vidyut didn't swim today as he was expected to meet Prince Vijayendra later.

Dhruva and Veera were to leave for the archery competition in a few days' time at Charanvasi. In their absence, it was decided that Vidyut would remain in charge of the army. It was a very convenient decision for the royal court. Though Dhruva was a better choice to be out in charge, neither he nor the royals would ever agree to it. For Veera, Dhruva at her side was confidence reinforced. She was more than happy with the arrangement.

Dhruva could hold his breath for a long time under water. Years of practice had made his movements not just fast but also graceful in water. Vidyut rubbed his abdomen as his stomach let out a soft rumble. He was hungry after the ride. The two horses were now grazing on the grass after drinking their fill of water from the river.

'We should have brought something to eat,' he mumbled. His companion on the other hand was in a state of bliss in the river. Vidyut smiled at him and looked up. The sky was clear and the sun was glowing warmly. Just then he saw the two horses getting a little restless. He propped up on his elbows and saw a horse rider approaching. After a few moments he relaxed his stance. He could easily recognise the rider. He sat up.

'Dhruva! She is here!'

But he didn't seem to hear Vidyut. Veera dismounted from her horse. She walked up to him with a smile. Her eyes fell on Dhruva's clothes on the shore and nodded her head. Looking at the river, she spotted him.

'How long?'

'He has not stepped out ever since we came here.'

Veera placed her bow on the ground. Then she unstrapped her quiver of arrows and placed it down. Veera untied the angavastram tied to her waist and it was not empty.

'Here, take this Vidyut,' she said handing him the fruits that she had collectively tied in her angavastram. Vidyut was overjoyed as he took them.

'You are a saviour Chief. I am starving.'

He began biting into the fruit hungrily. Veera walked to the river and washed her hands and legs. Then she splashed the cool water on her face. It was such a relief after the rigorous training and the ride. She splashed the water a few more times and then drank some water. Just then Dhruva saw her and began swimming back to the riverbank. She smiled at him and walked back to Vidyut.

Veera sat down and started eating a fruit.

'It's good that you have picked ripe fruits. It's really sweet!'

'Yeah. I actually smelt them before plucking,' she replied smugly. Dhruva rose from the water and began wading through to them. His violet dhoti, now wet was clinging to his long muscular legs. His well sculpted upper torso was glistening with water droplets. He pushed his wet hair back with his hands.

'Spare me something too! Look at the way you both are hogging!' he complained raising an eyebrow. Veera threw his angavastram at him. Dhruva caught it and wiped his face. He didn't bother wiping his chest.

'We thought you would fill your stomach with water,' teased Vidyut. Dhruva gave him a bored look and picked up a fruit.

'How did it go?' asked Dhruva sitting in front of Veera and biting into his fruit.

'I have practised every technique I know with different ranges of target. Next I have to practise with different bows,' she said shrugging her shoulders.

'You could go to the artillery, Chief. There you will find every type of bows and arrows.'

Veera nodded in agreement. Then suddenly her eyes lit up looking at him.

'By the way, how is Sinhika?'

A smile entered Vidyut's face. He had married Sinhika just a few days ago. She was actually a warrior in their army. Veera had been instrumental in arranging the wedding.

'She is good. Sini changed my life. I am happily married,' he said with quiet satisfaction. Veera gave Dhruva a sharp look. But he seemed to be unperturbed and concentrated on relishing his fruit. Then suddenly he caught her staring at him.

'What?!'

'Nothing,' she said dismissively but held his gaze. Vidyut finished eating his fruit. He walked to the river and drank some water. The evening began to set in.

'I have to go. I am expected to meet his Highness before nightfall. I will see you in the morning.'

'Of course! You have to. Better be early. After marriage you seem to take a really long time to get out of your bed,' teased Dhruva with a lopsided grin. Veera rolled her eyes at him.

'Shut up you rogue!' admonished Vidyut embarrassedly. Dhruva winked at him. He mounted his horse and sped away.

'Aren't you feeling cold?' asked Veera seeing that he was still wet.

'No!' he said matter-of-factly. She finished eating and suddenly her eyes fell on her hands.

'Damn it!'

'Hey, what happened?'

'I left my amulets in the clearing. I will go and get them back.'

She stood up to go.

'Do you want me to come along?' asked Dhruva lazily.

'The place is really close. I know the way. I won't get lost!' she snapped. Veera began walking towards the clearing.

'Come back soon.'

Dhruva stretched himself out on the riverbank. He liked the sound of gushing water. He closed his eyes, his mind calm. After a while, Dhruva's eyes opened. He strained his ears. Someone was approaching. It was a woman for sure. He could hear the sweet music of her tinkling anklets. It was dusk and the sky had a beautiful pinkish hue. He turned his head in the direction of the sound. A slender lady, draped in a sari was walking towards the riverbank. He sat up with interest. She was still far away, for him to recognize her face. Dhruva looked at her keenly. There was something really familiar about her walk. He stood up and his lips curved into a smile. She walked with a rhythm. He didn't fail to recognize, she was Menakini, a dancer at the royal court.

Menakini walked leisurely towards him though she had recognised him already. She was very beautiful. She had lovely curves as a result of years of dancing. Dhruva stood there, waiting for her to come closer. He was well acquainted with the attitude of royal court dancers. She had draped a sari made of sheer red fabric. It accentuated her curvy hips. Her long hair had been loosely knotted into a bun. Her kohl-rimmed eyes were sparkling. She let a seductive smile rest on her lips as she stood in front of him.

'What a surprise Commander Dhruva! I really didn't expect to be rewarded in this way...' she said slowly letting her eyes take in his bare torso and wet dhoti.

'What a pity! I wish I could say the same,' he said with his characteristic lopsided smile.

'Well, you don't have to. I can see it in your eyes.'

She moved a step closer to him. But he didn't move. He stood there with the same arrogance.

'How can I help you?' asked Dhruva casually.

'You can help me in more ways than you can imagine.' Menakini let out a long drawn breath.

'Oh really? Then I won't disappoint you,' he said with a mischievous twinkle in his eyes. She slowly went and put her arms around his neck. Her sweet perfume overwhelmed Dhruva, but he still remained confident as usual.

'I have lost my way. Will you take me home?'

He could feel her breath. He had clearly not missed that she just said home and not *her* home. Dhruva raised an eyebrow at her amused. Unwrapping her hands from his neck, he stepped back. She pouted her face at him. No man had ever done that to her before.

'I am extremely sorry, my lady. You see, I am waiting for my friend. I am not alone.' He stressed unnecessarily on his last words. Before Menakini could respond, Veera walked up to them. She smiled at Menakini.

'Good evening Menakini.'

'Good evening Chief Veera,' she said politely.

'I am sorry that I am late,' said Veera glancing at Dhruva.

'Yeah, you should have come earlier. Unfortunately Menakini has lost her way. Mithra could you kindly take her back home?' he said seriously. Veera frowned at him. She also noted the flash of anger on the dancer's face. Then suddenly an idea struck her.

'Dhruva actually, I am going to the artillery now. Its better I take a look at the bows there,' said Veera with an air of urgency.

'Are you going there alone?'

He was not ready to buy her lame excuse.

'Hmmmm... yeah...I mean Vidyut is already at the palace. I will send word for him to join me.'

'Let me come with you—'

She cut him short.

'No Dhruva! Be a gentleman. It's getting dark and it's certainly not safe to leave a beautiful dancer like Menakini alone. You should take her home.'

Veera went and strapped her quiver of arrows. Dhruva quickly went to her.

'This is not fair!' he hissed.

'See you tomorrow!' said Veera loudly to him. She smiled at Menakini who bowed to her.

'I am not going to spare you,' threatened Dhruva under his breath. She simply winked at him picking up her bow and swung it across her shoulder. Veera leapt onto her horse and rode away. He turned to Menakini who had her seductive smile back. Dhruva picked up his kurta and angavastram, but he didn't bother wearing his kurta. He just tied them around his waist. He mounted his horse and smiled at her.

'Let's go!'

Dhruva helped her get onto the horse and rode into the night.

***

CHAPTER 12

'That was an excellent shot, my lord,' gushed Devajit.

'It is a pity that princes and kings can't participate in the competition,' said Ashwasena.

'No Ashwa! I think it is justified that royals shouldn't participate. It is high time we got over praising the royals for their skills. It is just that we are privileged,' reasoned Shaurya.

Devajit was clearly impressed. Prince Shaurya was respected not just for his skills and leadership capability but also for his humility. That was a rare quality to be found in the royals. Moreover he was adored by the women for his charms and sturdy looks. Now, that was a deadly combination!

'I hope you are all set for the competition.'

'Yes my lord. It is indeed an honour for me. I am grateful that you chose me,' said Devajit bowing to Shaurya.

'I haven't done anything Deva. It is you who proved your excellence in archery. You are one of the best in our kingdom.'

'Only after you my lord.'

'Well, I won't argue with that,' said Shaurya smugly. The three of them went to sit on a boulder under a tree. Shaurya and Ashwasena sat down. But Devajit remained standing.

'Sit down Deva. Don't be formal here. It's just us,' said an exasperated Shaurya. He didn't protest and sat down with them.

'So when are we leaving?'

Ashwasena gave Shaurya a confused look.

'We? It's only Deva and me who are going.'

'Unfortunately you will have to accommodate one more person with you,' said Shaurya with a slight smile.

'Who is it my lord?' asked Devajit ignorantly. But Ashwasena clearly understood where this conversation was heading. He firmly shook his head in disapproval.

'No way Shaurya! You cannot come with us. You really can't be serious about it.'

'I am damn serious about it Ashwa! How can I miss this opportunity? It is already killing me enough that I can't participate. I am definitely going to watch the competition.' He was firm in his decision. Devajit looked at him dumbstruck. But Ashwasena was not ready to give in yet.

'Shaurya please try to understand. It's too big a risk. I can't take chances with your life. The rules clearly state that the participant can be accompanied by only a maximum of three. Letting a prince, without even his minimum entourage of guards, to roam in foreign land is dangerous.'

'Commander Ashwasena is right my lord. You are very precious to us,' reiterated Devajit.

'Oh come on! We are not going into a battlefield. It's only a competition. You both are just being paranoid,' said Shaurya casually.

'Enemies wait for an opportunity like this! With you there, we have every reason to suspect each one of them. Moreover his Highness will never agree to this,' rued Ashwasena. He thought this would certainly make Shaurya rethink his decision. But he was wrong, rather it provoked the prince even more. Shaurya smiled at them mischievously.

'Well that's why we are not going to tell anyone about this. I am going to sneak out of the palace at night. I will accompany you in disguise.'

Both his companions were stumped.

'Shaurya if his Highness gets to know, it will be disastrous for us. Even a small inconvenience to your life and we both will be as good as dead,' argued Ashwasena furiously. Shaurya grinned at him in response.

'As much as you guard me, so I guard you. Don't worry about the King. I will not let you both get into any trouble. I know how to handle it. Trust me.'

'But Shaurya—'

Shaurya raised his hand to stop him and stood up. They both also quickly stood up.

'No more arguments! You will do as I say. It is an order!' commanded the prince. This was always his last resort to convince them. He knew it would always work.

'As you wish my lord,' said the men grimly bowing to him.

'Deva I will need some of your clothes,' said Shaurya with a smirk.

***

'Here, we have reached your home. Now I hope next time you won't lose your way,' said Dhruva dismounting from his horse.

Menakini stayed at the quarters meant for the royal court dancers and singers. The stars were twinkling in the sky when they reached there. The place was enveloped in darkness and silence of the night.

'If it is you who would help me find my way back home, I don't mind losing my way often. It sure is worth the effort,' she said looking straight into his eyes. He stood there with an expressionless face.

'Have a pleasant night. I have to go.'

'Do you really want to go?' asked Menakini moving towards him.

'I think my night would be more than pleasant if you shared it with me,' she said seductively. Literally no man could resist this level of temptation. Dhruva had to use every ounce of his self-control to stay away from this seductress.

'I have promised myself a life of celibacy. I cannot break it!' he said in a controlled voice.

'Why are you trying so hard to keep up your promise? Who are you doing this for? Chief Veera?'

Dhruva didn't answer. But his eyes clearly answered her question. She placed her soft hand on his cold, hard chest. His body stiffened at her touch.

'Have you given her your heart? Do you love her?'

He caught a whiff of her overwhelming perfume. He put his hand around her waist and pulled her closer. Menakini's heart was fluttering at his aggression.

'It is something more than love, hard to explain,' said Dhruva gruffly. She could feel his hot breath on her face. Wrapping her arms around his neck, she instantly kissed him. Dhruva could no longer hold onto his stance. He wrapped his arms around her waist and gave into the temptation. He kissed her back passionately. After a few moments he released her from his hold. Menakini saw a wild excitement in his eyes. But soon his eyes returned to the darkness they always had. Her face still held that slight smile. Her eyes held expectation which was shattered the very next moment. Dhruva lightly stroked her cheek with his finger. He closed this eyes for a moment. With a long drawn breath he opened his eyes.

'This is all I can give you,' he said intensely. Dhruva no longer stood there. He mounted his horse in one leap and rode away. Menakini stood there looking at him disappear into the dark.

'The best night of my life,' she said with a smile of satisfaction. This was one man whom she would never forget...

***

'Damn this headache!' cursed Shaurya. He dropped his head into his hands. It was a warm morning. Trivika walked in with a glass of buttermilk. He took it and gestured her to leave. He took a sip.

'Have you sobered down or are you still high on liquor?' asked Ashwasena walking into his private chambers.

'Looks like that arrack liquor was really strong yesterday. My head is hammering!' rued Shaurya. Then he gulped down the buttermilk in one go.

'I did warn you last night, but you hardly listen.'

'Oh stop it Ashwa! I really enjoyed it! This headache won't last long. That drink was surely worth the pain,' he winked.

'I won't argue with that! Take, here are Deva's clothes...'

Ashwasena handed him a cloth bag which had a few kurtas and dhotis. Shaurya took a look at them.

'These are good. They will surely help me pass as a Major in the army.'

Ashwasena let out a sigh.

'I am still not convinced. I think you should give it a second thought.'

Shaurya stood up and walked up to him. He placed a hand on his friend's shoulder.

'You know me better Ashwa. I have made up my mind and I don't rethink my decisions. I am going to attend this competition.'

'Well, at least I tried to stop you. You are so stubborn!'

'Let's just say I am more determined to get what I want.'

Ashwasena smiled at this comrade.

'Later we will decide about when to leave for the competition. I also have to make some arrangements.'

'Sure. Right now my mind is bogged down by this headache!' said a frustrated Shaurya.

'I think right now you should bathe first! This whole place reeks of nasty liquor,' said Ashwasena pinching his nose. Shaurya punched him lightly.

'You smelt worse than me yesterday!'

'But nobody will believe it now,' he said shrugging his shoulders.

'Alright! I am starving. I will quickly bathe and eat breakfast.'

'I will meet you at the stables later. We need to pick horses.'

'Yeah. You are right. I definitely cannot ride on Vayu. His presence will be too conspicuous,' said Shaurya with a hint of pride in his voice. No amount of disguise can hide his identity if he rode on that black stallion…

***

CHAPTER 13

'You really left him there, with Menakini?' asked Vidyut disbelievingly.

'Yeah I did. He was angry no doubt, but I didn't budge,' said Veera smiling. Today early in the morning Veera had come to the artillery with Vidyut. After spending some time looking at the bows, she narrated him the last evening's events.

'Do you really think she could have been successful?'

'Well, let's hope for the best.'

'I doubt it because—' he suddenly stopped mid-sentence. Vidyut gestured her to look in the right. Dhruva was walking towards them dressed in an orange kurta and blue dhoti. His face was expressionless.

'You both were supposed to come here last evening, right? Looks like you couldn't make it,' he said sarcastically.

'Dhruva I was just trying to—'

'Trying to do what Mithra? I have very clearly told you what is in my mind. Don't you understand that?' thundered Dhruva.

'I think I should leave,' said Vidyut and moved away from them. For some reason he felt their conversation was too personal. He glanced at Veera and she gave him a slight nod. Veera walked up to Dhruva and placed her hand on his shoulder trying to placate his anger. But he pushed her hand off his shoulder.

'Don't touch me! You just stay away from me.' He looked away from her.

'I only wanted you to rethink your decision. I thought a beautiful woman like Menakini could make you do that. For me, it's hard to accept your decision Dhruva...'

'Even for me, it's hard to accept your decision. Yet I stood by you. I never asked you to rethink about it then why are you doing this to me?' he asked angrily. It took a moment for her to give him a reply.

'Because I want you to be happy,' she said looking into his eyes. Dhruva held her face in his hands.

'I am happy with my decision Mithra. Nothing can ever give me more happiness than being able to share this life with you.'

'I am sorry...' she said sheepishly. He smiled at her affectionately.

'At least now I hope you will stop trying to hook me up with every beautiful woman you come across,' he said with a lopsided smile. Veera laughed at him nodding her head.

'I am not the one who will give up so easily!'

Dhruva rolled his eyes at her.

'Let's get back to your training,' he said pulling her by her hand towards the bows exhibited there. Veera smiled at him. But her heart weighed heavy with guilt. Dhruva's decision was something that would never let her heart be at peace.

***

'What do you mean? How can the soldiers not find them?' thundered King Kritiverman.

'They have probably gone in a different route to Charanvasi. They had crossed the border of our kingdom well before our soldiers could go in search of them your Highness,' said Prime Minister Agniverma hesitantly.

Shaurya, Ashwasena and Devajit had left Indragiri at midnight. Since the prince was in the disguise of a Major nobody had seen him go. He had secretly slipped out of the palace. From a narrow entrance behind the stables he rode out on a horse without being conspicuous. But before leaving he had left a message for the king telling the truth about his absence. He knew the King could not stop him once he was out of their kingdom. Kritiverman crushed the papyrus scroll in a fit of rage.

'What do we do now Agni?'

'Your Highness, we know that royals are not allowed inside Charanvasi for the competition. But the prince has gone there in disguise and there are very little chances of anyone finding out his identity. Moreover Devajit and Ashwasena are there to protect him. Prince Shaurya himself is an exceptional warrior. It is better we wait for their return,' reasoned Agniverma.

'Wait for their return!? Doing nothing? For heaven's sake Agni! Shaurya is the crown Prince of Indragiri and he is out there in a foreign land without even a bare minimum of his guards,' growled Kritiverman.

'Forgive my impudence your Highness. But if we try to send our guards or search for the prince in any other way it could prove to be dangerous to him. Revealing his identity will only complicate things.'

Kritiverman paced across the royal chamber impatiently. Queen Arunadevi was sitting worried on a chair clasping her hands. At last Kritiverman stopped to look at Agniverma.

'Alright! I think you are right. Don't send any search groups. But do send a spy to keep a watch on him.'

'As you say, your Highness,' said Agniverma. He bowed to them and walked out of the royal chamber. Kritiverman shot any angry look at his wife.

'I suppose you knew about this,' he said coldly. Arunadevi glared at him.

'I would never have let him go, had I known. He never told me.'

'Shaurya is becoming very rebellious and reckless. It is time he showed some dignity of being the crown Prince.'

'He is still young. We should give him some time...' she said softly.

'Time? Shaurya is a grown up man Aruna. Stop being just an indulgent mother. He is no longer just a son. He is a prince,' he said intensely.

'Being crowned a prince doesn't imply that he ceases to be our son,' she replied acridly. Kritiverman winced at her words. He clearly understood the undercurrent of anger behind her words. Arunadevi loved her son immensely and she wished her husband loved Shaurya more as a father and less as a king.

***

'Where is Dhruva?' asked Veera frowning.

'Commander Dhruva went to bathe in the river my Lady. He has not yet returned,' replied the beautiful attendant at the travel inn. Veera and Dhruva had left Virpur four days ago. They rode hard and rested little. Now they were just a day's journey away from Charanvasi. Last night they had stopped by a travel inn and decided to stay there. Veera thought they would leave the inn after eating breakfast. But when Veera bathed and came to eat breakfast, she could not find Dhruva there.

'Did you send someone?'

'Yes my Lady. I sent one of the guards to call him. But the commander sent a message for you. He said he would join you in a while,' she relied politely. Veera nodded at her.

'Shall I serve you breakfast?'

'No. it's alright. I will eat with him. You may leave.'

The attendant bowed to her and left. Veera sat on the wooden bench and decided to wait for Dhruva. She knew he wanted some time alone. There have been instances in the past when she had seen him sitting alone deep in thought. Dhruva preferred to be left alone when he wanted to clear his mind of some disturbing thoughts. Veera understood his mind and she never disturbed him during that time. Though they never spoke about it later, it was an understanding they always had.

A long time passed and the sun was up high in the sky now. Veera paced up and down in the porch of the travel inn looking every now and then at the path that led to the river. She stopped pacing and let out a long drawn breath. She began walking towards the river. Veera could no longer stay there waiting for him.

It was a warm morning. As usual Veera was dressed in dhoti and kurta. The attendant at the inn was quite taken aback last night when she saw that one of the men entering the inn was actually a woman. She looked at Veera with a new found respect when they introduced themselves. All the more, she was interested in the handsome, but indifferent Commander Dhruva. He never showed any interest in the special attention she was giving him. Though she knew who Veera was, she couldn't get used to seeing a woman dressed as a man.

A few steps had been built at the riverbank leading to the river. These steps were meant to facilitate during rituals performed there. Dhruva sat on one of these steps looking at the river pensively. He had bathed and changed into a blue dhoti. Though the sun was shining above, there were enough trees to provide shade on the steps. Soft breeze was blowing. He lost track of time after he sent back the guard with his message. Though the water on his bare torso had evaporated, his hair was still a little damp. There was a cuckoo singing somewhere in the distance. But Dhruva was oblivious to his surroundings, his mind was lost somewhere in the depth.

Veera stood at a distance looking at a pensive Dhruva. She expected him to look up at her. She was sure he would have heard her come there. But he didn't move. Veera went to him and sat down one step below him. She didn't look at him and rather gazed at the river instead. He still didn't move. There was silence except for the musical flow of the river and the singing cuckoo.

'We kissed...' said Dhruva breaking the silence still looking away. Veera didn't react.

'That evening, when I went to leave Menakini at her home, I ... she kissed me and I lost my self-control. I gave in to the temptation...'

There were a few moments of long silence.

'Mithra... say something,' he implored. After a moment Veera turned to sit facing him. She placed her hand on his clenched fist.

'It was hard, wasn't it?' she asked softly. Dhruva closed his eyes and let out a long drawn breath.

'Very hard.'

'This is exactly what I want you to understand. It is not easy to practise celibacy, Dhruva. You can still change your decision...'

He opened his eyes and gave her a tortured look.

'Will you rethink your decision? Is it not equally hard for you?' he snapped. But Veera smiled at him indulgently.

'You have to believe me when I say that it is not hard for me. I grew up in seclusion. I don't know what it means to fall in love. So being a spinster is easy for me since there is no man who can have such feelings for me. I haven't seen a man who can fall in love with a warrior woman and being the Chief only makes it easier for me.'

Dhruva unclenched his fists. Though his heart refused to accept her reason, his mind understood the truth in her words. Veera could feel the change in his stance. She took his hand and squeezed it lightly.

'As easy as it is for me, this is equally difficult for you. You being a handsome and invincible warrior will only attract women more. The same reasons which work in my favour will go against you. Now, do you understand why I want you to change your mind? It is not easy to give up the simple desires you crave as a man.' She spoke like a mature individual. For a moment, seeing Dhruva not arguing, she hoped that he would heed to her words.

'I won't deny that I do have desires and temptations. But I have the will to control them. Nothing is bigger than my vow to stand by you in every decision you make. These temptations only make those challenges more interesting!'

he said with his characteristic smile crinkling his eyes. Veera shook her head in defeat. She should have known better than to hope in vain.

'If you had no intention of changing your mind, why did you tell me about it?' she complained. A sombre look entered his eyes.

'It was weighing heavy on my mind Mithra. I didn't want to hide it from you. I had to get it off my chest.'

Veera could understand his feelings. Though it was a trivial incident, it did mean a lot more between them. She stood up and pulled him up holding his hand.

'Let's go. I am starving.'

But Dhruva didn't stand up. He pulled her hand down and made her sit next to him. She looked at him confused.

'What? Did you kiss someone else too? I did notice that lovely attendant eyeing you last night,' said Veera with mock impatience. He looked at her surprised for a moment and then both burst out laughing.

'Well, I didn't notice that she was interested in me. But I did notice that she is indeed lovely! Rest assured that I would certainly let you know if she...' said Dhruva winking at her.

'Shameless!' said Veera punching his arm.

'Now come on, get it off your chest. I know there is something more important that want to tell me. You look disturbed,' said Veera caressing his head once. He averted her eyes and looked at the flowing water. He took a deep breath and slowly let it out.

'Guruji never told me anything about your training, Mithra. The last time he spoke to me about you, I promised him that I would always protect you. Back then, I didn't know you were a warrior. The first time when I saw you in the battlefield after Guruji's death…' Dhruva's voice shook slightly.

'I was stunned! You were exceptional despite the fact that it was your first battle. Later I was dumbstruck by the way you displayed your skills in archery. I am proud of you Mithra,' he said looking at her. Veera smiled at him. Dhruva smiled at her lightly.

'But now, I am worried. It may just be a competition but it will be nothing less than a battlefield. Men will not only compete for the honor of their kingdoms but also for their individual honor. Though it is supposed to be fair game, they will never hesitate to go to any length just to ensure their victory.'

'I don't stand a chance before them, do I?' asked Veera softly. Dhruva rolled his eyes at her.

'Fool! I am not worried about you losing the competition. You have every chance to win Mithra. Do you want me to keep saying this every time? Stop underestimating yourself!' Veera frowned at hm.

'Then what is it that you are worried about?'

'You! We are going to be on our own in Charanavasi. It is going to be the first time that a woman will compete against them. Having such an exceptional female competition will only complicate things. I am worried about your safety,' said Dhruva intensely.

'What do you want me to do?' asked Veera understanding his predicament. Dhruva took her hand in his.

'I want to keep up the promise I made to Guruji. You will not wander about there alone. As long as we are together we are safe. You will do everything you can to keep yourself out of trouble, will you?'

Veera squeezed his hand in return.

'I promise, I will always be with you!' said Veera intensely. Dhruva nodded his head in agreement.

'Let's go. You must be hungry' said Dhruva standing up. He picked up the cloth bundle.

'Let's eat breakfast and leave for Chranavasi. We will reach there by nightfall, won't we?'

'We are not leaving today. We leave early tomorrow morning' said Dhruva seriously.

'Tomorrow!? But why? The competition starts the day after tomorrow. It is better to go there at least one day in advance,' protested Veera. Dhruva let out a tired breath. The look in his eyes suddenly made him look much older than his age.

'Try to understand Mithra. Taking you there early is too big a risk. It is better we reach there tomorrow night. With competition the next day, people will just think a little less about you! I mean they won't have time to plot against us,' reasoned Dhruva. Veera understood his logic and smiled at him. They both knew that this competition was a dangerous challenge. But what they didn't know was that, it would change their lives forever.

CHAPTER 14

'You could have easily won this completion,' said Shaurya languidly.

'But I never learnt how to use a bow,' said the lady in a voice laced with amusement. She filled his glass with wine standing near him closer than necessary.

'You don't have to. Your eyes seem to be shooting arrows accurately at their target,' he said huskily. She smiled at him seductively clearly aware of the charms men used on her. But this one was quite quick in impressing her. She looked at Shaurya who had a confident smile of a man who was used to having women swoon over him. But what surprised her was that he was only a Major in the army!

Shaurya was sitting leisurely in the tent allotted to Devajit. At Charanavasi, one tent was provided to every participant and his companions. It was a spacious tent with three separate rooms and common meeting space in the middle of the tent. Shaurya was disguised as a Major in the army of Indragiri and he told them to call him Chandravarun. After dinner, Shaurya and Ashwasenasena had returned to the tent. There were female attendants to serve and entertain the men. One such beautiful attendant had come to serve them wine. As usual Shaurya had taken to flirting with her. Ashwasenasena sipped his wine and glanced at Shaurya. He nodded his head smiling. Just then Devajit barged into the tent.

'My Lo—' began Devajit but he was silenced by an angry look Ashwasenasena cast on him. Shaurya remained unperturbed and looked up at her, who was frowning at Devajit.

'I think we should meet later without these disturbances,' said Shaurya winking at her. She smiled at him nodding her head and left the tent.

'Have you lost your mind Devajit? How could you be so reckless?' admonished Ashwasenasena. Devajit lowered his head.

'Please forgive me my lord. I will not repeat it again. I will be more alert now on.'

'That's okay Deva. But what happened?' asked Shaurya.

'A woman my lord!'

Shaurya laughed at him

'Well there are so many women here. But which one made you go crazy like this?'

'She is no ordinary woman my lord. She is unique,' said Devajit stressing his last word.

'What makes you to say so?' asked a curious Ashwasenasena.

'Is she very beautiful?' asked Shaurya still not as curious as Ashwasenasena. Shaurya had seen many beautiful women in his life.

'She is beautiful but more than that, she is special. She is dressed like a man!'

'What! But why?'

'She is here to participate in the competition my lord'

'What?!' cried Ashwasenasena standing at once.

'This is unbelievable! Are you sure about it?'

'Yes Commander. I saw her just now. I also enquired with the member of organizing committee about her. He confirmed it.'

'Where is she from? Who has accompanied her?'

'She is from Virpur. She is the chief of their army. Commander Dhruva accompanies her.'

Shaurya was dumbstruck by what he had heard. He was clearly impressed. It was not easy to impress Prince Shaurya!

'Who is she?' he asked softly.

'Veera,' said Devajit with respect in his voice.

'Veera...' said Shaurya slowly letting the name linger on his tongue. His heart was burning with curiosity. He let out a sigh and closed his eyes trying to picture a woman with bow and arrow. He smiled at his imagination.

***

'Anything else my lady?' asked the attendant politely.

'No. You may leave,' said Veera curtly taking the glass of milk from her. The attendant smiled at Veera and left.

'Damn it!' cursed Veera under her breath. She knew exactly why the attendant had smiled. Her dress!

Yesterday when Veera had tethered her horse and walked with Dhruva into the archery camp, the moon was up high in the sky. Most of the men had retired to their tents. Very few were actually seated around the camp fire chatting. The guards at the entrance had mistaken her for a man. But Dhruva introduced themselves and said that they wanted to meet the organizer. One of the surprised guards looked mockingly at her. But Veera averted his eyes. He would have passed a snide comment had it not been for Dhruva's threatening look. Along the way the men gave her similar kind of looks and passed comments on her. But she turned a deaf ear to them and walked with her head held high. Though she knew that all their eyes were on her, she kept a calm façade. Dhruva glanced at her making sure that she was fine. He could sense her discomfort but was satisfied that she didn't quite show it out. He clenched his fists at the comments passed on her but did not lose his temper. He knew it would only worsen the situation. He had already made up his mind to exercise every ounce of his self-control.

Veera gulped down the contents of her glass and wiped her mouth with the back of her hand. She was dressed in a red silk dhoti and a purple kurta. She tied the leather scabbard which had her dagger to her waist. She tied her hair into a tight bun and secured it with a pin. She wore her amulets and picked up her bow. She passed her hand over it lovingly. Though she won't be using it today, she couldn't help caressing it. The bow had very intricate carving and it also held her name 'Veera'. That bow was gifted to her by her father. She closed her eyes, as her mind seeked the blessing of her father.

'All set?' asked Dhruva as he walked into her room. Veera turned around and smiled at him tentatively. Dhruva smiled at her with a look of assurance.

'I think so,' she said sheepishly.

'Well, not until you have this.'

Dhruva held a brown leather armor in his hand. Veera looked at him baffled.

'But we usually don't wear an armor in a competition!'

'I know that's why I got this light weight leather armor made for you. I can't let you go in there totally unprotected!'

Veera took it from him. She put it on and smiled at him. It fit her perfectly. Dhruva fastened the strings on the side to secure the armor on her torso. He then held her by her shoulders.

'Today is an opportunity to prove that you are no less than any man. It is time to show the world that a woman can fight a war. It is a chance for you to show gratitude for your teacher, to make your father proud. You are born to do this Mithra!' said Dhruva looking into her eyes. In a moment Veera's mind was wiped clean of all apprehensions. Dhruva had actually echoed her father's wards. She was born to do this!

'I will do my best!' said Veera confidently.

'All the best Mithra!' said Dhruva and kissed her forehead. He held out his hand and Veera placed her hand in his. Dhruva held her hand securely and they both walked out into the broad daylight. All eyes were pinned on them but they stood there fearlessly looking at them. Nothing mattered as long as they stayed hand in hand...

***

'There she comes,' said Devajit pointing towards his right. Shaurya quickly turned but he didn't see a woman at first in the crowd. He saw a tall man dressed in a blue silk dhoti and a cream colored sleeveless kurta make his way towards the arena. Shaurya noted that his right hand was holding something behind. Then the men around began making way and there was an unusual disturbance there. Then she stepped beside the handsome man.

Ashwasenasena let out an involuntary gasp. Shaurya whistled in amusement. Devajit stood there, his eyes fixed on her still unable to believe that she was indeed a participant. Shaurya noted that despite being dressed as a man, she was indeed beautiful with a dusky complexion. She was slender yet curvaceous at the right places, though her curves were camouflaged by her attire. Her walk was not just graceful but also confident bordering with slight arrogance. Shaurya appraised her with a hawk's eye. Then his eyes fell on her left hand holding Dhruva's right hand. He didn't let go of her hand even once until they stood near the arena. Shaurya suddenly felt a pang of jealousy, though he didn't fathom why.

Veera sat down on the stone bench with Dhruva. Though she managed to keep her appearance unperturbed, her heart was drumming inside. Had it not been for Dhruva's hard hands holding hers, she could never have pulled it off. Dhruva was constantly observing their surrounding scrutinizing for threats. Shesha, the broad, muscular man walked to the center of the arena. He was the organizer of this competition and also the Chief Commander of Charanvasi.

'Good morning warriors! Today we all have assembled here for the annual archery competition. This competition is held to honor the best archer amongst you. With the blessings of Lord Shiva I declare this competition open!' bellowed his voice. All the men cheered in delight and applauded. Then all the participants were asked to assemble in the arena.

'All the best Deva!' said Shaurya and patted him on the back. Ashwasenasena embraced Devajit. He then walked into the arena. Veera stood up and so did Dhruva. When she looked up at Dhruva, nervousness was clearly written on her face. He squeezed her hand.

'You will surely win this! Don't worry, I will be right here.'

He stroked her cheek affectionately. Veera managed a smile and nodded her head. She then walked into the arena letting go of his hand. Shaurya eyed her as she walked into the arena confidently or so she tried to appear. He still couldn't get his head around the fact that she was a warrior. A woman with a bow seemed ridiculous to him. A smile of mockery played around his lips.

***

'Yes!' said Dhruva punching his first in the air. He was grinning widely. She lowered her bow and let out a self-satisfactory smile. She looked at Dhruva and mirrored his grin. She then slowly looked around her dumbstruck audience. Shaurya was still gaping at her wide eyed.

'Bravo!' bellowed Shesha applauding her feat. Veera bowed to the audience. Everyone present in the audience began applauding. The other participants were not very happy with the outcome yet they grudgingly applauded. Veera clearly deserved it. She had cleared three rounds in the competition. There were about twenty participants, the best archers from the kingdoms far and wide. After the three rounds on the first day, the competition was down to the final five contestants. Now Veera was one among them. She had easily cleared the rounds. Devajit had also secured a place among the final five.

Veera placed the bow down in its place. It was a special bow made of iron especially for the event. It was heavier than Veera's bow but since she had trained with various types of bows in the artillery, she could handle this without much trouble. Veera then walked back and sat on the stone bench among the other participations. Few men had a pleasant smile of appreciation while others gave her an egoistic look. But she held a calm expression. Shesha announced the events for the day over. Now the final five would compete the day after tomorrow in the final contest. The men began dispersing. The participants walked to their companions seated in the audience. Veera quickly walked towards a beaming Dhruva. He put his arms around her in a warm embrace. She rested her head on his chest feeling relieved and secure.

'See! It wasn't that hard. You were brilliant!'

'You were right about everything. Now I think I can win this,' she said smiling. He released her from his embrace and nodded at her appreciatively. Shesha then walked towards them.

'Commander Dhruva! We have met before. You were unbelievable today Veera,' he said looking at her.

'Thank you sir. It is indeed an honor to hear you say this,' she said politely.

'You have made your father proud. I knew Agneyastra. He was a great man. I am eagerly waiting for the final contest. May the best archer win! Best of luck to you.'

'Thank you sir.'

Then he went towards the camp. A few other warriors too walked up to them and congratulated her. Dhruva stood right next to her with a proud smile etched on his face. Then Devajit walked up to her before going to his companions.

'I am Major Devajit from Indragiri. You were fantastic today Chief Veera.'

'Thank you Major. Your skill was no less in keeping us spellbound,' she said appreciatively.

'Well, I think you were the hero of the day. I can still see everyone's eyes pinned on you,' he said glancing around. Veera laughed lightly.

'I have to admit that when I first came to know that a woman was competing, I laughed at the idea. But you proved me wrong.'

'I think she has proved everyone wrong here!' snapped Dhruva.

'I am commander Dhruva from Virpur!'

'Yes of course I know you Commander. Your presence too has been more than conspicuous especially since you are the companion of female participant,' he said in a teasing tone. Dhruva narrowed his eyes. Veera sensed the tension in air.

'Major Devajit, it was nice meeting you. I think we should get going. Everyone needs a break after a long day,' she said smiling slightly.

'Pleasure was all mine Chief Veera. I hope to meet you later during the competition,' he said and left.

'Thank God! You didn't break his teeth,' said Veera raising her eyebrow. Dhruva relaxed his stance at her words.

'It was tempting! But I think it is better he be in good shape for the competition. I don't want to miss the pleasure of seeing him lose!' said Dhruva with lopsided smile.

'You better get hold on your temper until we finish this competition. Else you will ruin all the fun!'

He simply shrugged and began walking towards their tent tugging her along.

Shaurya stood rooted to his place seeing all that happened around Veera. Until that day he had never thought that a woman with a bow could set his heart on fire. Her poise as she released the arrow was intense and graceful. She looked every bit confident as a man but at the same time beautiful. Shaurya wanted to touch her slender hands just to know how they felt on that bow! His heart was overcome with desire at that moment. Prince Shaurya wanted her!

'Well done,' said Ashwasenasena as Devajit walked towards him. He smiled at him.

'So what do you think?' asked Ashwasenasena gesturing towards Veera with whom he was talking earlier.

'Arrogant!' said Devajit bitterly.

'Well, that's not surprising. With such talent, she is allowed to be arrogant!' he said casually.

'It is not Veera that I am talking about. She is humble and polite. It is her companion, who is arrogant. Commander Dhruva, I don't like him.'

'I don't like him either,' said Shaurya who was quiet until then. The only reason for that was he was still staring at Veera whose hand was locked in Dhruva's tight grip. He wished that it was his hand which held her at that moment.

'Shaurya don't,' whispered Ashwasenasena clearly understanding his train of thoughts. He frowned at Ashwasenasena but nodded his head slightly. He knew Ashwasena was right. Shaurya had to stop thinking about her. He let out a long drawn breath and closed his eyes momentarily to throw that ridiculous desire out of his mind. Yet his heart echoed *Veera*.

***

CHAPTER 15

'Heading out?' asked Veera looking at Dhruva quizzically. He was putting on his amulets.

'Yes. I am going to meet commander Shambhu of Brihanga. Their kingdom is one of our allies and he is an old friend of mine. I want to catch up with him since it has been a long time. The last time we met was during a war which we fought together and won,' he said looking up at her. It was a hot afternoon and they had just finished their lunch some time ago. Veera was leaning against a cushion on the wooden cot. The previous day had exhausted her and she wanted to rest today to be prepared for tomorrow.

'Well then have a good time.'

'I hope you will not plan any mischief in my absence!' he said critically. Veera rolled her eyes at him.

'You have got to stop treating me like a child!'

'It isn't my fault. You don't act like grown up sometimes,' he said trying hard to suppress a smile. She stuck out her tongue at him.

'See! This is what I meant!' he said laughing. Veera couldn't help smiling at his child like glee.

'I hope you are strapped.'

He gave her an exasperated look.

'I am going to meet a friend. You can take it easy.'

'It doesn't take long for friends to turn foes. You said that to me once,' she said smugly. He nodded his head at her giving up.

'Yes, I have strapped my dagger to my waist.'

He pointed to the leather strapper which held his dagger. But for others it would only look like an accessory hiding its contents.

'See you later.'

'See you later. Take care and be alert,' said Dhruva and walked out of the tent. Veera smiled at him.

Father was indeed right in choosing him. Dhruva has more than made up for the loss of father in my life. Without him....

Veera didn't even want to think about it. She closed her eyes and decided to take a nap.

Suddenly Veera opened her eyes. She had almost fallen asleep when she was woken up by the clanking sound of bangles. A beautiful woman was standing before her. She was dressed in a lovely pink sari. She looked at Veera apologetically. Veera frowned at her.

'What is it?' asked Veera curtly.

'Please forgive me for disturbing you my lady,' she said in a tone indeed apologetic. Veera sat up straight and smiled at her lightly.

'It's ok. Tell me, what made you come here?'

'I… I want to apologize my lady,' she said lowering her eyes.

'Apologize? For what?'

'For insulting you by looking down on you. I underestimated your skills…'

Veer's face took a somber look. She let out a sigh.

'I don't mind. After all you are not the first one to do so.'

'I will never be able to forgive myself for it.'

'What is your name?' asked Veera.

'Everyone calls me Supratika,' she said softly.

'Come, sit here,' invited Veera gesturing to the place next to her on the cot. But Supratika looked at her taken a back.

'No my lady. I don't have the slightest quality to have the honor to sit beside you,' she said in a painful tone.

'Supratika, you either sit beside me or leave the tent immediately. Don't ever show your face again to me. The choice is yours,' said Veera shrugging. Supratika hesitated for a moment and then obliged.

'Don't be hard on yourself. I can understand. It was not your fault. Not everyone can know about me initially. Only later do they realize what I am capable of.'

'You are indeed a brave woman. You must be blessed to lead such a life, unlike us.'

Veera looked at her baffled.

'What do you mean?'

Supratika smiled at her dryly.

'You know who we are Chief Veera. We are attendants and most of the time courtesans to men. All we have is beauty and that is nothing but a curse. There have been times when I wished I was ugly. I don't live a life worthy enough to be spoken of…' trailed Supratika, her voice breaking down. Veera placed a hand on hers and squeezed it lightly. 'You don't have to be ashamed of who you are Supratika. Each one of us have our own drawbacks in our life. All that matters is what we think about ourselves and not what this world thinks about us.'

Supratika was clearly impressed by Veera's words. She smiled at her.

'I have seen many men Chief Veera. All I see in their eyes is lust and greed. But today when a few men looked at you, there was respect and awe. Now that is something I thought was impossible until today.'

'Didn't you notice? Some even looked at me with fear,' said Veera winking at her. Both of them laughed heartily. Supratika then stood up, to leave.

'Why don't you stay longer?' insisted Veera.

'Today you have time to rest. But I never get a day off like this. In fact I have more work to do,' she said mischievously.

'But do visit me when you have leisure time. It's good to have a friend to talk. Moreover I am tired of only interacting with men here,' said Veera puckering her face. Supratika nodded in agreement. She bowed to Veera and walked towards the entrance. Then she stopped and turned to look at Veera. She looked at her raising an eyebrow questioningly. Supratika hesitated for a moment.

'Well… Commander Dhruva is a handsome man. Is he your…?'

Veera understood her incomplete question.

'He is my companion!' she answered straightly. Supratika still had a confused look on her face.

'Do you think he will be interested —?'

'In you?' completed Veera suppressing a smile.

'I have no objection if you want to try,' said Veera playfully. Supratika grinned at her.

'He hardly notices any woman other than you! But I really cannot fathom the look his eyes hold for you, Chief Veera. It's deep,' she said intensely.

'Deeper than you think,' said Veera softly. Supratika left glancing at her one last time. Veera closed her eyes and let out a long drown breath.

***

Veera was making shadows on the wall with her fingers placed before the lamp. She had finished eating dinner and was trying to kill time before going to sleep. Just then Dhruva walked into the tent. Veera narrowed her eyes looking up at him. He was surprised to see her awake.

'What are you doing Mithra? Why haven't you slept yet?'

'You are drunk!'

'What?! No!'

'Don't lie to me. You smell odd,' complained Veera shrinking her nose.

'Come on Mithra! It's just wine!' said Dhruva rolling his eyes at her. Veera smiled at him mischievously raising her eyebrows.

'Who said drinking wine doesn't make you drunk!'

'If I am drunk like you say, I wouldn't have found my way back so easily. My eyes would have turned bloodshot and my vision would be disturbed. Most of all I wouldn't be standing so steadily!'

Veera burst out laughing Dhruva sat down in front of her shaking his head.

'Tell me, how does it taste? I am curious,' said Veera with a childlike glee.

'It tastes more like grape juice but is stronger. Do you want to try?'

'Of course not! I haven't touched any form of liquor in my life,' said Veera proudly. Dhruva smiled at her.

'Good for you! I think you should sleep now. It is late already.'

'I know, but I am not sleepy. I hope you had a good time with your friends.'

'Yes indeed. But today everyone spoke mostly about only one person. You!' said a smiling Dhruva.

'We should be surprised only if they don't talk about me! Not every day they get to see a woman defeat them.'

'I totally agree with you. Now focus on tomorrow and I know it shouldn't be difficult for you.'

Veera let out a sigh and looked down. Dhruva caringly stroked her cheek.

'Hey, are you alright?' he asked gently.

'I don't know. Those men out there don't accept me, do they? Many just hate me, I can see it in their eyes,' mumbled Veera.

'Damn them! You don't think about them. Who cares about what they think? Men do not accept changes easily Mithra. Sometimes you have to simply force it down their throat. You should give them no choice but to accept you as a warrior. For that, you should win this competition hands down. We can't afford to lose now,' said Dhruva, intensity burning in his eyes. His confidence was infectious and it instilled a new vigor in her.

'We always win!' said Veera grinning. They punched their clenched fists together.

'Chief Agneyastra,' said Ashwasenasena. The three were seated in their tent drinking wine.

'She is Chief Agneyastra's daughter. He must have trained her too. Impressive!' said Shaurya his eyes gleaning with interest.

'What do you think Deva? Does she stand a chance?'

'Well, it was not easy to come into the final five. If she could make it here, then she certainly has a chance to win. I don't make the mistake of underestimating my competitors,' said Devajit sipping his wine.

'But I doubt she can win tomorrow. We know that the final test is very difficult. Even the most skilled men stumble.'

'You can never know the expertise of an archer until it is put to test. Veera's skills are still unknown to the world Ashwa. Virpur has chosen her as its representative after considering its best archers in the kingdom. If one kingdom has its hopes pinned on her, then she must be exceptionally skilled,' reasoned Shaurya.

'Maybe or maybe not. Only tomorrow's competition can answer that,' said Ashwasena finishing his wine.

'I can't wait to see her tomorrow,' breathed Shaurya. Ashwasena narrowed his eyes slightly at Shaurya but he ignored it. Shaurya knew he should not be thinking about Veera. She is not someone you desire for. Everything about her was aimed at repelling men from her. But for Shaurya it was exactly opposite. He was drawn to her irresistibly! The more he tried to shut her out of his mind, the more his mind thought about her. He tried to convince his mind that it was temporary and would not last long. Had Veera just been a passing cloud in Shaurya's life, they would never have crossed each other's way. But it was never meant to be that way.

***

'Promise me, you will do as I say,' said Agneyastra outstretching his palm. Veera placed her hand in his palm instantly.

'I promise father.'

'*Then go and pick up that bow,*' *said Agneyastra smiling serenely. Veera went and stood before the bow. It was a huge bow. She looked at her father with doubt and fear.*

'*Pick up that bow Veera,*' *said he with an unchanging expression and tone. She hesitantly touched the bow. It was hard and cold. Veera tried to lift it up, but she couldn't. It was heavy. She tried several times but failed to lift it. Her hands seemed to slip from the bow every time.*

'*Mithra…*' *called out a familiar voice. Veera looked up to see Dhruva.*

'*You can do it,*' *he said looking into her eyes. His eyes bored into hers. Veera bent down and picked up the bow easily this time. She positioned the arrow securely on the bow and stood ready.*

'*Shoot,*' *commanded Agneyastra. She instantly released her arrow. Veera turned to look at her father. But his face was blank and he was staring down at her hands. She followed his gaze and looked down at her hands. They were stained with blood! Terrified she looked up at Dhruva. His face was contorted in pain. Blood continuously oozed from the wound, where her arrow had pierced his chest.*

'Dhruva!' cried out Veera flashing her eyes open and sitting up. Her breathing was heavy. Her body was soaked in sweat. Her room in the tent was dark except for a small lamp glowing in the corner. Realizing that it was a nightmare, she slowly calmed her breathing. Veera drank little water from the copper jug placed beside her bed. She stood up and walked to the small window. It was still dark outside but she could see a few priests going to the river for their morning bath and prayers. Veera slowly walked to Dhruva's room. He was still fast asleep, sprawling on his bed. His face had a soft glow to it in the dim light of the lamp. Veera knew that previous night's wine still had its effects on him. She was glad, her scream had not woken him up. She closed her eyes in a silent prayer.

Keep him safe. He is all that I have.

She then slowly walked out of his room noiselessly. There was no use going back to bed now. She went into the bathing chamber and bathed in the cold water. She dressed in her kurtha and dhoti and stepped out. Veera walked straight to the Shiva temple near the river.

***

Kshini took a look at her sari once more and pressed it slightly at the folds. She then turned to leave. Before that she looked at Major Chandravarun once more. He was lost in his thoughts staring into the dark outside the window.

'Chandra, who is she?'

He looked at her taken aback.

'Who?'

'The one you are thinking about,' she said calmly.

'How did you…?'

Kshini smiled at him.

'You were in my arms, but there was someone else on your mind.'

'Well yes, there is someone,' said Shaurya slowly.

'She is very lucky to have a man think about her even when he is in another woman's arms…' said Kshini and walked towards the entrance of the tent. Before stepping out she turned back and smiled at him bashfully. Shaurya turned to look outside the window again. The cool breeze caressed his bare torso. He ran his hand through his disheveled hair.

Sleep was far from entering his eyes. He saw small flickering lamps in the Shiva temple at a distance. He knew it would be dawn after some time. He bathed and dressed in Devajit's blue cotton dhoti. While stepping out of the tent, he noted that Ashwasena and Devajit were still fast asleep. He walked towards the Shiva temple with bare feet, in the dark.

Shaurya washed his feet in the river outside and stepped inside the temple. It was an old temple made of stone. There were many stone pillars arranged in four columns outside the sanctum sanctorum. All the lamps inside were lighted and the carvings on these pillars were delicate and beautiful. The sanctum sanctorum had a black stone idol of lord Shiva seated in penance. Though it was a statue of penance, the Lord's characteristic weapon, the Trishul was fixed to the ground beside him. It was an idol which instilled peace and fighting spirit equally in the worshipper's heart. Shaurya didn't go near the sanctum sanctorum. The priests were chanting hymns and pouring milk on the Lord Shiva's idol. The temple was empty except for the priests and their assistants. Shaurya decided to sit near a pillar. When he turned to his right, he let out an involuntary gasp. His heart skipped beat! Veera was sitting there leaning against another pillar with her eyes closed. A tear had escaped her eye lid and was resting on her cheek delicately. She seemed oblivious to her surroundings. Her wet hair was not tied and gathered to fall on her left shoulder. She sat there cross legged with hands on her thighs. Her fingers were long and slender with neatly clipped pink nails. Now that was unusual because most women that he had been with had longer nails, well-shaped and preserved. Her dusky face had a golden glow in the light of the lamps. She had fuller pink lips…. Shaurya suddenly closed his eyes and shook his head to stop himself from ogling at her. He was standing in a temple for God's sake! How could he let his mind wander like that? He slowly opened his eyes, but she remained unmoved. Shaurya stood rooted to the spot. He couldn't tear his eyes away from her. He could spend days just looking at her. All he wanted to do now was take her in his arms and kiss away the tear from her cheek.

Dan! Dan! Dan!

Shaurya was abruptly pulled away from his reverie. The priests had begun the arti to the Lord and their assistants were striking the bronze bells in the temple. Veera stirred slightly. Shaurya quickly hid behind a pillar. He was not willing to meet her then. His heart was filled with an untold nervousness. She slowly opened her eyes and wiped the tear. She then walked to the sanctum and joined the others in the arti with folded hands. Veera stood in that position until the arti was over. Then she bowed to the Lord. The priest blessed her and offered the Lord's blessings as the sacred vermilion. She took it in her finger tips and applied it on her forehead reverentially. Once again she bowed and turned around to leave. Suddenly she saw a man smiling at her. He was standing just a few feet away from her. His hair had been knotted on the crown of his head. He sported a long beard, neatly kept. Veera noticed his well-toned physique under his ochre saffron robes. That was very unusual for a scholar. More than any of this, it was the sharp look in his eyes which was unsettling for Veera.

'That was indeed a long prayer for a warrior to make,' said the scholar calmly.

'Well you must have already known that I am an exception Acharya!'

'You have a quick tongue Veera. Interesting!'

'How do you—?'

'Is there anyone here who doesn't know you?'

Veera just smiled at him.

'Acharya kindly forgive me, but I don't know you.'

'I am Rudrapriyapriya, a scholar. But I can see that you find it hard to believe, don't you?' asked he with a gleam in his eyes.

'It's quite obvious that your appearance doesn't match your occupation Acharya,' she said politely.

'I think we are attracting undue attention standing here. Why don't we sit down and I will answer all your questions?'

Veera nodded and sat down near a pillar away from the sanctum. The scholar fixed his gaze on Veera.

'I am not a scholar by chance but by choice. I am a warrior by birth Veera. But I chose to become a scholar after I began studying the Vedas. I was quite absorbed by them.'

Veera looked at him with interest. Now that explained his toned physique.

'It's hard to take you for a scholar Acharya.'

'I know and that's why I am a misfit among scholars. No matter how vast my knowledge is, they will not accept me as one among them. I can see that you face the same crisis,' he said smiling genially. Veera was shocked at how he had read her mind. She looked at him wide eyed.

'Don't look so shocked Veera. I can know what is on your mind partly from your eyes and partly from the way people talk about you. It didn't take long for me to empathize with you.'

'But why Acharya? Why me?' she asked in a pained voice.

'Is this what you were asking Him?' asked Rudrapriya gesturing at Lord Shiva.

'I ask Him every time, but He never answers...'

Rudrapriya laughed at her quietly.

'He won't Veera. It is very unfair to question him. You never asked Him why, when you were happy. You never asked Him why he chose to give you Dhruva. Then now why are you questioning Him?'

But Veera could not accept his argument.

'Why has He cursed me like this?' she snapped.

'The Lord only blesses the life that comes into this world. A boon or a curse is what you make of your life. He never interferes with it,' said Rudrapriya with mature eyes.

'Then why do we call Him the supreme power when He does nothing?' questioned Veera still not ready to accept his words.

'He is the supreme being because He does nothing when He has the power to do everything. Only the Lord can resist the urge of using such power. He wants us to find our destiny. He will only give us hope,' said Rudrapriya patiently. Veera took a moment to analyze his words. Maybe he was right. She had found her answers. She smiled at him slowly.

'Thank you Acharya.'

'It in my duty Veera. This is what scholars are meant to do. Answer questions of people for which they can't find answers. But most of the time the answers are within us. It's just that we refuse to accept them.'

Veera now looked at the Lord's idol. He seemed to be smiling at her how. She would never question Him again. Lord Shiva would always reside in her heart as hope.

'I have to leave,' she said and stood up. Rudrapriya too stood up. Veera bent down to touch his feet. He affectionately placed a hand on her head.

'Victory will be yours,' he blessed her.

'Go Veera. There is someone out there waiting for you,' said Rudrapriya intensely.

'I know Acharya. I must hurry. Dhruva will be looking for me,' said Veera and quickly strode out of the temple. After she was out of his sight Rudrapriya let out a sigh.

'It is not Dhruva. There is someone else Veera...' whispered Rudrapriya looking at Shaurya. But he was now looking in the direction of the steps where Veera had been just a few seconds before vanishing from his sight. Shaurya quickly shot a glance at the scholar and left immediately. Rudrapriya smiled at him. He then turned to look at the Lord's idol.

'Desire always gets the better of a man,' he said slowly.

***

CHAPTER 16

Clang! The copper glass of water slipped from Dhruva's hand. He stood there, his mouth open and wide-eyed.

'What have you done to her?' he said slowly, looking at Supratika. She gave him a smug smile and looked at her muse. Veera was grinning widely clearly enjoying the expression on Dhruva's face. Supratika had completely transformed Veera's appearance. Dhruva ran his eyes from her head to toe. Her usually clumsily draped dhoti had been replaced with a correct fitting around her waist. Supratika had tightly draped her dhoti such that it accentuated her shapely hips without hindering the movement of her legs. The kurta that she now wore fit her perfectly and it had beautiful hand-embroidered designs on it. The kurta was short sleeved and embellished with beads. The red color of her kurta was a stark contrast to the flame colored silk dhoti. More than everything it was her eyes which held his attention. Supratika had applied kohl to Veera's dove eyes. Her eyes looked smoldering. Her hair was beautifully plaited.

'We are going to be eliminated from the competition accused of cheating,' said Dhruva recovering from his initial shock.

'Why?' asked a shocked Supratika.

'She is going to have her influence on them. Veera will be the biggest distraction. This is not fair!' quipped Dhruva.

'I don't care, as long as I win,' said Veera coolly. Dhruva smiled at her.

'You seemed to be in good spirits after visiting the temple,' he noted.

'We should get going,' said Veera on a serious note. Dhruva nodded his head. He took the leather armor from Supratika and strapped it on Veera. Supratika looked amused at the way Dhruva interacted with Veera. His demeanor around her reeked of love and affection. But with other woman he showed nothing more than basic courtesy. She felt a ridiculous pang of jealousy.

Dhruva stood in front of Veera and held her shoulders firmly. He closed his eyes and let out a long drawn breadth. He slowly opened his eyes and looked straight at her.

'This is a big day for us Mithra. Guruji fought this world for you. Today you fight for him. For us. We can't afford to lose after coming this far. You have to win!'

'I will, Dhruva.'

He held out his hand and she placed her hand in his. He squeezed her hand assuredly. It was a simple gesture of saying 'No matter what, I am always there for you!'

Supratika quietly watched as they both headed out. Suddenly she was overwhelmed with pain. She knew no man would ever hold her hand like that. It was not just a touch but a promise of companionship for a lifetime and beyond...

***

Veera confidently walked up to the bow in the centre of the arena. The bow was different today, it was bigger and she knew it would be heavier too. She looked up at her target placed at a distance. There were two wheels with six spokes each. The wheel at the back was fixed and had a bird carved out of metal fixed to each spoke. The front wheel was rotating with a fixed speed. The participant will be given six identical arrows. Each bird has to be shot with the given arrows. The arrow once touched cannot be used again by the participant. Six chances will be given to shoot, one each for a bird using an arrow only once. The first four contestants had finished their turns. The best performance was a score of three out of six. Veera had to shoot four birds to win. Dhruva sat on the edge of the stone bench with his hand cupping his chin. His eyes were fixed on Veera.

Breath was knocked out of Shaurya when he saw Veera walk into the arena. She looked so beautiful! Her kohl-rimmed eyes were scorching. In that tight fitting dhoti, her shapely hips swayed gracefully as she walked. Even the brown leather armour looked so attractive, matching her outfit. He closed his eyes in frustration and dropped his face into his hands.

This is so wrong! How can she do this to me?

Shaurya had still not recovered from seeing her this morning. Now, just after a few hours she was here killing him with her looks! He was completely smitten by her. After a few moments he lifted his head up. His lips curved into a quiet smile as he admired his Goddess of fire. His heart was in the throes of burning passion…

Veera looked at the bow and froze! It reminded her of her nightmare. An unknown fear gripped her heart. Nervousness engulfed her entire being. Her hand shivered and she knew she won't be able to lift that bow. Her vision seemed to blur and she saw the image of her father with a strange expression on his face. Her breathing was heavy and she immediately closed her eyes. She took in deep breaths and then opened her eyes. Veera knew how to get out of her predicament. She immediately looked at Dhruva. He understood. He blinked once and nodded his head slightly. That was all she needed. She smiled and looked at the bow with renewed vigour. Placing her hand firmly on the bow, Veera lifted it. As expected it was heavy, but she held it in position firmly. She picked up an arrow and fixed it to the bow. She pulled at the string so that the tension on it was maximum. Veera keenly observed the two wheels for a few moments. With lightning speed she released the arrow. It hit the first bird accurately. No one stirred in the audience. Similarly she shot the second bird. Most of them knew this was an impossible test and they were certain that Veera would lose. Many were of the opinion that the first two attempts were a success only by fluke.

Whoosh!

The third arrow unerringly hit its target. Dhruva's lips curved into a slow smile.

Four, five and six!

Veera had shot all the six birds. She placed the bow down. Looking at her target she was overwhelmed. Veera had won! Tears stung her eyes and she fell on her knees closing her eyes.

The crowd rose in jubilation and gave a thundering applause. Her competitors though shocked, couldn't stop themselves from appreciating her achievement.

'What a woman!' breathed Shaurya standing up.

'You did it Mithra!' screamed Dhruva. He was beyond jubilant. Veera heard him and stood up, tears streaming down her eyes. Dhruva! It was because of him she had done it. Unmindful of her surroundings, Veera ran straight into his arms like a lost child running to its mother. He held her in a tight embrace and she wrapped her arms around his neck.

'I am so proud of you, Mithra!'

After a few moments he released her. He took her face in his hands and tenderly wiped her tears.

'It is over now. You have won this competition. You did it Mithra!'

'It never would have been possible without you. Just stay with me and I can conquer his world.'

'I am not leaving you, ever,' said Dhruva emphasizing on his last word and kissed her forehead. They stood looking into each other's eyes with a smile of satisfaction. Shaurya had seen this entire exchange between the two and so had the other men in the audience. Though he couldn't hear their words, their actions spoke volumes. Everyone there was clearly shocked by the turn of events. Though they did not like it, they could not deny the fact that Veera had defeated them. A woman had proved to be better than them! Quite unacceptable until that day, but not anymore. It was not her victory that bothered Shaurya. It was the hold that Dhruva had on Veera which tortured him. With clenched fists and his lips pressed into a hard line, Shaurya stared at them, his eyes spewing fire.

***

The fire crackled gloriously with its flames mercilessly devouring the wood. Veera sat on the ground leaning against a boulder. The noise of men's laughter and loud merriment floated to her ears from a distance behind her. She knew their celebrations would continue well into the night and maybe even until dawn. Chief Shesha had awarded Veera with a special bow as a prize for her victory. He made an elaborate speech about her skills and valour. Veera accepted the bow and thanked him humbly. Then she made a short victory speech and she attributed her victory to her companion Dhruva. He stood beside her all through the proceedings with a proud smile etched on his face. Shortly after that Chief Shesha invited all of them to be a part of the celebrations of the successful commencement of the competition. Veera stayed there for a while but soon felt out of place. She whispered to Dhruva that she was leaving. He simply smiled at her nodding his head and let her go. She politely excused herself from Shesha and quietly left unnoticed. But of course, Shaurya had seen her leave. He quickly turned to leave.

'Chandra, where are you going?' questioned Commander Ashwasena aware of the men around them. Shaurya looked at him irritated but quickly regained his composure.

'Kindly excuse me Commander. I will be back in a few moments.'

'This night won't last long, Chandra. Come back soon,' he said as casually as possible. For Devajit standing right there, everything he said was obvious. Even for a few other men around them, there was nothing unusual in it. But Shaurya clearly understood what Ashwasena meant. He had made his concern quite clear in that cryptic warning. He just nodded his head at him and quickly left the place.

There were small fires lit up around the camp. Veera sat near one such fire lit up a little away from the camp. There was no one very close to that place. She liked that quiet atmosphere. She spent time there just looking at the fire without thinking about anything else. Shaurya slowly sneaked up to the place. She looked radiant in the glow of fire. He stood there spellbound! For a man who could charm any woman, from a courtesan to a princess, standing spellbound was a first. Veera suddenly felt intent gaze on her and looked in the direction of her discomfort. She was surprised to see a tall man wearing a dark blue dhoti and a cream coloured sleeveless kurta, standing a few feet away from her. His face was partially covered with a thick stubble. An angavastram had been tied on his head in a fashionable way. He had a well-toned physique and muscles rippled on his arms. Veera looked at him quizzically raising an eyebrow. His experience with women kicked in and helped him come to his senses. He gave her a charming smile.

'Would you mind, if I sit here?' he asked confidently.

'Well, for now I have no reason to be disturbed by your presence. You may sit as you please,' she replied politely. Shaurya sat down, consciously not making an eye contact with her.

'It's surprising to see you sitting here alone, Veera.'

Veera looked at him taken aback.

'Did you call me just Veera?'

'Hmmmm? Yes. Would you like to be called Chief Veera?'

'No! Not at all. I prefer Veera. Kindly do away with my title,' she said in a tired voice.

'As you wish, Veera.'

'So why is it surprising for you?'

'You are always seen with your bodyguard. He never leaves your side,' he said with dislike. Veera frowned at him.

'Dhruva is not my bodyguard. He is my companion. Who are you?' she snapped. Shaurya gave her a lopsided smile.

'I am Major Chandravarun from Indragiri.'

She looked at him suspiciously. His outfit certainly qualified to be worn by a Major. But his physique, attitude and confidence screamed of royalty. Yet she dismissed those thoughts from her mind.

I am overthinking.

'You are too audacious to be a Major.'

'Thank you. I will as well take it as a compliment.'

Veera slowly smiled at him.

This man clearly has a way with words.

She could see that he was indeed a handsome man. The stubble on his face gave him a characteristic look, though warriors were most of the time clean-shaven. It was a protocol to be followed strictly. But he seemed to defy every trait of being a Major.

'You were exceptional today Veera. You are—'

Veera raised her hand to stop him.

'If you are here to praise me, then kindly stop right now. I have already heard enough of it. There is nothing more than you can add to what has already been said. Don't waste your energy in repeating it and kindly spare me the trouble of hearing it again,' she said exasperated.

'I am impressed. Never seen anyone who dislikes appreciation. But I have a question for you.'

'Go ahead.'

'How did you accurately shoot all the six metal birds when the others couldn't even come close to your achievement?'

His voice was filled with curiosity. Veera laughed at him lightly.

'I can wager that every other man out there wants to know the answer. But their ego will never let them ask me. I appreciate your inquisitive thinking. What I did was just analyse a trick! The wheel which was rotating in the front had six spokes and at one particular angle, all the spokes will be positioned such that they don't block the birds. If you had keenly observed that wheel, it makes a characteristic noise of a squeak. I aimed my arrow accurately and released it exactly when I heard that noise. It hit the targets without getting obstructed by the spokes of the front wheel.'

Shaurya was dumbstruck. He looked at her wide-eyed. What he had just heard was unbelievable! Veera calmly continued to gaze at the fire. She knew he would need a few moments to recover from the shock.

'You are gifted, Veera,' he said at last finding his voice. She smiled dryly.

'Today must have been the happiest day ever for you, isn't it?'

'I don't know...' she said in a voice heavy with pain. She looked at him. Her scorching, enigmatic, kohl-rimmed eyes stared at him. His eyes bore into hers with untold longing. Shaurya was lost in the depth of her eyes. After a moment, Veera averted her eyes feeling awkward. She stood up.

'I should go now.'

'No! Please stay,' blurted out Shaurya. She shot him an authoritative look.

'I better leave before Dhruva comes here. He may not be so cordial with an audacious Major.'

'Dhruva is always on your mind,' he said, his voice laced with bitterness.

'Yes indeed! I don't see any reason why it should bother you. Dhruva means the world to me.'

'I won't stop you. You may go as you please. It was nice meeting you Chief Veera.'

His formal tone was more than necessary.

'Thank you for your time, Major Chandravarun.'

'The pleasure is all mine. Anything for you...' said Shaurya in a gravelly voice. Veera glanced at him and walked away. He stood there watching her disappear into the darkness. He used every ounce of his self-control to resist the urge of holding her hand to stop her. To not let her go! This could be the last time that he ever spoke to her. The last time that he ever saw her! He closed his eyes as his entire being was being engulfed in excruciating pain. It was no longer the wood, but his own heart burning in that fire of separation. He fell on his knees and opened his eyes. A tear slid down his cheek. She was gone but the fire continued to burn.

***

CHAPTER 17

'We are doomed,' rued Ashwasena.

'How will I face his Highness? I have lost the competition and that too against a woman!'

'You should be honoured to have competed against Veera.'

'My lord, you should stop obsessing about her. I don't think his Highness will like it.'

'Stop it Ashwa! I know what I am doing.'

Devajit, Ashwasena and Prince Shaurya were walking towards the royal chambers of King Kritiverman. They were escorted to the palace the moment the three entered the border of Indragiri. The King had ordered that they be brought before him at once.

'I think we should first concentrate on other problems at hand,' reasoned a worried Ashwasena.

'I will handle it. You both will just have to keep your mouth shut!' snapped the Prince. Shaurya was still dressed in Devajit's clothes. His hair was dishevelled and shabby. His beard was unkempt, partly to help in disguise. The guards in the corridor saluted Shaurya as he passed them. He acknowledged them with only a nod. They entered the royal chamber. Devajit and Ashwasena bowed to the King.

King Kritiverman was seated on a beautifully carved chair. Prime Minister Agniverma was standing next to him. Shaurya glanced at him and smiled lightly. Agniverma returned the gesture. Kritiverman's wrath doubled when he took in his son's appearance. But he reigned in his temper, aware of the audience present in the room. He looked straight at Devajit.

'Major Devajit, you have disappointed me. You lost the competition and that too against a woman. I think you could have done better than that!'

Devajit lowered his head in shame.

'Kindly forgive me, your Highness.'

'Forgiveness will not change the fact that you have had an embarrassing defeat. And you Commander Ashwasena, I didn't expect you to be such an imbecile! How can you take a Prince unprotected to a foreign land?' he thundered.

'I take full responsibility for my action, your Highness. I am obliged to serve my punishment,' said Ashwasena sincerely.

'Of course you will be punished. You both will be stripped off your ranks.'

Shaurya could no longer take it.

'I object, your Highness. Deva and Ashwa did everything because I told them to do so. They take direct orders from me and all they did was obey my orders. I don't think they committed any crime by doing so.'

'Prince Shaurya, do you even understand the grave risks involved in having you unprotected? Their recklessness certainly necessitates punishment.'

'Your Highness, they are my bodyguards and their prime duty is to obey me. They both have been very sincere and dedicated in their service. The very fact that I have returned unharmed is a proof of it. I would really appreciate it, if your Highness does not interfere with my decisions,' said Shaurya with finality in his words. King Kritiverman clenched his teeth in anger. It was becoming a nightmare for him to tame the Prince.

'You both may leave,' hissed the King. Devajit and Ashwasena bowed to him. Before going Ashwasena glanced at Shaurya who nodded his head discreetly. They both then left the place.

'Have you lost your mind Shaurya? Look at yourself! Is this the way a prince behaves?' roared the King.

'I was well aware of what I was doing.'

'You are being very reckless, Shaurya! Don't forget that you do have responsibilities. Its time you stand up to them.'

'You have already reminded me about them on many occasions your Highness. May I leave now?'

'You may. But before that I have one more important thing to say. I have decided that you will command our troops from tomorrow. The army of Indragiri is in your hands. It is time you be given some real responsibilities,' said Kritiverman authoritatively. Though Shaurya was surprised, he did not show it.

'I accept it with pleasure, your Highness,' said Shaurya with a slight smile. Just then Arunadevi stormed into the royal chamber. Shaurya grinned at her widely. He quickly strode across to her and embraced her.

'You look so dirty! I was very worried about you. Why didn't you tell me before leaving?' she scolded him affectionately.

'Would you have let me go, if I had told you?'

'Certainly not!'

'That's why I didn't tell you, Mother. But don't worry I am back, safe and sound. Your son is brave enough to protect himself.'

Arunadevi smiled at him and kissed his forehead.

'Quickly have a bath. You should be hungry.'

Shaurya nodded his head and left. She glanced once at her husband and followed her son. She knew, she would have a tough time dealing with him later. But for now, her heart was over brimming with joy on seeing her son after a long time.

'Do you think he can handle it?'

'Prince Shaurya is very efficient, your Highness. He will perform his duties well,' assured Agniverma.

'He has let me down on many occasions in the past. This time if he does it again it is not just me but the whole kingdom which will be affected. I want him to understand that it is not easy to rule a kingdom.'

'He will surely make you proud your Highness.'

'He should, for I have no choice Agni. I have already lost a son. I cannot lose Shaurya,' said Kritiverman closing his eyes. Agniverma's heart also weighed heavy with grief.

***

'Steady! Don't hold back. No mercy!' said Dhruva holding his sword in position.

'No mercy!' repeated Veera coldly, tightening her grip on the sword. They both eyed each other intently. They slowly moved in a circle holding forth their swords. Dhruva had insisted on not using shields. Though Vidyut was against it, Dhruva was stubborn. Both Dhruva and Veera had tied their angavastram to their head, to keep their hair from falling on their eyes. The soldiers, both men and women had gathered to form a circle around the sword fighting arena. They both were going to demonstrate a duel. Vidyut stood there tense. Dhruva wielded his sword first. But Veera quickly matched his moves. For a few moments their swords clanged against each other. After sometime they were no longer defensive. Their fight shifted to offense and became more intense. Vidyut watched them amazed. They were no longer companions, they fought like cold-blooded enemies! They swayed their swords at each other and momentarily pulling back only when they were about to land a lethal blow on their opponent. Achuta watched them with bated breath. She couldn't take her eyes off Dhruva. Everyone in the audience watched them keenly. Initially they expected the fight to be only a demonstration. But this was lethal! They both were literally going for the kill.

At one instance Veera's sword cut into Dhruva's skin on his left arm where he had raised it to avoid a strike from her sword. Veera suddenly stopped wielding her sword. But he shook his head at her and moved his sword forward. She was forced to continue the duel. Achuta held her breath as she saw Dhruva's arm bleed. She intertwined her fingers in tension.

Why doesn't she stop? Can't she see that he is hurt?

Suddenly Veera made a mistake of loosening her grip on the sword. That was the opening he was looking for. Dhruva hit her sword and the impact made her drop it to the ground. Her hand recoiled in pain and he quickly pointed his sword at her neck. The duel was over. Veera was panting for breath and sweat beaded on her forehead. His breathing was heavy and his bare torso was sweaty. He lowered his sword with grin.

'You win!' declared Veera grudgingly.

'Not surprising, isn't it?'

He winked at her. She nodded her head in disapproval and removed the angavastram from her head. She picked up her sword and handed it to a woman soldier.

'Get water and herbs!' she called out. Dhruva handed his sword to Vidyut. Veera quickly strode to Dhruva and held his injured hand. Though the wound was nothing serious, the cut was deep. She quickly tied her angavastram to stop the blood loss. Veera and Dhruva went to sit on a stone bench nearby. Vidyut gave orders for the soldiers to disperse and resume their training. Achuta brought a bowl of clean water, cloth bandage and some dry herbs ground into a paste with water. She stood a little away watching Veera tending to Dhruva's wound. Vidyut glanced at her and then went to stand beside Dhruva.

'Aahh!'

Dhruva let out a soft cry as Veera began cleaning his wound.

'I am so sorry Dhruva! I should have been more careful.'

'Mithra, don't ever make the mistake of feeling sorry for your opponent. The moment you empathize with your enemy, you lose the fight! Be alert and go for the kill!'

Veera applied the herbs paste and tied the cloth bandage.

'Your words hold well in a real fight. Seeing you in pain hurts me,' said Veera softly. Dhruva squeezed her hand lightly.

'It's just a small cut. It really doesn't hurt much dear.'

Achuta flinched at the term of endearment he had used for Veera.

'Chief Veera, you really amaze me. I am well aware of Dhruva's sword fighting skills. But you are equally dangerous! You both care so much for each other. How can you fight so lethally?' asked a curious Vidyut.

'We both fought so intently only because we trust each other moves. There is no way we will harm each other. Of course, had it been someone else duelling with Mithra like that, I wouldn't have endured watching it. I duel with her so spontaneously only because I know I won't hurt her,' said Dhruva calmly. Vidyut looked at Veera who smiled at him.

'And I trust his instincts.'

'By the way Vidyut, any news from the border?'

Dhruva wanted to get down to business.

'Nothing to worry about. Only trade and exchange along the border. No immediate threats.'

'Yet we should be alert and prepared. We may not be invaded, but I doubt the King will be satisfied with this calm environment. We cannot predict, when he will want to conquer a new land for loving his son,' said Dhruva with distaste. Veera frowned at him.

'What is it with you and the King? Why do you always antagonize him?'

'Simple. I don't like him,' he said shrugging his shoulders.

'It doesn't matter, if you like or dislike him. But be smart enough to not be blatantly honest about it. The consequences may not be very amiable,' warned Vidyut.

'I don't give a damn about it! Let's go.'

Dhruva stood up to leave. Vidyut looked at Veera with exasperation. She smiled at him shrugging her shoulders. Before going he once again glanced Achuta. She was standing at a distance staring at Dhruva. Vidyut looked at Veera and gestured her to go to Achuta and left. Veera looked at Achuta and noticed the longing in her eyes. She went to her. Achuta was startled to have Veera so close. She lowered her head. Veera placed a hand on her shoulder.

'He is a strong willed man. For me, he is way too precious. If you persist, it is a long journey of pain. I really hope you have the strength to not give up. I know I am being selfish. I am sorry,' she said in a voice thick with emotion. Achuta looked at her baffled. Veera shot her a pained look and left the place to join Dhruva. Achuta stood there still looking at Chief. She couldn't really comprehend her words.

***

Madhumathi lovingly caressed her abdomen, the bump on her stomach was quite pronounced now. She smiled in quiet satisfaction. Ever since the day, she was aware of her pregnancy her life centred around her child. Her smile broadened as she thought about Prince Vijayendra. His joy was boundless. Both eagerly awaited the birth of their first child. The heir to the throne of Virpur!

Vijayendra slowly walked up to her from behind and tenderly wrapped his arms around her. She closed her eyes feeling his warmth.

'So what is my son telling you?' he asked nuzzling her hair.

'Well, he is angry that you made his mother wait.'

He laughed lightly. He turned her to face him.

'I am sorry Madhu. I had some unfinished work at the royal court. It needed my attention and I was delayed.'

She simply smiled at him in return.

'Come.'

She held his hand. They both went and sat on a couch.

'Can I ask you something?'

'Anything darling!' he said and stroked her cheek lovingly.

'What if it is a daughter and not a son?' asked Madhumathi hesitantly.

'Is this what is bothering you?'

She looked at him with a timid expression.

'Madhu, I prefer a son so that he can succeed me. But I think even a daughter is no less. The only reason I dare say this is Veera. She is exceptional! Should I have a daughter, I want her to grow up to be like Veera,' said Vijayendra honestly. Madhumathi was surprised by his answer. Though his answer was unexpected, it had not put her at ease. But she managed to bring a smile on her face.

'Don't worry dear! Be it a son or a daughter I will be happy to be a father. I promise to love our child unconditionally.'

'I love you,' she said looking straight into his eyes.

'I love you too. I really need a bath now. I will be back in a few minutes,' he said and kissed her. Then he stood up and went to the bathing chamber. Madhumathi let out a long drawn breath.

'I am fortunate to have you as my husband. But I will never want a life like Veera's for my daughter. The sacrifice she has made for it is unimaginable,' whispered Madhumathi. She placed her hand protectively again on her abdomen with a heavy heart.

***

'We have to expand the infantry and cavalry.'

'But it is not easy, my lord. Training animals involves more resources and it is time consuming.'

Commander Vikraman looked up at Ashwasena a little taken aback at his words. Vikraman knew that it was Ashwasena's friendship with the Prince which allowed him to boldly interact with him.

'I know Ashwa, but it surely can save a lot of men in the battle for us. Don't worry about the resources. We can manage it. Start implementing my orders.'

'As you say, my lord,' replied Ashwasena and Vikraman.

'My lord, shall we proceed to the artillery?'

Shaurya rolled his eyes at Vikraman.

'I am done with today's work. We really should call it a day. Tomorrow morning I will meet you at the artillery. You may leave now.'

Vikraman saluted Shaurya and left. Ashwasena looked at him hesitantly.

'My lord, are we going to the palace now?'

Shaurya eyed him suspiciously.

'Do you have other plans for the evening Ashwa?'

'Well... er...yes. I have to meet Nahusha...' said he, unsure about Shaurya's response. He gave him a crooked smile.

'I see! That's the reason why you are so eager to send me home. I relieve you of your duties for the day. Stop blushing and get out of here!'

'My lord, I cannot leave before making certain that you have safely reached the palace. Your safety is my priority.'

Shaurya was about to admonish him, when his eyes fell on Devajit. He was quickly walking towards them. Ashwasena's lips curved into a smile.

'Well, I see that you have already found your substitute!'

Devajit came and bowed to Shaurya.

'Deva, don't take any chances. All of you should be alert. Do not leave the Prince alone,' he said stressing on his last words.

'Don't worry Commander. I will carry out your orders with utmost care.'

'If you are finished with this ridiculous dialogue on my safety, kindly leave,' said Shaurya, his tone clearly betraying the warmth in his words. Ashwasena bowed to him with a smile and walked away.

'He always thinks about me before everything else,' said Shaurya fondly. Devajit nodded his head in agreement. Both began walking towards the stables to take their horses. Shaurya turned to look at Devajit. He was a man of medium built and a very warm personality. He was a few years older than Shaurya.

'Deva shall I ask you something?'

'With pleasure, my lord.'

'Since how long have you been married?'

Devajit smiled at him.

'A little over five years.'

'Don't you think it's a little too long to stay with a woman?' he asked with a lopsided smile. Devajit laughed slowly.

'Maybe. But I have seen men who have lived with a woman for an even longer time.'

'Yeah… I wonder how a man can spend his entire life with only one woman! It must be really boring!'

'No my lord…'

Shaurya stopped in his way. Devajit too stopped and turned to face him.

'Come on Deva! Don't tell me that you don't miss all the fun and excitement you had before marriage,' he challenged raising an eyebrow.

'Before marriage, I have flirted with women and also courted a few. I don't deny that I do miss it.'

Shaurya smiled superiorly at him. But then he noticed the change of expression on Devajit's face. It was intense now.

'But now, I have a woman who is mine. I know that when I get back home, my wife will be there waiting for me. She understands my pain even without me telling it out. The happiness she gives me is worth much more than all that excitement. It is a lovely feeling to belong to someone you can call yours.'

Devajit's eyes were burning with intensity as he said those words. Shaurya stood there with his heart squeezing in pain. Suddenly he felt a weird loneliness in his life. Shaurya averted his eyes and turned to look ahead. He didn't want Devajit to see the effect his words had on him.

'Get the others to assemble near the entrance, Deva. I will join you in a few moments.'

Devajit bowed to him and left. Shaurya slowly looked around him. He was standing there. Alone. He closed his eyes and Veera's image filled his mind. That night when Veera walked away from him, he didn't understand why it had caused him so much pain. But today he realised what he had let go! When he was with her, he had felt a unique sense of companionship. His heart longed to see her again. Certainly this was not lust! Though he had tried to convince himself to believe it to be so. For Shaurya, lust was an easy emotion to deal with. Lust was something he could control. But the feelings he had for Veera were unfathomable and stronger than lust. Shaurya had never felt so desperate in his life and that too for a woman! Until now he had only wanted women but never longed for one. Initially he thought, her influence on him would subside with passing days. But the more he tried to ignore her, the more she occupied his mind. His own feelings were tearing him apart from inside. He knew there was nothing he could do to get her. Having her in his life was next to impossible.

Why are you doing this to me Veera?

Shaurya clenched his fist and let out a long drawn breath. The evening breeze caressed his hair. When he opened his eyes he was still standing alone with the evening sun going down in the horizon.

***

CHAPTER 18

Ashwasena cracked his knuckles sitting on the broken wall. The evening was still bright. The sun would set in a few minutes. He was fervently hoping that she would make it there before dusk. Ashwasena was waiting for Nahusha in the old ruins of a stable. This stable was meant for tethering of horses, but now it lay in ruins and made a good rendezvous place for these lovers. Usually no one wandered around that place as it was isolated from the bustling centre of Indragiri. Normally Nahusha used to be waiting for him but today she had not yet come. Ashwasena was impatient to see her as it had been a really long time since they had last met. He had last seen her three days before he left for Charanvasi. Suddenly he straightened his ears. He could hear soft footsteps. His heart leapt with joy! He stood up when he saw Nahusha hurriedly walking to him. She had wrapped a shawl around her and also over her head, partially covering her face. On seeing him, she let the shawl fall back from her face. She smiled at him and threw her arms around his neck. He embraced her warmly.

'I missed you so much!'

'I missed you too,' said Nahusha in a muffled voice. Ashwasena released her and held her shoulders.

'How are you Nahu? I am so sorry that I didn't come to see you.'

Seeing her was such a comfort to him.

'I am fine. I am glad that you could make it today. But Ashwa I should leave,' she said urgently.

'What!? So soon? You only came now!' he complained.

'Father came home early today. I made an excuse saying that I had to go to the temple. I have to go back before he decides to look for me at the temple.'

Ashwasena's face fell in disappointment. He didn't want her to go. At least not so soon! He held her face and bent forward, their foreheads touching. He closed his eyes and breathed in her fragrance.

'Let's meet again soon. I love you.'

He kissed her on her cheek.

'I love you too. Take care Ashwa,' she said softly. With a heavy heart he let her go the next moment. Nahusha once again wrapped the shawl securely around her head and left glancing at him once more. It was these small moments of bliss, that both of them patiently waited for days together. This satisfaction of seeing each other gave them strength to spend the coming days in separation. Ashwasena would readily wait a lifetime just to have Nahusha with him for a few moments. He slowly breathed in the cool air. He could still smell the fragrance of jasmine that adorned her hair, though she was long gone.

***

Veera dismounted from her horse and handed the reins to one of the guards at the entrance. She told him to tether it at the stable. Dhruva's horse was already tethered there. She untied the cloth bundle that slung across her torso. She was beautifully dressed in a blue silk dhoti and a contrasting orange kurta. Her forehead still bore the mark of vermillion. It was the night of Shivarathri festival. The whole kingdom of Virpur was revelling in the joy of festivities. There was a special puja organized at the Shiva temple late in the night. Though Veera tried hard to convince Dhruva to come along with her, he didn't oblige. She went to the temple alone, but was later joined by Vidyut and his wife Sinhika there. Though the rituals were still underway, Veera didn't stay for long. She collected the prasad of the Lord which contained vermillion, pieces of coconut, little flowers and bananas. The priest tied them in a cloth bundle and handed it to Veera, as she had requested. She bid farewell to Vidyut and his wife and made her way through the crowd.

There was an eerie silence at Dhruva's home. She knew there would only be a few essential guards. All the attendants and servants would have left early to take part in the festivities. It was almost past midnight, but Dhruva wouldn't have slept. She had already informed him that she would be coming to see him straight from the temple. On not finding him in the portico, she walked to his room noiselessly, half-suspecting that he must have fallen asleep. When she entered his room, she found him sitting on his bed gazing outside the window. He didn't notice her.

'You should have come to the temple Dhruva. It was so good to enjoy the festival with so many people. I also met Vidyut and Sinhika. I left the temple, though there were still more rituals to be performed. Had you been with me, I would have stayed until everything was completed. But you hardly step inside that temple,' she complained. Then she untied the cloth bundle and took a pinch of vermillion. Walking up to him she applied it on his forehead. Dhruva didn't speak a word. He closed his eyes on her touch and then slowly opened them. She handed him the banana. But he refused shaking his head. Veera frowned at him.

'Why are you refusing it? It's the Lord's blessing, you shouldn't refuse it.'

Dhruva closed his eyes.

'Please Mithra, leave me alone today,' he said clenching his teeth. Veera was startled. She sat down beside him and placed her hand on his shoulder. She knew something must terribly wrong.

'Dhruva, what happened?' she asked softly. He let out a tired breath and looked at her. His eyes were moist clearly reflecting his pain.

'What is hurting you so much?' Her voice was a hushed whisper now.

'I was born on Shivarathri.'

'Really? It is a special day. But why do you look so pained about it? Are you sad because your parents are not here with you today?'

He looked away from her and swallowed hard.

'I am not their son…' he said at last.

'What!?'

'They were my foster parents. My father found me in that very Shiva temple where you had been today.'

Veera stared at him astounded! Now she understood why he had never stepped into that temple. There was silence. Both of them didn't want to break that silence. After a few moments she spoke.

'Do you know who your birth parents are?'

'Yes.'

'Who?'

Dhruva clenched his fists. He didn't want to say it. But he knew he couldn't hide it from Veera. He didn't want to lie to her. She was the only one with whom he could share this truth.

'The woman who gave birth to me was a dancer in the royal court. The man responsible for my birth is King Devarata,' he said in a detached lifeless tone. Veera turned as still as a stone hearing his words.

Dhruva is the King's son!

She couldn't wrap her head around that truth. She gaped at him without even batting her eyelids.

'She had once come to the royal court from another kingdom. She was a famed dancer. The King fancied her. They had an affair and she gave birth to me as a result of their desire. But she didn't want me, I was a burden to her. She abandoned me at the rear corner of the temple, where usually unwanted babies are left. These children will then belong to the kingdom. They will be raised at the gurukul and later trained in the field which suits their abilities.'

Dhruva was still gazing into the darkness outside. Veera looked at him with a tortured look.

'How did your…?'

'Sankhaji nursed her during childbirth. She had disclosed to him the decision to abandon me. For him, that was not shocking. He had seen many mothers do that before. But he was very close to my foster father who was childless even after many years of being married. So Sankhaji told him about me and my father then found me at the temple before anybody else could. He brought me home and then I came to be known as their son to the world outside.'

'What about the King? Does he know about you?'

Dhruva smiled wryly.

'He doesn't even know that she bore his child. He was out on a war during the time of my birth. He had left the kingdom well before anyone knew that she was pregnant and came back many months after she had disappeared from Virpur. By then he must have long forgotten her.'

'How did you know all this?' she asked slowly.

'My father died when he was out on a battle. My mother didn't live long after his death. I was so unfortunate that I was orphaned a second time at a very young age. I didn't know anything about my birth until one day Sankhaji visited me at the gurukul. He disclosed to me everything about my birth. He said it weighed heavy on his heart and he could no longer carry that burden. That day the burden of this truth fell on my shoulders.'

He let out a long drawn breath. But he was still far from being at ease.

'Who else knows this?'

'No one except Sankhaji and myself. Not even Guruji. Now you know it. I made Sankhaji promise me that he would never tell it to anyone.'

'Why me?'

Dhruva slowly turned to look at her. His eyes filled with dark misery.

'I didn't want to hide it from you. Not anymore! This is who I am. I am an unwanted child born out of an illegitimate relationship. I was living aimlessly when Guruji came into my life and he gave it a direction. My life found a new meaning when he handed your responsibility to me. Every night I wondered if my life was worth living, for I had none to claim to be mine. That was when you came into my life...'

He took her hand in both his hands and held it close to him.

'You gave me the warmth of the felling that I have someone to live for and I actually belonged to that person. When I was drowning in this ocean of loneliness, it was your hand that pulled me out onto the shore of life. The two people responsible for my birth never cared for me. Mine was a shameful birth, a mere consequence of an illicit relationship! I never mattered to this world, but you made me a part of your life. You gave an anchor to hold onto.'

Dhruva was overwhelmed with emotions. A tear slid down his cheek. Veera could no longer bear to see him being so distraught. Her eyes welled up.

'Dhruva you mean everything to me. We are two halves of a whole. One is meaningless without the other. Nothing else matters so long as we are together,' she said wiping his tear. She gave him a warm hug.

'Who you were born as, will change nothing between us. You will always be precious to me. Don't ever be ashamed of your birth! For me, no man can ever reach the greatness that you have achieved. It is the actions of a man that will always be remembered, not his birth.'

'My heart always knew that even after knowing this truth, you would still be the same...'

Veera smiled at him affectionately. It was well past midnight but she knew, she could not leave him alone and go back home. A man always hid a lot more in his heart than a woman. He is in the most vulnerable state the moment he bears his soul. That was exactly what Dhruva had done. Though he feared that her attitude towards him might change after he revealed the truth, somewhere deep down he was assured that she would understand him. It was this assurance which gave him the courage to tell her everything. It was a secret which had been locked in his heart for many years and festered in his mind. But today Veera had set him free. She caressed his head.

'I think you should sleep now. You need rest. You have spent many sleepless nights over this, Dhruva. But today you can sleep peacefully. You are not alone, I am with you. I won't leave you, ever,' she said, the last words echoing in his ears. He nodded his head slightly. He lied on the bed, his head resting on her lap. Dhruva was tired but he liked this exhaustion as his whole being was soaked in a quiet satisfaction. Veera slowly caressed his head with her hand. She was all that he had in this world. For her, he meant life. Sleep willingly entered his tired eyes in the warmth of her lap. The soft touch of her hand wrapped him securely in a safe cocoon. That was all he had ever yearned for, a caring hand to hold and a loving heart to live in.

***

'What is war?' asked the four years old Kritinandan innocently. Shaurya stiffened a little and stopped pushing the swing on which the little boy was seated.

'Uncle, what is war?' asked Kritinandan for the second time impatiently. Shaurya stopped the wooden swing steadily. He walked around it and stood in front of the boy. Shaurya carried him and sat on the swing resting him on his lap. He was mulling over answering the question. He knew he couldn't avoid it.

'Nanda... a war is a fight between two kingdoms.'

Kritinandan was quiet for a moment trying to understand. Shaurya lightly swung by applying the force with his feet on the ground. Kritinandan again turned to look up at Shaurya.

'Who fights in a war?'

Shaurya smiled at him with paternal affection.

'Soldiers and sometimes even the princes fight in a war.'

'Did you fight in war?' he asked wide-eyed. The Prince simply nodded his head in agreement.

'Did father also fight?'

Shaurya once again nodded his head in assent. Kritinandan's questions were making him uncomfortable.

'You fought in the war and came back. Then why did he die in the war?'

Shaurya froze. This was the question he didn't want to answer.

Your father died because my father was selfish!

But he couldn't tell it to the little boy. He felt a lump in his throat.

'Your father was a brave man Nanda. You should be proud of him. When you grow up, you will know why he didn't come back.'

'Why do they fight wars?'

Shaurya looked at the boy amused. His questions defied his age. He was a clear resemblance of his father, Prince Shruthamanyu, Shaurya's elder brother.

'I don't know,' he said in defeat. Kritinandan looked at him with pity.

'When I grow up, will I have to fight in a war like you?'

Shaurya smiled at him.

'Let us hope that there will be no more wars when you grow up, Nanda,' he said embracing him. Kritinandan smiled as he rested his head on Shaurya's chest. Prince Shruthamanyu was the eldest son of King Kritiverman. He was five years elder to Shaurya and crowned a prince at a very young age. The King loved Shruthamanyu more than Shaurya. He was very responsible and an obedient son unlike his younger brother. Yet the two brothers were really close. Both were exceptional in warfare. Shruthamanyu always defended Shaurya before the King. Though Shaurya defied his father, he never disobeyed his brother, for he understood Shaurya. Though Shaurya was irresponsible, he was morally right. If only the King had listened to him that once…

Shaurya's heart grieved in pain and anger. He closed his eyes to check his temper. He patted Kritinandan's back lovingly.

'Is my tiger hungry?' he asked playfully.

'No… I want to play!' said Kritinandan with a glee. Shaurya lifted him and made him stand on the swing.

'Of course we can play. But before that you should eat. Or else my tiger will start squeaking like a rat!' he said mockingly. Kritinandan gave out a carefree laugh. Shaurya grinned at him. He turned and helped the boy climb onto his back and he carried him in a piggyback.

'Let us go find mother and get you your favourite sweets.'

'Yay!' cried Kritinandan in joy. Shaurya began walking towards the Queen's quarters from the garden. He knew Kritinandan wouldn't question him anymore for the day. But he knew he could never escape from those questions which always haunted his mind. Shruthamanyu named his son Kritinandan after his father Kritiverman. But Shaurya always called him Nanda as a term of endearment. After Shruthamanyu's death, Shaurya took it on himself to give Kritinandan the paternal love and care. He adored the boy as much as he was his own son or perhaps even more. Though Kritinandan still remembered his father, Shaurya was soon taking his father's place. Shaurya never wanted to be the crown Prince but he had no choice other than stepping into his brother's shoes. Yet taking care of Kritinandan was something he did wholeheartedly. Shaurya will never forgive the King for what he did. But he would never let Kritinandan miss his father. That was the least he could do for his brother. Shaurya knew they both still had a long way to go. He let out a long drawn breath and continued walking. He could feel the soft weight of the blissful boy on his strong back.

***

CHAPTER 19

It was raining moderately. The rain drops were not very painful but also not very light to ignore. Veera sat on the hillock soaking wet in the rain. There were constant streams of tears from her eyes but they were hidden cleverly under the pattering raindrops on her face. She had been sitting like that for a long time. Straight from the palace she had come there in the afternoon. That day was the naming ceremony of Prince Vijayendra's son. The baby was named after Arjuna's mighty bow, Gandiva. Veera attended the ceremony at the royal court. Dhruva as expected, didn't accompany her there. Later she had visited Princess Madhumathi privately to wish her and her baby good health. It was there, when Veera held the little baby in her arms, that her heart was overwhelmed with emotions. Suddenly she realised the vacuum in her life. That was the moment when the real sense of loss crept into her mind. She made an excuse and quickly left the palace. She could no longer stay there. She rode aimlessly and stopped near the hillock. Tethering her horse to a tree she climbed atop the hillock. The rain didn't seem to cease. The evening was darker than usual, but Veera didn't move.

'You may leave. Inform others also to get back,' ordered Dhruva. The soldier who had accompanied him, nodded and rode away. Dhruva dismounted his horse and tethered it to a tree near Veera's horse. He had gone to her home, straight from the army camp in the evening. On not finding her there, he went to the palace. But the guards there informed him that she had left in the afternoon, alone. His mind immediately sensed that something was wrong. He gathered a group of soldiers who set out in all directions to search for her. One of the guards had found Veera and he quickly went back to bring Dhruva to the place.

Dhruva climbed the hillock drenching in the rain. He wondered what Veera was doing there.

'Mithra, why are you sitting in the rain? I don't like you getting wet like this. Come on, let's go,' he said loudly over the rain. But she didn't move. He sat down beside her and looked at her.

'Mithra…'

Veera slowly turned to look at him. He let out an involuntary gasp.

'You are crying!'

The rain could hide her tears from others, but not from Dhruva.

'You had gone to the palace right? Did something go wrong there? What happened?'

He was impatient. Veera closed her eyes.

'I will never be complete…' she whispered. Dhruva frowned at her. He didn't understand what she meant.

'I will never become a mother. I will never be able to carry my child in these arms!'

She looked down at her hands and then clenched her fists. Pain struck his heart like a bolt of lightning. Her sense of loss tore him apart. There was silence except for the pattering raindrops.

'We can leave,' he said after a few prolonged moments. Veera looked at him baffled.

'Just say yes and I will take you away from this. Away from all this madness. You can have a chance at a life you choose. You won't have to make any sacrifices. I will protect you in every way possible. We can go far away from here, so far that none of these rogues can find us again,' he said intensely. Veera looked at him incredulously. She couldn't believe that he had just said those words.

'And go where?'

'Anywhere! But let's not stay here. I cannot see you make sacrifices every day for those people who care only about their greed. They don't deserve it, Mithra!'

'You will leave all this behind just for me?'

'What am I leaving behind, Mithra? Virpur has no hold on me except you. I lose nothing as long as you are with me,' he said holding her hand.

'Dhruva… we can run away from this world. But we cannot run away from ourselves. If we make this decision we will certainly regret it for our entire lifetime. You know why? Because we are warriors and warriors don't run away from challenges. Every challenge demands its own share of sacrifice and we have to accept it. I will learn to live with this pain….'

She squeezed his hand gently. He let out a long drawn breath in defeat.

'Why don't you simply listen to me? You are so adamant! Fine! I will stand by your choice but only on one condition. You will not shed one more tear over this. I can bear a thousand arrows piercing my chest but not a single tear from your eyes. It kills me!'

Dhruva's voice broke down on the last words. Veera complied with him by wiping her face. The rain had now reduced to a drizzle. Nevertheless both were completely wet and water was dripping from their clothes.

'Today you refused to leave Mithra... but remember one thing, if ever you feel this is not how you want to lead your life, you can always count on me. Anytime you decide, we can leave,' he said looking straight into her eyes. Veera smiled at him wryly.

'I don't think, that is ever going to happen.'

'Life is an expert in throwing surprises! For now, let's go home.'

Dhruva stood up to leave and he held out his hand to her. Without second thoughts Veera placed her hand in his and stood up. Both of them climbed down and mounted their horses. The two riders sped into the darkness towards home.

***

Shaurya outstretched his legs and relaxed on the terrace of the palace. He sipped his wine and looked at the view before him. From this end of one of the many terraces of the palace, he could see a magnificent view of Indragiri. Though darkness had enveloped the sky, central Indragiri was alive with activity. There were lamps lighted in all homes. Men wandered about in the streets, gathering at a few places to engage in discussion with their friends. Women rarely ventured outside in the dark except when it was necessary. The music of various musical instruments from the Central Hall floated to his ears. There was a hint of smile at the corner of his lips. He hurled his angavastram aside and ran is hand through his messy hair. He took one more sip of the wine. Devajit walked onto the terrace and executed a royal salute.

'I think I gave the guards clear orders to not let anyone disturb me. I wonder what you threatened them with to let you come here.'

'Pardon me, my lord. But I carry the King's message. His Highness sends the message that your esteemed presence is expected at the Central Hall for the evening.'

'I am not coming there today. Go tell your Highness that I am not interested,' snapped Shaurya

'My lord, the—'

'That was an order Major Devajit. You may leave!'

Devajit bowed to him and left without making noise. Shaurya turned his irritated gaze towards the view of the kingdom before him. Lost in his thoughts he finished his drink.

Today the King had hosted an evening of entertainment at the Central Hall in the palace. Famed dancers and musicians had been invited from the length and breadth of Indragiri. Shaurya always had a penchant for art and music. He had never missed an opportunity to enjoy performances by the artistes. But today he never went to the Central Hall. Though he dutifully supervised the arrangements for the evening, he didn't wish to be a part of it. When he said Devajit that he was not interested, he had actually meant it. These days loneliness was his most preferred company. He didn't want to go into the crowd and put up an act of being excited. Most of the time his mind was filled with Veera. Every time he saw someone shoot an arrow accurately on the target in the shooting arena, all he could think of was Veera gracefully poised with the bow in her hand. Shaurya knew he was being foolish! He was doing everything he could to stop being distracted by her. But deep down in his heart he was always hoping to see her again. He kept searching for her dusky face in the crowds. What if Veera suddenly came before him out of nowhere! It would be nothing short of a miracle. The problem is, miracles don't happen every day. Yet Shaurya didn't stop wishing for a miracle.

'Don't you think you are missing out all the fun?' asked Ashwasena sitting beside the Prince.

'I know I am. But this is bearable…' he said softly.

'You look so disturbed. Why have you become such a recluse these days?'

Shaurya's jaws stiffened. He didn't want to talk about Veera with anyone. Not even Ashwasena. At least not now! He was not sure about his feelings for Veera. He was still counting on the hope that her influence on him would eventually subside.

'It's none of your business!'

'Yeah. It is none of my business until you come running to me to bail you out of your misery. I am sure that will not take very long.'

Shaurya gave him a lopsided smile shaking his head. Then he called out for an attendant and asked her to get another glass. She coyly brought it and poured the wine from the case. Before leaving she gave him a lovely smile. But Shaurya didn't pay attention to her. Ashwasena raised an eyebrow at his indifference.

'It's amusing to see you so disinterested!'

'I think I gave very strict orders to the guard to not let anyone disturb me,' said Shaurya in a drawling voice. Ashwasena laughed in reply.

'Don't be mad at him. He was very prompt in his duty. I had to literally threaten him to let me come in!'

Ashwasena sipped his wine.

'Hmmmm! This is good.'

Shaurya smiled at him dryly and refilled his glass with wine.

'Any new announcements today?'

'Nothing declared formally.'

'Formally? Why? Were there any significant informal discussions?'

'Just one,' said Ashwasena finishing his drink. Shaurya arched up an eyebrow in surprise.

'Do I know about it?'

'I don't think so... I got to know about it only today. You will be really interested in it.'

'Come on Ashwa. Spit it out! I hate suspense.'

Ashwasena smiled crookedly.

'His Highness is planning on an invasion.'

'What's interesting about it? He always does that,' sneered Shaurya.

'Planning an invasion may not be new. But it is the kingdom which will be invaded, makes this all the more interesting.'

Somewhere deep down Shaurya had a bad feeling about this invasion. A sense of discomfort crept into him.

'Which one?'

'Virpur!'

Shaurya let out an involuntary gasp. The glass of wine slipped from his hand and the broken pieces of glass splattered on the terrace. Ashwasena frowned at his reaction.

'The Virpur, whose Commander-in-Chief is Veera?' asked an incredulous Shaurya.

'The same one. But why do you look so worried? I thought you would be really excited about it. Don't you think it is a wonderful opportunity to defeat her? It was such a humiliation to lose the archery competition to her. This war will be a perfect setting to overpower her,' he said enthusiastically. Shaurya stood up in one swift motion. Surprised Ashwasena also stood up.

'What is the matter Shaurya?'

'I want to be alone. I will see you later!' he said in a detached voice.

'But—'

'Leave me alone Ashwa! Just go. It is an order!' barked the Prince. Ashwasena knew him better as a friend. He just bowed to him and left, still baffled by his reaction.

Shaurya clenched his fists and closed his eyes. The moment Ashwasena had uttered the word Virpur, breath was knocked out of Shaurya. A war with Virpur would undoubtedly end Veera. It would put an end to all his miseries, an end to his untold pain. Yet that was not what he wanted. He would have lived, at least if he was ignorant about her life. But now knowing that she would be in danger, twisted his heart in pain. The thought that he would lose her forever, killed him.

This is it!

At last the realisation hit him cold and hard. All these days he lived with a hope that he would see her someday. A hope that she was alive somewhere. Now if this war happened, his life would be wrenched away from him, for there was no way Virpur could defeat Indragiri and that only meant death for Veera. Shaurya's breathing quickened at that very thought. He stood there helpless and unable to move. He stood there numb, feeling no sensation at all. There was just one thought running through his mind.

I cannot let this war happen. I cannot lose Veera. This is probably also the only chance for me to get to her.

Shaurya slowly opened his eyes and looked up at the tranquil moon. He let out a long drawn breath.

'I love you Veera…' he whispered softly. He could suddenly feel the fire of love engulf his entire being as he uttered her name. He no longer felt numb. Shaurya was alive with unfathomable passion lighting up his desolate heart.

***

'Why am I not surprised that you are making me do this?' asked an exasperated Dhruva. Veera smiled at him smugly.

'Let us go in!'

'Do I even have a choice!' he said dryly. She held his wrist and gestured him to come. Dhruva took in a deep breath and stepped inside the temple. It was not the first time he was entering a temple. But it was the first time he was entering this Shiva temple after Sankha had disclosed the secret of his birth. This place always instilled a feeling of hatred in his heart. But today Veera had been very adamant about bringing him there along with her. He apprehensively looked around in the temple. His eyes fell on that flight of stairs at the farther end which lead down to the rear end corner of the temple, the place where his mother had abandoned him. Dhruva felt a lump in his throat. He swallowed hard. His body stiffened at once! Veera squeezed his hand lightly. He looked into her assuring eyes and nodded discreetly. That was all he could do from tears escaping his eyes. It was Veera's presence which gave him strength to tolerate the emotions overwhelming him. The priest began preforming arti to the Lord. It was the first arti of the day at dawn. There were very few people in the temple. The other priests began ringing the bells. Everyone folded their hands in prayer, including Dhruva. He closed his eyes. He didn't ask the Lord for anything. He felt a sense of gratitude towards his foster parents. He slowly opened his eyes and looked at Veera. She was still praying with her eyes closed. Her lips noiselessly murmured her prayer. A slight smile appeared on his face. Dhruva turned to look again at Lord Shiva's idol.

Thank You for sending her into my life. As long as she is with me, I will never ask You for anything more.

After bowing to the Lord they both walked towards the rear end corner of the temple. Dhruva stood there with intense eyes. Veera knew this was going to be difficult for him. She touched his shoulder.

'You will never find peace until you let go of this hatred, Dhruva. I know what I am going to say may sound impossible but that is the only way to end your misery. You have to forgive them for what they did. Only then can you move on in life.'

He looked at her disbelievingly.

'Forgive them? After all that they have done?'

'It will be hard for you, but if you don't forgive them, their actions will always be a burden for you. You will harbour hatred for them in your heart forever. Trust me, that hatred will never let you live in peace. They are no longer a part of your life and I don't want you to live in pain carrying that burden of hatred. Let go Dhruva...' she said softly. Dhruva could no longer argue about what she said because Veera was right. He stood there still, staring at those steps. She quietly walked away from him. She knew he needed to be alone to realise what he wanted to do. Dhruva looked up once and let out a sigh. He decided to let go. He made up his mind to try to forgive them or in the least, he would not to think more about his birth parents. Once again when he looked down at the steps, it didn't hurt more…

'Either you are not interested in Him or this place must hold a special significance in your life!'

Dhruva was startled by the deep tone of the voice that spoke. He turned around and saw a man in saffron ochre robes. His hair had been knotted on the crown of his head. He had a well-kept beard. His guise was clearly that of a scholar but his well-toned physique hinted at his warrior skills. Dhruva bowed to him apprehensively, out of respect for his appearance of a scholar.

'Forgive me Acharya. But have we met before?'

The scholar smiled at him warmly.

'I have not had the pleasure of meeting you before Dhruva. But I know you.'

'How do you kn—'

'Acharya Rudra!' called out a surprised Veera. She quickly strode towards him and touched his feet. He placed a caring hand on her head.

'May you always be happy!'

Veera stood up with an excited smile. Dhruva looked at them perplexed.

'Looks like you already know him!' he said timidly, still trying too hard to remember if he knew him.

'Of course I do! We met at the temple in Charanvasi on the final day of the competition.'

'But you never told me Mithra.'

'That day I was so preoccupied that I couldn't tell you. Later I never got an opportunity to talk about him. Well, he is Acharya Rudrapriya. He was a warrior before but now a scholar. This should explain your questions about his physique.'

Rudrapriya smiled at Veera indulgently. But Dhruva still eyed him apprehensively.

'How are you Veera?'

'I am fine Acharya. But I am surprised to see you here. What brings you to Virpur?'

'A scholar always travels in the search of knowledge. My quest for knowledge has brought me here. But today I set out in search of you. Ever since I last saw you at Charanvasi, I wanted to meet you again. There is lots that we have to talk about.'

'With pleasure Acharya. It is indeed an honour to be in your company. Acharya kindly visit my home during your stay in Virpur and give me the fortune of serving you,' she said earnestly.

'I will gladly come, but on one condition. You will stop calling me Acharya. Call me Rudra.'

Veera was taken aback.

'But Acharya—'

Rudrapriya raised his hand to stop her.

'Don't refuse Veera. I don't easily mingle with people. But I really value your acquaintance. I want you to treat me as your friend and not as a scholar. Nobody else has the liberty of calling me by my name. But you are the only exception to it. Just call me Rudra if you accept me as your friend.'

Veera obliged with a smile.

'As you wish Rudra.'

Dhruva was a silent spectator. Rudrapriya turned towards him now.

'Well, Dhruva looks disturbed today.'

Dhruva's lips set into a hard line. He didn't speak a word. The smile disappeared from Veera's face.

'It was not easy for him to come here,' she said softly.

'Dhruva, sometimes the toughest part of a journey is at the start. Once you start your journey and travel some distance, you will realise that it is not that difficult.'

Dhruva eyed Rudrapriya with interest.

'You are right, Acharya. Moreover with Mithra by my side, nothing is impossible for me.'

'I can see that,' said Rudrapriya intensely.

Just then a soldier walked up to them and bowed.

'My lady, Prince Vijayendra has asked you to meet him at the artillery this morning. I have orders to escort you.'

'Did the Prince tell you anything about this yesterday?' asked Dhruva as a matter of fact.

'No. It must be something to do with the new swords that were made for the soldiers. I must leave right away!'

'I am coming with you.'

But Veera shook her head in denial.

'No! You won't. Not today Dhruva! I think you should take it easy today.'

Dhruva narrowed his eyes at her.

'Mithra, let me come with you. Nothing can make me better as much as your presence,' implored Dhruva. Yet Veera was firm in her decision.

'With me, you can only find an escape from your emotions but you will never overcome them. For that, you will have to find strength within yourself. Trust me, Rudrapriya is an excellent company. At this point, he can probably help you in more ways than me. I will see you in the evening at home.'

Dhruva gave her a defeated look.

'Have a nice day and get back soon.'

Veera smiled at him and nodded in assent.

'Kindly excuse me Rudra. I will meet you tomorrow at the earliest possible.'

'Don't worry Veera, we will meet soon. I will be staying in Virpur for a few more days.'

Veera walked out of the temple with the soldier hurriedly.

'Veera, means a lot to you,' said Rudrapriya on a serious note. Dhruva looked at him calmly.

'She means everything to me. She is my strength.'

'No doubt Veera is your biggest strength, but do you realise that she is also your biggest weakness?'

Dhruva looked at him baffled.

'You are a strong man Dhruva but at the same time you are equally vulnerable. The easiest way to defeat you is through Veera. She is the only one who can hurt you the most.'

'Mithra, will never hurt me,' he said glaring at the scholar. But Rudrapriya remained unperturbed.

'The day you love someone unconditionally, you become vulnerable. You put yourself in a position where that person can easily hurt you. Courage to withstand pain should always accompany love.'

Dhruva smiled at him wryly.

'It is really amusing to see a scholar speak about love!'

'No one can ever escape love. There are no exceptions for love. I know what it means to love and to be loved. It's just that I have the will-power to stay away from it,' he said calmly. Dhruva gave him a cold look.

'Nevertheless Acharya, I am not interested in listening to your views. If you would kindly excuse me.'

'Wait Dhruva! I came to Virpur for a reason. I came here to warn you.'

Dhruva was taken aback.

'Warn me? About what?'

'You don't seem to refuse anything that Veera asks for, do you?'

'Of course not! Why would I refuse her? I would gladly give up my life for her!'

'Now, there lies the problem. She will never ask you to give your life. What she will ask for will be something more than that,' said Rudrapriya, for the first time passion burning in his eyes.

'What is it that you want to tell me Acharya?'

Dhruva was on the verge of losing his patience. Once again the serenity entered Rudrapriya's eyes.

'Veera is going to ask you for something that you value more than your life. I really hope that you refuse her for if you don't, everything that you both did for each other will come to a naught. Her decision will change your lives forever!'

Dhruva was stunned. Though he really couldn't comprehend Rudrapriya's words, an ill feeling crept into his mind. A strange fear gripped his heart.

'What should I do?' asked Dhruva in a helpless voice. That mystical smile was back on Rudrapriya's face.

'I can only tell you what to expect. I can't make decisions for you. It's too early to say anything more. You will understand my words when time comes. For now, all I can say is, don't let your heart command your mind. That will only spell disaster for you.'

Dhruva nodded his head slightly.

'It is going to be really hard.'

'I know, but it is not impossible. My work is over. I have to leave.'

'Thank you, Acharya,' said Dhruva and bent down to touch his feet.

'May you find peace in life,' blessed Rudrapriya placing a hand on his head. Then he walked out of the temple. Dhruva stood still for a moment and then turned to the Lord's idol. With folded hands he once again bowed to the Lord. With a quick glance at the rear corner of the temple he began walking out. There was only question on his mind.

What will Mithra ask me?

An answer that would alter their lives forever.

***

CHAPTER 20

Shaurya stood in the hallway cracking his knuckles. The royal guard had gone inside the royal chamber to announce his presence to the King. The guard came out after a few moments and bowed to him. Shaurya walked into the royal chamber. Surprisingly King Kritiverman was alone without Prime Minister Agniverma.

'What brings you here so early in the morning Shaurya?'

The Prince didn't beat about the bush.

'Is it true that an invasion is being planned on Virpur?'

'Yes.'

Shaurya narrowed his eyes in anger.

'When was this decided? Why is it that I, the Chief Commander of the army, not informed earlier? Didn't your Highness feel that I should be a part of the decision-making process?'

'Your presence was not necessary,' said Kritiverman evenly. Hearing these words Shaurya lost his temper.

'A hell yes! It was necessary! And you know it. Your Highness knew very well that I would object to this plan. I would never agree to invade a kingdom with the lame excuse of expanding your kingdom!'

'Kings fight wars for power. It is already shameful enough that your man lost the archery competition to that woman. This war will be a fitting reply for that defeat and show our prowess.'

'Show your prowess by wreaking havoc in her life! Your greed for power is boundless. Why don't you simply let them live in peace?'

'Look at the way you speak! You sound like a coward!'

Shaurya clenched his fists in fury.

'Yes I am coward! I don't want to be brave like you! The great King who could never save his son or rather killed his own son,' he said acidly.

'Hold your horses Shaurya!' roared the King.

'Don't you dare forget that I am the King of Indragiri! You are the crown Prince and Chief Commander of the army. I decide about the war and you lead the army to fight in the war. *You* take orders from *me*!' he said firmly.

'Damn the war!' swore Shaurya and stomped out.

'What a shame! He is such a coward,' hissed Kritiverman. He was once again disappointed with Shaurya.

***

'How long will this last?' asked an impatient Dhruva.

'Why do you ask me? I don't even know, why this meeting has been called for,' replied Veera smiling at him. He let out a sigh and looked around the royal court. It was a private meeting where only the ministers and Chief Commander were supposed to be present. But as usual Dhruva was an exception, for Veera was always adamant about him accompanying her. Though he always disliked entering the royal palace, he never refused Veera. The royal guard announced the arrival of the King and the Prince. Everyone stood up. King Devarata, Prince Vijayendra and Prime Minister Purumithra walked into the royal court. The gathering bowed to the King. Devarata sat on the highly

embellished throne and gestured at this audience to sit.
Prince Vijayendra occupied an ornate seat, one step below
the King on his right. Veera looked at the Prince and then
at Dhruva. His face wore a blank expression. Her mind
couldn't help comparing them.

*What a contrast! Prince Vijayendra earned the respect of a
Prince only from his attire and the identity of being the King's
son. Without those two attributes he had nothing to make him
look distinguished from the rest. On the other hand, Dhruva
had every sign on him that screamed of valour. Even with his
simple attire he looked nothing less than the King himself. See
the power of fate!*

Veera leaned in closer towards Dhruva.

'You should have been sitting there!' she whispered
glancing at Prince Vijayendra. Dhruva gave her a sharp look.

'I don't ever want to be there. Don't even think about it!'
he hissed at her. She simply shrugged her shoulders at him.
But he nodded his head at her discreetly.

'Gentlemen, we have assembled here for an emergency
meeting. We could be facing an invasion in the near future.
We have received a message from the kingdom of Indragiri.
King Kritiverman has sent an open declaration of war,'
said King Devarata, concern straining his voice. There was
a sudden restlessness among the audience. The Ministers
began discussing their opinions with each other. But Veera
sat still. The news of a war jolted her! She knew the might of
Indragiri's army as much as she knew hers. If it came down
to a war, there could only be one outcome. She would lose
and so would her kingdom. Fear began enveloping her. Just
then she could feel the warm touch of a hand holding hers.
Dhruva squeezed her hand gently. She looked at him and

his eyes held a comforting assured look. He gestured at her with his eyes which only meant that everything would be fine. She was not alone. Though the fear didn't vanish, Veera had found the strength to overcome it.

King Devarata raised his hand to silence the men. Purumithra stepped forward.

'Let us not jump to conclusions. For now, we have only received the declaration of war. There can be negotiations on diplomatic terms. We will do everything we can to protect our kingdom.'

'Nevertheless I want the army to be ready, Chief Veera. The safety of Virpur now lies in your hands. I hope you won't disappoint me.'

Veera stood up.

'It is an honour, your Highness. I will never give you an opportunity to be disappointed,' she said and bowed to him. Dhruva gritted his teeth. He knew what her words implied. It was easy for the King to speak because it won't be he who will fight in the battlefield.

'We should also make preparations to get our allies to join us,' suggested Prince Vijayendra.

'But I really hope negotiations work in our favour. Be prepared for any eventuality. You all may leave now,' ordered the Prince. Everyone bowed to them and left except Prime Minister Purumithra who stayed with the royals.

'Do you think diplomatic talks will work?' asked Veera. They both were walking towards the stables to take their horses.

'Diplomacy is for the cowards! Warriors don't talk, they let their weapons do the talking.'

She gave him an exasperated look.

'You men are all the same. The very thought of fight intoxicates you!'

'Stop being a hypocrite! We warriors are all the same. Don't you revel at the idea of a battle?' challenged Dhruva.

'Maybe I do. But not to the extent of ignoring the devastation it will cause,' she said softly. Dhruva stopped in his way and turned to look at her. Veera had a pained expression on her face. He placed a caring hand on her cheek.

'What is it that you fear? Do you fear defeat?'

'No… I fear the pain of loss this war will cause. We may or may not survive. But there are numerous soldiers who will be doomed. What will they gain by sacrificing themselves? What will we gain?'

'Nobody ever gains anything from a war, Mithra. But everyone will certainly lose something. Yet these soldiers fight bravely. We all fight. We are warriors either by choice or chance. We are destined to fight battles. We hold pride in the numerous scars that adorn our body. There is no escape from this! As long as life exists, there will be war. The sooner you accept this fact, the stronger you become.'

Veera looked into his cold eyes swallowing hard. Dhruva was not trying to comfort her. He was stating the bitter truth plainly so that she gets the courage to face reality. He could not afford to let her be vulnerable. It was time Veera toughened herself for the future challenges. Veera let out a long drawn breath.

'Let us prepare for war,' she said intensely.

'War or no war, we stay together,' he said stroking her cheek gently. Veera smiled at him slightly. It was those words which actually gave courage to both of them. They stayed together, beyond that nothing mattered.

***

'You have lost your mind Shaurya!' said an angry Ashwasena. Initially he was shocked by what Shaurya told him, but then anger overtook shock the minute he realised the implications of his words. The Prince remained unperturbed, sitting on the steps of an old ruined temple on the border of Indragiri. He had expected such a reaction from his friend.

'Don't be a fool Shaurya. The declaration of a war has already been sent to Virpur. You have no choice but to lead us into the battlefield. We cannot go back on this decision. It will ruin the reputation of Indragiri.'

'I never mentioned about going back on our word. But we can always have negotiations before war.'

'Negotiations!?? Do you really think the King will agree to this? People will laugh at us!'

'I don't care!' said Shaurya unflinchingly.

'How can *you* say that Shaurya? You are the crown Prince of Indragiri. The future of our people lies in your hands and you say you don't care! I never expected this from you.'

Prince Shaurya let out a sigh and closed his eyes.

'I am helpless Ashwa. I have no choice. I can't let her die. If this is what it takes to save her then so be it.'

Ashwasena looked at his friend who looked so helpless now. This was certainly not the daredevil Prince that he knew. There was not just a difference but something more. Shaurya had changed. Ashwasena sat beside him.

'What you are going to do is not right. It will hurt many people. More than others, even if you commit a small mistake in this, it will completely devastate you.'

'I know, but this is the only way.'

'You don't have to do this.'

'I don't have to but I want to!'

'All this for a woman?' asked Ashwasena softly. Shaurya turned and looked straight at him.

'All this for love! I will not survive if something happens to Veera,' he said his voice cracking on the last words. Ashwasena now believed completely that Shaurya was indeed in love. What he was going to do was not insanity but actually protecting the love of his life. Nobody could understand Shaurya better than him. He couldn't abandon his friend now. He held his hand.

'I am with you. We'll do everything we can to save Veera.'

Shaurya smiled at him and they embraced each other. Ashwasena knew it was not right but that was not going to stop him from backing his friend. Shaurya felt huge relief when he heard Ashwasena's words. His support meant a lot to him.

'I think we should leave, it will be completely dark in a few moments.'

'Wait Ashwa. I have told someone to meet me here,' he said carefully looking around.

'Who?'

'You'll see.'

Shaurya said nothing more. They sat in silence for some more time. It was now completely dark. Just then Ashwasena stiffened when he heard hooves of a horse. Instantly his hands moved to the hilt of his sword. But Shaurya smiled and gestured him to relax. The hooded rider came to a stop near the temple and dismounted from his horse. Ashwasena still could not recognise the rider. They both descended from the steps. Shaurya went forward to greet the rider who slid the hood back from his head.

'I hope I didn't keep you waiting for long, Shaurya.'

'You have come at the right time Ayush. I wanted to meet you in the dark. I didn't want anyone to notice you.'

'Ayush!' said a surprised Ashwasena. The man in saffron robes smiled at him cordially. The three of them had been in the Gurukul together in their childhood. But now, Ayush the son of the Chief Doctor of Indragiri had taken the position of his aging father. Even after many years the three still shared the same warmth in their friendship.

'What is the matter Shaurya? Why did you want to meet me here in this desolate place?'

Shaurya looked at him with a serious gaze.

'The situation demanded it. This is something really very important and meant to be done surreptitiously.'

'Well I, as much guessed it when you told me about meeting here. Go ahead. Tell me what it is.'

Shaurya let out a long drawn breath and explained his plan. Ashwasena's jaw dropped in horror. Ayush gaped at him wide-eyed.

'Can you do this for me Ayush?' asked Shaurya with a hint of doubt in his voice. Ayush took a few moments to regain his composure.

'Are you certain that you want to do this Shaurya?'

'I am. But it won't be possible unless you help me.'

Ayush looked at Ashwasena. He gave him a resigned expression.

'But you should consider the risk involved. Even a small mistake could either kill her or you,' he said urgently. But the Prince remained unperturbed.

'I am ready to take any risk than let her go into this war. I know what I am doing. Will you please help me?' he implored. Ayush had never seen Shaurya implore like this before. He could not refuse his friend.

'If I agree to do as you say then I will be cheating on my profession. Yet I will do it for my friend. I promise to do my best, the rest depends on you.'

Shaurya smiled at him in gratitude. But there was no trace of a smile on his friends' faces. They were still unconvinced about him succeeding in his endeavour. Yet they had decided to stand by him. The pain of leaving him alone would be more unbearable than what they were enduring now.

***

Nila was standing outside Veera's room, her forehead creased with worry. It was a moonless evening and lamps had been lighted in every corner of the house except in Veera's room. The door had been latched from inside. Once again she knocked on the door but there was no reply. She placed the earthen lamp at the door and went outside to see at the entrance. She was desperately expecting Dhruva to arrive. When Veera came home in the afternoon, she didn't greet Nila with her usual smile. Her face was expressionless and set into a hard line. She had ordered Nila not to disturb her at any cost. Then Veera walked into her bedding chamber and latched the door from inside. Nila thought she must be upset about something but would return to normal after some time. She began to worry when Veera did not come out even in the evening. She knocked twice on the door but there was no reply. Nila knew only Dhruva could make her come out. She impatiently began pacing in the porch waiting for him. She let out a sigh of relief when he came.

'Nila what are you doing here?' asked Dhruva, surprised to see here in the porch pacing up and down. She quickly bowed to him.

'My lord, I was waiting for you. Lady Veera has not come out of her room ever since she came home in the afternoon. I knocked thrice on the door but she gave no reply. She has given me clear orders to not disturb her. But I am worried, my lord. Please do something,' she said hurriedly. Dhruva thought for a moment. He knew that Veera had gone to the palace today because the King had summoned her. She stopped him from accompanying her as there were strict orders that Veera had to go to the royal court alone. He also did not press the issue too much as he had to oversee the preparation for the war. Later he was so absorbed with his work that he had completely forgotten about the summons. Now he had come to her home to have dinner with her. After hearing Nila's words, he guessed that something important must have happened at the royal court today.

Dhruva quickly walked into the house. He knocked on the door of Veera's room. No reply.

'Mithra, open the door!'

No reply. He knocked once again, harder this time.

'Mithra! What are you doing? Come on, open the door. Now!' he said raising his voice. Still there was no reply. He could wait no more. He banged on the door repeatedly. When it did not open, he used all his force and pushed at it. On the second attempt the latch gave away and the door opened. The room was completely dark inside and it took a few moments for his eyes to adjust to the darkness.

'Mithra…' he called out. But she didn't respond. Nila gave him the lamp. He held it high and scanned the room. Veera was not on the bed. She was sitting at the farther corner of the room with her knees folded. Her arms were wrapped around her legs and her head rested on her knees. She was facing down. Dhruva felt relief when he spotted her. But he was worried to see her like that. He gestured Nila to leave. She bowed to him and quietly left them alone. He went to her and placed the lamp beside her. Dhruva sat in front of her and placed his hand on her head caressing it softly.

'Mithra, what happened?'

She didn't look up.

'Why are you like this?'

Dhruva was running out of patience.

'Say something Mithra! Your silence is killing me!'

Veera slowly lifted her head. Her eyes were not red. She had not cried. But the expression on her face was cold, hard. He was startled.

'What did they say in the royal court today?' he asked with anger straining his voice. She picked up the papyrus scroll lying next to her and handed it to him. Dhruva quickly opened it and held it before the lamp. It bore the symbol of Indragiri, a bull. At the bottom was their royal seal. Veera kept her eyes fixed on him as he read through it. She could see anger building up into unadulterated rage on his face.

'Spineless rogues!' swore Dhruva. He tore the papyrus scroll into pieces.

'How dare they make such a proposal? I will kill him. I will tear that bastard Shaurya into pieces,' he growled. He clenched his fist in anger. After all he had every reason to be enraged.

The papyrus scroll contained the terms of negotiation for the war. Prince Shaurya had sent it under his seal. Instead of a full-fledged war, he wanted a duel to be fought. Since he was the Commander-in-Chief of Indragiri, he had challenged Commander-in-Chief of Virpur for a sword fighting duel. The conditions for the duel were also clearly stated. If Veera wins the duel, Indragiri would never again wage a war on Virpur. If Shaurya wins, he only wanted Veera. She would be taken to Indragiri. Nothing more.

Dhruva simply could not accept the fact that they could make such an outrageous negotiation. Now all he wanted to do was defeat Indragiri in the war though the odds were stacked against them. The room was still dark despite the single earthen lamp placed next to Veera. Dhruva stood up and went about lighting the remaining lamps in the room. In the brightness of these lamps he saw that Veera was still sitting unmoved with the same cold expression. He took in a few deep breaths. His temper was under control now.

'Get up! Come on now, let's go and eat,' he said casually. She gave him a sharp look.

'We still haven't come to a decision about this issue,' said Veera acidly.

'Decision? There is nothing left to decide unless… wait a minute! What did the royal court have to say about this?' he asked suspiciously.

'They have given me a day's time to decide.'

'Aah! One day… it's a lot of time, isn't it? We will go to the palace tomorrow. You will tell that selfish and inefficient lot that we will go to war. Our men have not been emasculated! There are still enough brave men left in Virpur to valiantly defend our land.'

'Yes indeed! There are more than enough men to die in a war!' snapped Veera standing up. Dhruva looked straight into her eyes. There was a clear look of defiance in them. He quickly strode to her and held her arms tightly.

'Look at me, Mithra! There is nothing more to think about it. Accepting this challenge is sheer insanity. For prince Shaurya, its nothing but satisfying his ego. For King Devarata, it's the only way he can save his throne. I can't let you go into it for their selfish motives.'

Veera looked up at him.

'But it will also mean a lot for our kingdom. Our people will be safe. Our warriors can spend some more days with their families.'

Dhruva's expression was that of excruciating pain and extreme anger. His hold tightened on her arms.

'You will say no to them tomorrow. I will not hear another word in support of this ludicrous proposal. This conversation is over!' he said through clenched teeth. His hands were pressing her arms so hard that she could no longer bear the pain.

'Dhruva, let go of my arms. You are hurting me!'

'So are you!' roared Dhruva and instantly he let go of her arms. He went and stood near the window. Veera stood rooted to the spot. She had never seen him lose his temper with her. Today he was literally shouting at her. He had been very hard on her. After a few moments he turned to face her. Veera's heart was filled with compassion for him. There was no trace of anger but only pain on his face.

'Mithra... why are you doing this to me? If you agree for this duel, nobody is going to lose anything. They don't care for your life. But I stand to lose everything. For me, you are life,' he said softly. A tear slid down his cheek as he spoke those last words. Breath was knocked out of Veera. She ran to him and swung her arms around his neck. Dhruva wrapped his arms around her.

'I am sorry Dhruva. I won't leave you!' said Veera with tears streaming down her cheeks. He closed his eyes in quiet satisfaction. They stood like that for a few moments. Then he released her from his embrace. He wiped her tears and she wiped his.

'I cannot live without you,' he said looking into her eyes.

'Do you think I can?' she said smiling. He smiled back and kissed her forehead.

Veera had just fallen asleep. Dhruva was sitting on the bed patting her head lightly to make her sleep. They had eaten their dinner together. Dhruva knew she was disturbed and he didn't want to leave her alone. So he stayed back with her. Dhruva sat there for some time watching her sleep. What a day! Even the very thought of she leaving him, suffocated him. He pushed aside the undesirable thought and let out a sigh. He pulled up the blanket up to her shoulder cautiously so as to not wake her. He caressed her head lightly. Later

Dhruva lied on the other cot in the room. Looking up at her once more, he closed his eyes. His mind was enveloped in the assurance of her soothing presence. The cool breeze lulled him to sleep. For a man who owned nothing, Dhruva now had everything to lose and somewhere deep down in his heart he knew it...

***

CHAPTER 21

Veera sat down on the steps leading to the river from the rear side of the Shiva temple. The moon was still bright in the sky with the twinkling stars. It was well before dawn. She had already bathed and wore a yellow dhoti with a green kurta. Her hair was still damp and she let it fall over her left shoulder. The person she was searching for was knee deep in the river. He was offering his early morning prayers to the Lord. She waited for him patiently. After his prayers he took three holy dips in the river and then began wading outside the water. He smiled with a hint of surprise on seeing Veera. His wet saffron dhoti stuck to his limbs. She noticed that he still maintained the physique many warriors longed for. She stood up as he climbed the steps. Veera bent down and touched his feet.

'May victory be yours!' he blessed placing his hand on her head.

'Acharya I—'

Rudrapriya raised his hand to stop her.

'I have already told you this. Call me Rudra.' Veera hesitated for a moment.

'Rudra... I need your help.' The smile on his face widened.

'I knew you would come. But this is too early!'

'I couldn't wait till dawn. This urgency was necessary.'

'Well, I am not complaining as long as I get to meet you. Sit down Veera. We can talk.'

Veera obliged and they both sat down on the step. The sweet music of the flowing water filled the air.

'You must be aware of the impending war with Indragiri.'

'The whole of Virpur is talking about it. Obviously even I have heard about it.'

'But... yesterday Prince Shaurya sent the terms of negotiation.'

'Hmmm... interesting! So what has he proposed?'

Veera explained to Rudrapriya about the duel and its conditions. Though he was initially surprised, there was only a smile once she finished.

'What have you decided?' he asked coolly.

'What do you think I should do?' Rudrapriya laughed softly.

'It's not about what I think. It's about what you want.'

'I thought you would give me straight answers,' she snapped.

'I don't give answers. You have all the answers within you. I can only help you search them.'

'Please Rudra... help me. I am confused. I don't know what to do!' He slowly shook his head.

'Don't you? As far as I know, you have already made your decision.' Veera frowned at him.

'To whom do you always go to find answers?' asked Rudrapriya with an expression that he already knew the answer.

'Dhruva,' said Veera instantly. He smiled at her indulgently.

'If I am not wrong, he must have clearly told you to reject this proposal,' he said calmly. She nodded her head in assent.

'Dhruva will be very firm his decision. Now, it is up to you.'

Veera let out a sigh.

'I think he is right.'

'If you really thought so, then why did you come to me?'

'It's just that if I agree for the duel, I could save my people, my warriors and most of all Virpur. If the war happens, many lives will be lost...'

'You may be willing to sacrifice yourself for their sake but that sacrifice is not yours to make. It is Dhruva who will be making the ultimate sacrifice. You mean everything to him and he will lose you. This will cause him extreme pain. Can you hurt him Veera?' asked Rudrapriya staring at her mercilessly. Veera closed her eyes in pain.

'I don't want to... but do I have a choice Rudra?'

'Life always gives you choices. You can choose to reject the proposal and go to war. But you know the consequence of your choice better than me. You should have the courage to live with the choices you make!'

'Will it be worth the pain?'

Rudrapriya gave her a piercing look.

'Your father, Agneyastra also made decisions in life which gave him a lot of pain. You and Dhruva, both are the consequences of his choice. Do you think the decisions he took were worth the pain he endured? The pain you are enduring?'

Veera knew the answer but she could not say it out loud. She averted his eyes.

'You don't have to answer that. Every choice comes with its own share of pain. All you have to do is pick the one you think you can live with.'

They sat in silence for some time. A few priests came to the river to offer their morning prayers. Some shot a look of disgust at Rudrapriya when they passed him on the way to the temple. Though he noticed them, he simply ignored. Rudrapriya was now quite acquainted with their animosity.

'What sort of a man is Prince Shaurya?' asked Veera suddenly. But he remained unperturbed.

'Prince Shaurya is a valiant warrior. He was crowned as the prince of Indragiri after the death of his brother Prince Shruthamanyu in a war. He is well known for his sword fighting skills. A charming personality with the women. But a daredevil with killer instincts.'

Veera raised her eyebrows in surprise at his knowledge.

'You do know a lot about him!'

'I travel a lot in search of knowledge, Veera. In the process I get to hear a lot of things. Yet all that I know about him is what people perceive about him. There is more to him. Every man has a face hidden to the world.'

'What sort of a man makes such a proposal? A duel for nothing to gain!' she said irritated.

'This duel may either mean nothing or everything to Shaurya. We don't know.'

Veera let out a long drawn breath.

'Dhruva will never agree to this.'

'He won't. You will be stabbing him straight in the heart by accepting this challenge.'

'I know. But it is inevitable. He will eventually understand. He always does,' said Veera softly. Her eyes welled up but she managed not to let a single tear escape her eyes. She stood up to leave and so did he.

'Remember one thing Veera, if there is one person who will do anything for you, it has to be Dhruva. Don't ever make the mistake of believing that your physical absence will change it. He will never let go of you.'

Veera swallowed hard. This was going to be harder than she thought. She quickly bowed to him and turned to leave. She strode towards her horse without turning back.

'You still have a long way to go, Veera. The bond that you both share was never meant to end here. You both are two halves of an entity. One has no meaning without the other,' whispered Rudrapriya. He turned to look at the horizon. The sun had begun spreading its light slowly into the dawn cutting through the darkness of the night.

***

'Shaurya, be careful. Please make sure that they don't get suspicious about your intentions,' cautioned Ashwasena.

Shaurya and Ashwasena were walking towards the royal court. Shaurya had sent the terms of negotiation for the war with Virpur under the royal seal. But the King was unaware of it. Being the crown prince, he had the authority to use the royal seal other than the King. Yet it is expected of him, that he consults the king before using it. The next day after he sent the message through his confidante, Kritiverman got the news. Today he had ordered Prince Shaurya to be present in the royal court. The guard at the entrance announced the arrival of the prince to the royal court. All the ministers, Prime Minister Agniverma and Commander Vikraman were present in the royal court. Shaurya sat on the ornate chair meant for him, placed one step below the King's throne. Ashwasena took his place behind Shaurya. He gave a cursory nod to Vikraman. Shaurya did not once look at the King Kritiverman in the eye. Kritiverman gestured at Agniverma to begin. He stood up and moved one step forward to address the gathering.

'Gentlemen, a few days ago we had consensually decided to wage a war against Virpur. A message about the war was also sent under the royal seal. But two days ago another message was sent under the royal seal about negotiation. This time it was sent by Prince Shaurya without consulting the royal court. The terms of negotiation are as follows,' said Agniverma and took out a papyrus scroll. He read its contents. Shaurya sat calm and composed gauging the reaction of the audience. First the men were shocked to hear it. Once he finished reading, there was an expected unrest among them. Most of them began vehemently opposing the proposal. The King gave Shaurya an angry look. Then he raised his hand to silence the audience.

'Ministers, I know that Prince Shaurya has committed an act of foolishness. You are free to voice your objection.'

One of the Ministers stood up.

'Kindly forgive my impudence your Highness. But this proposal is unacceptable. We have made a mockery of ourselves by challenging a woman to a duel instead of waging a war.'

Kritiverman looked at Shaurya.

'What do you have to say for this Prince?'

Shaurya stood up and faced them undeterred.

'Chief Veera is no ordinary woman! She has proved her mettle on more than one occasion. Moreover I think waging a war for your greed is more shameful than challenging a woman!'

Another Minister stood up.

'But we have every chance to win this war. Then why make this proposal and exhibit ourselves as cowards?'

The Prince looked at him evenly.

'And do you think waging a war against a kingdom weaker than ours will make us no less cowards?'

'Yet the royal court should have been consulted before sending such a message,' reasoned the first Minister.

'If the royal court can decide on planning an invasion without the knowledge of the crown Prince, then I think the prince at least has the privilege to make negotiations!' said Shaurya sarcastically.

'Shaurya! Can you give one single reason behind your actions?' thundered King Kritiverman.

'Of course, your Highness! If I am not wrong, this invasion was supposedly planned to defeat Chief Veera. Your aim was to show that, a woman cannot be better than a man. You wanted to settle scores with her for the defeat we faced in the archery challenge. I think I have just fulfilled your wish by challenging her for the duel. All I did was stop the unnecessary bloodshed this war would cause.'

'Why are you doing this Shaurya?' asked Kritiverman through clenched teeth. He noticed the flicker of change on his son's face.

'It is necessary, your Highness. It is necessary... nevertheless we cannot go back on our word now. I suppose we should wait for their reply.'

'What if I withdraw your proposal?' asked the King looking straight into his eyes.

'You may do as you wish your Highness. But then, I will not lead the army. I will give up my crown. The decision is yours to make now,' said Shaurya unflinchingly. The royal court fell silent. They stared at him in disbelief. But Kritiverman knew too well about Shaurya's obstinacy. He knew that his son meant every single word he had just uttered. He let out a long drawn breath in defeat.

'There will be no changes made in the terms of negotiation. Further decisions will be made once a response is received from Virpur. Today's meeting ends for now.'

The Ministers were still not convinced but they had to obey the King's words. Shaurya let out a slight smile of victory. He turned around and winked at Ashwasena who gave him a discrete nod. Quickly they bowed to the King and departed. King Kritiverman looked at Prime Minister Agniverma who shared his helplessness.

'This is only the beginning. He is going to make us go through more disgrace than this. How I wish Shrutha was alive today!'

'My Lord, I think Prince Shaurya has to be given a chance. He is young and acts very impulsively. He is bound to have his share of mistakes before he can learn,' he said trying to convince the King. But Kritiverman laughed wryly.

'You cannot afford to make mistakes when you are a crown Prince Agni! You should not be reckless when you are in power and Shaurya is doing just that…' he said letting out a sigh. Kritiverman could not tame the disobedience of Shaurya. It became impossible after Shruthamanyu's death. He also knew that Shaurya would never forgive him.

***

Prince Vijayendra was dumbfounded! There was an eerie silence in the royal court of Virpur. The heavily sculpted ceiling did not reverberate any noise. King Devarata could not still believe what he had just heard. Veera stood in front of him with the same expressionless face she had, before announcing her decision. Dhruva had not accompanied her today or rather she had come to the palace without telling him. It was Prime Minister Purumithra who broke that silence.

'Chief Veera, your courage marvels us. Yet it is my duty to question you again. Are you completely aware of the consequences you will have to face?'

'There can only be three possible consequences. I may win the duel. Or in the event of me losing I will be taken to Indragiri as a captive. Or I may die fighting. I am well aware of the consequences.'

'Do you still want to accept the challenge? You may convey your decision tomorrow if you want to have second thoughts,' said Vijayendra.

'I am humbled by your generosity, my Lord. But I have already made up my mind. One more day will make no difference to me,' answered Veera politely.

'I am proud of you Veera!' praised the King admiring her valour. Just then, there was some commotion at the entrance and the next moment Dhruva stormed into the royal court. King Devarata was enraged at his impudence.

'Commander Dhruva, you cannot barge into the royal court at your will!' admonished Prince Vijayendra. Dhruva shot him a sharp look. He walked straight to Veera.

'What the hell do you think you are doing?' hissed Dhruva.

'Dhruva we can discuss this later. Please be patient until we get out of here. I will explain it to you,' she implored. She was trying her level best to pacify him. But he had already lost his temper the moment he got to know what she had decided to do.

'There is nothing left to explain, Mithra. I have told you that this conversation is over. You say right away that you are not going to accept the challenge. We are going to fight the war!'

Veera averted his eyes.

'We are not going to war Dhruva. I have decided to fight in the duel.'

'You cannot decide it on your own! Who gave you the right to do so?' he thundered. She looked up at him. She would have to be assertive now.

'It is my life Dhruva! You can't dictate terms to me,' she reverted. Dhruva narrowed his eyes at her with anger saturating his mind. He held her wrist tightly and turned to leave.

'Dhruva, let go of Veera. You are violating the code of conduct of the royal court,' said Vijayendra trying to block his way. Dhruva glared at him, his eyes spewing fire with raw fury.

'Stay where you are! Don't you dare stop me today! If you stop me, I will destroy the distance between the King and a commoner. That won't be good to any of you here,' he threatened. A terrorised Prince Vijayendra stepped back stunned by his words. Dhruva looked around at his audience once.

'All of you remember one thing. Mithra will not fight in this duel! This is a war and the warriors of Virpur will fight to defend their motherland. Only spineless cowards will sit behind and watch!' roared Dhruva glancing at King

Devarata. Veera tried to free her hand in vain. He tightened is hold.

'Dhruva listen to me—'

'I am not leaving you and that is final!'

He pulled her along and stormed out of the royal court. Prime Minister Purumithra looked up at the king. He was angry and disappointed with the turn of events.

'Don't worry my lord. She will do it. Veera is Agneyastra's daughter. Blood is always thicker than water!'

'You are right Purumithra. But there are some bonds stronger than blood relations. It's not easy to break them...' he said looking at the entrance. Yet he still hoped that she would come back, for Devarata knew Agneyastra too well to think otherwise.

***

Veera was sitting on an ornate wooden stool in her home. Dhruva was standing with his back to her. He was staring at the wall. They had not spoken ever since they came home from the palace.

'You have decided to leave me...' said Dhruva coldly.

'Dhruva... please don't see it that way.'

He turned quickly to face her.

'I have no other way to see it Mithra! Let's face it. If you fight in this duel, your chances of winning is almost zero. Shaurya's sword fighting capabilities are unmatched. That man's sword is stained with the blood of many courageous warriors. Death doesn't dither him!'

'Maybe you are right. But if I accept this challenge, either I win or lose, Virpur will survive. Sacrificing one woman for a kingdom, after all is worth the effort.'

'Stop this nonsense of sacrifice, Mithra! Nobody will lose anything, they are all only going to gain from this stupid proposal. It is only me who will lose you!'

His body was taut with anger and pain. He clenched his fists. Veera looked into his eyes. Tears welled up in hers. She knew her next words would tear through his heart.

'I think you can live through it...' she said almost choking on her words. Her own words were stabbing her heart. She could not see the pain he was going through.

Can you hurt him?

Rudrapriya's words echoed in her ears. Veera had chosen to hurt him. There was no way she could do it without hurting herself. Hearing her words Dhruva fell on his knees. His eyes were lifeless.

'You could have killed me before saying those words...' he said meekly. Breath was knocked out of Veera. The welled up tears streamed down her cheeks. She went and knelt before him. He looked into her eyes.

'Guruji will never forgive me. Had he been alive, he would never have let this happen. I won't be able to keep up my promise. I have failed him.'

'Dhruva, until now in my life I have lived with decisions others made for me. I know father would never have agreed to this. But first time in life, I have made a choice on my own. Let me live with the decision I make,' she implored.

Dhruva closed his eyes. He held her face in his hands and placed his forehead on hers.

'I will always stand by your decision. But this time you have chosen wrong. I cannot accept it.'

'Please Dhruva, this is all I will ever ask from you,' she said closing her eyes. They stayed like that for some time. Then he released her from his hold.

'You are asking for my life, Mithra. There will be nothing left to give after this,' he said in a lifeless tone and banged his fist to the earthen lamp placed on the floor. The lamp broke into pieces and wounded his hand which began to bleed.

'DHRUVA!' shrieked a petrified Veera and moved forward to hold his hand.

'Don't!' said Dhruva standing up immediately. He outstretched his bloodied palm before her to stop her from nearing him.

'Don't come near me! You have chosen to leave me, then learn to see me in pain. We both can never suffer in solitude. Your pain will agonize me before tormenting you. This fire of sacrifice will consume both of us!'

Dhruva walked out without looking back. Tears streamed down Veera's face continuously. She bent down and touched the drops of his blood. She collapsed onto the floor. Veera looked at her hands stained with his blood and sobbed ceaselessly. First time in life, she felt abandoned…

***

CHAPTER 22

Veera was woken up by the light tapping on her shoulders. With difficulty she opened her eyes. Nila was kneeling beside her with a worried face.

'My lady, what happened? Why are you lying on the floor? And look at your eyes! They are swollen and bloodshot. Have you been crying the whole night?' she asked in a terrified voice. Veera slowly sat up and her body was sore. She looked at her blood stained hand, though the blood had dried now.

'Oh my God! Have you hurt yourself my lady?'

Veera meekly shook her head in denial.

'It's not my blood,' she replied in a life less tone. She stood up and walked mechanically towards the bathing chamber. Nila looked at her with concern. She had never seen Veera so lost! So broken! She was certain something must have gone wrong between Dhruva and Veera. Nila began cleaning the place and removed the remains of the broken earthen lamp.

After a while, Veera came to the living space in her house when Nila was placing the plantain leaf for her breakfast. Nila looked up and was surprised to see her dressed in a neat white dhoti and red kurta, all set to go to work. Except that her eyes did not have the twinkle they usually have. Veera looked hard and cold.

'I don't want breakfast Nila. I am not hungry.'

'My lady, you have not eaten anything since yesterday. If you are going to work, please eat something or else you will be exhausted.'

Veera let out a sigh.

'Please Nila…I am not hungry. Don't force me.'

But she didn't give up.

'Please my lady, you need strength to shoulder huge responsibilities. At least drink this milk,' she said and gave her a glass of milk with a pinch of turmeric added to it. Veera did not want to argue any further. She quickly gulped the milk and left. Nila stood there wondering what Commander Dhruva did to hurt her so much…

Veera walked into the army camp slowly. She looked around to see if she could find Dhruva anywhere though she knew very well that he would not come. Yet she never stopped hoping. Prince Vijayendra saw her and came to her. She saluted him with the usual discipline but the Prince did not fail to notice the pain on her face.

'We need to talk, Chief Veera,' he said and led her towards the farther end of the camp away from the soldiers. She quietly followed him.

'So what have you decided at last?' he asked doubted. Veera looked straight at him.

'I stand by my decision, your Highness. I agree to fight in the duel,' she said evenly. He gave her a slight smile of satisfaction.

'You are a brave warrior Veera, not a coward like Commander Dhruva!' said the Prince haughtily. Veera shot him a displeased look.

'Dhruva is not a coward, your Highness. It takes immense courage to silence a prince in the royal court. It's just that he listens to his heart more than his brain,' she said acidly. Though Vijayendra flinched at her words, he did not show it.

'Looks like Dhruva has not come to work today. Did he give any valid reason for it?

'No, your Highness.'

'Look Veera, if he doesn't change his audacious behaviour, I will find a way to change him. He may not like the consequences,' he said with malice.

'Forgive my impudence, your Highness. But Commander Dhruva takes orders from me. I am always there for him. Nobody will interfere in his affairs other than me. You have every right to order me, but not him.'

Vijayendra raised an eyebrow at her words. Then he gave her a crooked smile.

'For how long will you save his back?'

'As long as... I am alive,' said Veera swallowing hard. She looked at Prince Vijayendra and suddenly a thought struck her.

Though Dhruva and the prince are both sons of the same father, they are so different. What if Dhruva was the crown prince? Would he have been as insensitive as Vijayendra? Never! Dhruva is a better man. He has a genuine heart worth living for! Certainly he would have been a better prince, a better king.

Veera tried to take out the impossible thought from her mind but failed. At last she just saluted the prince and walked towards the infantry.

'You cannot shield Dhruva for long, Veera,' uttered Prince Vijayendra slowly seeing her go. He was waiting for an opportunity to punish Dhruva for his impertinence the previous day at the royal court!

***

Dhruva walked into his house with a bleeding hand. Vani bowed to him.

'My lord, the lunch is ready. Would you like to—?'

She stopped in her sentence when her eyes fell on his bleeding hand. She gasped.

'My lord, your hand is bleeding,' she whispered. But he did not respond. He stood there like a lifeless statue. She quickly went inside and brought some turmeric made into a paste with a few medicinal herbs. She cleaned his wound with water and applied the paste. Vani expected him to flinch at the burning sensation caused by the medicine. Yet he did not move. She then bandaged his wound with a clean cloth. She looked at him. His eyes were blank and he looked lost.

'What is wrong my lord?' she asked softly, though she least expected him to answer. Dhruva turned to look at her. His pain was clearly evident in his eyes. Vani felt a lump in her throat.

'She decided to leave me...' he said and went into his bedding chamber. Vani did not ask who he was referring to, for it was obvious to her. It must be Chief Veera! There was no other woman in his life who could slash through him like this.

Dhruva latched the door of his bedding chamber once he was inside. He no longer had the strength to stand. His legs gave way and he collapsed to the floor. He looked at his bandaged palm and then his wrist. It had a leather wristband. There was beautiful engraving of bow and an arrow on it. Veera had tied it around his wrist as a symbol of their bond. A bow would be useless without the arrow and an arrow could never exist without the bow. His eyes welled up and tears came unhinged from his eyes. Dhruva never cries! The last time he had shed tears was when Agneyastra had died. But that loss was bearable because then he had Veera to share his grief. But now he had none.

'Why? Why are You doing this to me? Why are You orphaning me again? I can't live without her...' he cried. Excruciating pain tugged at his heart. Life was knocked out of his body.

Two days passed but Dhruva never came out of his bedding chamber. Vani tried hard to get him out. Her insistent knocking on the door only resulted in Dhruva shrieking at her to leave him alone. He lay on the floor exhausted. The tears had dried. He was in and out of consciousness every now and then. It looked like he had given up all the desire to live. Without Veera world did not exist for him. Finally exhaustion and starvation overtook his grief and he fell asleep...

There was mist all around him. Dhruva could only see the fog in front of him. Then he felt pain in his right hand. He turned to his right and saw Veera holding his hand tightly. She was wearing the leather armour that he had given her. There was a sword in her other hand. It was Guruji's sword. Veera was not looking at him. She was staring into the fog before them. Veera stepped forward but he tightened his hold on her hand though it hurt him.

'Mithra don't go...' he implored. She looked back at him with fear.

'Are you going to let me go alone?' she asked frightened.

'Don't go!' he said, but this time it was an order. Yet she turned away from him and took another step forward. Pain

shot through his heart. He let go of her hand. Dhruva then turned and started walking away from her, without looking back.

'DHRUVA!' screamed Veera. He stopped and turned immediately. The sight in front of him made him feel like someone had thrust a sword right into his chest. There were numerous cuts on her body and blood was oozing out of every single cut. She was shrieking his name in pain. Dhruva ran towards her, but a strong hand pulled her away from him. He kept running but she was being pulled deeper into the fog. His legs became weak and he was exhausted yet he didn't want to give up. He fell to the ground and she vanished into the fog, leaving behind her bloodied sword.

'MITHRA!' screamed Dhruva and his eyes flew open. His breathing was erratic. Fresh tears were streaming down his eyes and his body was soaked in sweat. He quickly sat up. His head was hammering with pain. He held his head and looked around. He was still on the floor of his bedding chamber. He took a few long breaths to calm himself.

I shouldn't have left her.

He closed his eyes in pain.

I should have known that she won't fight for herself if I let her go. Like me, she too will give up on life. This pain of separation will do nothing but kill us both! I can't let her do that. She will have to fight for her life, fight for both of us. I stand by her no matter what. I will never let go of her... never.

Dhruva held onto Veera like she was his only reason to live. This world will exist even without Veera. Dhruva might live even after she is gone but it won't be much of a life without her, for him. It was this simple truth which would make all the difference in the days to come...

***

'Shaurya… Shaurya!' called out an anxious Ashwasena. He patted Shaurya's face frantically. Ayush quickly applied the paste made of some medicinal herbs on his arm where he had sustained an injury. He tied a cloth bandage over the wound tightly. Ayush then took out a copper container and sprinkled its contents on Shaurya's face. That liquid was brown in colour and had a pungent odour.

'Why isn't he regaining his consciousness?' asked a worried Ashwasena. Ayush lightly patted Shaurya's cheeks.

'The medicine will take some time to show its effects. Moreover I think the cut on his arm is a little deep. He should come around in a few moments.'

'I always knew this was a risky affair.'

'Well, as did he.'

Shaurya, Ashwasena, Ayush and the royal bodyguards had come to the forest. Ashwasena instructed the soldiers to form a perimeter around the forest. Only the three of them went deeper into the woods to come to a clearing. The previous day they had received the royal message from Virpur. King Devarata had accepted the challenge for the duel. Though Shaurya knew that King Devarata would certainly agree, he was a little sceptical about Veera. In the message there was a special mention of her accepting the challenge bravely. His respect for her increased after this. More than respect it was his love for her which grew boundlessly. Today he had come there to train for the duel. Ayush had laced Shaurya's sword with a diluted mixture of herbs. He practised sword fighting with Ashwasena. During the combat Shaurya's sword made a cut on his own arm. Ayush sprinkled some more of the liquid on his face.

Shaurya's fingers twitched slightly. With some effort, he slowly opened his eyes.

'Shaurya… how are you feeling?' asked Ayush placing a hand on his forehead. He did not seem to have developed fever. That was a relief. Shaurya began sitting up and Ashwasena supported him against his chest.

'Shoot!' cursed Shaurya as the pain shot through his arm. He let out a sigh and leaned against his friend. Then he looked straight at the doctor.

'Now, explain!' He pointed at his wound.

'I have never tried anything like this before! All I did was a conjecture based on the knowledge I have about these herbs. I didn't expect it to be so potent. I am sorry.'

'Please don't be apologetic, Ayush. You have honoured my illegitimate request against your ideals. That by itself means a lot to me. I can understand that it involves a lot of complexities. Can you make this better? I don't want this to affect her more…' he said with a rare softness colouring his tone.

'I can dilute its effect a little more but I cannot do it beyond a limit. If I dilute it too much, then it won't serve the purpose. Moreover you can't achieve your goal without hurting her. You will have to injure her to allow the medicine penetrate into her body,' stated Ayush. Shaurya flinched at that thought.

'Take care that you don't hurt yourself with this sword again,' said a concerned Ashwasena. The prince was quiet for a few moments.

'She will survive, won't she?' he asked slowly with an untold fear filling his eyes.

'Veera will survive as long as you don't cause very grievous injuries to her. But she will have to endure a lot of pain. That is inevitable.'

'Pain is something we can endure but not loss…'

Ayush glanced at Ashwasena who shared his amusement. This was not the prince that they knew. Even during the death of Shruthamanyu, he had not been vulnerable. Though his sorrow filled his heart, he never let it show. But his feelings for Veera were quite evident even if he did not tell it out loud.

'If you feel better now, we can go to the palace. I think you need to rest.'

'Ashwa is right Shaurya. You will have to take it easy for the day. You may feel a little exhausted or even dizzy for some time, but it will last only for today. Just take care not to wet your wound. I will change the bandage tomorrow.'

Shaurya nodded his head in agreement. He stood up but the sudden movement made him a little unsteady. But Ashwasena was quick to hold him.

'It's okay Ashwa, I can manage,' said Shaurya and let go of him. Ayush was right about the exhaustion. But he could manage to walk on his own without any help. The injury on his arm was hurting Shaurya. Yet more than that, the very thought of inflicting pain to Veera hurt him more. He would have even fought the entire world had there been any other way to save her. Though success was not guaranteed, at least there was a chance. It was this chance which decided their lives now.

***

All the five arrows had hit the target board accurately. Veera stood there with closed eyes and picked one more arrow from the quiver strapped to her back. She strung the arrow to her bow and was ready to shoot. Just then, she heard approaching footsteps and she relaxed her stance.

'Chief Veera,' said the man and saluted her. Veera opened her eyes to see Major Vidyut standing beside her. She acknowledged him with a nod. She placed the bow on the stone bench and unstrapped the quiver and placed it next to her bow.

'Chief, Prince Vijayendra has sent word for you to go to the royal palace today. They have arranged a feast in your honour.'

There was no change on Veera's blank face. There seemed to be no life in her eyes anymore. She looked like a mere shadow of the cheerful and valiant warrior she once was.

'Tell them I am honoured but I can't accept their invitation,' she said plainly. He was baffled.

'Why Chief?'

'Do I have to spell out everything? I think you can understand,' she snapped at him. Vidyut let out a sigh.

'He is not coming back,' he stated flatly.

'He will never forgive me, will he?' she asked softly.

'Dhruva has already been orphaned once. Being orphaned for a second time is not easy to accept. It's not about whether you are right or wrong. But it's about him losing you! None of us will ever know what it means for him to lose that one person he ever called his.'

'Did you go to meet him?' she asked hopefully.

'I did go… he had given clear instructions to his guards to not let anyone inside. He has locked himself inside the house. He hasn't come out for the past three days.'

They both knew nothing could be done to change his decision. In the past three days, though Veera wanted to see him, she could not make up her mind about it. She did not want to hurt him more than she already had. Yet every day she kept looking for him in the artillery, or in the army camp hoping against hope. An emptiness had filled her heart ever since Dhruva had left her home that day. Seeing him walk away was the hardest thing she had ever done. She let out a long drawn breath and looked at Vidyut.

'Will you be able to handle the training for the rest of the day? I am going home.'

'I will Chief. Moreover there are other commanders and majors overseeing the training.'

Veera gave him a slight nod. He saluted her and then she walked to her horse. She looked exhausted. Though Veera had come to work from the very next day, her thoughts always revolved around Dhruva. Vidyut could see how much their separation was torturing her. Yet he admired the courage of this woman.

It was a sweltering afternoon. Veera rode her horse slower than usual. The hot sun scorched her skin but it did not bother her. When she reached home, she handed the reins of her horse to one of her guards and walked towards the house. She did not go inside. Standing on the porch 'Nila!' she called out. Nila quickly walked to her and was surprised to her come back home so early.

'What can I do for you my lady?'

Veera unstrapped her sword from her waist and handed it to her.

'Get me a pitcher of water.'

Nila quietly returned with a pitcher full of water. Veera washed her hands and legs. Then she splashed the cool water on her face. She quenched her thirst by drinking the remaining water and gave the pitcher to her.

'Shall I serve your lunch?'

Veera shook her head.

'I am not hungry…'

'But—'

'Please Nila, I want to be alone,' said an exasperated Veera. Nila bowed to her and went inside. Veera sat down on the steps of the porch. She didn't want to go inside the house. Yes, that's what it was for her now. Just a house and not home! Ever since he had left her, she felt repulsive about her home. It was no longer home without him. She leaned her head against the wooden pillar and closed her eyes. Her thoughts went back to the day she had last seen Dhruva. A tear escaped her closed eyelid. After some time sheer exhaustion overwhelmed her and she fell asleep.

Veera felt a hand touch her head. She opened her eyes and looked up. She couldn't believe her eyes! A sudden sense of happiness coursed through her. Dhruva was standing before her. She looked into those affectionate eyes which always held a promise of boundless love. It felt like a dream to her. After seeing him she realised how much she actually missed him. Neither did he speak a word nor did she. There was no need for words! Veera took his bandaged hand in her hands and placed her forehead on it. Dhruva caressed her head with his other hand. He sat down next to her.

She rested her head on his shoulder. He securely wrapped his hand around her. It felt like heaven! They sat like that for a long time. Either of them did not want to break that comforting silence. They feared that even a small movement would disturb their peaceful world. If only time would freeze at that moment forever! This was the life they wanted. Being together, it just felt right…

'You thought I would never come…' said Dhruva softly.

'After all that I did, I felt you would never forgive me,' she whispered.

'I still have not forgiven you, Mithra.'

Veera sat up straight and looked at him confused.

'Then why?'

'For you,' he said placing his hand on her cheek. She looked at him astounded.

'Mithra… I am angry with your decision and I will never forgive you for it. I was so overwhelmed with rage that day, I just left you. But after that every moment of separation tortured me. I tried everything I could to live without you, but I failed miserably. Once the anger subsided I started thinking. Then I realised that this was never about me! This decision was yours to make and you did it. Though I don't agree with you, as a true companion I should stand by your choice. When I said I would remain a celibate forever, you never agreed to it. You opposed me but you never left me. Then how can I leave you? Moreover I know you are also going through the same pain of separation. I can never see you in pain. I may despise your decision but I can never hate you for that. I will stand with you even if it means I stand to lose everything!' he said looking into her eyes.

'How can you do this Dhruva? How can you be so selfless?' she asked still unable to accept his words. He gave her a lopsided smile.

'Selfless? Of course not! I am very selfish Mithra and that is why I will do everything I can to make sure you win.'

Veera smiled back at him. She had smiled after many days.

'Nothing is impossible when we are together!'

Dhruva nodded his head in assent and kissed her forehead.

'Did you eat lunch?' he asked suspiciously.

'No…' she said sheepishly.

'How will you fight if you don't stay healthy? Let's go and devour the food Nila has cooked. Moreover I am also starving,' he said patting his stomach. Veera laughed at him and then both of them stood up. He slung his arm over her shoulder and they walked into the house. The only difference was that now it felt like home. Veera's world was complete with him. Though Dhruva agonized every moment over her decision, he endured it, for Veera was above everything for him. Her will was all that mattered to him even though he writhed in silence to fulfil it.

***

CHAPTER 23

'*Bhrathra, this sword is long and it looks heavy too. I don't think I can wield it,' said a doubtful Shaurya. Shruthamanyu smiled at his fifteen-year old younger brother.*

'*It will seem difficult if you just keep looking at it. Move beyond your fear. Don't think, just go for it.*'

Shaurya looked at his brother once more, still unsure. But he trusted his brother. He moved forward and picked up the sword. A bull was ornately inscribed on the hilt. The sword was heavy but he could handle it. He was happy with his strength and a smile appeared on his face. Shaurya swung the sword twice. His movements were not swift due to the weight of the sword. Shruthamanyu held his brother's shoulder.

'*This sword is yours Shaurya. From now on, it will bear your name. Practise hard with it. You can excel as a warrior only when these weapons become a part of your body. You should use them with the same ease as you use your limbs.*'

Shaurya listened to his brother's words with full concentration. He regarded Shruthamanyu as his teacher also. It was he who first showed Shaurya how to wield a sword.

'*You should also prepare your mind equally as your body to accustom to this sword. It won't be long before you make your first kill. You will be responsible for every drop of blood that stains your sword! It gives you the power to either save or destroy lives. You will decide the fate of the one standing on the other end of your sword. Use it wisely,' said Shruthamanyu staring straight into his eyes. An obedient Shaurya gave a slight nod and once again looked at the sword in his hand. Though he was young to completely comprehend Shruthamanyu's words, he understood what his brother wanted to convey him. Every time he used his sword, his brother's words would echo in his thoughts.*

Use it wisely...

Shruthamanyu's words once again rang in his ears. Shaurya opened his eyes instantly. He saw the delicate carving on the ceiling. The hall was quiet. He was lying on his back. His hands were folded and placed below his head. The marble floor was cool below his bare upper torso. Shaurya's sword was lying on the floor beside him. He was in the hall which was used for martial arts and sword fighting. This was the place his brother taught him martial arts and sword fighting. After Shruthamanyu's death, he rarely visited this hall in the palace. But today he simply walked in. It wore a deserted look and he could still feel his brother's presence there. He knew very well why he avoided coming here. This place brought back the memories so intensely that it made it hard for him to accept that Shruthamanyu was no more.

'Bhrathra...' whispered Shaurya and closed his eyes once again in pain. After a while he heard someone coming.

'Whatever it is that you want to tell me, I don't want to hear it. Don't disturb me. Just leave,' he said impatiently without opening his eyes presuming that it must be one of the royal attendants.

'Well, I don't take orders from you,' said a caring voice. He immediately opened his eyes.

'Mother... I am sorry. I thought it was—how did you know I was here?' he asked quickly sitting up. Arunadevi sat down near him.

'I am the Queen, obviously I have my sources.'

Shaurya smiled at her wryly. Arunadevi's eyes fell on his wounded arm. The bandage had been removed and it was beginning to heal. She lightly placed her fingers near the wound.

'Does it hurt?'

'No.'

He was not lying about it. For he knew, there was more pain to come.

'You are very disturbed these days, Shaurya. What is bothering you so much?'

'Nothing mother, I am fine.' He averted her eyes.

'You wouldn't have walked in here if you were fine. The last time you were here was when Kritinanda went to Gurukul.'

Shaurya let out a sigh. He again lay down on the floor placing his head on her lap, she caressed his head lovingly. He looked up at his mother.

'Can I ask you something?'

She smiled at him.

'Anything...'

'Do you love him?'

Shaurya did not have to say about who he was asking. Arunadevi understood the contempt in his tone. She was quiet for a moment.

'Yes I do.'

But he was not ready to accept her answer, he raised his eyebrows in doubt.

'Had anyone asked me this question when I married the King, my answer would have been different. But time changes everything. I understand him better now. I agree that he is not always right. Still he is a good man, Shaurya. Everyone makes mistakes and he has committed a few serious ones indeed. Sometimes circumstances rule us and we cannot control fate, can we?'

Shaurya looked at his mother disappointed.

'Fate? How can you blame fate for his actions, mother? He had the power to make decisions. Had he done the right thing, life would have been different for us.'

Arunadevi shook her head in disapproval.

'Your decisions are not entirely yours to make. The elements around you govern them. You are just a tool to implement such decisions. If you are a King then it is only going to complicate it further,' she said empathizing with her husband. Yet Shaurya was not convinced. He did not argue further. His mother held the King in a very high regard to agree with him. There was silence except for the faint footsteps of the royal guards around the palace.

'Do you really want to do this?' she asked after some time. He frowned at her open ended question.

'Do what, mother?'

'Fight in this duel,' she said calmly. Shaurya didn't reply, he quickly woke up. He stood up and turned away from her.

'I have to,' he replied in a blunt tone. She stood up.

'I usually don't question your actions, Shaurya. You have been rebellious even as a child. Everyone said you are mischievous and disobedient. But I have always loved you more than Shrutha, because you always stood for what is right. It might have been unacceptable but that never deterred you. Yet I feel this duel is not right. If you have made this choice then there must be a strong reason behind it. What is it Shaurya?'

Shaurya did not want to tell her the truth. She would never approve of his decision. Moreover the King might get to know his intensions through her. That would be disastrous! He would have to lie!

'The King wants to settle scores with Veera for the embarrassment at the archery competition. So he sent the declaration of an invasion. I didn't want unnecessary bloodshed just for the purpose of satisfying his ego. Therefore I challenged Veera for a duel. That's it!' he said briefly. He kept his tone expressionless lest his mother should suspect his reason. But Arunadevi was not convinced with it. She knew her son better than that.

'But Shaurya—'

'Mother, everything is decided about this duel and it will happen at the said time and place. Nothing can stop it now. I don't want to discuss anything more about it!' said Shaurya firmly. He stormed out of the hall without looking back.

'You can run away from me but not from yourself,' whispered Arunadevi. She knew he will not be able to hide the truth for long.

***

Achuta's heart skipped a beat seeing him. He made his way through the crowd dressed in white dhoti and white sleeveless kurta. The kurta did not have the disciplined look of a warrior attire which was his usual appearance. Rather it gave him a casual rugged look. He did not carry his sword today. But she was well aware that he had his dagger hidden under the red angavastram tied to his waist. His short wavy hair was unruly and windswept unlike other men who had a little longer hair and they usually kept it neatly oiled. He easily walked through the crowd as the soldiers made way saluting him. He kept searching for someone in the crowd and Achuta could easily guess who it was. She let out a sigh in longing!

Dhruva continued scanning the gathering at the central square in Virpur. People had gathered to celebrate Holi, the festival of colours. Large containers containing coloured water had been placed there. Large plates with turmeric and vermillion were also kept. Nobody had begun applying colours to each other as yet. The high priest of the Vishnu temple was performing the puja for the festival. Only when he finished it, people could start playing with colours. Most of them were dressed in white as was the custom. The royal family was present at the gathering. Vidyut waved at Dhruva from a distance. He waved back at him and once again looked around, but did not find Veera anywhere. He stood there waiting for the puja to be completed. Once it was over King Devarata began the celebrations by applying vermillion to Queen Lakshmipriya and Prince Vijayendra. They both returned the gesture. The crowd cheered them enthusiastically. But Dhruva was least interested in it. His eyes still kept looking around frantically.

'Searching for me?'

He was startled by the voice and immediately turned around. A smiling Veera applied the vermillion tilak on his forehead. Then she lightly smeared his cheeks with it. She was dressed in a similar attire like his. The expression of shock still remained on his face.

'Where were you all this while? I was so worried.'

'I was hiding from you. I wanted to give you a surprise and the expression on your face was indeed worth the effort,' she replied with a childish grin. Dhruva could not help smiling back. He softly rubbed his palms on her coloured palms and then applied the vermillion on her cheeks.

'May this Holi, fill your life with colours,' he wished her affectionately and embraced her.

'I wish you add more colours to your life,' she said softly. He released her and noticed the shadow of grief on her face. He wanted to say something but before that someone had splashed coloured water on them. Surprised, they turned to see Vidyut standing there with a pitcher. He winked at Dhruva mischievously.

'I am not going to spare you!' roared Dhruva chasing him. On the way he filled a pitcher of coloured water and ran through the crowd. Veera stood there watching with a smile on her face. Then the women and men alike began splashing colours on each other and exchanged good wishes.

Veera also enjoyed playing with colours. She applied colour to Sinhika and other soldiers. It was a festival which everyone celebrated with joy. Achuta too took part in the festivities but she always kept an eye on Dhruva. His dress was now wet and stained with colours. She decided to make a brave move today. The colours masking her face boosted her confidence. She took some turmeric and went to him. He was splashing colours on a few soldiers with Vidyut. When she went near him, he was surprised. He could not recognize her. Achuta's heart was pacing.

'May this Holi, bring you happiness, my lord.'

Before she could run out of her courage, she quickly applied turmeric on his face and turned to flee from the place. But Dhruva quickly grabbed her wrist. She was completely taken aback by his response. He pulled her closer. Her heart was literally fluttering. She locked her eyes with his. Dhruva took some turmeric from the plate nearby and applied it on her cheeks.

'May this Holi colour your life,' he said with a smile. Achuta was spellbound by the turn of events. Then he let go of her hand having completely beguiled her. He again went about playing with colours. She slowly placed her hand on cheek, trying to feel his touch. The moment he had touched her, felt heavenly. For the first time she had felt life course through her! Achuta closed her eyes standing there in an attempt to hold onto that moment forever. Deep down she knew this was the closest she could ever get to him…

Vidyut gulped down the remaining Bhang from his earthen pot. Bhang is an intoxicating drink made especially during this festival. Men drank Bhang as per the custom. But it was more of an amusement than custom. He was feeling light-hearted. Dhruva was seated next to him and he also was savouring his drink. Every now and then his eyes flitted across to the place where Veera was enjoying Holi. Vidyut signalled the attendant to refill his earthen pot.

'It must be hard, isn't it?'

Dhruva turned at him baffled.

'Hmmmm? What?'

'Letting her fight in that duel,' he said gesturing at Veera with his eyes. Dhruva's body stiffened.

'Hard? It's killing me!'

'You know you could have stopped her.'

'I know… but this is what she wants,' said Dhruva looking at Veera with a tortured expression.

'Her decision is only going to give you both pain. I don't doubt Chief Veera's skills but you know better about her chances of winning this duel. She is unparalleled in archery but in sword fighting? That too against an excellent and ruthless warrior like Prince Shaurya! Will you be able to forgive yourself if something happened to her? You don't have to do this Dhruva...'

Vidyut placed his hand on Dhruva's shoulder. Surely Bhang was showing its effects and helping Vidyut open up.

'I don't have to but I want to Vidyu... the woman you see there has endured more pain than any of us can ever imagine. She has been making sacrifices every single day just to keep up that one promise she made her father. She never had a say in his decision. The decision to fight in this duel is the only one she has ever made! This is what she wants... at least for once Mithra wants to be in control of her life. I don't want to ruin it. If I impose my wish on her, then there won't be any difference between me and her father. I also will be giving her pain like him. She is way too precious for me and I cannot hurt her. I will always stand by her decision even if it spells doom for me,' he said still looking at Veera. She was lost in her merriment. His heart was heavy with anguish.

'Don't you think you have to be more pragmatic?'

Dhruva laughed at his words. Vidyut frowned at him.

'You don't seem to understand us. There is nothing pragmatic about the bond I share with her. It is not just extreme adoration but far beyond that!' he said his eyes burning with intensity. Vidyut was completely astounded by his words. He knew there was nothing more he could do to convince Dhruva. Vidyut just gave up! Dhruva finished the contents of his earthen pot and then stood up.

'Leaving so early?'

'It is getting dark and I don't think it's safe for Mithra to stay out in this crowd for long. Moreover if I stay any longer, I will certainly get drunk!'

Vidyut smiled at his reply.

'I won't argue with that! I know both of us too well to think otherwise.'

'You enjoy the day. Also keep an eye on the surroundings. I will see you tomorrow.'

'Actually I want to discuss a few things about the weapons before we head to the palace tomorrow. I will come to your home and then we can go together,' said Vidyut standing up.

'I am not going home now. I am going to Guruji's home. You can come there tomorrow.'

Vidyut eyed him with disbelief.

'Are you staying with Chief Veera?!'

'Yes. I can't leave her alone especially when I know that she will be….,' said Dhruva swallowing hard. He could not finish the sentence.

'I want to spend every moment with her as long as she is here.'

'But Dhruva, people will not understand it. Gossips will spread like wild fire in the kingdom!'

'Like I care! I don't give a damn about what they think. People always talk behind our backs no matter what we do! But that has never bothered me until now nor will it ever dither me hereafter,' he said casually.

'I know… well see you tomorrow,' said Vidyut at last seeing the futility of any further discussion on the issue. Dhruva gave him a nod and left. He walked up to Veera and whispered something in her ear. She looked at him with a smile. Then taking leave from others present there they both left the celebration, hand in hand. They did not look like two people who knew they could be separated forever within a few days' time. They walked like they had all the time in the world to live together, hand in hand forever…

***

The night was gloriously dark. It was a no moon night. He did not carry a burning wooden log or a lamp with him. Though he could not see the path, he still knew he was moving in the right direction. He noiselessly passed behind the stables, down the narrow uneven path. Then he knew he had reached the spot when it strongly smelt of garbage and dung. It was the place meant for dumping waste which would later be used as manure. Yet he did not flinch at the odour, he was so accustomed to it that it no longer mattered to him. Faultlessly he reached the tamarind tree at the far end of the dumping yard. To confirm that he was at the right location, he moved his hands around the bark of the tree. One, two, three, four, five… he counted the holes on the bark. Smiling smugly he began clearing the garbage under the tree with a wooden stick. After some time he could feel the surface of the iron door. Slowly he tapped on the door in a specific sequence. There was complete silence for a moment. Then there was a tapping noise heard from the other side of the door in reply. Once again he tapped on the door to give a coded reply. After a few moments he heard a slow screeching sound. The iron door opened downwards, he quickly looked around and jumped through the opening after confirming that there was no one around. The tunnel was dimly lit. Holding a small lamp was Prime Minister Agniverma. He quickly closed the door and locked it by placing a metal wheel in the groove and turned it right and left in a peculiar sequence. The door was now secured. Agniverma placed the metal wheel back safely into the folds of his dhoti near his dagger. He turned to face the masked man.

'Reveal yourself!' Agniverma ordered softly.

The man untied the cloth from his face and bowed to him.

'I hope you didn't attract any attention on your way, Ghana.'

'No, my lord. I have been extremely cautious.'

'His Highness is here. Follow me.'

Agniverma started walking through the tunnel.

His Highness is here! This must be really big.

Ghana was surprised. Until then he had taken orders only from Agniverma at this place. Though he only delivered orders on behalf of the King, he never mentioned the King's involvement. But today the presence of King Kritiverman himself there was really astonishing.

King Kritiverman was seated on a boulder in the tunnel. There was a small lamp burning a few feet away from him. Ghana bowed to him bending as low as he could. Kritiverman gave him a cursory nod.

'Will he be able to finish the task?' he asked Agniverma unsure.

'He is one of the best, my lord. Till this day he has carried out our orders successfully,' assured Agniverma. The King looked at Ghana critically.

'This time you have to complete this task without even the slightest mistake. Even a small error could lead to huge losses. There is too much at stake to go wrong!'

'Just command me, your Highness. I will finish it even if I have to gamble with my life!' said Ghana loyally.

'You have to kill a person who does not belong to our kingdom. Can you?'

'I have done this in the past also. Who is it, my lord?'

King Kritiverman let out a long drawn breath.

'Veera... Chief Veera of Virpur!' he said at last. Ghana was astounded.

'Pardon my impudence, your Highness. But isn't she the one whom his Highness Prince Shaurya has challenged for the duel?'

'Yes... the same one.'

'My lord, but—'

'Ghana your job is only to carry out orders and not analyse them!' scolded Agniverma.

'I am sorry, your Highness. It will be done.'

'Don't underestimate your target Ghana. It's not so easy. Commander Dhruva always shields her. If you have to reach her, you will have to first get through him. So seize the opportunity when he is not near her.'

'I will do as you say, your Highness,' replied Ghana seriously.

'Be careful and finish this as soon as possible. There is no much time left!' warned the King.

'I will your Highness.'

'Take this as a token advance. You will be rewarded generously once you complete the task successfully,' said Agniverma and tossed a pouch of gold coins into his hands. Then he gestured Ghana to leave. He bowed to the king greedily and followed Agniverma. After a few moments he returned having secured the iron door.

'Is this necessary, my lord? We all know that Prince Shaurya will surely win this duel,' said Agniverma with hesitation. King Kritiverman gave him a stern look.

'This is not just about winning the duel Agni. Shaurya didn't challenge Chief Veera just to make amends for our defeat in the archery competition. I know him too well to buy that explanation! He has some hidden motive behind this challenge. Shaurya didn't reveal it even to Aruna. I don't trust his decision to agree to this. Kings wage wars and not let their princes to fight some ridiculous duel with a woman! He has made a mockery of our kingdom. The only way to salvage the situation is by not letting this duel happen. We have to invade Virpur and establish our prowess. That can be possible only if Chief Veera is eliminated!' he said acidly.

'What if Prince Shaurya gets to know?'

'Under no circumstance should he even get a whiff of this plan. Shaurya is unpredictable and will go to any extent to get what he wants.'

'You need not worry my lord. Prince will never know about it,' assured Agniverma.

'Agni I really hope everything goes as planned. The duel should not happen at any cost because if it does nothing will remain the same after that. In Shaurya's life, Veera is a storm which can only spell destruction and it is better he stays away from her,' said a tormented Kritiverman. His instincts have never been wrong about his son. Though Agniverma was not sure if the King was right, he still empathized with him. Agniverma was also against the duel, but still it was not a reason enough to justify this deed.

***

Sinhika slowly lit up all the lamps inside her home. She had washed her face and neatly braided her hair. She had draped a plum coloured sari and tied a small string of jasmine flowers around her braid at the top. Sinhika had cooked some rotis, rice and curry for dinner. One more time she looked at herself in the mirror with a slight smile. Then she went and sat down on one of the steps on the porch, waiting for her husband.

It was a breezy evening and the moon was up in the sky. Sinhika liked the feel of cool air on her skin. She rubbed her hands to warm them up and her eyes fell on the fading henna on her hands. It reminded her of her wedding henna. Only this time she had applied it for Holi. Instantly the memories of her wedding flooded her mind. It had just been a little over two months since her wedding. She had seen Vidyut during her days as a soldier under Chief Veera. He had accompanied Veera and Dhruva most of the time. But she had not spoken to him. When her father decided to get her married, it was Veera who suggested Vidyut's name. Today Sinhika is happily married. This would not have been possible had it not been for Chief Veera.

Chief Veera…

Suddenly a shadow of grief enveloped her face. Though Sinhika had started liking Vidyut, she still hesitated to open up with him. The initial days of awkwardness in a marriage was still present between them. She knew that Veera was going for the duel but had never brought herself to discuss it with her husband.

Just then she heard the noise of hooves and she quickly looked up. It was Vidyut. She smiled as she stood up. He dismounted from his horse and tethered it at the small shed inside the compound of his horse. Walking to the porch, a smile spread across his face. He was pleased to see her. She looked beautiful and it felt good to see her after a tiring day of work.

'Sini, its cold outside. Why are you sitting here?'

'I was… waiting for you.'

An expression of surprise crossed his face.

'I am sorry that I couldn't come home early. I was held up in the artillery,' he said apologetically.

'You don't have to be sorry. I was a soldier too. I know how demanding the work is. I can understand. Let's go in,' she said and walked inside. Vidyut felt a sense of relief. It was indeed easy living with Sinhika. She was a simple woman and most of all she also was a soldier. She neither demanded explanations for his late arrivals nor did she complain about it.

They finished their dinner in silence. Sinhika was not a very good cook but she was not a bad one either. She was still in the process of learning to cook. But that did not make Vidyut like her any less. He was sitting on a wooden chair relaxed.

'Do you want anything else?' asked Sinhika.

'No. my stomach is full.'

She turned to go but he held her hand.

'Sit with me...' he said expectantly. She obliged not because she could not refuse him but because she also wanted to spend time with him.

'You are looking very beautiful today, Sini,' he said intensely. She blushed at his words. Sinhika was sitting on the wooden chair near him. He angled his chair such that they were facing each other.

'Sini, I hope you are comfortable here. I know I haven't been able to give you time but my work demands complete attention now, given that Chief Veera is practising for the duel most of the time,' he said and let out a sigh. Sinhika knew this was the right opportunity.

'Shall I ask you something?' she asked timidly. He leaned in towards her and took her hand in his.

'I think I need to keep reminding you that we both are married. You don't have to take my permission. Just ask...'

He squeezed her hand gently.

'Why should Chief Veera agree to this duel?' she asked looking straight into his eyes. Vidyut's soft expression suddenly hardened.

'Because Prince Shaurya challenged her,' he replied flatly. Sinhika could notice the change in his stance. But she did not stop because she wanted answers.

'But should we let her do it? What message will it send out to other kingdoms? It will only be projected that men in our kingdom are cowards who can't protect their land!' she pointed out. Vidyut let go of her hand and abruptly stood up. She also stood up hurriedly.

'Sinhika, none of us forced Veera to do it. Even Dhruva couldn't stop her!' he said barely controlling his temper.

'This is not right...'

'Damn it! Who care about what is right or wrong? All people worry about is their own survival! I don't want to discuss more on this,' he thundered and stormed out of the place into his bedding chamber. Sinhika stood there paralyzed by the impact of his anger. He had never been rude to her until then. Her eyes welled up but she tried hard not to cry. She simply walked out.

Though Vidyut had angrily come into his bedding chamber, after a few moments he regretted his behaviour. He decided to apologise when she came in. but when Sinhika didn't come in even after a long time, he came out looking for her. She was sitting on the steps of the porch placing her head on her folded knees. Vidyut sat beside her.

'Hey…' said he softly placing his hand on her shoulder. She immediately stood and tried to go inside. He quickly stood and grasped her wrist. Vidyut stood in front of her and took her face in his hands.

'Sini… I am sorry. I shouldn't have been so rude to you,' he said affectionately. She looked at him with her distraught eyes.

'I am sorry too,' she whispered. He smiled at her nodding his head.

'Don't be. I can understand what you feel. But we have to accept the truth.'

She agreed with him though she did not like the truth.

'So, have I been forgiven?' he asked with mischief.

'Yes.'

Sinhika smiled at him lovingly. They both looked at each other for a moment. Slowly Vidyut's eyes burned with intensity. She blushed. He leaned in closer to her and she lowered her eyes. He kissed his wife on the porch with the moon watching them unabashed. This beautiful intimacy washed out all the awkwardness between them. Two strangers with different ideologies had become inseparable now. This is the magic of marriage!

***

CHAPTER 24

'I thought you didn't like milk with turmeric…' said a frowning Veera taking the copper glass from Vani. Dhruva was strapping his sword to his waist.

'Of course I don't like! That is for you, not for me. So drink it,' he said engrossed in his work. She smiled at Vani and drank the milk. Ever since Dhruva had started staying at her home, Vani too joined Nila and worked with her there. She gave her a polite smile and handed the milk boiled with jaggery for Dhruva. He quickly gulped down the milk. When he turned, he saw Veera keenly looking at her sword which she had inherited from her father. She cautiously moved her finger along the blade.

'You will have to sharpen it before the duel.'

'I know… that way he will have clean cuts,' she said still examining her sword.

'I don't care about his wounds! It's just that sharper swords help you make more number of cuts easily,' he said shrugging his shoulders. Veera gave him a patronizing smile. She had always been taught to respect her opponent. Moreover she felt that she was honoured to have Prince Shaurya challenging her. Therefore Veera showed some courtesy towards Shaurya. But Dhruva was never bound by any rules. He did not let go of any opportunity when he could make his contempt for Shaurya obvious. This was nothing compared to his hatred for Shaurya which was bottled up in his heart.

Nila walked in from the garden.

'My lady, Major Vidyut has come,' she announced.

'Major Vidyut? That's surprising… let's see what news he has got for us,' wondered Veera.

'Actually I told him to come,' said Dhruva looking up.

'But why?'

Before he could answer Vidyut walked inside.

'To accompany you for the practice, Chief,' answered Vidyut. Veera stood up at once, anger and surprise writ on her face.

'So you are not coming with me?' she asked in a controlled voice crossing her arms across her chest.

'No. I am not coming,' he replied flatly. Vidyut frowned at him. He thought Dhruva had already informed her about this.

'Give me one good reason!' she demanded. Dhruva let out a long drawn breath.

'I have not been to the army camp for some time now. My spies have reported that other kingdoms are likely to take advantage of your duel and mount a surprise attack. Though we don't have solid information, we should still be prepared. If both of us don't go to the camp then it won't serve the purpose. So I have to go.'

Veera eyed him critically. But the expression on his face was indeed sincere. Yet she found it hard to believe him. What if he was actually speaking the truth? Either way, it was better if he went to the camp. Moreover Vidyut also was a good warrior and she could practise with him though he was not as good as Dhruva.

'Fine. Go to the camp. I will see you in the evening,' she said at last. Dhruva nodded with a smile which did not reach his eyes.

'Take care Mithra. Don't hurt yourself.'

He said it with earnest concern. Veera looked at him for a moment and then turned to Vidyut.

'Let's go Vidyut.'

She walked towards her horse.

'That was a smart lie,' remarked Vidyut once Veera was out of the house.

'I had to come up with something clever for her to believe.'

'But you won't be able to keep up the farce for long.'

'I know. I just need some time to be able to accept the truth that she indeed is going into the duel alone. I have to prepare myself to be able to stand that helplessness...' said Dhruva closing his eyes in pain. Vidyut could see the hardship his friend was going through. Dhruva ran his hand through his unruly hair and opened his eyes.

'Stay with her. You will bring her back to me, safe.'

It was a subtle order. Vidyut nodded his head in assent and hurried out lest Veera should be waiting for hm. He did not want her to suspect Dhruva's intentions. At least not yet.

Dhruva looked down at his right hand. His eyes fell on the leather wristband with the bow and arrow engraved on it. He ran his fingers over the wristband. It felt like she was holding his hand...

***

Shaurya let out a breath of exasperation as he entered the bedding chamber. He closed the doors behind him. Hurling his angavastram to the floor, he quickly eased out of his blue silk kurta and tossed his gold amulets on a low table. He looked around the room. Obviously it was not as big as his own royal private chamber in Indragiri. In fact its size was just a little over the quarter of his bedding chamber. Yet it had a comfortable bed and a bathing chamber. There were ornate windows and ceiling. Though the walls were just plain. But that hardly bothered Shaurya for he never obsessed about interiors of a place, as long as it was comfortable. He walked onto the balcony and stretched out on the floor though there was an easy chair there. He lay there star-gazing trying to shut his mind out from the merriment happening in the banquet hall in the other end of the palace.

King Kritiverman, Queen Arunadevi and Prince Shaurya had come to the kingdom of Madhupur, the previous day. They were special guests of King Chitraksha. They had come to attend the wedding of his son, Prince Prahasta. King Chitraksha and King Kritiverman had been allies for some years now. This wedding served as a wonderful opportunity for Chitraksha to propose the wedding of Prince Shaurya and his daughter Princess Pritha. Even King Kritiverman wanted their friendship to be strengthened by this bond. It would seal their deal forever. Usually Prince Shaurya did not attend such events. Shruthamanyu accompanied the King on such occasions. But now it was inevitable that Shaurya continue to do it. Moreover he did not want to irk the King beyond what he had already done. Shaurya wanted to now play safe with the King, at least until the duel. The two Kings had already decided that Shaurya would wed Pritha. It was not a bad proposal except that Prince Shaurya was unaware of it…

This morning, the wedding commemorated at the royal palace with grandiose. Kings had arrived from far and wide along with their families to bless the couple. They all were accommodated in the eastern wing of the palace meant for the guests. King Kritiverman introduced his family to King Chitraksha and his family. Shaurya congratulated Prince Prahasta and greeted Pritha warmly. She was indeed a beautiful Princess. She was more than sweet while greeting Shaurya. Though he noticed it, he did not give it much thought. He was used to being treated special by women. In the evening the King had organised the grand feast for his guests in the banquet hall. The Kings were busy drinking and interacting with each other to make some strategic gains. The young princes were boisterously drinking and enjoying the feast. There were beautiful attendants and dancers keeping them engaged. Shaurya was a sport and enjoyed himself though he was not interested in any of it. When he was moving around talking to the other princes, briefly his eyes caught Princess Pritha staring at him. He gave her one of his charming smiles and moved ahead. Pritha smiled back as she blushed at him. After some time the merriment went to an extent where Shaurya could no longer stand it. He quietly slipped out of the banquet hall unnoticed.

There was just a little over a fortnight left for the duel. Shaurya closed his eyes and Veera's image filled his mind. The way she stood there with the bow in her hand on the final day of the competition made him breathless even now. The tear on her cheek in that Shiva temple, still bothered him. Above all the image of her when she left him on that night beside the fire filled his mind. That was the last time he had seen her, those enigmatic kohl-rimmed eyes…

'Don't you like this chair?' asked a sweet voice interrupting his reverie. Shaurya quickly opened his eyes and saw Princess Pritha standing before him. He stood up at once.

'I think we did our level best to make our guests comfortable. But if you are not happy with it then I will have it replaced according to your preference.'

He gave her a pleasant smile.

'Please don't take that trouble Princess. I am comfortable here. It's just that I like the floor more.'

'Don't you think lying on the floor is a little unorthodox for a Prince?'

'I am everything that a Prince should not be,' he said wryly. Pritha was baffled by his words but she kept the smile on her face. He was not very happy to have her interrupting his solitude.

'May I know what brings you here, Princess?'

'Can we go inside and talk? I don't want people gossiping about how boring Prince Shaurya is to have left the feast midway,' she said smirking.

'Or rather you don't want people talking about how Princess Pritha was alone with Prince Shaurya. I think that would make an interesting gossip,' he teased her. Pritha just frowned at him and walked inside. He followed her.

'Would you like some wine?'

'Yes indeed. Thank you.'

Pritha poured wine from the brass jug into two intricately designed brass glasses. Shaurya sat on the bed and she handed him a glass. She sat on the wooden chair facing him and took a sip.

'You still haven't answered my question,' said he sipping the wine. She looked at him and hesitated for a moment.

'I saw you sneaking out of the banquet hall. I was curious as to why you would do that when all other princes were enjoying the feast.

'Well, there were so many princes in the hall. What made you keep looking out for me?'

Pritha slightly turned crimson at his words. She thought he was just teasing her.

'I am interested in only that Prince who would be marrying me...'

Shaurya was surprised and baffled.

'I beg your pardon Princess. But what made you think that I would marry you?'

Pritha was offended by his words.

'Prince if this is a joke then it certainly is in bad taste,' she said sharply. He frowned at her in confusion.

'I have no intention of offending you. I really don't know what you are trying to tell me.'

Pritha looked at him critically. Shaurya had an earnest expression of confusion on his handsome face. But how could he be unaware of their wedding proposal?

'Prince Shaurya, aren't you aware that King Chitraksha and King Kritiverman have decided to get us married? This wedding today served as an opportunity for us to get to know each other better.'

Shaurya was shocked! Now he clearly understood why he was being given special attention by the King and his family, especially by Princess Pritha. He placed the unfinished wine glass on the table and ran his hand through his hair. Pritha looked at the change of expression on his face and her heart sank.

'I am sorry. I didn't' know anything about this,' he said honestly. There was complete silence for a moment. Then Pritha regained her composure.

'I hope you are not opposed to our wedding.'

Shaurya closed his eyes and let out a long drawn breath. He knew he was going to break her heart right there.

'I don't want to marry. I am sorry,' he said flatly without beating about the bush. Pritha froze! He had rejected her! She could not believe it. She never imagined that he would refuse to marry her! The beautiful Princess of Madhupur! There were many princes vying to be her husband, a few had even expressed their intentions directly to her. But Pritha had very politely and diplomatically handled such situations. When her father had told her about Prince Shaurya, she was genuinely interested in him. She had eagerly waited to meet him. When Pritha first saw Shaurya, he looked way better than she had imagined. The charm he exuded had actually swept her off her feet. Pritha had almost fallen in love with Shaurya…

'Why?' she asked looking straight into his eyes. Her eyes were burning with the pain of rejection and anger.

'Princess Pritha, I had no idea about this proposal. Had I known, I would ever have come here. I would surely have made my decision very clear to King Kritiverman. I never meant to hurt you.'

'You have hurt me Prince. You owe me an answer at least. Tell me why won't you marry me? Am I not beautiful? Why do you think that I can't be your Princess?' asked Pritha not giving him a chance to escape from her questions. She was not going to let him go until he answered her. Shaurya had no choice.

'It's not you, it's me,' he said slowly and stood up looking away from her.

'What do you mean?'

'You are indeed a beautiful princess. You are graceful and I am sure you will make a worthy wife. But I can't marry you because I will never be able to value your love. I cannot be a good husband. I won't be able to keep you happy and I don't believe in a marriage where staying together actually gives us pain.'

'What makes you think so? You don't even know me,' she argued.

'You are right. I don't know you but I know myself. All I am trying to say is that I am not the one for you!'

Princess Pritha stood up at last. She had one last question for him.

'Who is that princess in your life?'

Shaurya turned to look at her immediately.

'Don't look so shocked Prince Shaurya. If you are refusing to marry me then there has to be a strong reason for it. For me, it's not very hard to guess the reason. Who is that princess?'

Shaurya smiled at her wryly.

'She is not a Princess…'

'Interesting! I have heard tales about your unpredictability, but today I saw it for myself,' she said swallowing hard.

'I am sorry…' whispered Shaurya again. She looked at him and smiled slightly. He was indeed a man of compassion.

'You are a good man Shaurya. I really appreciate your honesty with me. I have never met a man who could value a woman's heart like you. I will certainly carry this pain of not marrying you, for a long time,' she said, a tear sliding down her cheek. Shaurya felt pathetic for causing her so much pain. He walked up to her and placed a hand on her cheek wiping her tear.

'Your tears are very precious. Don't shed them over a man who can never be a part of your life. You deserve a better man Pritha. A man who will value your love and who can love you forever. I am not that man,' he said tenderly. She closed her eyes feeling his hard hand on her cheek. She was overwhelmed by the urge to hold onto him. He was the first man she had ever allowed to come so close to her. For a moment she completely forgot that she was a princess. Instantly she moved forward and kissed him for a fraction of a moment. Shaurya dropped his hand taken aback. Pritha stepped back and opened her eyes.

'I will never forget you... the man who broke my heart,' she said intensely and strode out of the bedding chamber. He never thought his day would end like this. He clenched his fist as anger against King Kritiverman boiled in his heart. Though unintentional, Shaurya had become the reason for Pritha's heartbreak. This made him hate the King even more. Still Shaurya would never know the depth of pain he had given to Pritha by breaking her heart.

***

CHAPTER 25

Vidyut gasped in horror. His heart was beating fast and his body soaked in sweat. He moved his eyes down gingerly. Veera's sword glistened in the sunlight. The tip of her sword was touching his throat. Her eyes were blazing and she was breathing hard. After a moment the wild excitement subsided from her eyes and her lips curled into a smile. She withdrew her sword and grinned at him. Vidyut relaxed and gave her a smile picking up his sword.

'You win, Chief,' he said sitting on a boulder in the clearing.

'Thank you,' she said smugly. Veera was indeed happy with the way she had fought today. She made Vidyut drop his sword and even before he could move she had pointed her sword to his neck defeating him.

'So what do you think about my performance today?'

'Get some water!' yelled Vidyut at one of the ten soldiers who had accompanied them. The soldier brought a leather case of water and handed it to Vidyut. He drank some and gave it to Veera. She drank greedily as she quenched her thirst.

'You fought well Veera. But there is one thing I am not happy about. You are out rightly offensive in the duel. Your defence is weak,' he pointed out. She frowned at him and thought about it. Maybe he was right. Vidyut was not a very skilled swordsman. So she never gave much thought about defending herself. She used every opportunity to surge forward and make him defensive.

'I am not very attacking in my approach. So you could easily go for the kill. But with Prince Shaurya it will be completely different. He will be more than eager to make killer moves. If you don't master defence then you will be prone to injuries... start working on being defensive too,' he advised. Veera listened to him keenly absorbing every word that he had said. Then she looked at him with curiosity.

'Vidyut, what more do you know about Prince Shaurya?'

'I have never seen him but heard a lot about him from reliable sources. He is a beast when it comes to sword fighting. His sword is his fifth limb! Wielding a sword is second to his nature. He has been ruthless in battles and wars.'

There was a slight flicker of fear on Veera's face. Then instantly a new feeling of determination replaced it.

'I am honoured! An impossible opponent for an interesting duel!' she said zealously. Vidyut had to admit that he indeed admired her courage.

A soldier walked up to him hurriedly and bowed. Vidyut knitted his eyebrows in surprise. He was not one among the ten soldiers who had accompanied them.

'Why are you here?' he questioned sternly.

'Major, his Highness Prince has sent a message for you to be present at the royal palace as soon as possible.'

Vidyut and Veera stood up.

'Did his Highness tell the reason for this?'

'No Major. I was ordered to escort you along with me right away.'

Vidyut thought for a moment.

'Chief Veera I have to leave now. If you have finished your practice for the day then I will come along till your home and then go to the palace.'

But Veera refused.

'You are right about my defence, Major. I have to practise more. You may go. I will leave only by evening,' she insisted.

'As you say Chief. I will take five soldiers along with me and leave the rest for your protection.'

'That'll do.'

Vidyut saluted her. Then he left the place riding on his horse along with the soldiers. The five soldiers left behind spread along the clearing. Veera decided that she would rest for a while and then resume her practice. She began biting into the fruit that the soldier had brought for her. The clearing was quiet except for the branches and leaves of trees swaying in the occasional breeze.

Ghana watched keenly as Vidyut and his men left. His eyes were now fixed on Veera. Except the five soldiers spread out in the clearing, she was alone. He and his accomplice were hiding behind thickets surrounding huge boulders. Four of his men were strategically placed around the place. They could see the happenings in the clearing but nobody would be able to spot them from there. They all had dressed in green coloured clothes so that they could not be easily spotted.

'My lord, this is the right time she is alone without him,' whispered Ghana's man.

'Yes. Dhruva was always with her but today he is not here. Yet he might come here anytime if he gets to know that Vidyut has left. We have to finish our job as soon as possible. There should be no mistake, we won't get another chance like this,' hissed Ghana.

Ghana and his men had entered into Virpur a week ago. They had entered in the garb of shepherds, merchants and also two of them as saints. They had kept a watch on Veera and acquainted themselves with her routine. But they soon discovered that their task was indeed a very difficult one for Dhruva was always with her. Ghana had initially planned to kill Veera in her house at night when they could easily overpower her guards. But he realised that this plan would indeed be a failure, when one of his men saw that Dhruva stayed with her. As a result, even Dhruva's guards were stationed at her house. There was no way they could fight that many soldiers without creating a ruckus. Moreover facing Dhruva would certainly have been fatal for them. At last Ghana decided to wait and watch. They kept a hawk's eye on Veera for the right opportunity. Today was their day!

Ghana slightly nodded at his man. He let out a screech which sounded almost like a parrot. The other four men became alert and kept their weapons ready. Veera did hear the screech but she actually mistook it for a parrot. She did not find anything amiss. Only three of his men carried bows and arrows. The others including himself had a sword and a dagger. Those were the only weapons they had managed to smuggle into Virpur. Ghana felt they were more than enough to take on Veera. Two of Veera's soldiers had bows and arrows. The other three carried only their swords. He decided that the men with bows had to be killed first. Then it would be easy for him to outnumber and overpower them. Since this was an unplanned attack in the clearing as he actually did not expect Vidyut to leave Veera, he had to make the first move to guide his men. He wanted to take on Veera with the element of surprise.

'Shoot her,' he whispered to his man. The archer released the poison-tipped arrow from his bow. But due to it passing through the leaves of a bush it diverted from its path slightly. That would have gone unnoticed had it been someone else. Veera was way too familiar with the sound of a whooshing arrow. Reflexively she fell on her back from the boulder and the arrow missed its target.

'Damn it!' cursed Ghana. It was indeed a colossal mistake. He was very certain the arrow would get her except that he never expected her to respond like that. His other two men with the bows released their arrows and killed Veera's archers unerringly. She was astounded. Even before she could sit up on the ground, two of her men were down. She sat hiding behind the boulder and assessed the situation quickly. The directions from which the arrows had been shot confirmed the presence of three men. But she was certain there would be more. The remaining three soldiers had drawn their swords and were ready to fight looking around the clearing to spot any movement. Veera knew she had to act quickly. One of her archers had died just a few steps away from her. Luckily there were a few boulders and bushes which could help her crawl to up to him. Still there were chances of at least one of the arrows to get her. If they wanted to kill her then they would first try to kill all her soldiers. So the next round of arrows could be aimed at them. She had to take this chance.

Veera quickly crawled up to the archer and a moment after she laid her hand on the bow, the next round of arrows were released. Veera heard the sound and yelled.

'Down!'

The three soldiers went down on their knees at once. Two arrows missed their targets but one pierced through a soldier's arm. Veera knew he would survive. She quickly knelt on one knee and released an arrow towards the direction of one of the archers. The arrow pierced through his abdomen and he tumbled down from his hiding spot. Ghana was shocked. He was quite sure Veera could not see them, then how did she aim at his archer accurately? Now, she and her soldiers were not clearly visible to them as they were partly hidden behind those boulders and bushes. He became desperate to kill her as he knew this could be his only opportunity.

'Out!' he cried. All his men stormed out of their spots towards the clearing. Veera shot an arrow in the direction of Ghana's voice but it missed him. It hit the leg of the archer who was with him. The two archers who were now out of their hiding spots could clearly see her soldiers. Their arrows took down two of Veera's men. Now there was just one soldier left with her. She quickly loaded another arrow to the bow and shot at one of his archers. Ghana was out in the clearing with his two swordsmen. But Veera did not shoot at them. She used the last arrow in the quiver to shoot the archer whose leg she had injured. He fell dead on the ground. The lone soldier with Veera pounced on one of the men and engaged him in sword fighting. The other man and Ghana ran towards her with their swords drawn. The accomplice flung his dagger towards her but she deftly dodged it. Veera could not take her sword as it lay near the boulder she had been sitting on, some time ago. Now there was no way she could go near it. Ghana and his man closed the distance between her and them. From the corner of her eye she saw that her soldier had been injured and was on the verge of getting killed. He would not come to her help. But Veera quickly pulled out the dagger from the folds of her dhoti and flung it at the man fighting her soldier. It pierced his chest and incapacitated him. It was a neat throw. Veera knew she would have to use her martial arts training to save herself and she could not have killed with her dagger, the two men running towards her with their swords drawn. They would have easily moved away from it. Rather than wasting that attempt, she used it to save at least one of her soldiers. She indeed saved him but he was too injured to move. Veera stood there ready with clenched fists to punch in killer blows when they got closer to her. But there was very little hope. Without any weapon fighting two armed men was next to impossible. But she was certain she would not go down before giving a tough fight.

Veera stood rooted to the spot. She waited for them, channelling all her energy to her fists. For a moment Dhruva's image clouded her eyes.

'Dhruva...' she breathed and cleared her eyes. Ghana's man swung his sword trying to behead Veera when he got closer. She bent low and punched really hard into his gut. He let out a bloodcurdling cry and dropped his sword falling back holding his abdomen. Yet it was too late. Ghana caught up with his man and slashed a cut on her arm that had punched. She stumbled back a few steps with the pain. He inched forward with malice in his eyes. Veera quickly bent down and picked up the fallen man's sword and held it in her unhurt left hand. She stood up ready to fight him single-handed. For a moment, Ghana stood there in awe of his opponent, a woman for the first time! Her eyes were spewing fire with no trace of fear. Veera took advantage of his distraction and swung her sword which superficially cut his torso, tearing through his green kurta. Ghana was brought back to his senses and he furiously wielded his sword. Veera matched his moves but with difficulty as she could use only her left hand. At one instant the sword slipped out of her tired and aching hand. Quickly Veera fell on her back to avoid his sword cutting through her torso. A vicious smile appeared on his face. She was down and there was no way she could escape now. Veera knew it too. But she did not fear death. Her eyes still held the same fire of challenge. He lifted his sword to go for the kill. Veera looked into the eyes of her murderer defying him. She was going to die and she was not ashamed of it. Even in her last moment she would die defying a man…

Whoosh! Whoosh!

Veera heard the sound even before she could see the arrows. Two arrows consecutively pierced through the upper torso of her murderer. His sword dropped to the ground and he fell beside her without even being able to scream. Another arrow was shot at the man whom she had punched in the gut. Veera was astonished. She could not believe her eyes. Just a moment ago she was certain she would die. She quickly sat up and looked at the spot where her injured soldier was lying. He was still half unconscious.

Then who shot these arrows?

Veera quickly turned around and saw him. He was standing there with a bow in his hand. His long beard had been trimmed a little. His hair had been tied up into that characteristic bun on his head. The man was bare chested and had worn the saffron dhoti. His ochre upper robes were missing, exposing his rippling physique. His eyes were burning with rage without even a trace of the usual serenity they always held.

'Rudra...' whispered a stunned Veera.

***

'There has been some amount of blood loss. But let me clean your wound first. Most of the time an unclean wound appears a lot worse than it actually is,' said Sankha looking at Veera's wound on her right arm. Though Rudrapriya had tied her angavastram around the wound to prevent blood loss, she had bled along the way to Sankha's ashram. The only way to immediately get medical help for Veera and the injured soldier was to take them to Sankha. Though Veera was hurt she could still manage to ride a horse. Rudrapriya carried the soldier and helped him mount a horse. He also got onto that horse and rode to the ashram. There were a few cottages housing Sankha's students and his family in the ashram. The remaining cottages were meant for treating the sick and the injured. The soldier was being treated in one of these cottages. Sankha had assured Veera that he would survive though he had sustained many wounds. Now he was tending to her wound in another cottage. Rudrapriya sat on a wooden stool placed near her cot. He had borrowed an angavastram from Sankha and wrapped it around his torso. The tranquillity was back in his eyes but he still looked slightly disturbed. He did not take his eyes off Veera even once. She sat there on the cot leaning against a pillow. She was hard as a rock. She did not look shaken from the incident that had almost killed her. Sankha began cleaning her wound but she did not flinch even a little. It was like her whole body had become numb. Suddenly she looked at Rudrapriya.

'What were you doing there?'

He outstretched his legs and leaned back against the wall.

'I usually meditate in the forest. Unusually I heard the noise of hooves and saw Vidyut riding out of the forest with a few soldiers. I wouldn't have given it much thought, but one of the soldiers looked back for a moment and then rode away. I was curious and started walking in that direction. Then I saw some birds flying out of the trees at a distance. I knew something was happening there. Later, I heard you screaming. Quickly I rushed to the clearing. When I reached there I saw dead men first. Then I saw you deftly flinging your dagger to kill the one fighting your soldier. The other two scoundrels were running towards you. I knew I wouldn't be able to save you if I took the sword because I was too far to reach you. By the time I laid my hands on the bow and arrow, you had punched one of your opponents and you were bravely fighting the other. But you fell to the ground and I moved a little further to be able to clearly aim at him. Then I released the arrows,' said Rudrapriya as a matter of fact. He made it sound so casual as though he was just commenting about the weather. Sankha looked at him in awe. This man was no less a warrior, except that he did not have the insolence.

'Your aim was good,' appreciated Veera.

'I have been trained in archery,' he said shrugging his shoulders.

'Thank you. You saved my life,' she said with heart-felt gratitude.

'I did what I had to. My presence there was purely by chance. You shouldn't have taken such a big risk. Why were you alone with a meagre five soldiers guarding you?' asked Rudrapriya rebuking her.

'I didn't go to the clearing alone. Vidyut was with me.'

'But he did leave you later. Why didn't just go back with him?'

'I wanted to—'

'Wanted to kill me along with you!' roared Dhruva barging into the cottage. Veera looked at him startled. His eyes were wild and his body taut with tension. His eyes fell on her wounded arm and he clenched his fists.

'Bastards!' he swore.

'Dhruva listen to me...'

She was trying to calm him. He gestured with his hand to stop her. He looked around at Sankha, Rudrapriya and Sankha's two assistants in the cottage.

'Leave us alone,' he ordered in a cold tone.

They walked out quietly. Rudrapriya glanced back at Veera once and then stepped out. He could see the change in Veera once Dhruva was before her. That hard rock, now had life blooming in it...

Dhruva slowly walked up to her, his eyes filled with anger and affection. She looked at him with relief and excruciating pain. He stood near her and held her head to his chest. She wrapped her unhurt hand around his waist. Tears streamed down her cheeks. He wrapped his hands around her securely. Veera felt safe again.

Sahana L.

'I thought I would never see you again. I knew I was going to die...' she said choking on her words.

'I am sorry,' he said in a painful voice.

'Four of my guards died for me today and the one I barely saved is battling for his life! My hand gave up very soon on the sword. He was towering over me and raised his sword to thrust it right into my chest. I could do nothing. I almost died...'

Veera was sobbing like a child. Now she was not that brave warrior who had fought strong men just a few hours ago. She too felt vulnerable and wanted to be protected.

'Ssshhh... you are safe now. I am not leaving you alone,' said Dhruva rubbing her shoulder to soothe her. He held her that way until she stopped sobbing. After some time Veera calmed down. The incident had indeed traumatized her but she never let her emotions out until Dhruva came. It was only with him that she never hid her emotions. She did not pretend with him nor did he.

Dhruva released her from his hold and sat on the cot before her, holding her unhurt hand.

'I am sorry I didn't come with you,' he said tortured.

'Don't blame yourself. It was not your fault.'

'Of course it's my fault! I lied to you!'

Veera let out a sigh.

'I knew it,' she said coolly. Dhruva was startled.

'Then why didn't you question me?'

'For what? I can understand why you did that. Dhruva, I didn't want to make you feel more miserable than you already are. When you do something I know there is always a reason behind it. There was no need for questions.'

'I am so sorry...' whispered Dhruva closing his eyes in agony. Veera withdrew her hand from his and stroked his cheeks affectionately.

'Don't be. You did nothing wrong. You sent Vidyut and the guards with me. This was something waiting to happen... either way we weren't prepared for it. It was an unexpected incident.'

'I will never forgive myself for this!'

Veera gave him a stern look.

'Stop your self-loathing Dhruva! I am not going to hear another word against you. Moreover this incident has actually tested my skills effectively. Now I know what I need to work on. So it was not all that bad,' she said with a weak smile.

'You have been incredible today! You are a born warrior Mithra but just stupid enough to not believe it. You are always my brave tigress!' he said with a smile. She grinned at him but suddenly her face contorted as pain shot through her right arm.

'Aahh!' she gasped. Dhruva was distraught.

'It's hurting you a lot! Let's quickly get Sankhaji to treat it,' he said urgently.

'It's paining a lot Dhruva.'

He stood up and bent down holding her face in his hands. He looked straight into her eyes.

'This pain won't last long. You are going to be fine Mithra. Trust me!' he said ardently. His words actually gave her strength to tolerate the pain. She nodded her head in agreement. Dhruva quickly went out and came back with Sankha and his assistants. Rudrapriya followed them inside. Before going out Sankha had actually cleaned her wound and applied medicinal paste to stop the blood loss. He once again took a keen look at the wound. Dhruva was eagerly waiting for him to talk, standing next to Veera.

'Veera, the cut is deep. If I only bandage it, healing will not occur. Rather it could cause more infections. I have to suture it,' said Sankha with a detachment demanded by his profession.

'As you say Sankhaji,' she agreed. Dhruva squeezed her left hand reassuringly.

'I will give you a concoction to drink. It will make you unconscious and you won't feel any pain. You will partially regain your consciousness after a day. After two or three days you will completely regain your consciousness. But it will take more than a week for you to start using your hand.'

Veera was flabbergasted.

'Sankhaji, that is too long to recover! I can't afford to lose so many days. Is there any other way to speed up the process?' she implored. Dhruva looked at her in disagreement. But he did not object to her. He grudgingly agreed with her that she indeed had to get better soon. Sankha glanced at Dhruva once.

'This is the only way we can reduce your pain. Yet there is a way you could get better soon but I have to warn you that it will be a lot more painful.'

'Just tell me what it is,' she said adamantly.

'I can suture your wounds without making you unconscious. The concoction given to make you unconscious actually slows down the healing process. If I don't give it, your wound will heal faster and you can use your hand after about just three days. But the pain will be worse than you can ever imagine.'

Dhruva could not let Sankha do it.

'Mithra you should let him give you the concoction. I don't want you in more pain.'

'Please don't object Dhruva. You know how important this is for us. We don't have much time.'

'But Mithra you—'

'Do it,' said Rudrapriya who was quiet until then. Dhruva shot him an irritated look.

'You have no right to say it!' he shot back.

'Don't be rude to him. Had it not been for Rudra, I wouldn't be here now,' she scolded.

'I agree and I will be ever grateful to him but that doesn't qualify him to interfere!'

Rudrapriya remained unperturbed and calm.

'Let Sankhaji do it Dhruva. It is better for both of you. Veera should learn to tolerate pain and you should get used to seeing her in pain.'

Dhruva was not convinced. He looked at Veera and he knew how much she wanted it. He let out a long drawn breath.

'Go ahead Sankhaji,' he said and sat on the cot beside Veera. He wrapped one hand around her shoulder and held her left hand in the other.

'It will be over soon,' whispered Dhruva and kissed her forehead. She rested her head on his shoulder and outstretched her wounded arm for Sankha. When he began suturing her wound Veera shut her eyes tightly and her lips were set into a hard line. Dhruva tightened his hold on her and a tear slid down his eye. Rudrapriya looked at them incredulously.

She didn't let out a cry so that he wouldn't know how painful it was for her. Yet he is enduring more pain than her!

How can you love a person to an extent where you no longer differentiate between yourself and the one you love?

***

Shaurya opened his eyes with difficulty. His eyelids were heavy and they protested from opening. After some struggle he succeeded. He sat up on the bed with a throbbing head. Looking around he was unable to recognise the room he was in. His kurta was lying on the floor and his dhoti was untied. The room was dingy with very little light inside. Only one lamp was still glowing.

'Shoot!' cursed Shaurya and tied his dhoti around his waist. Empty liquor earthen pots were lying on the floor. The cotton sheets on the bed were messed up. He tried hard to remember about last night but the headache was making it impossible. Yet it was not hard to guess what must have happened.

Who was with me last night?

He let out a sigh and walked into the small bathing chamber.

After talking to Princess Pritha, Shaurya could no longer stay there. He was furious at King Kritiverman. He traded his clothes with his trusted guard. The Prince wore the attire of the soldier and slipped out of Madhupur that night. He had ridden on Vayu, so it was not hard for him to leave the place quickly. He knew that the whole kingdom was still revelling in the celebrations of the wedding. His absence would not be noticed at least until morning. It was a two-day's journey from Madhupur to Indragiri. Shaurya rode hard for a day and covered considerable distance. He stopped just twice to let Vayu drink some water and graze. He ate some fruits on the way. After a day's journey he reached a dingy inn, little outside the border of Indragiri. He was half a day's journey away from his palace. But Shaurya did not want to go home. He wanted a break from all the stressful events that had occurred in the past few days. The inn was not a very decent one. It was actually for thieves, robbers, dacoits, murderers and some soldiers who were in search of wild excitement. It was a dark place with vicious people enjoying hard liquor and prostitutes. A place not meant for people who lead a decent life and no way could a prince even think of stepping into it. But none of it hardly mattered to Prince Shaurya!

Shaurya pressed some gold coins that he was carrying into the hands of the heavy man who managed the inn. He happily gave Shaurya a room to stay and assigned a beautiful attendant to serve him. He drank the hard liquor without any restrain. It made him forget his problems at least for a few hours. He drank so much that he was not even aware of where or with whom he was. Shaurya wanted to lose himself somewhere, so that nothing ever bothered him. A beautiful woman beside him only made it too easy to get lost…

Shaurya walked out of the bathing chamber. He had bathed in cold water. He wore the same dhoti he had worn the previous day. He picked up his kurta and wore it. His head was still aching. He ran his hands through his wet hair in irritation.

Damn it! How could I do this?

Regret and guilt filled his mind. Just then the creaky door opened and a beautiful woman walked in. She was dressed in a pink sari of sheer fabric. She gave him a lopsided smile and handed him an earthen glass full of buttermilk.

'Not bad! I expected you to sleep through the day,' she said in a low voice. Shaurya could now remember that she was the one who had served him yesterday. She walked to the window and drew the curtains apart. Bright sunlight shone into the small room. The bright light hurt Shaurya's eyes. He held his hand reflexively before his eyes and turned away from it. He sat on the bed and drank the buttermilk. It eased his head a little.

'What is your name?'

She turned to look at him. She was struck by his features. Last night the dimly lit room had done no justice to this handsome man. He was such a misfit in that dirty place!

'Hardly matters! Some call me Shlena!' she said with an edge to her voice. He let out a long drawn breath.

'About last night, I am sorry,' he said earnestly. Shlena was surprised at his words and laughed softly.

'Don't be. I am not! Last night was pure amusement except for the part where you kept calling me Veera.'

Shaurya was astonished.

'Did I say that name very often?'

'Often? Your every sentence ended with that name. You spoke really lovely things but I know all those were meant for her.'

'Crap!' he cursed under his breath and dropped his head into his palms.

'Your lady love is really lucky!' said Shlena with jealousy colouring her tone. He let out a sigh and stood up.

'I have to go now.'

Shaurya handed some gold coins to her.

'I really wish you would come back sometime but I know you won't,' she said with a smile. He quickly strode out of the room. He walked to the stable where he had tethered Vayu. But there was a man standing near his stallion. It did not take him long to find out who it was.

'Let's go,' whispered Ashwasena as Shaurya neared him. They both mounted their horses and rode away into the afternoon. Once they were inside Indragiri, Ashwasena stopped by the river bank. Shaurya dismounted from his horse. They led their horses to drink water. Shaurya washed his face and drank some water. Ashwasena stood near him, impatience clearly writ on his face.

'What the hell do you think you were doing Shaurya?' he demanded. Shaurya sat down on the river bank.

'King has decided to get Princess Pritha married to me. I straightaway refused to marry her when she came and spoke to me. I could no longer stay there. I was disturbed...'

He was staring at Vayu as he spoke.

'So? Just because you were disturbed, you recklessly walk into some dingy inn. Do you even know what sort of a place it is? Why can't you just care for our life?'

Ashwasena was speaking in a raised voice. Right now he was speaking to his friend and not the Prince. He was clearly enraged by Shaurya's thoughtless attitude.

'I just needed some distraction. I drank hard and—'

'And bedded some whore for the night!'

Shaurya stood up and glared at Ashwasena.

'Last night was a big mistake, Ashwa! I was completely drunk and out of my mind.'

'That is surprising! You have never admitted it as a mistake before. What happened now?' he asked intensely.

'The whole time I believed I was with her…'

'Who?'

'Veera,' whispered Shaurya. Ashwasena was shocked. He did not know what to say next. Shaurya had changed.

'What are you doing Shaurya? This is utter foolishness. You are a Prince and she is the Chief Commander of your enemy kingdom. There is no way she can ever be yours. Why don't you just understand this?'

'I know that everything you said now is true. But it's my heart which refuses to accept it. Whatever! I feel miserable…,' he said closing his eyes. Ashwasena went to him and squeezed his shoulder.

'Do you think what you are doing is right?'

'I know it's wrong. Had there been another choice, I would certainly have chosen it! But now, this is the only opportunity for me to get her. I will do everything it takes to have her in my life…,' he said fiercely. Ashwasena always knew that the Prince was strong willed. He always got what he wanted. Love complicated his obstinacy further. Nothing could stop Shaurya!

***

CHAPTER 26

'Bastard! I would have torn him into pieces had he been alive!' said Dhruva fiercely, looking at the dead murderer. The previous day after Dhruva got to know about what had happened in the clearing, he had sent a few soldiers to guard the corpses. He wanted to personally take a closer look at the place. He stayed with Veera in Sankha's ashram after her wound had been sutured. She was in extreme pain. He did not leave her side even for a moment. At night Sankha gave her some medicines which could make her sleep. But the pain persisted. Dhruva felt his heart squeeze every time her face contorted in pain. He so wished that he could take all her pain! For Veera, having him by her side, gave her strength and support to go through the ordeal. Sankha said that she would have to endure so much pain for another day and then her wound would start healing, gradually reducing her pain. He insisted on Veera staying in his ashram for two more days so that he could personally tend to her. Dhruva did not want to take any chances and he too stayed with her. It did raise many questions but he was not the one to budge.

In the morning when Veera was still asleep he left the ashram with a few soldiers to the clearing. Vidyut was already present there inspecting the corpses with his guards. Dhruva had told Rudrapriya to also come there. He arrived a few minutes after Dhruva. The three of them now stood looking at the man whom Rudrapriya pointed out as the one who had attempted to thrust his sword into Veera's chest. Dhruva clenched his fists as raw anger flashed across his face. Vidyut bent down and checked the wrists of the corpse. There was no sign of any tattoo.

'They don't belong to any army. Must be mercenaries,' he said looking at Dhruva. He did not look at Vidyut. Dhruva had not spoken to him ever since he came. Vidyut knew he was very angry with him.

'Not any random mercenaries. They had been sent here with the sole purpose of killing Mithra. Maybe this attempt was not well planned. But they certainly had been well prepared for this,' said Dhruva still looking at the dead man.

'There could be more men of their group still roaming around in the kingdom. We will have to increase security for the Chief.'

Dhruva glared at Vidyut.

'Oh really? I think that was the reason why I sent you with her yesterday. Had you not left her, none of these low lives would have even neared her!'

Vidyut stood up, offended by his words.

'I had to go to the palace immediately. I even insisted on the Chief coming along with me so that I could leave her at home and then go. But she didn't agree to it. It was not my fault, Dhruva.'

'A hell yes! It was indeed your fault!' roared Dhruva. Vidyut did not speak back and lowered his head. Dhruva was admonishing him in front of Rudrapriya and all the soldiers present there. Dhruva ran his hand through his hair in frustration and let out a long drawn breath.

'Vidyu, you know I can't bear if something happened to Mithra. I would have never let her come here without me had it not been for you. I trusted you with her safety. I am disappointed...' he said in a lower tone. Vidyut looked up at him.

'I am sorry, Dhruva. I should have been more careful.'

'I really hope you will not repeat it. Send the corpses of our soldiers to their respected families. Bury these mercenaries according to the rituals. Mithra insisted on it. Otherwise I would have burnt them all alive,' he said coldly. Vidyut set out to follow his instructions. Dhruva keenly inspected the place with Rudrapriya. He was about to touch an arrow used by the mercenaries when Rudrapriya stopped him.

'Don't touch these arrows. They are poison-tipped. The venom used is very potent. Even a small cut can be dangerous. That is exactly why one shot was more than enough to kill a man.'

Dhruva nodded his head and did not touch the tip. He checked to see if he could find any mark or engraving on the arrow but found none. Then he went around and closely observed the faces of each and every mercenary. He could recognise none.

'They all must have come into Virpur at least a few days ago. Our guards couldn't suspect even one of them. How can there be such a huge security lapse?'

He was irritated. Rudrapriya smiled at him wryly.

'Maybe there was no lapse. Either someone from your kingdom must have purposely overlooked or even worse, decided to help them.'

Dhruva looked at him startled. But he did not deny. There was no way he could disagree with him, for not everyone liked Veera in Virpur. He gave a serious thought to Rudrapriya's suggestion. Just then Vidyut came to him.

'The bullock carts have arrived and the soldiers have placed the corpses in them. I will go with them and finish the work. Anything else Dhruva?'

'Nothing more. You may leave. I will see you later.'

Vidyut left with the soldiers and the carriages.

After complete inspection of the place Dhruva decided to leave. He started walking towards his horse when the scholar called out to him. He stopped in his way and looked at him quizzically.

'We need to talk.'

Dhruva frowned at him but agreed. They both sat on the boulders facing each other.

'What is it that you want to speak about, Acharya?'

Rudrapriya looked into his eyes.

'What is it between you and Veera?'

Dhruva smiled at him slightly.

'As far as I know, you can very well read people's minds. You must have figured it out pretty much the very first time you saw us together,' said Dhruva slowly.

'I don't read minds Dhruva. I simply observe their eyes and actions. People usually give away subtle clues when they communicate. I have learnt to pay attention to those signs and it makes it easy for me to gauge the person in front of me.'

Dhruva looked at him puzzled.

'Do you mean to say Mithra and I are hard to read for you?'

'Individually you both are not very complicated. But when you are together, your bond is unfathomable. The more I try to understand, the more complex it gets. I want to hear it from you...'

Dhruva let out a long drawn breath and looked into the distance at the jungle.

'The first time I saw Mithra, I was dumbstruck in the battlefield. She wielded Guruji's sword. When he had made me promise to take care of her in his absence, it was a commitment I willingly made. His death struck me like thunderbolt! He was a fatherly figure to me. I cried until there were no more tears left. But I knew I had to compose myself to support her. When I went to see her, she was sitting there like a rock, not a single tear shed. I spoke to break her stance and then she sobbed like a child... but that day we both were nothing but orphaned children. She leaned on my shoulder and wept for a long time. After a few hours I realised she had fallen asleep. I slowly rested her head on my lap. I could have made her sleep on the bed but I didn't do it. I was scared that the moment I move her away from me, the grief would overwhelm me. I feared that emptiness and loneliness. Her head on my lap reminded me that I was not alone. Her presence kept me sane...'

Soft breeze blew over their faces. Rudrapriya was keenly observing Dhruva. He did not intervene.

'That was the first day I spent with her. The next morning when I woke up, she was no longer a stranger to me. It felt like I had known her since a very long time. Mithra was the strength for me to go through the toughest day of my life until then. I went to her every single day. Mithra was the one whom I could get back to at the end of the day. I knew there was someone to whom I mattered. I had someone whom I could call mine. I don't know when exactly she became a part of me. Mithra is like the air I breathe...' said Dhruva earnestly.

'Do you really think you both would have still shared this bond even if you had not made that promise to Agneyastra?'

Dhruva looked at him with a flicker of doubt. There was silence for a few moments.

'Yes. We would still have been the same even without the promise. I cannot think that we could have been any different. There was nobody else for us. One single day had orphaned us both. Maybe the promise made it a lot easier for us,' he said thoughtfully. Now Rudrapriya was going to shoot his most important question.

'Do you love Veera?'

Dhruva looked straight into Rudrapriya's eyes.

'I love Mithra beyond anything. She is everything to me.'

Rudrapriya stroked his chin, deep in thought.

'People have raised questions about your relationship. Doesn't it bother you? Don't you want to give it a name?'

Dhruva laughed at him wryly.

'Why should we? I don't care about what others think. When you give a name to a relationship it limits the number of ways in which you love that person. In every relationship there is some amount of mystery. Be it between friends, between lovers, between a husband and wife or even between a mother and child! Everyone have their share of secrets to keep their relationship alive. But we both know the darkest secrets about each other and yet nothing changed between us. We don't pretend to each other because we know no matter what we do, we won't leave each other. She accepts me as I am. There is no need for explanations.'

Rudrapriya took some time to comprehend his words.

'But you do fight with each other, don't you?'

'Of course we do! We argue a lot. There are so many issues that we don't agree on. But we don't grudge each other for that. Together we come to a conclusion and sometimes it is painful for both of us. But it doesn't hurt as long as we are together in it.'

'Dhruva, don't you think this amount of vulnerability is dangerous?'

'Nobody wants to be the vulnerable one in a relationship. It makes the other powerful enough to push you into pain. People always use power to their advantage. Between us, we have seen each other's vulnerability in the worst possible circumstances. That level of trust is hard to achieve. I know that she is the only one in this world who can hurt me the most. No matter what happens, I know she will never let go of me and neither will I. Yet I trust Mithra with my heart knowing that she is the only one who can break it. That is because she will never do it!'

Rudrapriya looked at Dhruva in awe. He had never seen any man and woman share such a bond before.

'I am glad you let me see into your bond with Veera. You both are indeed special. People may never understand because they cannot even imagine that such a bond can ever exist between a man and woman. You bond is between two individuals who are equals and not between a man and woman.'

Dhruva looked up at the sky and closed his eyes.

'We don't belong to each other, Acharya. Mithra and I are a part of each other.'

Rudrapriya smiled at him serenely.

'I was right. You both are two halves of a single entity. One has no meaning without the other.'

Dhruva smiled back at him. Looking at the sun he realised that he was running late. He had been away from Veera for a long time and she must have woken up by now, still in pain. He immediately stood up to leave.

'I really have to go now. It is very late already.'

Rudrapriya stood up and nodded at him.

'One more thing Dhruva, don't leave Veera alone now on. You will always be with her. Don't trust anyone when it comes to her safety, not even Vidyut,' he said sternly. Dhruva thought for a moment. He knew that Rudrapriya clearly did not trust Vidyut.

'I won't leave her alone, Acharya. Even now I left fifty of my most trusted and efficient guards at the Ashram for her security. I left her because I really had to take a look at this place personally. I will guard her every moment,' said Dhruva deeply. He touched Rudrapriya's feet to seek his blessings. Dhruva then mounted his horse and rode away. Rudrapriya let out a sigh and looked up.

They both deserve to be together. Why is life so unfair?

He stood there as the cool breeze blew around him. That was the only answer he could get…

***

The sun had just risen in the horizon. The chirping of the birds was musical in the air. Slowly Indragiri was coming to life. But the guards and the attendants were bustling about their routine in the royal palace. Shaurya was in the quadrangle, practising martial arts. He had tied the cotton dhoti tightly around his waist and it reached only up to his knee. Small streams of sweat adorned his back and chest. He was rigorously practising. It was so strenuous that it hardly looked like a routine practice. Rather it looked like he was punishing his body! Shaurya was trying to forget his night at the inn two days ago. He was indeed punishing himself for his mistake. He stopped after some time, nearly breathless. He sat down on a stone bench there breathing heavily. His torso was soaked in sweat. The rigorous physical exercise actually made him feel better. He untied the angavastram from his waist and wiped his face. Then he wiped his neck and chest. The cool morning breeze was soothing. He closed his eyes and savoured the moment. Just then he felt someone sit next to him on the bench. He quickly opened his eyes and was dumbstruck to see the man next to him.

'Shaurya…' said the King slowly. Shaurya immediately stood up to leave the place.

'Shaurya wait! I want to talk to you.'

'We can talk in the royal court, your Highness,' he said acridly.

'I am here to talk to my son, not the prince.'

Shaurya's anger came unleashed from his heart. He turned to look at the King with hatred filled in his eyes.

'Son? Your son died long ago… actually the truth is, you killed him!'

King Kritiverman gave him a defeated look.

'Why are you doing this to me Shaurya? Do you really want to see me in pain? Is that why you are doing this?'

'No. But it sure is comforting to see that the man, responsible for my brother's death, is actually pain.'

Kritiverman let out a sigh. There was no use arguing with Shaurya over the past.

'I am here to talk about Princess Pritha,' said the King standing up.

'There is nothing to talk about her. I won't marry her. I think you got my answer the moment you realised that I had slipped out of the palace in disguise, that night.'

'Give me one good reason for your decision,' he demanded. Shaurya still maintained his cool demeanour.

'Of course I have my reasons. But I don't have to tell that to you!'

'Watch your words, Prince Shaurya! Don't forget that you are talking to the King,' he glared. Shaurya gave him a sneer.

'Really? I thought you were here to speak to your son. Good for us, that you realised you are no longer my father.'

King Kritiverman clenched his fists in frustration.

'You are a Prince, start acting like one. The people of our kingdom always look up to us. You should show them that you can make commitments. You should prove that you can shoulder responsibilities. You have to marry Princess Pritha!'

'Do you really think I will agree to this?'

Kritiverman lost his temper.

'Why don't you understand Shaurya? King Chitraksha has been our ally for a long time. This wedding will bind our kingdoms together forever. We will get unconditional assistance from him in every battle and war that we fight. This is a diplomatic way of—'

'To hell with your diplomacy!' roared Shaurya. He threw his angavastram to the ground.

'You are so greedy for power. You will do anything for it! You will never change. I was right! I will never regret saying that you killed my brother!'

Shaurya stormed out of the place. King Kritiverman sat on the bench quietly. He stroked his chin deep in thought. Arunadevi covered her mouth with her hand and sobbed quietly. She had heard everything, standing behind a pillar unseen by them. It never felt like a conversation between a father and son even for a minute. The two men she loved so much, could not stand each other.

***

'Aahh!' screamed Veera in pain. Dhruva stumbled back on his feet.

'Excellent!' he exclaimed with a victorious smile. But she hardly noticed it. Veera dropped her sword and held her bandaged arm tightly. Pain pierced through her hand. Dhruva dropped his sword and ran to her side.

'Nila! Vani!' he called out as he held her hand. The two attendants quickly rushed to the spot.

'Nila get that medicinal paste which Sankhaji gave. Also get clean cotton cloth. We have to replace this bandage. Vani take back the swords and place them safely in their scabbards,' ordered Dhruva hurriedly. They both immediately followed his orders. He made Veera sit on the wooden swing. Dhruva writhed seeing her face contort in pain.

'Mithra, don't worry. Your pain will subside once I apply the medicine. This won't last for long, just a few more moments. Nila! Come fast!' he yelled impatiently. Nila rushed there with a bowl containing the medicine. Dhruva quickly removed the bandage from her hand.

'It hurts,' breathed Veera. But this pain was not new to her. Sankha had actually warned her beforehand, but no amount of preparation could reduce the pain. At least now she had learnt to tolerate it better. Yet for him, every time she flinched, the pain stabbed his heart with a new vengeance. Seeing your loved one in pain was a lot worse than actually being in pain.

After spending three days in Sankha's ashram, Veera and Dhruva had come home two days ago. From the very next day itself Veera had insisted on resuming her sword fighting practice. Dhruva knew no amount of argument could convince her against it. So he obliged to practise with her. He did not want to take any chances this time. Veera wanted to strengthen her defence, so Dhruva had to attack her. The two days she had mostly defended by ducking or moving away from his sword. She could not use her sword for defence due to the injury. Dhruva knew very well that, it was not a very efficient way of defending. But today she had done exactly what he wanted her to do. Though the consequence was not very good!

Dhruva knelt on the ground and applied the medicinal paste on her injury. Veera had shut her eyes tightly and her lips were set into a hard line so as to not let out a cry. He looked up at her and felt a lump in his throat. She looked so vulnerable. Veera looked like any other delicate woman of her age. Yet she was extraordinary!

You deserve so much better than this.

He tied the cloth bandage carefully. She opened her eyes after a few moments. She was feeling better. Veera smiled slightly at Dhruva who was kneeling down. He took her hand in his hands.

'How bad is the pain?' he asked in a strained voice.

'I am better now.'

He kissed her hand lightly.

'You don't have to do this,' he implored looking into her eyes. She let out a long drawn breath.

'We have spoken enough about this. You know I won't change my mind. Every time you say this, it is only going to hurt us more because we both know nothing is going to change.'

'You are so stubborn!'

'And you never give up,' she said with a smile and stroked his cheek. Then suddenly Veera remembered something.

'By the way, why did you exclaim in joy when I shrieked in pain?'

Dhruva grinned at a frowning Veera and stood up.

'Today you have mastered your defence!'

'What? Really? What makes you say that?'

'You usually avoided my sword to defend yourself. But today you used your sword to block mine. Not just that you also managed to push me back with that contact. Given that you are injured if you could do that, then without the injury you can indeed make your opponent fall to ground with that attempt,' he said enthusiastically. Veera grinned at him overjoyed. She knew that he actually meant what he said.

'Now I am feeling confident!' she said with relief.

'Believe in yourself, Mithra. You will win the duel. I know you can!'

'I know that I can't afford to lose this duel. I can't lose you, Dhruva! I have to win for us!' she said mirroring his intensity.

'Nobody can separate us. It is going to take more than just a hare-brained fool with a sword to steal you away from me,' he said winking at her. Veera laughed at the words he had chosen to describe Prince Shaurya. Right then she heard approaching footsteps and looked back. Vidyut and Sinhika were walking towards her. She smiled at them warmly.

'What a surprise to see you Sini!'

'I was waiting eagerly to come and see you, ever since I heard about the attack on you. How are you, Chief?' asked a concerned Sinhika.

'I am as fit as a fiddle! Don't worry.'

'I am so sorry Chief…' said Vidyut full of regret. Veera let out a sigh.

'Will you keep apologising every time you see me? It's not your fault Major. Don't blame yourself. You were just doing your duty. This would have happened sometime later had you been with me that day. It was an unfortunate incident waiting to happen. We should be thankful that I survived it. Had it happened some other time, I may not have been so lucky.'

Dhruva gave Vidyut a dirty look. Words boiled on his lips but he did not spit it out. He did not want to embarrass Vidyut in front of his wife. He had still not forgiven Vidyut. Veera noticed Dhruva's expression.

'And you are not going to admonish him anymore for this. It is over and let's just forget it!'

'Forget it? Are you serious? We still have not found out the identity of those bastards,' thundered Dhruva.

'Do you suspect anyone?' asked Vidyut curiously.

'They are outsiders for sure. But they couldn't have come this far without the assistance of someone from our own kingdom. I suspect that there are still more from their gang fanned out throughout Virpur. We cannot rule out a second attempt,' said Dhruva thoughtfully.

'I'll have our men keep a close watch all around. We'll not let down our guard even for a moment.'

'I know you will. By the way Sini, I hope our Major is taking good care of you,' said a smiling Veera.

'Indeed he is,' replied a blissful Sinhika.

'Actually Chief I want to tell you that what you are doing is really great. Your sacrifice is unmatched,' said Sinhika full of admiration.

'You can make a sacrifice only when you are selfless. But there is selfishness in my decision. I am doing this for my motherland. Anyone in my place would have done the same. It's just that I got the opportunity and they didn't.'

'I doubt anybody else could do it, Chief. Not everyone has your courage. You were born special. Your name will be worshipped in every heart of Virpur. Only you deserve it!' said Sinhika idolizing the woman before her.

'Thank you so much for your adulation Sini. I really hope I live up to it...' said Veera wryly. She looked at Dhruva. He made no efforts to conceal the anger in his eyes. Sinhika did not miss the silent exchange of glances between them. Rumours about them had reached her ears too. But she never believed them. Sinhika always knew that the bond between Veera and Dhruva was beyond comprehension for a commoner. It was something as pure as the nectar in a just bloomed flower...

'Chief, I have a message for you from the royal court,' said Vidyut breaking the silence. Veera and Dhruva looked at him curiously.

'His Highness enquired about your health. He has sent fruits and vegetables from the royal garden for you. I have handed them to Vani. You have been summoned to the royal court tomorrow morning.'

Dhruva smiled wryly.

'I can see that his Highness indeed cares about Mithra. Why wouldn't he? She has literally saved his throne!' he said bitterly. Veera shook her head in disapproval.

'How many times do I have to tell you not to go public with your hatred for the King? Vidyut we will be at the royal court tomorrow.'

'We'll take leave now, Chief. I think you need some rest. I will see you tomorrow,' said Vidyut.

'Take care, Chief,' said Sinhika.

'You too Sini,' said Veera cordially. Then they both left the place.

'Now can we go inside? You must be tired,' said an impatient Dhruva.

'Yes indeed. Actually I am hungry. I can't wait to eat the fruits from the royal garden. I am certain they taste heavenly!' said Veera mischievously. Dhruva threw up his hands in exasperation.

'You don't let go of even one opportunity to annoy me, do you? Fine, let's go!' he said rolling his eyes at her.

'Come on Dhruva! You are being very hard on the King. He doesn't even know that you are his son.'

'I don't want him to ever know about it! It's not going to make any difference to me. Either way I hate him,' he said coolly. Veera did not say anything more. She knew this conversation was over. He outstretched his hand and she placed her hand in his. Veera stood up and they both walked into the home in silence. Dhruva barely cared for anyone other than Veera. For him, the only person he lived for was the one holding his hand. He would do anything to hold onto her forever.

***

CHAPTER 27

'Do you love me?' asked Nahusha looking straight at Ashwasena.

'What sort of a question is this?' he asked shocked. Nahusha had sent him a message through her pigeon to meet her at the old ruins of the stable which was usually their rendezvous spot. Ashwasena rode to the place as soon as he had escorted Shaurya to the palace at the end of the day. Therefore he was very late and he half expected that Nahusha would still be waiting for him. Usually if he did not come at the said time, she could not wait. She would write her message on the wall of the ruins and leave. But today she was determined to meet him at any cost. Though he was surprised that she had waited, he was actually overjoyed to meet her. But her very first question put an end to that joy.

'I know you don't love me!' she said critically.

'Please don't say that again Nahu! Every time you utter those words, it kills me.'

'Then why didn't you come to meet me at all? Do you know how long it's been since the last time we both met? Even today, had I not waited for you here, we would not have met. Why are you so late?'

'I could not leave the Prince before he goes into the palace. It is my duty to guard him.'

'You are so obsessed with your duty that you have no time to even think about me. Why did you even fall in love with me if you can't spare time for me?'

Ashwasena let out a defeated sigh.

'Please try to understand Nahu. There are only a few days left for the duel and I am in charge of all the arrangements. I should also assist the Prince in practising sword fighting. I have no time for myself! Despite that I came riding so fast only to see you!'

'Had your Prince not challenged her for a duel, all the soldiers would have been preparing for war! He is being ridiculously coward!'

Ashwasena glared at her.

'Mind your words Nahusha! It is because of Shaurya that the man you love will only be watching when he fights. Had it been a battle, I will be the one to die before him. It is easy for the royal court to declare a war because they are not going to fight in the battlefield. They only make decisions! But Shaurya has saved so many lives by proposing that duel. He did so because he values every life equally, be it a foot soldier or a Commander. He has given his men an opportunity to spend more time with their loved ones. Not every man has the courage to make such a decision!' thundered Ashwasena. Nahusha looked at him dumbstruck, shaken by his outburst. Seeing her shocked face, he let out a long drawn breath to control his temper. He ran his hand through his hair in frustration. Ashwasena walked up to her and held her shoulders softly.

'I am sorry Nahu. But you know that Shaurya is my best friend. He means a lot to me and I cannot tolerate a single word against him. Why don't you just understand that?'

Nahusha's eyes welled up and a tear slid down her cheek.

'Why don't you understand how much I miss you? I spend days thinking about you. All I want is to see you at least once in a fortnight!'

'I miss you too,' whispered Ashwasena and wiped her tear.

'I promise to try my level best to see you as often as I can. But always remember one thing. I love you!'

'I love you too,' she said and flung her arms around his neck. He wrapped his hands around her in a tight embrace. After a few moments he released her from his embrace but held her close.

'I will be leaving soon for the duel. So I can meet you again only after I come back...' he said softly. Nahusha's face fell in disappointment. He took her face in his hands and looked into her eyes.

'Hey... don't be sad. I will come back as soon as I can. But if you don't smile now, then I am not letting you go,' he said with a slight smile.

'Really? Then I won't smile. Take me with you.'

'I wish I could, but you know I can't. One day you will be mine forever. Then nobody can stop me from taking you with me. Until then...'

'I will be waiting for that day,' said Nahusha smiling. Ashwasena kissed her cheek. They looked at each other for a long moment.

'I have to go,' she said at last. Ashwasena let go of her with a heavy heart. She covered her face with her veil and looked at him. He could only see her eyes on her masked face.

'Take care Nahu. I will come back soon,' he assured. Nahusha nodded her head and quickly strode away. Ashwasena did not want to let her go but he had to. She was his, yet he could not reveal it to the world. Though he loved her, he was not yet committed. Their courtship would not remain a secret for long. Ashwasena knew he had to do something about it. But he decided, that he would think about it only after the duel between Shaurya and Veera was over. For Ashwasena, Shaurya mattered more than Nahusha, not just now, but always. Though Nahusha knew this, it was hard to accept.

***

The rain was pounding the earth. The thunder roared and lightning lit up the sky every now and then. It was evening. Usually it would have had a pinkish glow to it but today the sun was shrouded by the dark clouds. Yet it was not dark. Shaurya looked at the sprawling Indragiri before him. Not a soul outside in the rain! Everyone had taken shelter except him. He was seated on one of the high terraces. He held up his face to the rain and closed his eyes. The rain drops pattered on his bare upper torso and wet dhoti. But that did not bother him, rather it was comforting.

She slid her hand into his. A smile appeared on his face and he held her hand firmly. He turned and looked at her kohl-rimmed dove eyes. Those sparkling enigmatic eyes! She was not bothered about the rain either. Her lovely pink lips curved into a smile.

'Stay with me please,' he said deeply. She leaned closer and rested her head on his shoulder.

'I am not going anywhere,' she said lovingly. Even in the rain her hand felt warm in his grip.

'You are lovely, my love…' he whispered softly. She did not say anything but he could feel her smile.

'You will come with me, won't you?' he asked hesitantly.

'I will come,' she assured.

'Am I doing the right thing?'

She did not reply. There was silence except for the pattering rain drops.

'Will you forgive me?'

'Maybe,' she said promptly.

'Are you going to hate me for what I do?'

'Yes I will,' she said serenely. He was disappointed a little.

'Will you ever... fall in love with me?' he asked with his voice thick with emotion. She sat up straight and looked into his eyes.

'Will I?' she asked him doubtfully. He was quiet. There was no way she could love him after all that he would do to her. He looked at her in distress. She released her hand from his hold and placed it on his hard chest. Her warm hand felt like fire on his cold chest. It was comforting.

'Your heart is pounding. You are scared...' she said softly.

'I don't want to lose you!' he implored.

'You won't,' she said, her hand still on his chest. He pulled her closer. Her eyes widened in surprise but she did not protest. He looked at her face, so close to his. Those eyes which he always loved, those cheeks which he always wanted to touch and those lips which he longed to kiss! He placed his hands on her cheeks. They were soft as a flower. Their faces were just inches away. His breathing was heavy and so was hers. He could feel her hot breath on his skin and smell her earthy fragrance.

'I love you Veera...' he said in a gravelly tone. He leaned in closer to her and she closed her eyes. He closed his eyes taking in her overwhelming fragrance...

The lightning struck and the thunder roared! Shaurya opened his eyes. He looked around, she was not there. The rain drops hit him hard and cold. It was not dark and he could still see Indragiri below from the terrace. He let out a long drawn breath. He pushed back the wet hair from his forehead.

It cannot be a dream. It felt so real!

A weird pain was tugging at his heart. Right before the moment he opened his eyes, she was with him or so it felt. He had not felt lonely at all. But now after opening his eyes, the reality hit him hard and cold like the rain. With her, the rain was comforting. Now every drop stung him with pain. It felt too real to be a fantasy! Yet that was the truth. This was how he had started living with her. Shaurya so badly wanted to be with her. That was the difference between Veera and other women for him. Shaurya could see himself sharing his life with Veera. He wanted a future, a life with her. He was ready to do anything to have her in his life. Even if it meant pushing himself along with her into peril, he would do it.

Shaurya could no longer take the pain. He once again closed his eyes. After a few moments his lips curved into a slight smile.

He could feel the warmth of her hand on his throbbing chest...

***

'Are you ready for the duel Veera?' asked King Devarata.

'Yes, your Highness,' said Veera with a smile.

The royal court was filled with the royal family and all the ministers of court. Veera stood in the centre facing the King along with Dhruva. Vidyut was standing at the farther end of the hall.

'You have always been exceptional like your father. You have won battles for us and also that archery competition at Charanvasi for the first time ever. Now you are going to fight in this duel for our motherland. You will win it, Veera. Virpur will praise your valour for generations to come.'

'I am humbled by your words, your Highness. It is indeed an honour for me.'

Dhruva shot the king an irritated look.

'When are you reaching Kaalvan?' asked Prince Vijayendra.

'A day before the duel, your Highness.'

'Only one day before? Why won't you leave early?'

'What is the point in leaving early? She will be there a day before the duel. That is more than enough. I don't want to risk her safety,' intruded Dhruva. The Prince narrowed his eyes.

'I asked her the question, not you.'

Veera looked at Dhruva in exasperation.

'You will keep your mouth shut until we walk out of here,' she whispered to him. He gave her a lopsided smile.

'Dhruva is right, your Highness. Given that I have been attacked in our own kingdom, we shouldn't be taking chances there,' she said politely.

'Alright. All the arrangements have been made, Veera. You only focus on winning this duel. We want you to come back victorious. Virpur needs you!'

She bowed to the king respectfully.

'Veera if you want to ask for anything you can do it now. We won't refuse you,' announced Prince Vijayendra generously. Veera smiled at his words.

'I already have more than I can ever ask for,' she said looking at Dhruva.

'I have only one request to make. If I don't come back, everything that belonged to me, will be Dhruva's. He will be the heir to my family legacy.'

Dhruva looked into her eyes as she said those words. He swallowed hard and looked away from her.

'Your request will be honoured,' assured the King.

'Thank you, your Highness.'

'Tomorrow evening I have arranged for a grand feast in your honour Veera. I invite every one of you to come and support our Chief.'

'I am honoured, your Highness.'

'If he is done with his display of generosity, can we leave?' mumbled Dhruva impatiently.

'Shut up!' she whispered.

'The assembly for the day is over. You may leave and we expect to see each one of you at the feast tomorrow,' announced the Prince. Veera and Dhruva bowed to the King and left.

'This is going to land you in deep trouble,' blurted Veera once they were out of the palace.

'What did I do?' asked Dhruva shrugging his shoulder.

'You have to hold your tongue when you stand before the King. If not for the man, show some respect at least for the throne he is seated on!'

'He did nothing great to earn that place except being born as the royal couple's son.'

'I will handle the situation for you as long as I am here. But once I am gone—'

Dhruva raised his hand to stop her.

'Shut up! You are not going anywhere. You are going to come back. You are not leaving me. So don't even try telling me what I should do after you are gone,' he said sternly. Veera stood there speechless looking at him. He was not going to listen anymore. Right then a soldier came and saluted her.

'My Lady, a boy and his mother want to meet you. He claims that you know him.'

'Really? Bring them here.'

She waited curiously and Dhruva also looked in the direction of the soldier with curiosity and suspicion. After a few moments a boy and a woman were coming towards them. Veera stared hard at the boy aged around thirteen years. He smiled at her. Her eyebrows knitted into a frown.

'Do you know him?' asked Dhruva trying hard to remember if he could recognise them.

'I think... I have seen him before. But I can't remember where and when I saw him,' she said still thinking hard. The boy saluted and bowed to them. His smile widened seeing her confusion.

'I think you don't remember me, sister. It's me, Bahu.'

The name rang a bell in her mind. He had met her before her first battle as a Chief with a request to keep his father safe.

'Oh my God! Bahu! You have grown so tall!' she exclaimed and embraced him warmly. Then she released him and looked at him keenly. He had lost some weight. There was no roundness in his face. He looked leaner and his taut arms indicated that he has been training for a while now. There was no twinkle of innocence in his eyes anymore.

His eyes held a mature look of responsibility. Dhruva still looked puzzled.

'Dhruva do you remember? I had told you about Bahu before our first battle. He is that brave boy I spoke about!'

Dhruva remembered him and gave him a warm smile.

'Are you training in the army now?'

'Yes Commander. I joined the army after my father died in that battle. I am undergoing training at the Gurukul.'

Though Veera did not have any knowledge about his father, it still hurt her that he had died in the battle.

'Bahu, I am sorry I couldn't save your father...'

The boy shook his head.

'You don't have to be sorry about it. He always wanted to die a warrior. We are very proud of him. I shouldn't have made that request to you. Now that I am in the army I realise how immature I was.'

Veera looked at Bahu in awe. He had changed so much. He was a completely different boy now. Then she looked at his middle aged mother. She was short and fair. Every time she looked at her son, there was pride in her eyes. This woman had lost her husband in a battle and yet she had sent her son into the army.

How can she be so brave?

'This is my mother, Chief. She wanted to meet you,' said Bahu looking at his mother. His mother smiled at Veera and stepped forward. She took Veera's hand and bowed to her. Veera was taken back.

'What are you doing, aunt?'

'I am bowing to that woman who saved my son. Not just my son but also so many soldiers! You have saved Virpur! Had there been a war now, Bahu would have fought in it.

But now I can be with my son for some more time. Thank you Chief,' she said with heartfelt gratitude. Veera squeezed her hand lightly and smiled.

'All I am doing is my duty. You don't have to thank me.'

'Your sacrifice will not be forgotten, my child. Every mother in Virpur will bless you. Victory will be yours!'

'Thank you aunt.'

Veer then turned to the boy.

'Your father is proud of you Bahu and so am I. One day you will be a great warrior. Don't ever give up your fighting spirit.'

'I won't, sister. One day I want to be a warrior under your command and we will win battles together,' he spoke enthusiastically. Veera smiled at him. She looked at Dhruva. He had a blank expression on his face. He simply could not be so hopeful like the boy because deep down in his heart there was always the fear of losing her.

'We'll take leave now, Chief. I have to head back to my training for the day.'

Bahu bent down to touch Veera's feet to take her blessing. But she held his shoulder and stopped him from doing so. She hugged him affectionately.

'May God bless you with happiness! Take care, brother.'

Bahu smiled at her and saluted them. Veera bowed to his mother who blessed her. Then he left the place with his mother. Veera and Dhruva stood there looking at them.

'What a courageous boy!'

'Courage? I would rather say compulsion,' quipped Dhruva. Veera raised an eyebrow questioning him.

'What do you mean?'

'He would have still been the same innocent boy enjoying his childhood, had his father not died in the battle. In the name of courage we just robbed him of his childhood, his innocence!'

'But it's inevitable Dhruva. Every warrior has to endure this.'

'Why? Just because he was born to a warrior? If he had been a peasant or a goldsmith or a charioteer, wouldn't his life be simpler? We are pushing innocent children to train for a war. It's just not right!' he argued furiously.

'We do not get to choose our parents. We cannot change who we are born as.'

'All I am asking is, why should our birth decide our life? Why can't we decide what we want to become? In the name of war all we do is prepare soldiers to die!' he snapped. Veera let out a sigh and went to stand in front of him.

'So this is what it is all about…death? Everyone has to die someday.'

'I know. But it is not right to live with the sole aim of preparing to die in a war. A glorified warrior death! Just to have history sing praises about your bravery! There is nothing glorious about death. People glorify it simply to brainwash young men to sacrifice their lives. If we told them the real truth about war, then nobody would ever die in it for nothing.'

Veera smiled wryly and took his face in her hands.

'People always fear death except warriors. We are prepared to see death straight in the face. We don't run away from it. We are ready to throw ourselves into peril to save someone else. Like everyone warriors also value life. The only difference is we value others life more than ours.'

Dhruva was impressed by her explanation. She was right. But he had never thought about it like her. She had answered the question troubling his heart with so much ease.

'If I say you are my life, would you refuse to go into the duel to save me?' he asked intensely. Veera was silenced. She was quiet for a moment.

'If I say you are my life, would you let me go into the duel to save my life?' she asked with the intensity matching his.

'Of course not!' he snapped. Veera's smile widened.

'Then even my answer is a no!' she said smugly.

'You are such a brat,' she said smacking his cheek.

'You are no less,' said Dhruva with his lopsided smile. Veera stuck out her tongue at him in protest.

'Behave yourself kid! This is not our home. Damn Shaurya! Shame on him to be challenging an immature child like you for a duel,' he said mocking her.

'Oh really? Let's go back to practice. I'll show you who is a child,' said Veera pointing at him.

'We'll see!'

Dhruva was grinning at her. Together they began walking towards the stable to take their horses. It was just like any other day in their life. They were happy being together. There was no problem so big that they both could not overcome. But their days of companionship were numbered. Veera and Dhruva would walk hand in hand as long as they were destined to and maybe even after that. Their bond defied fate!

***

CHAPTER 28

'What?! She survived?' asked King Kritiverman disbelievingly. Agniverma was equally shocked.

'Yes my lord. She killed them,' said Vatsan looking down.

Agniverma and Kritiverman were in the royal chamber. The door was securely latched from inside. They both were speaking to Vatsan, one of Ghana's men. He had not accompanied them to kill Veera. Vatsan went with them only to act as a messenger for the King. On the day of the attack he was on one of the trees bordering the clearing. He was so still, watching the events that he did not make any noise. He had come to the palace to give the King the message about their failed attempt. He stood nervously before the King.

'She is a woman for God's sake! There were six men and not even one succeeded? Shame on you! Cowards!' reprimanded Kritiverman clenching his teeth.

'But that is impossible. Tell us what exactly happened there, Vatsan,' demanded Agniverma.

'They almost had her, my lord. She was alone that day except being guarded by a meagre five soldiers. But the very first arrow she dodged. The aim was accurate yet she miraculously escaped. Then she cleverly moved and laid her hands on a bow and quiver of arrows. She accurately shot arrows at our archers though I am quite certain that she couldn't see them from her position.'

'Wait a minute!'

Kritiverman was deep in thought.

'She didn't doge the first arrow miraculously. Veera knew where it was coming from. She didn't have to see the arrow, she only had to hear it. No doubt she won that archery competition...' said the King with realisation dawning on him. Agniverma looked at him baffled.

'What do you mean, your Highness?'

'Veera has mastered the art of Shabdavedhi.'

Agniverma was dumbstruck.

'That's impossible, your Highness. There are barely any men who have even heard about it, let alone mastering it. It is next to impossible for anyone to learn it.'

The Prime Minister was not ready to agree with the King.

'Who said she is not special, Agni? What happened later?'

'She killed our archers and a swordsman. She punched one in the gut and incapacitated him. But Ghana managed to cut through her arm. Yet she picked up a sword and fought him with only using her left hand. But she couldn't hold up for long. The sword slipped from her hand and she fell to ground. Ghana was about to thrust a sword into her chest, when he was shot by an arrow.'

'Who shot him? Was it any of her soldiers?'

'No, my lord. He was dressed as a scholar.'

King Kritiverman was stumped.

A scholar!?

'Who was he?' asked Agniverma suspiciously.

'Later I found out who he was. His name is Rudrapriya. He was a warrior but now a scholar, my lord.'

'How does it even matter to us? Despite all the effort, Veera survived. There is nothing we can do about that,' said Kritiverman disappointed.

'You may leave now. You will not let out even a single word about this incident to anyone. Leave Indragiri and I don't want to see you here ever again. Take this,' said Agniverma and handed him a pouch of gold coins. Vatsan nervously bowed to them and walked out.

'Veera just got lucky, your Highness.'

'No Agni. Fortune favours the brave. I really wish Ghana had succeeded in killing her.'

The King let out a dejected sigh.

'Your Highness, I still think this was not necessary. Prince Shaurya will easily defeat her and I don't think she will survive this duel. Your Highness should not worry so much about her.'

'It's not as simple as it seems to be. Shaurya certainly is reckless but he is not a fool. At least not in choosing his opponent! He has chosen Veera for a reason. We will have to soon find out what it is or else we are in trouble.'

Agniverma felt that the King was unnecessarily worrying about Veera. He could foresee no danger from her at all.

'All we can do now is wait for the duel, my lord. It is not wise to take any step without actually knowing what the danger is.'

Kritiverman nodded his head in agreement.

'Nevertheless, Veera should not survive the duel,' said Kritiverman coldly. He knew he could not trust Shaurya, who was unpredictable.

***

'How do you feel now?' asked Sankha slowly removing the bandage on Veera's right arm.

'The pain has almost reduced. But my hand still feels sore when I use my sword. It is hindering the free movement of my sword,' she said disappointed. He took a close look at her wound which had begun to heal.

'The medicine which I gave you will numb the pain and aid healing. But the soreness will persist especially if you strain your hand.'

'But it's worrying me a lot, Sankhaji. I can't go into the duel with a sore hand. It's not a wise thing to do. Is there anything at all you can do about it?'

She was sitting there with expectation but he shook his head in denial.

'I am sorry Veera. I will give you the medicinal paste. Apply it on the wound for three more days. Let's hope your pain will subside completely.'

Veera was dejected. This was not what she had wanted. The pain was affecting her mind more than her body.

Veera and Sankha were seated on a cot in one of the cottages in his ashram. One of his assistants was standing beside him with a bowl containing the medicine. Sankha took the medicine from him. A young lady rushed inside the cottage. She was slim with a fair complexion. She had draped an orange cotton sari. Her hair was tied into a knot and the free end of her hair reached just above her hip.

'Guruji, that soldier is in pain and panting for breath,' she said hurriedly. Sankha frowned.

'But he was recovering well. What happened suddenly? Where is Chirayuhastha?'

'I don't know Guruji. But we could do nothing to make him better. You have to treat him.'

He looked at Veera. He could not leave without treating her.

'Sankhaji I think you should go to him. He needs you now more than me. I shall wait,' said Veera empathising with him.

'Guruji, I will apply the medicine and bandage Chief Veera's hand,' offered the woman. Sankha thought for a moment. That was not a bad idea indeed.

'Veera, this is my student Damayanti. She is also a good doctor. She will take care of your wound. I will come back as soon as I treat him. Damayanti, take good care of Veera. You will stay with her until I come back. And Veera, you will not leave until Dhruva comes to take you home. I will be back before that.'

Veera agreed with a polite smile. He handed the bowl of medicine to Damayanti. Then he went out of the cottage with his assistant in tow. Veera smiled at Damayanti. But she looked nervous. She stood at the entrance as if she was expecting someone. Suddenly Veera was alert and suspicious. She was about to question the doctor when a man suddenly stepped inside. He was of medium build with sun-tanned skin. He was wearing a cream coloured cotton sleeveless kurta and a saffron dhoti. He glanced at Veera once and then went near Damayanti. Veera had not seen him before.

'Give it to me and leave,' he ordered.

'Why are you making me do this? Guruji trusts me so much. If he gets to know that I let you in, he is going to be so angry.'

He rolled his eyes at her.

'You know this is not wrong. Had you not believed it, you wouldn't have agreed to do this. Don't worry about him! You can say that I threatened to poison you if you didn't do as I told. I am certain he will believe the lie,' he said smirking. She let out a sigh and turned to face a baffled Veera.

'Chief Veera, this is Chirayuhastha, Guruji's son. He... he wants to talk to you,' she said hesitantly. Veera looked at him disbelievingly. He looked nothing like Sankha's assistant or even student, let alone being his son. Moreover she had not seen him even once before. He appeared to be as old as Dhruva. He had his shoulder length hair tied into a tight knot unlike Sankha whose long hair had been tied into a round bun on the crown of his head. He smiled at her warmly. Veera could not help smiling back though she still looked confused.

'Finish your work as soon as possible. Guruji might come back anytime.'

'I doubt that... don't worry dear! I will finish my work long before he comes back,' he said winking at her. Damayanti blushed and walked out embarrassed as Veera had witnessed him flirting with her. Chirayuhastha went and sat on the cot facing Veera.

'It was about you that Sankhaji was asking when she told him about that soldier. What are you doing here?'

'I am here to meet you. He wouldn't let me anywhere near you,' he said as a matter of fact. Veera looked at him knitting her eyebrows.

'Where were you all these days? I haven't seen you before in the ashram especially since I had stayed here for a few days recently.'

'I was living in Chitravan forest. I was there living with the Rathsu tribal group. I wanted to learn about the medicines they use.'

'But... Sankhaji himself has a vast knowledge about medicines. There are so many students learning about medicines under him. Being his son, what was the need for you to go there?' she asked, still not convinced. He smiled at her wryly.

'I was learning about medicine under father. But a few years ago I came across the medicine made by one of these tribal when I was in the forest to collect some herbs. It was very intriguing for me. I slowly befriended him and gained his trust. Then he let me go to their settlement deep in the forest. Their medicines are far more potent than ours. We had no access to those plants and herbs deep in the forest. So those medicines were unheard of here. I wanted to learn about them. Therefore I left the ashram some years ago and went to live with the tribes to learn. I came back a month ago,' he said letting out a sigh. Veera looked at him with a raised eyebrow.

This is interesting! Now that explains his sun-tanned skin. He must have been wandering outside in the sun given his inquisitive nature.

'I am assuming that Sankhaji is not very happy with what you did.'

'Being unhappy is an understatement. He disowned me when I said I was going to live with the tribes. He doesn't believe in their medicine. For him, they are nothing but uncivilized nomads. How can they have knowledge about medicine which he considers to be utmost sacred? According to father, medicine is something that needs to be worshipped. He simply cannot come to terms with the fact that a flesh-eating nomad can also treat the sick and injured people,' said Chirayuhastha shrugging his shoulders.

'So has he forgiven you now? Given that he has let you stay here.'

'No. He will never forgive me. It's just that he wants his son to be with him as he is getting old. Although I am disobedient, I am still his son,' he said coolly. Veera was impressed by his deeds. She could understand the rebellion he must have undergone.

'Well, there must be a reason for you to meet me. What is it?'

'I know your hand still hurts. I can put an end to it,' he said calmly. Veera was shocked.

'What?! But how?'

Chirayuhastha took a small pouch from the folds of his dhoti. He opened the pouch and held it to her. It had a brown paste with a pungent odour. She moved away her nose from it reflexively,

'This medicine can relieve the soreness from your hand completely.'

He spoke earnestly but she looked at him doubtfully.

'If what you say is true, why didn't you tell it to Sankhaji? I am sure he wouldn't have refused to this if he believed that it would work.' Chirayuhastha let out a long drawn breath.

'He doesn't trust the medicines that I suggest because they are unconventional. He won't even accept them as medicines because they defy his knowledge. He doesn't want to take chances with the lives of people with these because he has not witnessed their effects. I am not allowed to treat anyone here. I treated that soldier you saved the other day.

That was possible only because father's medicines couldn't help save him. He had given up on the soldier, but I didn't. I debated and protested to an extent where he wanted me out of this place at once. At last mother convinced him to agree saying that there was no harm in letting me treat a dying man. I succeeded and now that soldier is recovering fast,' he said smugly.

'Isn't it the same soldier that Sankhaji has gone to treat now?' she asked quickly. He gave her a mischievous smile.

'Actually it's a ruse. I told him to pretend to be in pain so that father would go to him. Damayanti is also a part of this act.'

Now, that was something Veera had not expected. He was too clever to be a conventional doctor.

'You are very smart. You proved your skill by saving my soldier. Yet why won't Sankhaji let you treat me?'

'Father is very cautious when it comes to your wellbeing. You are way too important for Virpur now. Moreover you are not dying, for him to let me treat you!'

Veera still had many questions on her mind. She was not yet convinced enough to trust him.

'I still cannot comprehend why he won't accept your medicine.'

Chirayuhastha hesitated for a moment. If he wanted her to agree then he would have to gain her trust. For that he would have to come clean with the truth.

'Actually, some of these medicines use not just plants but also animal extracts. That is what makes them so potent. But this is completely against my father's principles and ideology. In some conditions… these medicines have been fatal,' he confessed. It was very clear to her as to why Sankhaji was against him. Veera looked straight into his eyes.

'Despite all this, do you still think I should take your medicine?'

'I wouldn't be here if I didn't think so. This medicine will lead to quick healing of your wound. I have nothing against you Veera. I couldn't back out after knowing that I can cure you.'

'Chirayu, can I trust you?'

Though she was no fully convinced, she wanted to take a chance. Veera knew the importance of her hand in the duel.

'Yes,' he said unflinchingly. Veera held out her wounded arm to him. He took some paste from the pouch and pressed it to her wound. He held it in place tightly. Veera's eyes widened in horror and she gasped. The paste made the wound burn fiercely. The burning sensation radiated to her entire arm.

'Aahh!! What the hell is this? Why didn't you tell me it would burn so badly?' she shrieked at him.

'I have spoken enough to make you agree for the medicine. I couldn't risk you having second thoughts.'

Chirayuhastha pressed the paste firmly to her hand. She could no longer bear it. Veera tried to take his hand off her using her left hand. But he did not budge. She dug her nails into his skin in desperation.

'You are a rogue!' she swore.

'I know,' he said unperturbed. He placed his other hand on her left hand in assurance.

'It will last only for a few moments. Once it enters into your wound the burning sensation will subside. Calm down, Veera.'

A few more painful moments passed for Veera. She took in deep breaths to control her heartbeat. Suddenly an aghast Sankha walked in. He was furious.

'Chirayu what are you doing? Get your hands off her!'

'Father, just stay out of this. It will be over in few moments,' he replied evenly. Slowly Veera could feel the burning sensation reduce. He was right.

'Sankhaji, I agreed to let him treat me. I am sorry.'

'But Veera, it's very dangerous. If something happens to you I will never forgive him. I have no idea what rubbish he has applied to your wound!'

She could feel her pain disappear slowly.

'Feeling better?' asked Chirayuhastha ignoring his father. She nodded her head in assent. He withdrew his hand and tied a cloth bandage over the medicine.

'Flex your hands,' said Chirayuhastha confidently. Veera flexed her muscles slowly still unsure that his medicine might work. There was no pain. She stretched and folded her hand to test it. Then she moved her hand fast. There was absolutely no pain. Just to be doubly sure she pulled out her sword from the scabbard. Then with quick reflexes she swung her sword. Her face lit up with joy.

'I don't feel any pain at all!'

Chirayuhastha gave her a broad smile.

'I always keep up my word,' he said looking at Sankha. His father looked with disbelief. Sankha still thought it was just luck that it worked, there could be side effects.

'Thank you so much Chirayu! Sankhaji your son has done a huge favour for me. I am so grateful to both of you. I think we should appreciate his knowledge.'

But Sankha let out a sigh.

'He may have succeeded now Veera. But that doesn't change the fact that many have died in his hands. I still can't approve his methods. You take care my child,' he said looking at Veera. Sankha walked out after giving a hostile look to his son. Chirayuhastha stood there motionless. His demeanour was calm but his eyes looked disturbed. Veera eyed him seriously.

'Is it true that many people have died during your treatment?'

He ran his hand over his face in dejection.

'Yes... but there was nothing I could do about it,' he said in a detached tone.

'I really don't know how much it must be hurting you. You must be regretting—'

'Regret? I don't regret what I did. It's not easy to live in a forest. There are so many animals and creatures which are dangerous. People become sick or come with snake bites for which we may have no particular medicine. I tried everything I could do to save each one of them. So I don't regret that they died. If I keep worrying about the dead, I won't be able to think about those who still have a chance to live. I simply consider it as an opportunity to learn.'

Veera looked at him in awe. She had killed men in battles and seen hundreds die in a war. But she still could not help being affected by death. Yet here was a man with a noble gift of saving lives and he had managed to stay unaffected by death. It was not easy to develop that mind-set.

How stone-hearted can he be?

'Are you saying that you don't consider yourself responsible for their death?'

Chirayuhastha let out a long drawn breath.

'My father thinks that it's a boon to become doctors. He thinks that God chose him to give him the power to save lives and he is just a tool in God's hands. So neither does he take credit when he saves a life nor does he blame himself when someone dies at his hands. For him, it's all God's wish! I don't believe in it, because if I did then I would give up too soon. I am a doctor because I have worked hard to become one. So I do everything I can until the person is still breathing. If he lives it's because of my efforts and if he dies its only because I did not know what could actually save him. Either way I don't hand it over to God.'

There was silence in the cottage. Sometime ago this man was a stranger to her but now he was here revealing the details about his life. Veera was thinking how different he was from Sankha. Instantly she turned to see a surprised Dhruva at the door. His eyes were on her bandaged hand holding the sword. He quickly came inside.

'What are you doing with your sword here? And doesn't your hand ache?'

Veera swung her sword twice and grinned at him. He raised his eyebrows in surprise.

'Wow! I can't believe this! You really don't seem to be in pain. What did Sankhaji do to you?'

Veera put back her sword into the scabbard. She looked at Chirayuhastha and Dhruva looked at him baffled.

'Who is this?'

'He is Chirayuhastha, Sankhaji's son. It is because of him that I am able to use my hand without pain.'

'Really? I knew that Sankhaji had a son but I was not aware that you had come back. The last thing I heard about you was that you had gone to live in a jungle. Thank you so much,' said Dhruva with sincere gratitude.

'It is my duty. You don't have to thank me for that Commander,' he said formally.

'You have no idea how happy I am to see Mithra relieved of pain. I am very grateful to you. I really don't know how to repay for your favour.'

'Of course you can repay me right now. I am going to ask you for a favour in return. Obviously I did not put so much efforts for nothing,' said Chirayuhastha evenly. Veera looked at him slightly shocked. She had not expected him to ask for a repayment. Though Dhruva was surprised he did not let it show. He was more than eager to do anything for him at that moment.

'Go ahead and ask,' he said with a smile.

'You will have to make sure that I will accompany you and Veera to the duel and not my father as decided by the King. I need a bigger opportunity to prove myself and this could be the one.'

Veera looked at Dhruva who was now looking at her. They both were unsure about Chirayuhastha. Trusting a man with such a huge responsibility just after having been with him for a few hours, was not easy. They both knew Sankhaji well and trusted him unconditionally. But Dhruva was a man of his word and he felt indebted to Chirayuhastha.

'You can have my word, you are coming with us, Chirayuhastha.'

A smile of ultimate satisfaction appeared on Chirayuhastha's face. He was happy that his efforts had paid off.

'Thank you so much.'

They both smiled back at him.

'We have to leave now Chirayu. We hope to see you soon,' said Veera politely. Chirayuhastha nodded his head in assent. Veera and Dhruva walked out of the cottage. They both mounted their horses and rode away. The platoon of guards who had surrounded the ashram to guard Veera also rode with them.

After they both walked out, Damayanti came in. She smiled looking at a happy Chirayuhastha.

'Looks like you got what you wanted. Your plan worked.'

'Of course my plan worked! There is no way he could refuse me the favour after all that I did for Veera,' he replied with his usual smugness.

'You are very cunning, Chirayu!' she said playfully. Chirayuhastha quickly held her and pulled her closer to him. She tried hard to free herself but he wrapped his hands around her waist.

'Stop wriggling! You know I won't free you so easily. At least not until I get what I want…' he drawled in a husky voice. Damayanti blushed and her heart was fluttering. She could no longer protest. He was as untamed as the wild forest. His turbulent behaviour had swept her off her feet within the first few days of his return. Chirayuhastha uninhibitedly bent and kissed her. He kissed her passionately until she lost all sense of her surroundings and kissed him back. In that calm, serene ashram, Chirayuhastha was a fresh breath of tempest. Sankha was ready to die to uphold his principles but Chirayuhastha was born just to break them.

***

'You think this will work better?' asked Shaurya.

'This will work better in incapacitating her quicker,' answered Ayush. But Shaurya and Ashwasena were horrified. The three friends had surreptitiously assembled on the riverbank in the wee hours of the morning. It was dark and the moon was still bright in the sky.

'Then why are you suggesting me this?'

'That concoction of herbs with which I had laced your sword before, is very unstable. It will quickly lose its properties if I dilute it. I am not very certain about its effect. But the venom that I suggest now will not lose its properties on dilution. Moreover I know exactly which antidote I should use to save her,' reasoned Ayush.

'Snake venom is more dangerous, isn't it?' asked Ashwasena. Ayush hesitated for a moment.

'A venom is defined by its antidote. As much as I know how to save her, there is an equal chance of it being fatal.'

Shaurya was frustrated. He ran his hand through his messy hair.

'What are her chances Ayush?' asked a troubled Shaurya.

'Her chance of surviving this venom is better than the previous one. But this will hold well only if you don't cut her very deep with your sword. Yet the venom should enter her blood. After that it will spread throughout her body and she will lose consciousness. Make sure you defeat her soon so that we can treat her with the antidote quickly.'

'This is way too dangerous for you also, Shaurya. Please think again about what you are doing,' implored Ashwasena. Shaurya was in deep thought for a few moments.

'No second thoughts Ashwa. I have to do this. I know that I will have an edge over her in sword fighting. So many years my sword killed men to save me. For the first time let it fight to save the love of my life. Only this time it won't kill but do just the opposite.'

Ashwasena silently prayed that his friend would come out of it safe. Ayush fervently hoped that his skill and knowledge would save both the lives. If the duel ends badly for either of them, Ayush will never be able to forgive himself, for what he had agreed to do was against everything he had ever believed in his profession. The duel was going to be crucial not only for Veera and Shaurya but also for each one of them whose life was entwined with theirs.

***

CHAPTER 29

Dhruva casually walked through the bustling market. People were moving around buying and selling things. The market had rows of stalls of vegetables, fruits, clothes, earthen pots, copper and brass utensils etc. there were also some men selling sheep, goats fowls and fish. He was not there to buy anything. A few guards in the market saluted him as he passed them. The sun was overhead and the sales in the market of Virpur was in full swing. Dhruva kept looking to his left and right as though he was inspecting the place. Then between a shop selling rice and another one selling clothes there was a shoddy path. He quickly turned and was out of the noisy place. The path was very narrow and a little dark even in the broad daylight. He kept looking back a few times to make sure he was not being followed. After walking a few yards he turned to his left. The path led into a shed which housed livestock to be sold in the market the next day. The place was dirty and the floor had generous animal and bird droppings. It smelt nasty, but Dhruva did not flinch. Seeing an intruder there was some unrest among the animals but since they were used to human presence they did not make much noise. Dhruva walked in the path at the middle of the shed and reached the farther end. It was completely dark except for a sole burning lamp. Rudrapriya was sitting on a stone. He gestured Dhruva to come over there. When he went near him he realised that Rudrapriya was not alone. There was another man next to him. But it did not take long for Dhruva to recognise him.

'Chirayuhastha? This is surprising! I thought you sent a secret message only to me,' said a surprised Dhruva looking at Rudrapriya.

'Sit down Dhruva. I don't want anyone to notice you. Where is Veera? What did you tell her?' asked the scholar on a serious note.

'She has gone to the blacksmith to get her sword sharpened. I lied to her that I was going to have a meeting with the soldiers guarding the marketplace as I had to give them some instructions before we leave for Kaalvan. Mithra didn't suspect anything amiss. Be quick! Why did you want to meet me here?'

'Show him,' said Chirayuhastha. Rudrapriya took out a cloth with something wrapped in it. He unwrapped the cloth on the floor and there was an arrow in it. Chirayuhastha held the lamp above the arrow.

'Do you recognise this?'

Dhruva bent and took a closer look at it. His eyes indicated that he knew which arrow it was.

'This is the arrow those scoundrels used during the attack on Veera. What is it with this?'

'Dhruva, that day I told you that these arrows were poison-tipped but I did not know what they had used to make it so fatal. Later that day I saw Chirayuhastha at Sankhaji's ashram. Then he told me that he had lived with the Rathsu tribes. These tribal people also make dangerous poison tipped weapons. I took him to the spot and showed him the arrow. He instantly recognised it.'

'What do you know about this? Tell me everything,' ordered Dhruva looking at the doctor.

'The venom used to lace this arrow is very strong and rare. Even a small cut on the body with it is enough to kill a man. Also the antidote is not very easily available. So had Veera been hit by even one of these arrows, death was certain.'

'Cruel bastards!' cursed Dhruva.

'It doesn't end there, Dhruva. I took this arrow to my tribal friend Kanchu. He confirmed that they had sold these arrows to a man a few weeks ago. That man was a native of Indragiri!'

Dhruva clenched his fist and banged it to the floor. Pure rage was burning in his eyes.

'Shaurya! That spineless coward! I will shred him to pieces!' he swore. Rudrapriya placed a hand on his shoulder.

'Calm down Dhruva. Just because the man was from Indragiri doesn't mean that Shaurya was behind this,' reasoned Rudrapriya. Dhruva looked at him in disbelief.

'Are you serious Acharya? If it is certainly someone from Indragiri, it has to be him. He is the one keen on making life hell for Mithra. I have no doubt that it is Shaurya!'

'But he was the one who challenged Veera to the duel. Then why would he want to kill her before that?' asked a mystified Chirayuhastha.

'The duel is just an eyewash! If he killed Mithra before the duel then it would certainly lead to war. Without the Chief, the army will be in chaos if led into a war on such a short notice. This is exactly what he wanted!'

Rudrapriya let out a long drawn breath.

'Nevertheless, Veera was saved. I am still not convinced that Shaurya could have done this. All we have to make sure is Veera wins this duel,' said Rudrapriya.

'Veera should know nothing about this,' cautioned Chirayuhastha. Dhruva nodded his head in agreement.

'Mithra will know nothing about this. I want her to only focus on the duel. I want her to kill that wimp in the duel. Unfortunately if he survives, his death will be so horrific that he will regret the very thought of hurting Mithra,' threatened Dhruva in a cold tone looking at the arrow. Chirayuhastha shared Dhruva's anger in agreement. But Rudrapriya was in distress! He knew Shaurya was not behind this. Rudrapriya had recognised Shaurya that day in the Shiva temple at Charanvasi. Shaurya would never want to kill Veera. Rudrapriya knew there should be a deeper motive behind this duel. It was certainly not as simple as it looked...

**

Shaurya rode hard on Vayu, his black stallion. It was a cold, full moon night. He reached his destination after a long ride. The flowing river made a gurgling sound. He tethered Vayu to a tree on the riverbank. The moon made the water sparkle and look appealing. Without even a moment's hesitation Shaurya removed his kurta and hurled his angavastram to the ground. Then he dived into the cold river. At first his body flinched at the water's temperature. But after a few moments of swimming it was comforting. His mind now concentrated only on swimming and the water. He felt relaxed. His stressed mind was calm. He kept swimming until his limbs were tired of pushing against the water. Being alone was always comforting for Shaurya. Later, physically exhausted he waded out of the river. He pushed back the wet hair from his forehead and sat on the riverbank stretching out his legs. Once out of water he could feel the chill. But he sat there with the water droplets adorning his torso. Bearing the cold was better than having to burn in your heart...

Shaurya was staring at the moon when he heard the sound of hooves. Instantly he turned and saw Ashwasena riding towards him. He let out a sigh and continued staring at the moon. After a few moments Ashwasena was sitting beside him. He did not speak to break the silence. The wind whistled in their ears.

'How did you find me?'

'I didn't go home today. I decided to stay in the palace with your guards until we leave for Kaalvan. I was patrolling the palace when I saw someone ride away from the back entrance at the stables. It was not difficult to recognise Vayu. I quickly mounted on my horse and followed you but your horse is way too fast and I couldn't keep up. Yet once I was certain about the direction you rode in, I knew where you were heading to,' said Ashwasena as a matter of fact. There was silence again for a few more moments.

'You are trying to escape from reality Shaurya. That's not possible. You have to face it.'

Shaurya looked at his friend.

'Do you think I am not? This is my way of dealing with it!' he snapped. Ashwasena gave him a look of frustration.

'Yeah I can see that! Slipping out of the palace and jumping into a river to swim in rough waters in the middle of the night! Of course you are deftly dealing with reality!'

'You think I am wrong, don't you?' whispered the prince.

'I don't *think* you are wrong. I *know* you are wrong Shaurya.'

'Then why are you still doing everything I ask you to do? Why don't you just leave me?'

Ashwasena let out long drawn breath.

'Shaurya, I have seen you go through various circumstances in life. You have done outrageous deeds in the past but you were never morally wrong. Now you know very well that you have made a wrong decision. Yet I can't leave you because I have been caring for you ever since our childhood. Just because you are wrong now, I cannot abandon you. You are way too important for me. Under any circumstance I will stand by you,' he said, his voice was thick with emotion.

'Despite having a rational mind, you are foolish enough to stand by me. It is exactly for the same reason I challenged Veera for the duel. I did not come to this decision in the heat of the moment! I have spent days asking myself whether I love her or not. I struggled to get a yes or no from my heart. But once I got my answer, there was no looking back. I love her and I want to save her,' said Shaurya determined.

'You are just being insane!'

'Really? Now answer my question. Would you die for Nahusha?'

'I would happily give my life for my love,' said Ashwasena without second thoughts.

'But that is because Nahusha and I love each other. In your case, Veera doesn't even know you! I am certain there is not the slightest chance in the world that she is ever going to love you. Then why the hell are you doing this? You are just going overboard with your obsession!'

Shaurya smiled at him wryly.

'Just because she doesn't love me, doesn't mean my love is any less than yours. Love is love, even if the one you love doesn't love you! I will do anything for Veera who lives in my heart,' he said closing his eyes.

'Still, you cannot justify your deed.'

'People say all is fair in love. I think it's time we test it. If it is true, I will never ask for anything again from life. If not, I will never believe in love again, for this time I have put everything at stake just to save the love of my life...'

The two friends sat there looking at the flowing river.

'When are we leaving?' asked Shaurya.

'Day after tomorrow, early in the morning. Kaalvan is six days journey from here. I have already sent Devajit to supervise all arrangements there. Almost everyone from Indragiri and Virpur will be there to witness the duel. The fate of two kingdoms for the first time will be decided by two swords.'

'What about Ayush?'

'He has already gathered the required antidote and medicinal herbs. Ayush and two of his assistants will leave along with us.'

Shaurya ran his hand through his wet hair. The cold wind enveloped his bare torso with a vengeance. He shivered slightly. Picking up his waist-long sleeveless kurta, he dusted out the sand from it. Then he wore his kurta and tied the angavastram to his waist.

'How do you think this duel will end?' asked Ashwasena demurely. Shaurya thought for a moment and let out a long drawn breath.

'You may assume any number of consequences. But I know that there can only be two. Either we both come out of it alive or we both die,' said Shaurya coldly. Ashwasena was stunned. He slowly looked up at the sky with a silent prayer that they both should survive the duel. But he knew future was something nobody could predict. *If all our prayers are answered, we will no longer pray...*

***

The full moon was shedding its soft light on the river. Dhruva was sitting on a boulder on the riverbank, throwing pebbles into the water. He should have gone home a long time ago but he did not go. He had been preparing himself mentally for the day of the duel. Yet no amount of preparation was enough to face the reality. Tomorrow they would have to leave for Kaalvan. There was an untold fear lingering in his mind. Veera had really improved her sword fighting skills and she could use both her hands flexibly without pain, all thanks to Chirayuhastha. He believed she would win the duel

But what if she didn't?

That very thought made his body go limp with fear. But not once did he let Veera know about his fear. He had to put up a brave front to keep her going. Sitting alone he could feel this thoughts overpower him

What if Mithra doesn't come back?

Are my days with her numbered?

What if I don't get to see her ever again?

Dhruva closed his eyes shut in frustration. He simply wanted to run away from there, far away where he would never know the consequence of the duel! He heard someone coming and instantly knew it was Veera. He opened his eyes and took a deep breath to compose himself. There was no way he could let her see his vulnerability. Looking up at her, he smiled lightly. She sat beside him and reflected his smile.

'I have been waiting a long time for you to get back home.'

'I am sorry Mithra. I just lost track of time here. It's such a calm night...'

'Yeah. Do you remember the first time we both sat on this riverbank together?'

Dhruva ran his fingers through his tousled hair.

'How can I even forget it? It was the night before our first battle together against Suryapatna.'

Veera let out a sigh looking at the river.

'The night, this river, moon all look the same as they did that day. But so much has happened after that night. It feels like a lifetime ago...'

The breeze blew over them. Veera tucked a few strands of her lose hair behind her ear. Suddenly Dhruva looked at her knitting his eyebrows in tension.

'Did you come here alone?'

She raised an eyebrow at his question.

'As if your guards would let me come out alone? Six guards accompanied me. After I spotted you I told them to keep a watch around this place. They have surrounded us at a distance.'

'Good.'

Dhruva looked around and spotted four guards. The other two must be further ahead in the dark.

'Can I ask you something?' asked Veera timidly.

'What do you think would be my answer to that question?'

'I think you would say that I can ask you anything,' she said smiling.

'Then go on,' he said softly.

'Dhruva, you know exactly what to do, to not let me go. But you didn't push too hard to stop me. Why?' she asked intensely looking at him. Dhruva averted her eyes and looked ahead into the distance.

'I know you won't listen to me. You would anyway go into the duel. By forcing you against it, I will only be causing you more pain. I can't bear to hurt you,' he whispered.

'That's not the only reason. You agreed to this because you know I am not wrong. You know that this is the best chance to save our motherland, our people. You would have done the same thing had you been in my place.'

Dhruva looked at her with tormented eyes.

'Yes I would have! But I am not stubborn like you. One word from you and I would have stepped back without even a moment's hesitation!'

Veera swallowed hard. She never wanted to hurt him but she had thrust a dagger deep into his heart. Now she could not take it back...

'I am sorry Dhruva. I am sorry I am doing this to you. I am sorry I am doing this to us,' she said in a muffled voice. Dhruva looked into her eyes and put his arm around her shoulder. She moved closer and rested her head on his shoulder.

'Me too...' he said slowly. They sat in silence for a few minutes. If fate was considerate enough, time should have frozen at that moment without going forward. But time stops for none!

'Dhruva, if I don't—'

'Shut up Mithra! You are not going to speak a word of losing the duel.'

'Dhruva please… even I don't want to think about failure. But nothing is certain. If I don't come back—'

Dhruva dropped his hand from her shoulder and immediately stood up. Veera also stood up to face him.

'Please listen to me,' she implored.

'No, you listen to me!' snapped Dhruva. He held her shoulders tightly.

'Mithra, you are not going to tell me one word about what I should do if you don't come back. I don't know how to live without you! I want you to go into the duel with this thought. If you want me to live, you have to come back!' he said with absolute tenacity. A tear slid down Veera's eye.

'You are going to come back to me Mithra. Otherwise where ever you are, I am coming for you,' he said ardently.

'I will never let go of you Dhruva, not until my last breath,' said Veera almost choking on her words.

'I won't let go of you Mithra, even after I stop breathing,' said Dhruva his eyes welled up. Veera embraced him, tears streaming down her cheeks. He wrapped his arms around her more securely than the usual. They never feared the future but at that moment tomorrow scared them. This could be their last day together in Virpur. Yet they believed that they could never be separated because they were a part of each other. One simple truth was etched forever in their hearts. No matter what tomorrow brings with it, nothing ever changes between them.

***

CHAPTER 30

Shaurya looked at the sun from the window of his tent. He had already worn his armour and amulets. His sword was in the scabbard tied securely to his waist. The day he had been waiting for was here at last. All the preparation, plans and some hard decisions had led him to this day. The sunrise today held a new meaning for him, because tomorrow his life would no longer be the same. By the end of this day Shaurya would have either saved the love of his life or killed her. All the battles that he had won in the past would have no meaning if he lost this one. For once, he felt gratified to hold his sword. Determined to get Veera, Shaurya took in a deep breath and stepped out of his tent.

Kaalvan was a battlefield. It did not belong to any kingdom. On either ends of the battlefield, tents had been set up by both Virpur and Indragiri. Arrangements had been made for the people of both the kingdoms to watch the duel. A line had been drawn at the middle of the battlefield to divide it into two. The people from either of the kingdoms should not cross the line. They kept distance with each other. Barricades had been put up with wooden logs along the perimeter of the field. Almost all from Virpur and Indragiri had assembled to watch this epic duel. For Indragiri, it was a matter of ascertaining their superiority but for Virpur it was a question of survival. Indragiri was assured of victory whereas Virpur was in the hope of a miracle.

Queen Arunadevi was holding an arthi plate in her hand. King Kritiverman, Prime Minister Agniverma,

Commander Ashwasena and Chief Doctor Ayush were standing with her. Shaurya walked up to his mother. She moved the plate in three circular revolutions before his face and applied the vermillion streak on his forehead. There was pride in her eyes seeing her son in the armour. Arunadevi handed the plate to an attendant. He bent down touched his mother's feet. She caressed his head and blessed him.

'May victory be yours!'

Shaurya stood up and embraced her. Then he moved to the King but did not seek his blessing, rather he executed a royal salute.

'Come back victorious, Prince Shaurya!'

'I will, your Highness,' he said smugly. Shaurya went to Ayush who was standing a little away from the royals. Ashwasena followed him. Without waiting for Shaurya, Ayush stepped forward and embraced Shaurya. He was taken aback by that gesture.

'Be quick and don't cut very deep. The more you prolong, she won't survive,' whispered Ayush. Then he released him from his embrace quickly to avoid any suspicion.

'Be ready to save her,' whispered back Shaurya instantly. He gave a discreet nod to Ayush. Nobody heard their brief conversation except Ashwasena. For Ayush, it was clearly not just an order but also a request. He could not override either of them. Ashwasena climbed onto the royal chariot. Shaurya climbed in behind him. Ashwasena would ride the chariot to the centre of the battlefield for the duel.

Dhruva tied the straps of Veera's armour securely. The gold amulets glistened on her hands. He made sure that her scabbard was tied securely to her hip. He once again looked at her from head to toe. Veera was all set to go into the duel.

They looked into each other's eyes. Their emotions were well hidden and only confidence glowed in them. It was possible only because they were not yet ready for a farewell.

'Ready?' he asked outstretching his hand.

'Yes,' she said holding his hand. Together they stepped out of the tent.

Queen Lakshmipriya performed the arthi and applied vermillion on Veera's forehead. Veera sought the blessings of the King and Queen.

'May God bless you with victory, Veera. I know you will make us proud,' bellowed the King.

'I will, your Highness,' said Veera bowing to him.

'Give him hell, Veera!' beamed Prince Vijayendra. Veera executed a royal salute to them. Then she went to where Rudrapriya and Chirayuhastha were standing. She bent down and touched the scholar's feet. He placed his hand affectionately on her head.

'Aayushman Bhava!' said Rudrapriya blessing her with a long life. Dhruva frowned at him.

Long life? Why not victory?

But Veera smiled at the scholar.

'Thank you Rudra. I hope you won't forget me.'

'You were not born to be forgotten Veera. You are making history and you are going to live a long life to leave your name etched in this world forever!'

Then she looked at Chirayuhastha.

'Don't worry Chief Veera, I will do everything possible to save you. You only have to come back!'

'I will,' said Veera glancing at Dhruva. His demeanour was calm and composed. Yet she knew the pain was tearing him apart from inside. Veera and Dhruva climbed onto the chariot.

Dhruva was her charioteer leading her into the battlefield. But will he be able to take her out of that battlefield alive?

***

Dhruva stopped the chariot a few feet away from the middle of the battlefield where Ashwasena and Shaurya were standing. Veera and Dhruva stepped down from the chariot. They both started walking hand in hand towards Shaurya and his companion. Breath was knocked out of Shaurya when he saw her. He really did not expect her presence to have such a strong effect on him. His heart was drumming with joy on seeing her. Once in the past he had thought that he would never be able to see her again, but now here she was, so close to him! Ashwasena did not miss the change of expression on Shaurya's face.

'Any second thoughts Shaurya? You can stop this even now. It's not too late.'

'If she is willing to go with me, I will stop this right now. I will happily give up everything just for her. But life isn't that easy Ashwa,' said Shaurya still staring at Veera.

'Unfortunately not...' said a dejected Ashwasena.

Veera and Dhruva stood four steps away from their opponents. For the first time Veera looked at Prince Shaurya. Until that day she had heard a lot about him and today he was there, right in front of her. But he did not look anything close to what she had imagined. Firstly, Veera did not expect him to be so handsome! Since she had always pictured him to be a bad man, she also expected him to be ugly. Secondly, he was very tall, even taller than Dhruva. She was just a few inches shorter than Dhruva but she would probably only reach up to Shaurya's neck. His upper torso was covered by the sleeveless kurta and the armour above it. Yet she could see well-toned muscles on his arms. His face had chiselled features and he sported short wavy hair. But what actually caught Veera's attention were his sharp eyes! He did not once take his eyes off her and that was very unsettling for her. Veera was used to people staring at her but this was something more than that. It was like his eyes were piercing through her with some unfathomable yearning. Veera could feel Dhruva's hand tighten his hold. She squeezed his hand gently.

Shaurya took a moment to study Veera. She had worn a red cotton dhoti and white kurta. The shining armour covered her upper torso. Her hair had been tightly plaited. Gold amulets adorned her delicate looking hands. Her dusky skin was glowing in the sunlight. Though she had not applied kohl to her eyes, they had a rare sparkle in them. Her enigmatic dove eyes had a magnetic hold on him. Veera looked a lot more beautiful than she used to in his fantasies. Then his eyes fell on her hand holding Dhruva's hand. Shaurya did not miss the leather wristband on Dhruva's hand. He looked at Dhruva whose eyes were filled with pure rage and hatred. Dhruva would have ripped Shaurya apart if he had his way. For Shaurya it was more of jealousy than rage. That moment he would not have hesitated to kill Dhruva just to be able to hold Veera's hand. Though their reasons were different, these two men wanted to kill each other. Ashwasena could sense the tension in the environment.

'It's time for the salute,' announced Ashwasena. Dhruva released Veera's hand. Shaurya and Veera executed a warrior salute and bowed to each other. It was a gesture to respect their opponents.

'Invoking the blessings of Lord Shiva, let the duel begin. Both the warriors will adhere to the rules and conditions laid out for the duel. Do you agree?'

'I agree.'

'I agree.'

'May the best warrior win,' said Dhruva glancing at Veera. Ashwasena looked at Dhruva for a brief moment. Then he embraced Shaurya.

'Be alert. Don't hurt yourself with your sword. Come back with her,' he said softly so that Veera and Dhruva could not hear him.

'Thank you for everything, Ashwa,' said Shaurya to his friend. Then he took his sword and handed the scabbard to Ashwasena.

'See you soon,' said Ashwasena and began walking towards his chariot.

Dhruva hugged Veera and she embraced him back tightly.

'Kill him Mithra. Kill him!'

He held her for one more moment and then released her.

'Will you promise me something?' she asked looking into his eyes. He closed his eyes and placed his forehead on hers. She closed her eyes in tranquillity.

'Anything for you…' breathed Dhruva.

'After me, you own my sword,' she said, her voice pleading him.

'I promise! But you are coming back or else I am coming for you!'

'We are companions forever,' said Veera her voice on the verge of breaking down.

'Even beyond forever, Mithra.'

Dhruva kissed her forehead and let go of her. They looked into each other's eyes for a moment. One moment of life they would hold onto until their last breath. Veera took her sword and gave him the scabbard.

'Come back!' said Dhruva fiercely.

'I will!' assured Veera with confidence. He quickly turned around and strode towards his chariot before he would change his mind. Leaving behind Veera was the hardest thing he had ever done in his life. For Veera, seeing him walk away was worse than her father dying before her eyes. She vowed to herself that this certainly would not be her last day with Dhruva. Veera steeled herself for the duel. She looked into the eyes of her opponent with determination. If she had to kill Shaurya to get her life back, then so be it! This duel was going to be really hard for Shaurya. At that moment all he wanted to do was drop his sword and take her into his arms right there.

How can I fight with her when my heart is over brimming with love? Why is life so cruel?

Shaurya took a deep breath to focus on the fight. He would have to hurt her. If he wanted to save her, then he would have to give her so much pain that she might never forgive him. Yet he had no choice! On the other hand, an ignorant Veera was going to fight with an adversary who loved her beyond everything. While one will fight for patriotism, the other will fight for love…

***

CHAPTER 31

Almost all the people of Indragiri and Virpur had assembled to witness this epic duel. For people of Indragiri it was unbelievable to see a woman walk into the battlefield. They had not even heard of a woman becoming a warrior in their kingdom and here was a woman ready to duel with their crown prince. The people of Virpur were fervently hoping that their Chief Veera would win this. She had accomplished many impossible feats in the past. Veera will defeat Prince Shaurya too, nothing was impossible for her or so they believed. But the soldiers of both the kingdoms were filled with gratitude for their respective Chief because they alone could appreciate the value of their decision. By fighting this duel they both had saved the lives of thousands of warriors. Nobody wants a war, especially not the ones who fight in it.

For King Devarata, practically there was nothing to lose. If Veera lost the duel then Indragiri wanted only her and not Virpur. He was well aware that if it came down to a war, then there was no way he could retain his throne. Therefore the worst thing possible was that he would lose Chief Veera. Sacrificing a woman for his kingdom was indeed a good bargain. For King Kritiverman, this duel was nothing but yielding to his son's obstinacy. He tried to stop this in many ways but failed. Kritiverman was certain that Shaurya would win. For him, this duel was a mockery of his power as a king and he was not going to take it lightly. He would certainly avenge this humiliation by bringing Virpur under his rule.

There will be an opportunity to make it happen. Until then he would wait and watch.

Veera closed her eyes for a moment remembering her father Agneyastra and seeked his blessing. When she opened her eyes, they were burning with determination. Animosity emanated from every cell of her body. She looked her enemy in the eye and held her sword in a position ready to strike. There was no trace of fear at all. A mild shadow of smile crossed Shaurya's face. He had expected to see at least slight nervousness on her face. There was none! In the past he had fought many invincible warriors and he had seen some level of fear in their eyes. But this woman knew nothing about fear. Shaurya was impressed by her courage. One more reason to love her more! He wanted to get over with this duel as soon as possible. He held his sword in position.

Veera made the first move and Shaurya defended her strike well. For the first few moments he only defended her attacks. He had to admit that she was indeed going for the kill every time she struck. Then he could no longer just defend because he narrowly missed her sword twice. The swordsman in him overtook his emotions and he switched to offence. Now it was Veera's turn to defend and she deftly did that. Dhruva was standing behind the barricade and watching them keenly. He looked around and noticed the archers of both the kingdoms placed strategically around the field. If anyone crossed the barricade then they would be shot at right there. Not just that, even if one of the two warriors broke any rules of the duel, that person also would be shot dead. Dhruva clenched his fists in frustration. He could do nothing but helplessly just watch her fight. It was like his whole body was set on fire. The helplessness was killing him. Rudrapriya was diligently watching the duel.

'Will she make it?' asked Chirayuhastha doubtfully.

'Veera has proved us wrong on many occasions. She never fails to surprise me. But Shaurya, his sword is ruthless! Yet I really hope she wins,' he said earnestly.

Initially Shaurya was making the obvious moves and Veera easily defended, but then he upped the pace of his sword and at one instant his sword made a cut on her arm. She moved a step backwards. Though her wound started to bleed, Veera felt no pain, instead that part had gone numb. That was odd! Still she did not pay much attention to it, rather she moved forward and swung her sword. Ayush was watching with bated breath after Shaurya had injured her. He expected her to weaken but it seemed like the wound had no effect on her. Tension was building up for Ayush because this only meant that Shaurya had to cut her deeper for the venom to work. Both Shaurya and Veera were on the offensive now and desperate to hurt each other. She managed to injure Shaurya a few times but they were just superficial cuts.

Shaurya inflicted a few more wounds on Veera but her spirit was still the same. At one point the warrior in him completely forgot that he was fighting with the love of his life because she was a formidable opponent. Shaurya swung his sword hard and cut through her shoulder. Veera shrieked in pain. The venom had taken its time to penetrate into her blood. This deep cut on her shoulder actually sped up the process. Every wound on her body did not cause pain but began to burn. The burning sensation was new to her and unbearable. Shaurya stood there watching her face contort in pain. He realised that she would have to be taken to Ayush as soon as possible. He expected her to collapse at that moment.

Dhruva could no longer bear watching her in pain. He pulled out his dagger from the scabbard tied to his waist. He was about to fling it at Shaurya but by then two sets of strong hands held his arms tightly. Dhruva turned to look at them with unadulterated rage.

'What the hell are you doing? Let go of me!' he growled. But Rudrapriya and Chirayuhastha stood there without loosening their grip on him.

'Don't be stupid Dhruva! Archers are placed all around this place. One bad move is enough to kill you both!' warned Rudrapriya sternly.

'I can't stand here watching him kill her!'

'Veera is alive. He has not killed her yet, but if you do anything insane then she will surely die! Don't act in haste and lose her forever,' he reasoned. Dhruva was shaking with rage and helplessness. Though he did not want to listen to the scholar's words, he knew that was the truth. He looked at Veera, pain tearing him apart.

'Kill him, Mithra!' screamed Dhruva. Veera heard him and gathered all her strength. She rushed forward with full force to attack Shaurya who stood distracted by her pain. By the time he acted in defence it was too late. She was almost over him and in the process of avoiding her, he made a cut on his left hand with his own sword. Veera missed him and fell to the ground.

'Aagghh!' cried Shaurya. His wound was bleeding and he was in terrible pain. Ayush gasped in horror.

'Oh my God! He has cut his hand,' said Ashwasena slowly.

'He doesn't have much time. The venom will incapacitate him!' said a worried Ayush.

'But she didn't seem to be affected by the venom so soon. Maybe he also has time.'

'The venom is potent, Ashwa. I really don't know how she is managing to hold up for so long. But Shaurya may not be able to do it!'

Ashwasena and Ayush looked at them soaking in anxiety.

Veera did not give up. She once again stood up with great effort to face her adversary. Shaurya was dumbstruck! He was impressed by her bravery and courage. His wound was now burning so badly and he realised how much pain she was in. Veera deserved to live and now, only he could save her. She once again tried to strike him but he cut through her right arm more fiercely. When he saw that she was still holding onto her sword, he was astounded. Moreover the venom had begun to show its effects on him. He knew there was not much time left, yet she was not ready to give up. Veera would fight until her last breath but Shaurya could not let that happen. Her vision blurred and she could feel her mind slowly slip away. Veera desperately raised her sword for one last strike. She knew she was going to die and she wanted the death of a warrior. When she moved forward towards him, Shaurya struck her hard and his sword slashed her torso through her broken armour. It was a killer blow!

Everyone present were stunned. Shaurya recoiled back due to the effect of his own blow on Veera. He was stupefied! Veera collapsed to the ground letting out a bloodcurdling cry. Rudrapriya and Chirayuhastha dropped their hands from Dhruva's arms. He fell on his knees flabbergasted. It was like a lightning had struck him. He was too dazed to even breathe! Veera felt darkness envelope her.

'Dhruva...' she breathed closing her eyes. She was unconscious. Shaurya was pulled back to his senses when he felt his vision blur. The whole of Indragiri erupted in jubilation. For Virpur, the grief was unimaginable. All their hopes were shattered. A tear slid down Chirayuhastha's eye. Rudrapriya stood there unmoved, his eyes cold and hard. Though everyone belonging to Indragiri were excited about Shaurya's victory, Ashwasena and Ayush were horrified.

Shaurya quickly bent down and examined an unconscious Veera. Her breathing was heavy. The burning sensation of his wound was now radiating through his entire left arm. He tried lifting Veera using both his arms but he could not use his left hand flexibly. At last, Shaurya hoisted Veera on his right shoulder. He turned to look at Dhruva once. Dhruva was a lifeless rock. Shaurya then strode towards the tents meant for the royalty of Indragiri with a barely breathing Veera on his shoulder. Veera's bloodied sword lay on the battlefield.

Dhruva had lost sense of his surroundings that very moment when Veera collapsed. Shaurya had snatched away Dhruva's very reason for existence. Once Shaurya was out of the battlefield, Rudrapriya slowly placed a hand on Dhruva's shoulder. He was still on his knees, his eyes lifeless.

'Dhruva... let go,' whispered Rudrapriya. Dhruva moved his hand off his shoulder and slowly stood up. Then he mechanically began walking towards the centre of the battlefield. Rudrapriya quietly followed him. Dhruva went and picked up Veera's bloodied sword. He looked at it, his eyes glowing with fury.

'I let him go only because Mithra is alive. She has not come back but I will go to get her. Shaurya will have to pay for everything he did to ruin our life. He will repent every single day for hurting Mithra! We both were never meant to be separated. Today cannot be the end of our bond because this is not over yet...' said Dhruva fiercely looking into the horizon. He tightened his hold on Veera's sword which glistened in the evening sun. Rudrapriya looked at him in awe. The sun set in the horizon ending a momentous day. This dusk was destined to usher a new dawn. One single day had changed their lives forever. In this ever vacillating world Dhruva was certain about only one thing.

Between Mithra and Dhruva nothing ever changes...

***

EPILOGUE

'Drink this,' said Trivika handing a copper glass of milk with a pinch of turmeric in it. Veera had just then finished eating her dinner. She took the copper glass without looking at it. Then she took a sip of the milk. The moment she tasted turmeric in it, she felt a catch in her throat. She closed her eyes in pain.

Dhruva hated to drink milk with turmeric.

Dhruva's image filled her mind. Staying away from him was tearing her apart. Veera had never even imagined that she would have to live without seeing him. Though most of the time she was either in physical pain or her head was filled with unanswered questions, Dhruva was always on her mind. She agonized over how he would survive this separation.

I am coming for you...

His words always echoed in her ears. Veera knew that it was next to impossible for him to reach her. She actually wanted him to believe that she was dead. Veera hoped that if Dhruva knew that she was dead, maybe he might move on in life. She did not want him getting into danger. Sneaking into an enemy kingdom's palace only meant death! She shuddered at that thought. Yet somewhere deep in her heart she still believed that he would come for her...

'Veera are you in pain?' asked Trivika looking at tears streaming down from her closed eyes. Veera was instantly pulled back to the present. Immediately she opened her eyes and wiped the tears. Without speaking anything, she drank the milk. After a few minutes the attendant gave her a dark brown, bitter concoction to drink. Quickly Veera gulped it down at one go as usual. Trivika put off all the lamps in the room except the one placed a little away from Veera's bed. Wordlessly the royal attendant sat on the wooden chair near the cot. She stayed with Veera to take care of her until she got better. Veera slowly lay down on the bed. She closed her eyes thinking about Dhruva. After some time she fell asleep.

Veera was standing bare-feet in the sweltering battlefield. Dhruva was holding her hand and looking into her eyes. They were intense.

'I am coming for you,' he said. Then he let go of her hand and walked away from her. Veera looked at her hand. She was terrorized! Her hand was smeared with blood. When she looked up, she did not find him. Her bloodied hand began to turn cold.

'Don't leave me,' she said and ran wildly in that empty battlefield searching for him. Though the sun was scorching her whole body, her hand was cold. Suddenly she felt the warmth of a strong hand in hers...

Veera's eyes flew open. A sturdy hand was holding her right hand. She froze! That hand belonged to none other than Prince Shaurya. He was sitting on the chair where Trivika had been sitting before she fell asleep. Even in the dim light of the lone lamp, she could see the anxiety on his handsome face. She immediately withdrew her hand from his. Veera sat up on the bed facing him. She was furious and frightened.

'What are you doing here?' she asked, barely constraining her temper.

'Are you alright, Veera? I think you were having a nightmare,' said Shaurya slowly. He could not take his eyes off her. Her hair was tousled and her face had a lovely glow in the light of the lamp. She was burning along with the lamp under his scorching gaze. Veera took a deep breath to control her anger.

'Your Highness, what are you doing here, in the middle of the night?'

Meet you in the sequel…
Love,
Sahana